Unwanted Inheritance

Unwanted Inheritance

A Novel

Robert B. Bolin

iUniverse, Inc.
New York Lincoln Shanghai

Unwanted Inheritance

iUniverse books may be ordered through booksellers or by contacting:

iUniverse
2021 Pine Lake Road, Suite 100
Lincoln, NE 68512
www.iuniverse.com
1-800-Authors (1-800-288-4677)

Because of the dynamic nature of the Internet, any Web addresses or links contained in this book may have changed since publication and may no longer be valid.

This is a work of fiction. All of the characters, names, incidents, organizations, and dialogue in this novel are either the products of the author's imagination or are used fictitiously.

ISBN: 978-0-595-44375-8 (pbk)
ISBN: 978-0-595-68688-9 (cloth)
ISBN: 978-0-595-88704-0 (ebk)

Printed in the United States of America

To Sandy and Mila who taught me to quit trying to get there without enjoying the trip. May we learn from the likes of them and not fear the journey.

He who has a why to live can bear most any how.

Anonymous

Introduction

I am a gene—not just any gene, but a special one. Of course, all genes say that, because they all do something special. Just the same, I am different from the norm, and that is what makes me special. The funny thing is that there is only one small molecular change that does that. Without that change, I would just be another gene. With this change, I can survive—which is more than most altered genes can say—and I can hide until it's time to do something … different. It is a defect, I guess, in the grand scheme of things, this ability to pass on the code. I rather enjoy it.

Oh, I can't claim that my power to alter things is solely responsible for what happens, but it is a major role. In recent years, your scientists have made great strides in discovering my kind of defect, but they are still trying to figure out how I work; I am that complex in function, even though I am relatively simple in structure. They will figure it out. Someday, they may even figure out a way to correct my defect, having already discovered how to make artificial genes and new codes called oligonucleotides. Clever, that—but until they figure out how to get into the cell, I'm safe.

I can be detected before I can cause damage. Your scientists have proved that and have even developed tests. What's funny is that your nonscience people don't want to find me. Why? Strange folks you are. Maybe some don't want to find me because it is messing with nature. That's kind of fatalistic, if you ask me. Maybe some don't want to find me because of a silly value you humans have, called "cost," and you want to contain it. What is cost, anyway? Maybe some don't want to find me because they are afraid of me. That one I can understand, because if you lose your fear of me, I will cease to exist.

This is a story of what I can do if you ignore me. It is technical in places. After all, I am a technical entity. Can you find me?

Duplication Mutant, Exxon eight, Chromosome 13

May 11, 2007

Chapter 1

April 11, 1972

At first sight, the room brought back a flood of memories. Ann felt a tightness in her throat and panicked. Her impulse was to turn and run, but reason prevailed. The nurse's voice brought her back to reality.

"Please change into this patient gown, Mrs. Garrity. Then I'll come back and take you for your chest X-ray. Dr. Long ordered some other tests as well, so you'll have to go to the lab too." The nurse left and closed the door.

Ann hurried to get out of her street clothes and into the hospital gown before the nurse came back. She let the stylish, yellow mini-dress fall to the floor and removed her bra. *Thank goodness I can keep my panties on*, she thought, fumbling with the gown. As a young girl, she had been self-conscious about her nakedness. A date rape in high school had accentuated the feeling. *Should this open to the front or the back? It's cold in this room.*

She turned as the nurse reentered. "How do you get this thing to cover your back?"

"Here, let me tie it for you. These things are not designed for comfort, that's for sure. Are you ready to go?"

"I still feel exposed. You sure it's on right? Isn't there a robe I could wear?"

"You'll just have to take it off once we get to X-ray. It's okay."

Ann held the back closed with both hands as she followed the nurse down the hall. Impatient a minute ago, the nurse did not seem to be in a big rush now.

The X-ray technician was no more sympathetic. He appeared to be in his early thirties—Ann's age—and he seemed to linger as he eyed her with more than professional curiosity. The nurse interrupted by clearing her throat.

"Oh, come with me," he said. "You don't have to change. Just loosen the gown in the back, so I can take the picture. Then it will be all done, and you can be on your way."

Ann followed him into a dark room and faced the wall, as instructed. He maneuvered the X-ray machine at her back, placing a plate between her and the

1

wall. With an open hand, he pushed between her shoulder blades, bringing her chest into the plate. Her mouth went dry. She was at his mercy.

Before she could react, his distant voice commanded, "Take a deep breath, and hold it."

Instinctively reacting to the command, she took a deep breath. A swishing sound at her back reminded her of the opening in the gown. Like it or not, she could do nothing but stand and accept what was happening.

She felt his warm breath and smelled tobacco as he whispered, "Good. Now stand sideways, with your left side to the plate, and raise your arms."

He turned her shoulders with one hand and her waist with the other until she faced him, then positioned her left arm above her head. The gown slipped forward off her shoulders, exposing most of her body. She turned and looked toward the corner of the room to avoid his gaze.

He replaced the X-ray plate and left her alone in the dark. The empty room provided her temporary relief.

His distant voice commanded her to hold her breath again. Her heart pounded, and thoughts flooded her brain. She was helpless, like the night years ago when another boy (she suppressed his name) had ripped off her clothes. She had been in his car, ten miles from home, when he had demanded that she comply or walk. She had attempted to open the door, but he had held her left arm over her head. She had struggled but was unable to break free.

"Good," the distant voice called out. "You can go now."

Dismissed, just like that. A second ago, he had dominated her, and now she was free, like years ago. She tried to control her trembling fingers as she drew the gown around her and clutched the back with both hands. She rushed out the door toward her room, but the nurse rerouted her to the lab for some tests.

◆   ◆   ◆

Finally, she was alone in her hospital room with her memories. She sat on one of the two beds, relieved to be the only occupant. Thoughts raced through her mind. The similarity to the room eight years ago was uncanny. The same three colors: shades of cream, gray, and white. The floor was linoleum, gray with white marbling. The walls were cream-colored to match the privacy curtains between the beds. The beds were cream, same as the open-weave cotton blanket. Even Ann's gown was cream. When she sat down, the plastic mattress cover crinkled. The TV hanging from the wall at the foot of the bed was the only modern addition. Not a comforting atmosphere, but it would have to do.

"Hello. You okay?" A head with a nurse's cap poked through the door.

"Yeah, I guess. Who are you?"

"I'm the night nurse, Sharon. We just changed shifts. You look like you could use a friend about now."

Except in the movies, Ann had never seen a nurse wear a cap. The black-haired nurse wore white, even her stockings and shoes. Her dress looked so starched that it was a wonder she could move in it.

"Yeah, I guess. This is overwhelming. Can I call home, to be sure my girls are okay? My husband was supposed to pick them up at school, but he had a job interview this afternoon and may have missed them."

"Sure. There's a phone at the end of the hall. This is a small hospital, and we don't have all the conveniences, as you can tell. Just dial nine, and the operator will let you call for free if you tell her you're a patient. Okay?"

"It all seems so ... strange."

"You'll get used to it. Dr. Long usually makes rounds about six or so, and we serve dinner at five thirty, so you still have plenty of time. I need to go over some things with you before he gets here. But you can call first. Hit the nurse's call button when you're finished, and I'll come back. I'll get you a robe to wear."

"Why didn't that other nurse give me a robe?"

Sharon shrugged and fished a robe out of the small closet. She tossed it on the bed and left before Ann could ask any more questions.

Ann slapped her hands on her thighs and sighed as she rose from the bed. She put on the flimsy robe and went down the hall. The phone sat in a little alcove next to the waiting room. There was a sign overhead, proclaiming its use for patients and staff only: PLEASE LIMIT YOUR CALLS.

"Hello, Michelle. Things okay at home?" Ann cupped the phone close to her ear to hear the response.

"Okay, Mom, I guess. Holly's being a pill. She won't clean up the mess she made in the kitchen. When you coming home?"

"Tomorrow. Is your dad there?"

"No, just Holly and me. Can we have spaghetti for dinner? You know, that new canned stuff?"

"Your dad will make dinner when he gets home. You girls be good, okay?" She wanted to talk longer, but another patient had approached the phone. He leaned against the wall, sighing and looking at his watch. "I love you guys," she said in a low voice, her hands cupping the phone, so he couldn't hear.

She returned to her room and thought back to earlier that morning. The day had not started well. At breakfast, Bob had hardly spoken, and when he did, it was about the job interview. Maybe he was just scared, like her.

At least the girls weren't aware of the situation. They had eaten in silence, then grabbed their lunch sacks. Ann had heard them singing as they skipped through the snow, down the driveway, to the bus stop. She had wanted to hug them before they left, but Bob urged them on. Perhaps it was better; keep it routine.

Bob was too busy with his job interview to drive her to the hospital. She'd call a cab. He'd try to pick up the girls at school; otherwise, they would have to ride the bus. He had seemed impatient with Ann's concerns about the girls, and he had even admonished her for making a big deal out of the situation. His last words to her had been: *Just get on with it, and don't make it something it's not.* Ann felt empty, sitting on the crinkly hospital bed. *Sometimes he's too dense.*

She sighed, then continued her thoughts. Everything was up in the air. She had two children, a career, and the promise of a nice home on a little farm eight miles from town. Bob wanted to live in town, but that wouldn't do. She had grown up on a farm, and the girls would benefit from the same experience. Reluctantly, Bob had consented to the farm. At first it wasn't much, just a small cabin, but she was building it into a log home. *Maybe I should have given in a little. Maybe then he would be ... well, a part of ... us, me.* Everything would be all right if Bob got a job. Everything would be all right if this were over. All she had ever wanted was to teach, raise a family, and live on a farm, like her mother.

Funny, I never thought of it until now. Like Mom? Strong, yet soft. Domineering, yet loving. A leader, yet able to follow. Am I like that? At least Mom wasn't afraid.

In college, Ann was popular and respected. At five foot five and 120 pounds, she was a beautiful young woman with grace and poise, always cheerful. Her short blonde hair gave the impression of action and, except for thick ankles, she could pass for a beauty queen. Her only blemish was a pinpoint mole above her right eye. She was the homecoming queen, class president, and head of the student-faculty committee. People turned to Ann with their problems. She could solve them all, like Mom.

Oh, Mom, I wish you were here now. Guide me through this. Tell me everything is going to work out.

She glanced around once more, then got up; the only sound was the squeaking of the bed. The door looked inviting. If she just walked out, then this wouldn't happen. *No, that won't solve anything.* She tiptoed to the wall and looked at the only picture in the room that seemed small and insignificant from the bed. A caption on the bottom of the frame read: JESUS IS MY SAVIOR. Ann stared at the image until it appeared that he might be animate, but instead of seeing something spiritual, she saw the rapist. Blinking, she backed away.

"I'll follow no man!" She said it with conviction but immediately regretted it. Raised with a staunch religious background, she felt guilty and even looked around to be sure that no one had heard. Mom had made her go to church every Sunday and every Wednesday night, where she had interacted, almost comfortably, with boys in her life until college.

College was different, though, and without the security of home and parents, she was forced to be social. She had no trouble finding a date. But since the date rape in high school, she didn't seek out males, except if they were needed for social events.

That's how Bob came into her life. A year behind her in college, he had gawked at her whenever she walked by. He stood out, not because of social skills or popularity, but because of his awkwardness. He was withdrawn, so when she had needed a date for the prom, she had asked him. He was so malleable and passive that she had felt comfortable around him, like with her dad.

The sounds of the hospital brought her back to reality. She looked at her watch; it was four thirty. Nothing to do but sit. She glanced at the call button, then reached for it, but hesitated. She wanted to escape into her mind, like when she had been raped, but a siren outside interrupted.

She walked to the window. Valley Hospital was only three stories tall, and from her second-floor room, she could see the events outside. A white ambulance drove up to the emergency room door. She stared at the front door next to the emergency room. Was Bob coming?

It had been raining most of the day, and the snow had washed away, leaving gravel-covered streets with dirty white edges. Even the lawns were coated in granular gray. Her drab hospital room had more color. The dropping temperature was turning the water to sleet and ice. Ann glanced around, desperate for color, any color. But the shadows elongated to hide anything but black and white.

She scanned the view from the window and focused on a lot across from the hospital. A small spot of yellow caught her eye. A single glacier lily stood out, heralding something different. Had she not focused so hard, Ann would have missed it altogether. The flower shape was indistinguishable; only the color gave it away.

"You ready now?" The capped head of the nurse appeared in the doorway.

"Yeah, I guess so."

Sharon entered and motioned Ann back to the bed. The nurse stood at the foot of the bed, ready to give a lecture.

"You can have dinner tonight, Ann. Afterward, nothing to eat, though you can drink water until midnight. After that, nothing. It's important. We don't want anything in the stomach when you go to surgery. Before you go to bed, I will shave your right armpit, just in case."

"In case of what?"

"Dr. Long will explain later. If you need a sedative, just press the call button, and I'll give you one. Are you on any medicines?"

"No."

"Good."

Ann went back to the window. It was snowing lightly. In the waning light, the lily was almost imperceptible. Encased by ice, it seemed unreal.

"I just want my life back!" she said.

◆   ◆   ◆

Bob stopped by briefly, with the girls. At eight, they were interrupted by a booming electronic voice announcing that all visitors must leave. Dr. Long arrived at 8:30 PM to explain the procedure scheduled for 7:30 AM. He reassured her that it was just a routine biopsy and said that he did not anticipate anything. If the biopsy was positive, he would remove her entire right breast.

He stood up from sitting on her bed. "Do you have any questions, Ann?" The question was more of an exit salutation than a genuine question, and he was halfway to the door before she could reply.

"No, I guess not. I'm not sure I understand all this, Dr. Long."

He stopped and raised his voice, as if to indicate that she had not been listening in the first place. "Look, Ann. You have a lump in your right breast. Both you and I feel it. We need the biopsy, to make sure it's nothing. If it is something, we need to treat it. Do you understand now?"

"Okay, yes."

Later, she lay in bed, staring at the walls and ceiling. Sleep would not come, and she fought back tears. This was a new experience, and she was so confused. *Why can't they tell what it is without surgery? Why must the breast be removed if it is just a little lump I can hardly feel? What am I going to do if I wake up and find my breast gone? Why can't they wait until after the biopsy to remove the breast, so I can get used to the idea? Why didn't I ask him these things?* She rolled over again, but each toss and turn caused more thoughts.

Another ambulance passed under her window to the emergency entrance. Its rotating light shone through the trees, casting shadows on the walls on the right side of the room and swiftly passing to the left. Then they were gone. She remembered, as a child, seeing shadows on her bedroom walls and being scared. They had seemed alive, ready to consume her. She would call out to her mother, who would come and console her until sleep drove the shadows away. She wanted to shout now, realizing how ridiculous it was for a grown woman. It would do no good anyway.

Mom wasn't here anymore. The last time Ann had seen her was in a room like this, eight years ago. Memories flooded back. Try as she might to fight them off, they wouldn't leave. *I am what I experience.* She sighed and closed her eyes, but the thoughts would not go away, and she relived the past, as if in a dream.

◆   ◆   ◆

She peeked down the hall, trying not to make any noise, and tiptoed along the corridor. It was dark, and she had to grope the walls to feel her way. She stumbled but caught herself. Light came from the nurses' station, and a flashlight beamed at the end of the hall. It was so quiet that her footsteps seemed to echo as she tiptoed to the vacant station.

She stopped at a wheeled rack in the middle of the small room. Its metal charts showed names and numbers, presumably room numbers. She did not see her mother's name, but she noticed an empty slot on the rack. The slot was between charts numbered ten and twelve. The lighted rooms across from the station were four and six. Eleven must be down the hall on the same side as the nurses' station, where she had seen the light beam earlier.

A night-light in room eleven did not illuminate anyone in the single bed.

"Mom?" Ann groped for the switch, then flipped it. The room flooded with violating light. The body in the bed did not move. She approached the foot of the bed cautiously, not knowing what to expect. The name plaque confirmed it was her mother: BETTY GIMBLE. Even then, Ann didn't want to believe it. The patient was at least half the weight of her mother. Her eyes were so sunken into their orbits that her eyebrows dominated her upper face. Her temples were wasted, and the skin was drawn around her mouth, like mummification. How could this happen so fast?

"Mom?" she whispered.

Her eyelids fluttered and rose as if questioning, then glanced around and settled on Ann. Recognition was slow, but she smiled her old, familiar smile, rewarding Ann. Ann wanted to cry as the smile transformed into a grimace.

"What are you doing here!" a voice challenged at the door. A nurse in white stood there, menacing, but Ann was not afraid.

"This is my mother, and I haven't seen her for two years. She needs me, and I am staying here as long as it takes, visiting hours or not. So just accept it!"

The white thing wavered for a moment, then nodded and left the room.

Betty didn't die that night. Later, Ann learned Betty had broken her hip walking down the front steps of the house. She had collapsed, but even then, she did not want to go to the hospital until the pain was so intense that she had consented. The doctor called it a pathological fracture. They could do little for her except give her painkillers. Radiation would help, but the nearest radiation treatment was 120 miles away. With little money and no insurance, there was no option. Besides, X-rays showed that all her bones had cancer. She refused further treatment; she didn't want to leave Dan with a big debt.

Mom was always strong and always there. Now it was Ann's turn, and all she could do was be there. Every day, Betty tried to smile, until pain and fatigue intervened. Ann sat by the bed as her mother's life waned.

For two weeks, Ann felt anger, then helplessness and embarrassment. Could it be that she was angry because Betty hadn't told her about the cancer? Could it be the helplessness of the situation? She didn't understand, and she was ashamed of the feeling.

Dad joined Ann each day, but not for long. He always had some duty or excuse to leave, yet he always came back.

Although the hospital had rules about visitors, they allowed Ann special privileges and never questioned her presence. Ann suspected this generosity had more to do with nursing issues than compassion. It seemed that none of the staff wanted to attend to Betty. They entered the room awkward and uneasy. A dying patient required intense emotional support. Death issues were difficult to address without looking at one's own mortality. Ann and her mother were pariahs.

When Betty writhed in pain, Ann pressed the call button. "Mom needs another shot. She's in a lot of pain."

"Has it been four hours yet?"

After what seemed an eternity, a nurse entered the room, turned down the sheet, and gently rolled Betty onto her side to inject the painkiller into the remaining muscle of her outer buttock. Her buttock was so wasted, its skin so leathery with multiple needle puncture holes, that the painkiller oozed out through multiple holes. The nurse rolled her back and straightened the sheets, ready to retreat as fast as possible.

"Why do we have to wait four hours when the shot doesn't last that long? It seems to last only about an hour. Can't we give more?"

"Doctor's orders."

After the pain shot, her mother had a lucid moment.

"The hardest part is knowing," she announced to the ceiling.

"What do you mean, Mom?"

"For the past two years, since they removed my breast, I've had a crystal ball. I knew the ending. Now, I can't see the future. Can I have a drink of water? I'm so thirsty." She dosed off before Ann could respond.

Ann gradually replaced the anger with hope, hope that her mother would die soon. For days, she arrived in the morning, wishing Betty's room would be empty. Although she wanted her mother to die, she didn't want to see her in death. Betty was not eating and barely drinking. The week before, she had drunk copious amounts of water and complained of thirst all the time. She hadn't had a bowel movement for weeks. Her skin was a bronze color, even though she hadn't been in the sun for months. For the past two days, she had been confused, delusional, and restless, and she had had the dry heaves.

Yet every morning, Betty was still alive and trying to smile. Except today. She just stared at the ceiling. There was no response; still, she was breathing deeply.

"The time is near." The day nurse's proclamation sounded more like hope than fact.

Ann sat next to her mother and stared at the shell of a body, her mother who had meant so much to her. Whenever Ann wavered on an issue, she thought of her mother. She could face any issue, remembering her mother's resolve.

Her mother had worked so hard to become a schoolteacher. Mom had come to the small town thirty-eight years earlier to work and earn enough money to return to college. She had met Dad and stayed for the rest of her life. To get her college degree, Betty had packed up Ann and moved a hundred miles away, to the state teachers' college, every summer. Ann had obtained her degree at the same college a year before Betty, but Betty's determination and tenacity set an example.

Ann left the hospital numb with exhaustion. How much more suffering would it take? As she drove back to the house, she felt a new, alien feeling: her life was on hold. Was it resentment? Her two children were neglected, as was her career. Money was a problem. Their income depended on her teaching.

The following morning, Ann slept in. Going to the hospital one more time to sit with a living corpse was too much.

Michelle, her two-year-old, finally brought her back to reality as she peeked over the edge of the bed. "Mommy! Sick?"

How did she know about being sick? Ann rolled to her side and stroked Michelle's blond hair. "No, Mommy's not sick, sweetheart. Mommy's just tired."

She pulled Michelle into bed and held her tight until the child squirmed away. It was time for breakfast. Life was so precious and precarious, Ann thought as she dressed and followed her daughter down the stairs.

Looking darling in her Bambi pajamas, Michelle waddled to the stairs, then sat down, putting one leg on the next step down, scooted her bottom to the step, and repeated the process until she reached the bottom of the stairs. At the landing, she jumped up and waddled to the kitchen. Michelle's vibrancy was rejuvenating. Ann spent the whole morning with Michelle and Holly.

Anne dragged herself to the hospital, sorry she'd not received a call saying it was over. She walked in the room, aware of something different. The cream-colored curtain around Mom's bed was drawn, as were the window curtains. A nurse emerged from behind the curtain, startled to see Ann.

"Oh! I just cleaned your mother. She is incontinent now and has been having seizures all night." There was no eye contact as she delivered the message and gathered up the soiled bedding before hurrying out the door.

Ann pulled back the curtain. How could it get any worse? Betty's teeth were clenched and bared, her lips stretched back, with one corner twitching. Her eyes were wide open and vacant as she stared off into space. Her breath labored as she tried to exhale through closed jaws and inhale through her nostrils. A rattle sounded from her chest and throat.

Ann remembered the elk Dad had shot. As they had approached, it had lay with its eyes wide, breathing hard from a lung wound as it died.

"Oh, Mom. Oh, Mom," was all Ann could say as she stroked her brow and gave way to tears. The anger, frustration, and embarrassment left as she leaned in, forehead-to-forehead, and just cried. "God. Oh, God. Please stop this."

She heard sobbing at the foot of the bed and turned to see Dad standing with the nurse. Both were crying. He had never looked so helpless. He wore a blue herringbone suit with a white shirt and a blue tie. His face was tan to the forehead, a sharp delineation from brown to white. He looked out of character, standing with his head down and his shoulders stooped, wringing the brim of his Stetson. As the body before them stilled, they cried themselves into emotional dullness. The nurse hugged him, then Ann, and left without a word. There was nothing to say. Dan and Ann stood, one on each side of the bed, not knowing what to do.

◆   ◆   ◆

She woke in a sweat, threw back the covers, and jumped out of bed to run away. In the dark corridor, panic set in as her throat started to close and dizziness made her weak. She pressed her back to the wall, thinking that if she could press hard enough, she might escape.

"Ann? Ann? What are you doing out here in the hall? You all right?" Sharon broke the spell as she emerged from the nurses' station and walked toward Ann.

"I don't want … this. Can't sleep here."

"Here, I have an order for a sleeping pill. Let me give it to you now." The nurse retrieved the medicine as Ann stood in the shadows, stooped, her head bowed in resignation.

Chapter 2

April 12, 1972
Evening

Ann woke in a daze and peered around the room. Where was she? The walls were cream-colored, perhaps white at one time. A cobweb clung to a corner of the ceiling. She was surrounded by a curtain hanging from a ceiling track, lying in a bed that was not hers. Overall, the illusion was of total privacy. Yet she could hear labored breathing beyond the curtain and distant voices.

Was she in her mother's bed? She studied the cream-colored curtain for clues. Something was familiar. The bed was enameled cream. Chips exposed rust spots in the metal undersurface. She almost laughed to herself, *What color of cream don't you like? This place needs some contrast!* A breeze caused the lower canvas to undulate. The motion mesmerized her for a second, then she continued exploring.

The sheets were stiff with starch, and the ill-fitted sheet did not cover the plastic mattress cover. An ill-fitting pillowcase left her head to rest on plastic. She shifted, and the plastic stuck to her sweaty skin.

She tried to turn. Pain in her chest brought her closer to reality. Now she remembered. The surgical suite, the casual banter with the aide who had pushed the gurney, being scooted onto the operating table, someone yelling at her, "Come on, sweetie, breathe! Take a deep breath for me. That's a good girl."

How long ago was that? Pain brought the answer. She had had surgery and was waking up. The pain on the right side of her chest occurred with movement, especially breathing. It was hard to take a deep breath, as if something bound her chest. Was she back in the car with the high school boy? Breathing fast, panic gave way to reality as she tried to concentrate. There was another, different pain in the front of her right thigh, as if someone were pushing a hot poker into her leg. She lifted the sheet and looked down toward her leg. A huge bandage extended from her right breastplate to her armpit and from collarbone to the bottom of her ribcage. No wonder she couldn't breathe.

Her right breast. Gone. She panicked again. She did have cancer, and Dr. Long had removed it! Just like her mother! *Oh, God! I'm going to die just like Mom. Can I make it for two years like she did? I must—to raise the kids!*

The panic eased as she thought about her daughters. She tried to focus on them, but the pain kept bringing her back to the present. Why did her thigh hurt?

There was so much she didn't understand. But one thing was for sure: she had cancer, breast cancer, just like Mom. She too would die. She didn't want to die—not yet. Fear choked her. She wanted to take a deep breath but couldn't.

How could this happen to me? I'm only thirty-two, Mom was fifty-six. Why now, when my family needs me? They can't survive without me. Thoughts whirled through her brain like a tornado, and all the time, the pain worsened. It was punishing her for being a mother, a daughter, or even being alive.

"I don't deserve this!" she sobbed. "Why me?"

She felt guilty thinking about herself. She should be concentrating on her children's needs. She had to get well for them.

No sooner did one wave of fear subside than another appeared, looming larger, then collapsing with the thoughts of her children. Pain and fear ebbed and flowed. The battle wore her out.

Just then, the curtain flew back at the foot of the bed. It startled her. At first, she guessed it was a process of her own thoughts. An apparition stood at the opening. Was this an angel, come to take her beyond?

"Ah, you're awake. I thought I heard your voice."

After the initial start, Ann was relieved. Perhaps the nurse could help her understand what was going on.

The nurse asked, "Are you in pain?"

Ann couldn't gather up an answer fast enough.

"I'll get you a pain shot in a minute, but first, let's scoot you up in bed. You'll be more comfortable. You need to rest quietly, so as not to bleed any more. You must take deep breaths to prevent pneumonia. Dr. Long would not be happy if you got pneumonia."

The initial relief from the presence of another human was short-lived. *Am I bleeding to death? How can I take a deep breath? Who cares whether Dr. Long is happy?* She said nothing. The nurse grabbed her under the left arm and pulled her up the bed, all the while talking, without apparent regard to the pain associated with the maneuver.

Ann was relieved when the nurse left. She felt like some inanimate object, pushed, prodded, and conditioned not to displease others, particularly the doctor.

The nurse returned with a syringe and needle, pulled her over on her right side (with much more pain), and injected the syringe's contents into her left buttock. Scenes flashed through Ann's mind of her mother being turned for a pain shot. She was glad when the nurse left a second time and hoped there would not be a third visit. Despite the pain, she wanted to go home.

The injection was taking effect. She was groggy, and she dozed off.

Ann woke, hearing moaning and coughing coming from behind the curtain. She wanted to help, to get beyond her own pain to reach the call button. Before she could act, she heard a nurse's voice at the door, followed by a shout for help and a lot of activity behind the curtain. The voices were loud and anxious.

A male voice proclaimed the patient dead, and for the next few moments, there was no sound. Ann wanted to run away, wanted not to be a part of this experience. God knew she was facing her own mortality. Why did she have to be involved with someone else's death? *Why do we have to die? For that matter, why do we live? What does it all mean?* There were no answers, only feelings.

Just then, a voice beyond the curtain asked, "Ann? Are you awake?"

She wanted to pretend she was asleep. She felt she had intruded on the life-and-death event beyond the curtain, but her pain was real, and she needed reassurance of some reality. "Yes, I'm awake."

"You okay?"

The woman with the white nurse's cap slipped through the curtain and just as quickly, closed it again. Rustling noises on the other side persisted for a while, then there was silence.

The nurse asked, "Are you in pain?"

"Yes. I can't breathe."

"Did Dr. Long talk to you after the surgery?"

"No, all I've seen is the nurse who gave me a pain shot."

"Did she explain?"

"No, but I know."

"How do you know?"

"I have no right breast now."

"Oh, Ann, I'm so sorry."

"That's okay. I don't need it. Bob doesn't even look at me that way anymore."

The nurse drew her lips into a smile and just as quickly, let it go. "Do you have any questions?"

"Why does my leg hurt so badly?"

"I don't know for sure. There was no mention of your leg in the report. Let me take a look."

A large, blood-soaked bandage sat on top of her right thigh. Part of the dressing had pulled away to reveal raw, dimpled flesh.

The nurse said, "Dr. Long gave you a skin graft on your chest and took the skin from the leg. It's called a split thickness graft, because only the surface of the skin is removed for the graft, leaving the base to grow back. It can be painful, because the skin is shaved, splitting nerve endings. It will get better in time."

Ann was relieved. "Thank you for telling me. What's your name?"

"Sharon. I'm the night nurse. I saw you last night."

"I remember you. You're the only person I've met in here who doesn't treat me like a machine. Do you have a minute? Can I ask some questions?" It was like finding an oasis in the desert, this nurse.

"I have all night. Fire away, and I'll answer what I can. First, let me loosen the chest bandage and redress the thigh. You'll feel a lot better." Sharon peeled away the dressing on the chest, then rolled Ann to the left.

Again, Ann remembered her mother and that last day. Shame overtook her as she lay there, controlled by the other woman.

Sharon asked, "How many children do you have, Ann?"

"Two girls, ages ten and eight."

Sharon grabbed a chair from the closet. "Tell me about them while I work."

"No ... I can't. Just help me"

"We have a long night, Ann. I can help, but I want you to help me too. Tell me. Is that so hard?" Sharon said as she ripped off one of the bandages.

Ann flinched, then realized what Sharon was doing. She didn't want to think about it. "Well, Michelle is ten. She's tall and lanky...." She tried hard to conjure the images to describe her. "Much taller than other kids in her class ... and is determined. She leads the girls, while the boys dare not make fun of her. Boys can do that at that awkward age when girls start to mature." Concentrating now, Ann continued proudly, "She earned the nickname Bossy, but not to her face. I suspect many a boy would go home with a bloody nose for using that moniker within her earshot. The only person who can use that nickname without retribution is Holly. Even then, she's careful to be sure it sounds like a title and not an accusation."

There was more pain, but Sharon continued her ministrations. "Michelle sounds like quite the character."

Ann tried not to pay attention to what Sharon was doing. "Yes, Michelle is hardworking and intelligent. A good student. Teachers appreciate her in class. She behaves totally different from the others. She's quiet, rarely volunteering answers or asking questions. Her teacher knows Michelle's answers, however pithy, will be correct. She'll be a beauty someday, with her teardrop face, brown eyes, and black hair. For now, she's in an apprenticeship as the ugly duckling." *Think hard. Try not to be here. Think of the girls.*

Now Sharon appeared not to be listening. She cut away the bandage and focused on the wound. "Go on."

"What do you mean?" Ann said, focusing on what Sharon was doing.

"You know your daughter pretty well, I'd say. Now tell me about the other one."

I know them, I don't know myself. She reverted to her thoughts again as Sharon poked the wound. "I'm a schoolteacher at the same school. That's why I know so much. Holly? She's like her sister, but shorter. She's bright, only she doesn't care whether she uses it or not. She goes with the flow … not a self-starter. She takes her clues from Michelle, but even then, she may not comply. So she's earned her nickname—Brat. Unlike Michelle, she doesn't mind the moniker." Ann squeezed her eyes shut and pictured her daughter. "She has high cheekbones and a symmetrical face … and red hair. She'll be more attractive than her sister some-day. She's self-conscious about her hair, since no one else in the family has red hair. Bob used to joke about her parentage, much to Holly's despair."

Sharon kept up the distraction. "What about your husband?"

I can't go there. She doesn't need to know. Ouch! "Bob? Well, he is nice, but a dreamer. Always looking for the gold at the end of the rainbow. He had an interview for a new job yesterday … I don't know how it went. I hope he gets it. I've been the sole support for a few months, and now I won't be able to work for a while."

"I can relate. My ex didn't work for a year. Just sat home, drinking beer all day. I wanted to go back to school, but I had to drop out."

"You're not a nurse?"

"Don't worry, I'm licensed. I got my degree by work experience and corre-spondence. Now I want to go back to school part time and get a master's or a PhD, so I can teach."

Ann was silent as she watched. Sharon seemed to have power as she stood over the bed, and Ann recalled her mother. Both were ambitious and responsible.

"Tell me more about Bob," Sharon said as she continued to work.

Ann couldn't look down any longer. The room smelled like a butcher shop. Now there was another smell, like the Mercurochrome Mom used to use on her scrapes. "What's to tell? He's just Bob. I met him in college. He was so shy, seemed helpless. That's probably what attracted me. I was put off by most boys, really didn't want a relationship. He was so needy. He wasn't doing well in college, wanted to drop out, so I helped him. Even wrote a couple of his term papers. Looking back, it was wrong. We both got jobs as teachers. I had to sign a three-year contract so they'd take Bob too. He didn't like it, and it didn't last. The poor principal found him another job just to get rid of him. Bob has jumped from job to job ever since."

"Sounds high maintenance, like mine. Is he emotional?"

"He has two gears—high and low. I have to be careful when he's on a roll. He's so sensitive. If I say the wrong thing, he pouts and shifts into a low gear that can last for days." She felt her face flush at this confession. Her thigh felt better, even cool now. Ann lifted her leg off the bed.

"Hold still, I'm not done. Doesn't sound like a marriage made in heaven. Maybe you should have been a nun."

Ann laughed, then thought for a moment. "No, I'm not Catholic, and I really wanted children."

"I can understand that." Sharon stood up and looked at Ann. "Okay, you're all set. Press the call button if you need anything else." She patted Ann's hand and left.

◆   ◆   ◆

The following morning, Dr. Long, with Sharon in tow, entered the room. "Good morning, Ann! It's a beautiful day. How did you sleep?"

Before Ann could respond, he inspected the chest dressing, showing a sudden look of puzzlement at the redressed wound. He turned to Sharon and frowned.

Ann summoned the energy to intervene. "I couldn't breathe until Sharon changed the dressings. What a relief!"

He glanced over her chest to her leg, then removed the dressing to inspect the graft underneath but said nothing. He leaned over her bed and propped one arm over her body. "Ann, do you have any questions?"

"Yes. When can I get out of here?"

He pulled his arm away and chuckled. "Depends. If your operation heals without infection, I'd say a week. Any other questions? I talked to Bob yesterday."

She wasn't sure what he meant, but she assumed that a recapitulation of events was not forthcoming. "No, Sharon talked to me last night."

Dr. Long gave Sharon another stern look as he rose and turned to leave. "Just rest now, Ann," he said as he exited the room.

Ann searched out Sharon's eyes to ask what went wrong. Sharon shrugged and chased after the doctor.

Ann looked at the ceiling for the hundredth time. Why was Dr. Long upset? After a while, she figured it was his issue and let her mind wander. Would she live two years more, like her mother, and then die, as she did? What about the kids? Michelle was old enough to comprehend, but did she need to know? Holly would take her cue from Michelle. *Should I tell them?*

Her intuition was to protect them from the bad news. She'd wait and tell them—eventually. They had a right to know. She remembered being angry because her mother had not told her. Her children should know ahead of time, and she would prepare them … somehow.

An aide entered the room with a washbasin and a towel, then left. Ann wiped her face with soothing, tepid water. Her ruminations continued. *Who will care for them after I'm gone? Bob is not strong enough.* She wished he would be more practical. He was always looking around the corner for a better job, a better life. He had little interest in his family. *I hope I'll live beyond two years, so I can raise them. Ten years would be great.*

A terrible thought crossed her mind. *If I got cancer from Mom, I can pass it on to the girls. Is breast cancer preventable?* She would have to find out, to save her girls.

Dr. Larson, Mom's doctor, had told Ann that she needed to check her breasts, but he didn't say how. He had implied that Ann might get cancer someday, but at the time, it hadn't seemed relevant. She would make sure the girls realized the importance.

Would Bob understand her concerns? Would he support her? They never had "alone time." She couldn't remember their last intimacy or kiss. How would he react to the cancer and the fact that she only had one breast? Could he accept it? Would she be less of a woman in his eyes? Would she be desirable?

She remembered telling Sharon that Bob didn't look at her sexually anymore. She was being flippant, but it was true. She blamed their lack of intimacy on their lifestyle. It would resolve itself, maybe. Now he might find her repulsive; he wouldn't want her anymore.

Ann's ruminations ceased with a cough, causing her chest to hurt more. She pressed the call button; it was time for a pain shot.

♦   ♦   ♦

Something caused her to wake. Dan, her dad, stood at the foot of the bed with hat in hand, as he had eight years ago. The suit was the same, as was the tie. The blues didn't match. Ann grimaced when his thigh accidentally bumped the footboard. He fingered his Stetson. "Hello, Ann."

She wanted to cry. She hadn't realized how much he meant to her until now. She looked into his eyes as the tears started to flow.

Dan cleared his throat and looked around for the chair, then moved it to the foot of the bed and sat down. His forehead still was two-toned, his face tan ending where his hat brim protected his head. His face was weathered and plagued. Doctors said it was discoid lupus. As a child, Ann had thought his complexion looked like fried pork chops. Mom use to rub bear grease on his face and proclaim it worked.

The room was quiet. Ann wanted to speak, to tell him how much he meant to her and how afraid she was. They didn't talk much about the past. She remembered how he used to behave when a boyfriend came over to the house. Dad would come out to the porch, where she was entertaining, and interrupt her, asking her to rub liniment on his aching back. It had worked every time—the boy would leave. If she liked the boy, it was irritating. At times, it did ease her out of awkward circumstances. Unspoken communication was their style. Today would be no different.

"Did you want me to rub some liniment on your back?" she said with a slight smile.

He appeared startled at her sudden question. After a pause, he broke into a chuckle. They both started laughing. A nurse stuck her head through the door to see about the commotion. At the sight of the authority at the door, they stifled the laughter, but the amusement lingered in their eyes. After a while, they became pensive again.

Dan asked, "Whatever happened to that boyfriend of yours who was going to be a doctor?"

"You mean Ralph Bowen?"

"Yeah, I guess."

"I think he got killed in Vietnam. He was a doctor over there."

"Too bad."

She knew what he was thinking. He wanted her to get all the help she could. She smiled. "You asked me to rub your back, the last time I saw him."

They started laughing again. Warm moisture on her chest brought her back to reality. She rang for the nurse. After examining the dressing, the nurse proclaimed the bleeding minor, nothing serious, and left.

They sat in silence. Occasionally, a tear would dislodge and run down Dan's cheek. He wiped it away with a quick motion, as though it were a bothersome fly. Otherwise, there was no communication.

Chapter 3

April 13, 1972
Afternoon

Ann's mouth was dry. She imagined a cup of tea or a large glass of orange juice with moisture dripping down the sides of the glass. She felt a bit hungry too, but she still felt nauseous. When she asked for something, the reply was, "You passed any gas yet?"

What does gas have to do with it? Besides, women don't have gas, only men. A man could rip one sounding like thunder, then smile as if he'd done something monumental, whereas a woman worked hard to avoid detection.

She wanted to fib, just to get a drink. How would they know? It was her word against theirs.

The pain was more tolerable now. Her chest didn't hurt much since Sharon had loosened the dressings, but her thigh still felt like a hot poker. She didn't want to medicate. That stuff made her nauseous, like she wanted to jump out of her skin. When Sharon put an ice pack on her thigh, it was better, but the day nurse took it away. Now Ann's buttock hurt as much as the surgery sites. "I want to go home," she said aloud, to no one but God.

"Oh, you do, do you? I don't think so. This is just your first post-op day, and it will be a while before you can go home. So get used to it," a voice from the door replied.

Ann turned to respond as the big nurse entered the room, carrying a blood pressure cuff and a thermometer. "I didn't hear you come in. I wasn't really talking to anyone."

"That's okay. I talk to myself all the time. I'm the only one who understands me." She laughed. "Let's take your vital signs. We have an exciting afternoon planned here at Club Med. You want another roommate?"

"No."

"Too bad. I got a handsome, virile, eighty-two-year-old man in room 223 who is anxious to meet a beautiful young woman like you. He is particularly obsessed with bottom pinching. Sure you don't want to share him with me?"

Funny, last week I would have been offended. Now it would be nice to have the attention. The thought brought her back to Bob. "Is it visiting hours yet? I wish I had a phone to call my husband. I haven't seen him or my family since the surgery."

"You want a phone? Next you'll be wanting your own hairdresser and masseuse. We have a phone on a cart with a long cord to the nurses' station. If you're a really good girl, I'll wheel it in here later. Tomorrow, though, you will have to walk or take a wheelchair to the hall phone. Which reminds me—you been up yet? No? Well, guess what we're going to do next? Come on, let's do it."

This nurse was a pleasant change from the others, in her own sadistic way. Still, Ann wished Sharon were there. The nurse pulled her to a sitting position, slung Ann's left arm over her shoulder, placed her arm on Ann's waist, and lifted. Ann was surprised. She was so light that the motion seemed effortless to both of them. She started down the hall, leaning on the IV pole for support, like an old woman. The nurse grabbed her gown, holding it closed in the back. Ann wanted to return when she realized people could see her.

Afterward, she was exhausted, but the pain was not as bad. In a way, she felt a sense of accomplishment.

The nurse tucked Ann back in bed. "Ring the call button when you have to go, and I'll help you to the bathroom. It's time you were potty trained."

The sheets bound her like a mummy, but she felt secure. A nap would be nice. The only thing better would be to see Bob and the girls.

The nurse came back in the afternoon with the phone cart and handed her the receiver. "What's the number? I'll dial."

No one was at home. She let it ring until the nurse interrupted. "Let's try later, okay?"

As the nurse pushed the cart out of the room, she called over her shoulder, "I'll just put the tip on the bill. Guests need not worry about the gratuities here at Club Med."

Of course no one was home. Bob must have gotten the job, and the girls were still at school. They'd be there tonight for sure.

Last night's talk with Sharon came to mind. Putting it into words seemed to make her relationship with Bob more objective. *Why did I marry him? I will think about that.*

Both of them had graduated as teachers, but Bob never enjoyed teaching, and he resented her achievements. He wanted to be successful in his own right. He tried construction and made good wages, yet it wasn't him. He tried sales for a while and wanted to go back for a business degree. His math skills just weren't good enough. She hoped he had gotten this new job as regional manager for janitorial products. Although he would travel, he could be home most nights. His drinking would diminish if he had a job.

She remembered their first date: the senior prom. Bob had showed up at the dorm with an orchid corsage. He was nervous taking it out of the box; he had fumbled, not knowing what to do. Worse, she had worn a white strapless gown. He had raised the flower to her breast, too embarrassed to proceed. She had taken it from him and pinned it to her waist. The girls in the dorm had giggled at his discomfort, but Ann found it endearing. How would he act now that she had no décolletage?

A knock at the door interrupted her thoughts. Bob stood there with a long-stemmed rose in one hand and a rolled-up paper in the other. He seemed nervous and uneasy. His gaze never left her face as he offered the flower to her.

"Hello, Ann. I came last night with the girls, but you were out of it, so we went home. The girls had homework to do."

For a moment, his eyes dropped to her chest, then they returned to her face, as if he was embarrassed. His stare made Ann uneasy. She wished he would bend over and at least kiss her.

"My mom died of breast cancer, you know," he sputtered, as if nervous about the topic.

"Yes, I know. So did mine." She felt her throat tighten.

"Yeah, so did her sister, and I think an aunt did too," he continued, ignoring her comment. "We were never sure about her, though. One day, her belly began to grow like she was pregnant, but she was already past menopause. I think my granddad died of ca—"

"Bob, please. This is not the time."

He shifted his eyes to the window at the corner of the room, as if looking for a diversion. He walked over to it. With his back to the room, he continued, "Maybe you got it from us."

"What?"

"Maybe I gave you something that made you have cancer."

"Bob, that's the most ridiculous thing I have ever heard! Cancer isn't contagious. For Pete's sake, get off this talk. I don't want to hear about your family history and some harebrained idea about this being your fault!"

Ann didn't like the way this reunion was going. He remained at the window as they both fell silent. The best thing to do was nothing.

Bob turned and waved the paper in his hand. "Oh, I got the job! It's even better than I dreamed."

Some good news, finally. "Great. Tell me about it."

"Well, it entails a lot of responsibility. I have to manage other salesmen ..."

"You'll still have to travel a lot?"

"Yeah, and now I have other things to do too. They want to send me to Virginia for six months to learn how to run a computer. Then I'll come back to track sales and revenues for the company. Neat, huh?"

"Well, you don't know anything about computers." She wanted to say more, but it would just start a fight.

"They'll teach me. Ann, you don't sound too enthusiastic. It's my big chance. I can get off the farm with this job."

"What do you mean? The farm is our home."

"No, Ann, it's your idea of home. I don't want to live on a farm. I've been thinking a lot about this. I want to be in a big city. That's where the girls will get the best education and life experiences. This is *the* big opportunity. The company will pay to move us to the Bay Area when I get back from Virginia."

"I ... thought the job was regional. San Francisco is a long way from here. I can't deal with this now, Bob. How are the girls?" She wanted to cry; her whole world was shattering.

Looking at his watch, he moved away from the window and toward the door. "Speaking of the girls, I have to go get them. It's almost four. Can I get you something?" With that, he almost ran out the door.

Ann lay still, alone in the room. Tears ran from the corners of her eyes, draining to her cheeks and into her ears. What a strange feeling it was to have tears in her ears.

Sharon stood at the side of the bed. Ann wasn't even aware of her at first. Neither said anything as the nurse with the white cap drew up a chair and sat. "Tell me about it."

"What do you mean?" Ann tried to act dumb.

"Judy told me your husband came in a while ago. Tell me about it."

"Oh, it isn't anything. He just ..."

"Ann, cancer changes everyone who has to deal with it."

"You mean he is having trouble with it too? I figured that much, but I think there's more to it. Bob ... well, Bob is struggling to find himself, I guess. He has this new job and an opportunity to move to the Bay Area. He thinks moving will solve all his problems. Why did he have to dump it on me now? I have problems too."

"You're just beginning to realize that?"

"What do you mean?"

"Well, most people hear the word 'cancer,' and they go numb for a while, until they have to deal with it beyond the emotional level."

"You're right … I guess. I am still numb and so afraid, I can't even think at times. I want to run and hide. At the same time, I think I'm dying, so why even try? The only rational thing was raising my family on the farm, and now Bob wants to rip us away. I love it here. The thought of my farm, raising the girls, and working as a teacher is all I have to go on. I can't beat this fear if I have to face the loss of my dreams and who I am. My mom lived two years before she died of breast cancer. I don't know how long I have, but it isn't long enough, and I don't want to waste it starting all over again in another place. I'm so afraid."

Sharon looked at her. "Do you love him?"

"Yes, maybe. Does he love me now that I'm deformed? He wouldn't even kiss me today, and he never looked at anything but my eyes. Sometimes I think he wanted me as some kind of trophy. Something he could drag out and show off every now and then. Now I'm tarnished. I became the successful one professionally, and he can't accept it. He was so helpless when I met him. For some strange reason, I found it appealing. I'm sorry, I'm rambling now."

"You feel better?"

Ann reached over and squeezed Sharon's hand. "Yeah. Thanks. I need to get real, don't I?"

As Sharon rose to leave, Ann added, "Thank you so much for … being here for me. I value your friendship." Not since her mother had Ann felt so close to another human, and this friendship was only two days old.

Chapter 4

Friday, April 21, 1972

It felt good to be leaving the hospital. Ann sat in the wheelchair, as required, all her paraphernalia stacked in her lap. Over the past few days, she'd become adept at changing her own dressings. She felt in control, even comfortable, despite the persistent hot-poker pain in her thigh. Both surgical sites still drained, particularly her chest. According to Dr. Long, the two remaining tubes could be inched out a little each day.

"Listen, Club Med pampered you. Now you have to go back to reality," the day nurse said as she pushed the wheelchair toward the exit.

"What happened to Sharon? I haven't seen her since the day after my surgery."

"Oh, I don't know. Nurses come and nurses go," she announced for anyone to hear. Then she glanced side to side, leaned over the wheelchair, and whispered, "Frankly, I think Sharon was too good for this place." She straightened and resumed her normal, loud voice. "Just don't overdo it at first. Those dirty floors don't need scrubbing today. Chances are, they have been that way for a while. Make the old man do the dishes and the laundry for the next couple of weeks." The big nurse babbled on as she pushed Ann toward the door.

Ann cringed at the reference to Bob. Since that first encounter after surgery, he had not come back to the hospital. Dad had stayed on to look after the farm and the girls. Bob had never showed. Ann had asked Dad about Bob, but he'd just shrugged and said, "Ain't seen him."

Her dad was taking her home today. He was at the entrance in his 1946 International half-ton pickup. It had been green at one time—beautiful, actually—when Dan had first brought it home. Ann was six then. Now it was rusted and old. Still, it was reliable … like Dan. Always there when needed.

Eager now, Ann pushed out of the chair and swung into the passenger seat as the nurse and Dan both tried to help. No, she would do it herself. Sitting up high gave her a sense of command as she bade the nurse good-bye. "This must be how a prisoner feels when released! Come on, Dad, let's go!"

The snow had melted, and as he turned from the hospital road onto the main street, she glanced at the field. "Slow down for a minute, Dad."

It was hard to see with no patch in the snow as reference, but it was there. Somehow, it had survived the freeze. On its two-inch stem, the flower stood resplendent in bright yellow, as if to shout, "Look at me! I made it!"

She turned and smiled at her dad to encourage him to speed up again. "It's a beautiful day. Not a cloud. It has to be spring now, Dad."

"Oh, we'll probably get another snow before it's over. This winter wheat here in the valley hasn't grown much since last fall."

During the eight-mile trip home, she was a kid again, bouncing in the seat of the old International truck like it was a tractor heading out to the field, looking around at familiar sights with a different perspective.

"There it is!" Ann exclaimed as the farm came into sight. "This view is always breathtaking, isn't it, Dad?"

But he didn't answer; he was obviously lost in his own thoughts. She leaned against the window and recalled the first time she had seen it. *Bob and I lived in the old motel down by the railroad tracks when we first came here. Michelle was six and Holly four at the time. Bob wanted to get an apartment in town, then look for a house. The only apartments available were by the train tracks, and I was concerned about the girls' safety.*

A truck sped by in the opposite direction creating a shock wave that rattled the passenger window, hitting Ann's head. She straightened and then gazed down the road as she relived the first trip here. The road wasn't paved in those days.

My principal suggested this place. He planned to retire here eventually, but when his wife died, he decided to move out of the area. The place made him distraught with memories of their plans together, so he practically gave it to me. There was no water, sewer, or electricity, and the land was undeveloped. It was part of an old homestead. Nevertheless, it was ideal, eight miles from town, on an old dirt road, with the nearest neighbor a half-mile away. Since it's on a gentle western slope under a granite mountain, it's bathed in the morning sun. We could wake to the trees of golden brown, and the evenings would bring long shadows dancing in slow motion until they faded away. I loved it at first sight. Dad gave me the money for the down payment.

A bump in the road made her chest hurt but Ann laughed to cover up the pain. Dan looked sidewise at her. "I'm trying to relive the first time I saw this place, Dad. Don't you do that sometimes?"

"Nope, but I wondered about this place. No agriculture on this land, because of the rocks and the lack of water. But it was pretty with those large ponderosa pines and Douglas firs and the occasional tamarack tree."

"Don't you think the view is worth it? Besides, we have deer, elk, and turkeys to provide meat, while quail, songbirds, and owls provide background music for the heart. Flickers act as alarm clocks. The kids can raise livestock to help with expenses. I love this lifestyle. This is home."

"You sound like a radio commercial for one of them suburb developments," he said, as the truck came to a stop at the front of the house.

He helped her into the house, then brought in her supplies. The trip had been more fatiguing than Ann had realized, and her chest dressing was soaking again. She changed the dressing, put on the terry-cloth robe, and returned to the kitchen, where Dan was making a pot of tea.

"I love this farmhouse, Dad. I helped place every log here. Remember how I had to coerce the banker to give me a loan to build the log house?" She glanced around the room. "Rustic, but with all the modern amenities. This is all I ever wanted."

Dan stirred honey into his tea and offered the honey jar to Ann. "What did the doctor say?"

"He said he got it all and most likely it wouldn't come back."

"Doc Larson told Betty that too."

"They don't always know. Did Mom still worry after her operation?"

"What do you mean?"

"I don't know…. Intuitively, did she think she still had it?"

"We never talked about it. She came home and went back to work. Looking back, I guess she worried. Every now and then, she'd say something to make me think she was planning to check out before me. That what you mean?"

"I guess. I feel … I don't know what I feel. It's like part of me is gone, my soul. Like I'm living on borrowed time, and any day, the cancer could come back. I can't shake the feeling."

"That's nonsense. Be like your mom—get on with it."

"I would love to be like Mom, just get up and go to work, but I have two kids who need me. Mom didn't, and she had you to help." She could hear the spoon tinkle against the side of the cup. "Oh, look. There's a doe out by the barn. She looks swollen. Bet there's a fawn about to drop."

She turned her eyes to the window and watched the doe. It grazed on the hay sprinkles where the cows fed, then ambled over the berm next to the runoff pond and out of sight.

"Why didn't you tell me Mom had cancer? I didn't find out until that night you called about the broken hip."

"Your mom didn't want anyone to know. Just get on with life, was all." He got up and put his cup in the sink. "I best be getting back to the ranch. Old Earl's been feeding the cattle, but we're about out of alfalfa hay. Hope the weather changes, so I can turn them out. Earl'll want to get on with his own herd."

"Did your ... relationship with Mom change afterward?"

Dan's face turned beet red as he sat back down at the kitchen table. "Ah ... I don't know what you mean."

"Yes, you do. I mean, did you still have it for Mom?"

"Your mother and I took a vow for better or worse. She would have stood by me if I lost a leg or something. Beauty ain't everything. It's what's inside that counts. Nothing changed. She was a woman, and I was a man. That's all there was to it. Listen, it's late, and I got to get back. Old Earl don't mind helping, but enough is enough, and this has been a burden. You understand? Anything you want me to do before I go?"

"No, I guess not. I'm sorry, Dad, I didn't mean to get personal. I just.... Thanks for coming all this way. I appreciate it. You've always been there for me."

He gathered up his hat and jacket.

"Dad, did Bob tell you where he was going or why he never came back to the hospital?"

His eyes focused on the counter as he shook his head. "You know, sweetheart, you can always bring the kids and come home."

"No, this is my home," she said as he closed the door behind him.

Ann wandered from room to room, grateful for the house and the solitude. The girls would be home at four, and for now, it felt good to be alive in the comfort of her farm. Her stamina waned just walking about the house.

She slept most of the afternoon. Later, she struggled into a dress as the movement caused more thigh pain. She planned to meet the girls at the bus stop a quarter-mile down the path. It was chilly, and the sky had become overcast.

She put on boots, an overcoat, and gloves, but her exposed legs suffered. By the time she had walked down to the road, she was exhausted. Looking back at the house, she wondered if she could make it. As the bus approached, Ann half hid behind a tree. She wasn't ready to have others see her. The bus driver waved as the children got off, and Ann waved back, self-conscious. As the bus drove off, the girls rushed to meet her. Michelle ran faster, reaching her with outstretched arms, wrapping herself around Ann's waist and pressing into her injured right thigh. The pain was excruciating, causing her to cry out and pull away. Both girls froze in horror.

"I'm sorry, Michelle. You didn't do anything wrong." Ann didn't understand their puzzlement until she felt the warmth on her leg. A red stain appeared on her dress over her thigh. What to do? She turned away from them, pretending nothing had happened, and started back to the house. The girls didn't follow at first, and she yelled back over her shoulder, "Come on! Let's have a snack!" Still the girls lagged as she tried to make light of the situation.

Finally, Holly spoke. "Are you going to bleed to death?"

"No, dear. I'm fine. You guys want a peanut butter and jelly sandwich?"

"You okay?" Michelle ventured.

"Of course. Don't worry about it. It's cold. Let's hurry." Her stamina left her, and she had to stop every few steps to rest.

"What's happened to you, Mom?" Michelle asked.

"I had an operation, that's all. It's okay now."

"What kind of an operation?"

"Nothing serious, just an operation. I'm still tired from it, and it will take a couple of days to regain my strength. Can you help me for a while?"

"How?"

"Well, just clean up your room and things like that."

"Okay." Michelle was still skeptical. "You going to die?"

"No, of course not. Whatever gave you that idea?"

"The first night in the hospital, you said you'd be home the next morning. But you didn't come home. Dad said you were sick, and every time we visited, you looked ... you didn't talk much."

Holly chimed in, saying, "Yeah, and Daddy wouldn't talk either. It was a big secret. Then Grandpa came to look after us."

"When did your dad leave?" Ann asked Holly.

"After your operation, he put us in bed and listened to our prayers. I heard the car leave."

"Did he say when he would be back?"

"No. He took a lot of stuff, though."

Finally, they were at the steps of the house. Ann needed to lie down, but first she checked the closet. Bob's clothes were gone.

There wasn't even bread for sandwiches. Dad was like that. Sometimes at his house, all she could find were beans. She should have asked him to go to the store before he left. How could she go out, looking like this?

After bedtime, she dressed again, this time in a yellow dress with no waistline and black boots up to her knees. She stuffed tissue paper under her dress over the chest dressing and looked in the mirror. Not satisfied, she added more, until it looked almost normal and somewhat symmetrical. She paced around the room, coming back to look in the mirror again.

She waited until 11:00 PM, checked to be sure the girls were asleep and the fire had died out, then slipped away silently to the car. The local Safeway was open until midnight.

As she turned off the highway, she was relieved to see that there were only a few cars in the parking lot. This might work. The handful of shoppers appeared inattentive as she entered. She did not recognize anyone.

While shopping, she checked the makeshift prosthesis for authenticity. She wished she had some more tissue; activity had flattened it. She bought a roll, slipped into the bathroom, and reconstructed. Relieved, her confidence bolstered, she returned to shopping, only now the place was more crowded. The store was filled with night-shift workers from the plywood plant, shopping on their way home.

One man in particular seemed to be eyeing women as if this were an occasion to cruise. Ann was reaching to a top shelf when her chest started leaking profusely, staining her dress and causing the tissue to collapse, wet, against her clothing. As the incident unfolded, the man started down the aisle toward her. His lascivious grin turned to revulsion as he approached and viewed the front of her dress. Ann ran out the store, leaving her groceries in the cart.

Back in her bedroom, she was tearful as she undressed and removed the bandages. She stood in front of the mirror, wanting to see what others saw. She had refused to look at herself naked in the mirror before, dreading what she might see.

She gasped. It was the same body, but there was no right breast, only ribs. A patch of white skin the diameter of a grapefruit showed two thin rubber tubes poking out each side, the one closest to the armpit draining a thin, bloody yellow fluid. The muscle to her shoulder was gone. The exposed ribs under her white skin looked ghoulish. Her right side seemed to have melted away and died. The only sign of healing was the presence of scars, but even they gave the impression of desperate patching. Part of her was alive, and part of her was dead. Sobbing, she turned off the light.

The next morning, after the kids left for school, armed with money for breakfast and lunch, Ann noticed an envelope propped against the flour jar on the counter. The handwriting was Bob's.

Dear Ann:

I have to go to San Francisco for a week of orientation. Afterward, I will fly back to Virginia to begin training. If you want, I will get an apartment in the Bay Area for you and the kids. Then when I get back, we can be together again. I need this opportunity to be somebody.

Love, Bob

Ann looked out the window, absentmindedly tapping the note against her fingers. A sigh and a deep breath later, she threw the note into the fire. "Now the ball is in my court," she proclaimed to no one at all.

Chapter 5

May 16, 1972

Snow? It's May! Michelle looked out the window. The cold house had awakened her early, and she scrambled out of bed, dressed quickly, and descended the loft to start a fire in the stove. Mom was still asleep, or at least still in her bedroom. She didn't come out much, and when she did, it wasn't for a long time. Michelle had heard her the previous night, moving around the house, so she was probably still asleep.

The fire started crackling as flames leaped around the tamarack kindling. She piled on a log. Mesmerized by the fire, she knelt in front of it, occasionally poking the embers to stoke more heat. She turned around to warm her backside before heading to the kitchen to make breakfast and fix their lunches. *Plenty of time.*

"Yogurt again? I hate yogurt! Why can't we have eggs?" Holly came in the kitchen, still in her pajamas, peeking around Michelle to see the fare for breakfast.

"Why aren't you dressed? Go get dressed before we eat."

"But it's cold, and I want to be by the fire. Let me eat first, then I'll get dressed. I'm going to have Cheerios and milk. What kind of sandwich? I hope it isn't bologna again."

"You'll get what I make. Now, hurry up while I clean up the kitchen."

Later, they plowed through the snow to the bus stop. The snow was heavy, with about six inches on the ground. Holly dallied, dragging her feet and occasionally falling to make a snow angel. As she lay, looking up at the flakes coming toward her face, she asked, "You think Mom will ever be well again?" Her breath was foggy.

"I ... don't know."

"You think Dad is coming back?"

"I don't know."

"You don't know shit, do you?"

"Brat! Watch your mouth! I ought to—" Before she could finish, Holly stood and threw a snowball at her chest, then tried to run away. "Why, you—!"

Being taller with longer legs, it didn't take much effort for Michelle to catch her sister, pounce on her, and stuff snow down her back. She wanted to be sure that the punishment fit the crime. The snowball wasn't so bad, but the profanity was unacceptable. Michelle hadn't heard Holly use a bad word before, and she didn't want to hear it again. Those boys, whose fathers worked at the mill, used foul language. That must be where she had learned it. *I'll deal with them later.*

Holly was crying as she danced around, trying to get the snow out of her clothes. The scene didn't fit the emotion, and Michelle stood by, laughing.

"You're a bully, Bossy!" the younger girl screamed while trying to cry. Not getting any sympathy, she stopped. Both stood silently for a while. The bus was late. The only activity now was an occasional stamping of feet to keep warm.

Holly returned to her concerns. "Will Mom die?"

"She isn't getting better."

"Is that why Dad left? You think he knew she was going to die?"

"I don't know. Why are you asking all these silly questions? I don't know the answers!"

"I don't ... understand, I guess. Sometimes I just lie in bed and look out the window at the mountain and wonder. Sometimes I think Mom got sick because we ... I did something wrong. Maybe Dad wouldn't have left if we ... I didn't do it."

"That doesn't make sense," Michelle responded, but with some doubt, as if she had entertained similar thoughts.

"Oh, yeah? Then why is it a big secret?"

There was silence again. Michelle walked out and stood in the road, looking for the bus. If it didn't come soon, they would have to go back to the house, as both were now shivering.

"I'm cold," Holly said.

"Let's huddle. If the bus doesn't come in five minutes, we'll go back to the house. Okay?"

"What do you want to be when you grow up?" Holly asked as the shivering subsided.

"You ask the dumbest questions. Why can't you be quiet?"

"Well?"

"I ... want to be a teacher like Mom. Or a principal."

"You ought to be a general."

"Don't be silly. There's no such thing as a woman general. What do you want to be?"

"You remember when we went over to the Jensens' last Sunday and watched television? That show about the ballet? I want to be a ballerina! I want to travel and have people like me."

"You would be good at it, since you can't stand still. Hold still!"

"You ever think about running away, like go to Arizona or New York or, better yet, Alaska?"

"No, and you shouldn't either. Oh, good, here comes the bus."

◆   ◆   ◆

Michelle took small steps as she made her way to the principal's office. She was in trouble, and all the kids knew it. At noon, she had slugged Andrew, a millwright's son, and then stood over him, proclaimed that she'd knock his block off if he ever said another bad word in front of Holly again. He must have reported her.

Michelle opened the outer door to the office. "Yes, Mrs. Meyers?"

"Oh, come in, Michelle. I wanted to talk to you. How's your mother doing?"

"She's doing good." She was nervous now. Adults tended to ask funny questions before they punished you.

"The reason I ask is because I tried to call her this afternoon but didn't get an answer."

"She probably went to the store. Yeah, that's it. I remember her mentioning that." Michelle was more nervous now. *She is going to tell Mom.*

"Well, could you tell her to call me tomorrow?"

"Sure," she said, her heart thumping.

"I need to talk to her because her sick leave is about up, and I will have to put her on administrative leave for the rest of the year. I hope that she will come back next year. Can you remember all that?"

"Yes, ma'am." Her relief was obvious.

Mrs. Meyers said, "Is everything okay?"

"Sure, we are doing just fine."

"You have been acting … different since your mother became ill."

"No problem. I just got a lot on my plate right now." *Where did that come from? Oh, yeah. Dad always said that to Mom when they were fighting.*

Mrs. Meyers smiled. "Yes, I suspect you do. You had better go now, so you don't miss the bus. Please tell your mother, okay?"

"Yes, ma'am." *This isn't so bad.*

As she opened the door to leave, the principal added, "Oh, yes. There is one other thing, Michelle. Could you take it a bit easier on the boys?"

"Yes, ma'am."

The school halls were still empty as Michelle went to her locker. She would wait outside until the bell rang. She didn't want to go back into the classroom, not because she felt shame (which she didn't), but rather guilt. She would do anything to protect her family, even if it meant lying or beating the snot out of someone.

◆   ◆   ◆

A few nights later, Ann undressed in the dark, which was now her routine. Then she turned on the light to look at her body in the mirror, as others would see her. Assured there was no change, she would then go to bed. Tonight was different; the cancer had come back! At first, she wasn't sure, but that was because she didn't want to believe it. Try as she may, she couldn't explain what she saw, except to conclude that the cancer was back.

In the mirror, her ribs were the same, and even the white patch of skin was the same, except now, the drain tubes were gone; she had pulled them a week ago. Since then, there was a scar on the inside site and a small hole on the outside site. Every night, the outside hole seemed to be getting smaller as it healed, but now there was a large lump, about the size of a golf ball, below the hole. It hadn't been there the night before. It even hurt a little, and she remembered feeling discomfort at the site since afternoon.

What else could it be? She could think of no other option. No, the cancer was back. Sleep would not come, and she paced back and forth in the room. *This came back faster than I knew it would … but this fast? I have children! It didn't grow this fast when I first had cancer. Maybe the surgery caused it to grow more rapidly. I have to call Dr. Long! No, that's not a good idea, He'll just tell me to come in the morning. Besides, the girls might hear the call. I could go to the emergency room. No, they would just call Dr. Long.* She watched all night but it didn't grow any more.

She was so exhausted by morning that all she could do was lean by the door, but when she did, she thought she heard a sloshing sound. She leaned again. "There's water in this door." Again the same sound. "Wait a minute, that's not the door, it's in the wall. No, it's coming from … me. Oh, my god! What's it doing?"

At 9:00 AM precisely, she called the office. "Please … please … answer the phone," she said as it kept ringing.

Every few minutes, she called, until someone finally answered. "I need to see Dr. Long immediately! This is an emergency!"

There was a long pause from the other end. At first, Ann thought the line was disconnected. "Dr. Long is not with us. I can get you in at one this afternoon with Dr. Anderson, who is covering."

"You can't get me in sooner? This really is an emergency." She felt her grip on the phone tighten.

"Dr. Anderson is in surgery this morning. If you can't wait, go to the emergency room."

"No, I'll be there at one."

She hung up and gently walked back to the bedroom and eased down onto the bed. It sloshed again, even though she moved as carefully as she could. Ann didn't move again until it was time to go.

It was two thirty before Dr. Anderson entered the examining room. Her anxiety had stripped her of stamina, and the longer she waited, the worse it got. Dr. Anderson looked tired, but he was nice and sympathetic. He examined her chest wall carefully, then had her lie down. He took a syringe with a needle and plunged it into the tumor. Two tablespoons of straw-colored liquid came out. Afterward, the tumor was gone.

"This lump is called a seroma, Mrs. Garrity. Sometimes after surgery, an irritated spot will wall itself off then retain fluid and form a cyst. It shouldn't bother you again, but it can come back. If it does, come in, and we will drain it again."

"It isn't cancer?" Ann asked, for reassurance.

On the way home, she didn't know whether to laugh or cry. "Somehow, I have to get control. I'm so scared."

Chapter 6

Summer of 1972

Ann was standing at the kitchen counter when the phone started ringing. It would be best not to answer it, but curiosity got the better of her. She shuffled across the room, hoping it would stop. Her heart was pounding in her chest, but she was still ambivalent. As if taken over by an invisible force, she lifted the receiver, held it in silence for a moment, then almost whispered hello.

"That you, Ann? You still asleep?"

For the first time since coming home from the hospital almost two months ago, she wanted to talk. "Dad! Where are you?"

Dan was not one to use the telephone. He was a man of the earth who shunned most modern things in favor of the simple. He would rather ride a horse than his truck; he only drove it to get supplies. He was more comfortable communicating with his cow dogs with whistles and arm gestures than talking to other humans. She could only remember getting a call from him once before, when Mom died.

"I'm at home."

"You got a telephone at home? That's great, Dad!"

"Naw, I'm down at the switchboard in town. Elsie is letting me call."

"Elsie's still the operator? When are they going to get modern? Why did you call? Everything okay?"

"Fine. Just wanted to see how you're doing. Bob back?"

Ann felt flushed, and she hesitated. "Ah, no."

"You getting out? Back to work?"

"No, not yet. I am still pretty tired."

"You dressed?"

She looked down at the opened robe and slippers. There were stains on the front of her nightgown. She closed the robe, as if he could see. "No. I don't get out of the house, so I'm still in my … nightclothes."

"Your mother went back to work after a week."

"I ... can't. I need more time, Dad. How's your weather? Could you come visit?"

"Weather here's fine. We got lots of rain. Now the hills are green, and I got the cows out. Good thing too—low on hay."

"Could you come?" It was almost a sob.

"Three hours there, then three back. Can't now. Got to get the alfalfa in while I can. Been too wet to plant till now, and I'll need at least four cuttings this year to make it through next winter. I'll come when I can, promise."

"I miss you."

"Elsie's telling me to wrap it up. You do something for me? You get outside today. Nothing better than outdoors to get your mind off your troubles. Perk you up too. Promise?"

"I promise. Bye, Dad." She listened for a long time after the line went dead, until the phone started to beep.

She wanted a cup of tea and reached to the cupboard. Reaching up no longer caused drainage, but she now had limited motion in her right arm. Pain in her shoulder also made movement of her arm difficult, so she had to stand on her toes. She wanted to go back to bed. Usually, after shopping, she would flop in bed and stay there until noon, while Michelle and Holly continued their duties, independent of supervision. At first, Ann would call the doctor when a new symptom developed, but the nurse taking her call would just tell her that the symptom wasn't serious. After a while, Ann quit calling, even though, in her mind, any symptom or new finding by nocturnal self-examination suggested that the cancer was growing back. She wished the pains would go away.

The morning sun did look inviting as she stared out the window while stirring honey into her tea. There was a motion in the snowberry bushes at the top of the berm. At first, the movement was barely perceptible, and had she not be staring at that point then, she would have missed it. But there it was again: this time, the limbs of the shrubs shook. Still, there was nothing to see. She took a sip of sweetened tea, then moved out to the patio to sit in the sun; she had promised Dad she would.

The air smelled sweet, as it does when spring heralds new life. The ground was moist and the grasses heavy with early morning dew. Brown was giving way to green, and the tips of the evergreen trees were yellow-green with new growth. New life was everywhere.

The cry of a quail broke her thoughts. A mother quail with five chicks hopped upon the lower rail of the fence across from the little pond in the yard. The father quail was already there, and he crowded the mother as he scooted down the rail, displacing chicks as he went. He scurried down to the pond to drink. The family followed as he finished drinking, then he stood vigil for the rest. After a while, he chirped, and they all ran off, single file, into the tall grass. At first, Ann felt animosity toward the male, but as the scene unfolded, she could only admire the dynamics. *If only Bob were like Dad or that quail. Maybe I should have followed him.*

There was that movement on the berm again. Curious now, she decided to investigate, knowing the effort would be great. Something was wrong. Ann climbed the slope of the old catch dam, and about halfway up the effort proved considerable. She stopped, rested, then decided to turn back. There it was again, but now she could see little ears. She continued up. The fawn did not move now, and she knew it wouldn't. It was still, except for rapid breathing. Normally, a fawn would not even breathe perceptibly when approached.

As she reached the berm, she could see dry blood covering the fawn and a part of the birth membrane still wrapped around its body. Why had the mother abandoned it at birth? She looked around for answers. Animals used this runoff reservoir, and it was not uncommon to find them here in the early morning or late evening.

She slid down the steep inner slope of the dam toward the water's edge. There she found the answer. A dead doe lay there, with a protruding placenta. Blood was everywhere. It had hemorrhaged and died giving birth. The fawn had survived, at least for the moment, and had reached the berm, for some strange reason. How could it survive without the mother cleaning the amniotic membrane and severing the umbilical cord? Yet the fawn had gotten to the berm. There were fresh dog or coyote tracks. Somehow, a canine had appeared at the right time and dragged the fawn up the slope. She had probably scared it away earlier that morning before it could enjoy its feast.

She crawled back to the top to inspect the animal. Blood matted its fur, as did the amniotic membrane. The membrane was constricting its chest as it dried and shrunk, causing breathing difficulties. The fawn was a male. Close inspection showed the right back leg extended, with puncture wounds on the thigh. Two of the skin punctures were torn, exposing deep muscle. *Like my leg,* she thought.

Despite its plight, the fawn did not appear frightened. If anything, it lay in such a way as to suggest acceptance of death. His eyes were not wide with fear, and although his chest constriction was severe, he would occasionally sigh. Tears welled up and blurred her vision as she pulled away the membrane, using her index finger as a hook. With her dress hem, Ann wiped dirt from its eyes, but it did not blink. Standing, she removed her housedress, stooped, and wrapped the fawn with it. The dress absorbed some of the blood as her gentle hands massaged the little buck, hoping the stimulation would help. She stopped massaging to wipe away tears and blow her nose. The animal still did not respond, but it didn't seem any worse, either. She made a sling out of the dress and slowly dragged the animal back to the house.

Ann was exhausted. According to the clock, only fifteen minutes had passed since she made tea. How could so much happen in fifteen minutes? It seemed like two hours. With warm water and a hand towel, she cleaned the fawn's wounds and fur as the little animal shivered, lying on the kitchen rug. She rummaged in the utility room and found Holly's old day blanket. She warmed it in the dryer for a minute, then used it to cocoon the fawn. If it didn't get nourishment soon, it would die. An old baby bottle was in a box of things in the attic. Sugar water might work for a while.

The deer finally took the nipple after Ann held his head and stimulated his mouth with her finger. At first, it suckled weakly, but then it became more aggressive, nudging the bottle with nose thrusts when the amount was not as much as expected, and soon the bottle was empty. Before she could decide whether to refill the bottle, the animal closed its eyes, its breathing became regular for the first time, and it slept undisturbed.

Ann dressed again, deciding to call her neighbor, who lived about a mile down the road. Fred Block was the regional director of the state fish and game service. He would know what to do.

"Hello, Fred. This is Ann Garrity. Are you busy at the moment?"

"No, Ann. What's up?"

"I just found a dead doe with a fawn. The fawn is alive, but not by much. A dog or coyote has chewed its leg. What do I do with it?"

"How old do you think it is?"

"It's a newborn. Still had the membrane wrapping."

There was a pause. "Ann, it won't make it. Best to just leave it there for the coyotes."

Now it was her turn to pause.

"Ann. Ann? You still there?"

"That's not an option I want to take, Fred. Besides, I brought it home. What do I feed it? It has a gash in its leg. What do I do with that?" She realized, as she talked, that she wasn't asking Fred to take it, but instead asked what she should do. She was committed now.

"Ann, now, listen to me. We do not encourage people to take in wild animals. It's a mistake. You'll regret it. Please, let nature take its course. If it were older, we would relocate it, but even then, its chances of survival are slim. You can't play God. Besides, it's against the law."

That was his mistake. Now Ann knew she would try. Fred continued to convince her otherwise. "Even if we had facilities for situations like this, a wounded newborn won't make it."

"Thanks anyway, Fred."

"Look, Ann, I don't mean to be a hard-ass, but those are the facts. Keep it warm, and if it's still alive tonight, I'll drop by and see what you can do."

Ann was busy the whole day. She scrubbed the deer's open wounds with soap and water and doused them with a heavy dose of mercurochrome from the veterinarian box. She tried treating the wounds as she treated hers, but the chest dressings, called 4x4s, wouldn't stay in place. Finally, she just left the wounds open but cleaned them every couple of hours. For the first time since her surgery, she left the house during the day, going back to the store to buy baby formula, which she fed to the fawn every hour. Despite the exhaustion, she felt revitalized.

The children got off the bus at the usual time and found their mother in the kitchen, making snacks. Wiping her hands on a towel, Ann announced, "I have a surprise for you! Come."

In the wooden kindling box by the fireplace lay the fawn, wrapped in a blanket on a pillow. It could raise its head now, and it did so when three heads peered down.

"A baby deer!" exclaimed Holly.

Ann shushed the kids so as not to startle it. They stared until Holly mumbled, "Bambi."

"That's a stupid name," said Michelle. But she was excited. "Can we keep it?"

Ann had anticipated this. "It's not ours, dear. It belongs to Mother Nature. For now, though, we must take care of it until it is strong enough to care for itself. But it ..." She stopped talking.

Michelle looked at Ann and understood. "Did its mother die, Mom?"

"It was just born when its mother died. A dog or a coyote grabbed it away. Its leg is hurt, and it may not live. Do you understand?"

"Yes. We have to try, Mom. Let's call it Yoty, short for coyote."

"Yes, we have to try, but it isn't our fault if it dies. Life is precious but fragile. Yoty is not healthy, and you must realize that what we are doing may not save it. If it dies, it dies." Ann was frustrated that she could not express herself more clearly, but the kids seemed to understand and were up to the challenge. They were country kids now, and they had learned that life came with chores and hardships. Some of the chores were of their own choosing, such as caring for a baby deer.

◆   ◆   ◆

After dinner, Fred called back. "That fawn still alive?"

"Yes, Yoty seems to be doing okay."

"Oh, God, you've even named it. Do you know what you are doing?"

"Fred, damn it. I don't need you to judge. I need help." She surprised herself by saying it, but it did feel good. She was in control and taking on the responsibility.

"Okay, Ann. You want me to come over?"

She didn't, but they needed help. After hanging up the phone, she quickly made herself presentable. She changed into a clean housedress and prepared a prosthesis. After the supermarket incident, she had devised a new one: a balloon. She would blow up a small party balloon to about the size of her breast, then stick it under the blouse. She still could not wear a bra. The balloon would stick to her skin but would roll around, so she had to tape it in place. To give the appearance of symmetry, the real breast was packed with tissue to make it round like the balloon. The achieved symmetry was larger than real life, and wearing a balloon inconspicuously was not easy, even if it was taped down. She would have to squirm every now and then to keep it in place. To a casual observer, the behavior gave the appearance of a neurological disorder. The makeshift breast would only have to work for a little while, and she felt she could handle it for about an hour at most.

Hurry up, Fred! It seemed like an hour, but in actuality, Fred drove up in his official state pickup about fifteen minutes after hanging up. He had alcohol on his breath but was not drunk. She kept her arms folded to support the faux breast. It was easier than squirming.

He asked, "Where is it?"

The children sat at the kindling box, looking in, as the adults stepped into the room. Fred lifted the fawn and examined the wound. For the first time, the deer struggled.

Ann said, "That is a good sign, isn't it?"

At least it had the strength now to move. Fred placed the animal back in the box, straightened, and looked at Ann, indicating with a toss of his head that they should go to the kitchen to talk. There, he sighed and said, "Ann, please. This is not right. That animal is not going to make it. Those tears are all the way down to muscle and probably infected. It looks good now, but in a couple of days, gangrene will set in, and then it will get ugly. Let me take it and put it to sleep. That way, the kids won't know."

With her arms still folded, only now with resolve, she replied, "Thanks for coming over. We'll manage."

At the door, he half-turned and shrugged. "Okay, Ann. Keep it warm, and feed it every two hours. It will probably get diarrhea feeding on formula, but that is probably as good as anything for now. If you have any topical antibiotic …?"

"I have polymyxin ointment for the horse."

"Okay, put that in the wound. Not on the wound, but in the wound. Can you do that?"

"I'm not squeamish, if that's what you mean. Give me a break, Fred. I've taken care of animals before."

He looked at the floor. "Sorry, Ann. Watch for dehydration when it gets diarrhea. Put a pinch of salt in the formula when that happens, and give plenty of fluids. You might have to go to sugar water instead of formula. Other than that, I don't know what else you can do." He turned to leave, but again he hesitated. With his back to her, he asked, "How are you going to deal with the kids when it dies?"

"The children need to know that love involves death just as much as life. There are good times and bad times. If Yoty lives, we will celebrate, but if Yoty dies, we will mourn. That's life. They must learn that too."

Fred nodded and left. Ann unfolded her arms and dropped them to her sides with a large sigh. "Now I can get out of this costume." As she headed to the bedroom, she glanced in the hall mirror on the way. The balloon was over her collarbone, almost sitting on her shoulder. It looked more like a second head than a breast.

Later that night, Ann lay in bed, exhausted but thinking, as sleep would not come. She thought of Yoty, and how life was precarious. She reveled in her role to keep it alive and was thrilled by the enthusiasm of the children. For the first time in a long time, they were a family, and this newfound unity felt good. She thought about how Yoty could breathe after she had released the constricting membrane. Maybe her arm limitation was due to scarring like that; if so, loosening the scar might make her arm move better. She would try, starting tomorrow. Exercise might even help the numbness.

In all the excitement, she had not inspected herself tonight. She got up and undressed for the ritual. No, there was no change, despite the labor of the day. *I didn't injure anything!* Yes, exercise might help. She got back in bed as the door squeaked. Ever vigilant to noises, Ann interrupted her thoughts to listen.

"Mom, you awake?"

"Yes, dear. Come in."

Michelle jumped on the bed, almost bouncing Ann out of it. "Mom, can I ask you something?"

Ann drew the child to the crook of her left arm and hugged. "Shoot."

"Will Yoty live?"

Ann sighed inwardly. She thought carefully, then answered as honestly as she could. "Mr. Block doesn't think it will. Chances are not good for Yoty. Even if he makes it through the night, he faces infections and diarrhea. After that, he will grow and be too big to stay in the house. The dogs could kill him if he leaves the house. He won't be able to care for himself for many months, if ever. His life will be hard if he lives. But, my darling Michelle, we love him and will care for him as long as we can."

"I don't want him to die."

"If he dies, we must accept that as nature's way."

Michelle was silent for a while, then spoke with a soft and cracking voice. "Will you live, Mom?"

"Yes, I will."

They lay in each other's arms, both with drying tears on their cheeks. After Michelle went to sleep, Ann carefully extracted herself and went to the firewood box to check their ward.

◆　　◆　　◆

Yoty did live though the night. In fact, he woke Ann by making noise, trying to get out of the box. He could stand but could not support his weight with his right hind leg. It was stiff and swollen but seemed to move. The children were delighted. Both girls wanted to feed the hungry animal, so Ann made them take turns.

As the days passed, Yoty became stronger. He did not get gangrene, as Fred had predicted. Later that summer, his leg healed. The girls would put the deer out in the morning and watch during the day for dogs and coyotes. But at night, Yoty slept in the house, actually in a bed. He didn't discriminate; one night he'd be with Ann, but another night might be with Michelle or Holly.

Chapter 7

Fall 1972

Ann was becoming more comfortable with her body. She worked hard to break the scars. It was painful at first, but it was working. She could raise her right arm above her head normally, and the wounds finally healed that summer. The numbness didn't go away, but now she could wear a bra. She tried stuffing the right cup with tissue paper, but the effect was not satisfactory. A trip to the local department store to procure an enhancer improved the look. She wore it during the day as she became more active, but her back ached, and she felt lopsided.

Early that fall, just before school started, Dad drove through the gate and up to the house in the old Chevy truck. There was a passenger this time: Dan's older sister, June. This woman had two features that stuck in Ann's mind: asperity and one arm twice the size of the other. The last time she had seen June was thirteen years ago, at her college graduation party, where the older woman had displayed her usual popery, dampening the festivities. Ann helped her out of the car, feigning pleasant surprise while turning her head to Dan with a quizzical expression: *Why did you bring her here?* Dan smiled and just shrugged his shoulders as he headed to the house to greet the kids. It was obvious that his reason for this visit was to see them. It was also obvious that the passenger was not his primary concern.

"What's that damn deer doing in your yard?" June croaked as Ann helped her up the steps to the patio and kitchen door. Ann was surprised she had even noticed, with her bent head concentrating on the steps.

"That's the kids' pet deer, Yoty, Aunt June."

"You better get rid of it. It will eat your plants."

"It already has."

Indeed, Yoty was fond of the garden. None of the twenty prize Benjamin roses were thriving this year, for lack of buds and leaves. The marigolds were untouched, which gave the garden a yellow spottiness. They went into the house.

"Smells like piss in here," Aunt June pronounced.

◆   ◆   ◆

After two long days, the visitors gathered at the car to leave. As Dan said good-bye to the kids, June pulled Ann to the side. With uncharacteristic gentleness, she said, "I asked your father to bring me over here. Everyone knows you got cancer, Ann. It's nothin' to be ashamed of. Ain't your fault. You know, I had cancer too. They whacked off my breast back in 1949, and I'm still here. Hell, dearie, you don't need them anyway once the kids don't use a teat anymore. Who cares what men think? Face it, dearie, that's one appendage you don't need, and if you got to lose an appendage, it's the best one to lose. If you're going to look good for the men, though, you better do something about that falsie."

Ann just stood there, dumbfounded.

Later that night, she lay in bed, thinking. Aunt June was right. Better to lose a breast than an arm or leg. The problem of Yoty was on her mind. He was a mule deer, the biggest deer species found in this state, and he was growing fast. He was still just a fawn, but his spots were gone now, and his hooves were playing havoc with the linoleum kitchen floor. She hadn't been aware of the urine smell until Aunt June had pointed it out. Yoty had to move out.

The next day, Ann drove to town and mustered the courage to go into the department store and ask the salesperson what kind of bra women with mastectomies needed. The woman was kind and sympathetic, but she didn't have any postmastectomy bras and really didn't know much about them. She did know a woman, Alice, who might be able to help. Ann called that very night. For the first time since leaving the hospital, she felt comfortable talking to another person.

"I'm glad you called, Ann. I know exactly how you feel. I was ashamed to talk about it and had no idea want to do. I had Dr. Long too, but he was too busy to explain things. Finally, my daughter in Salt Lake took me to a surgical supply house, where I got a special bra, and my backaches subsided."

"Can anyone get these bras?"

Alice gave Ann the address of a surgical supply house, but it was two hundred miles away. Early the next morning, she packed the kids in the car, locked Yoty in the barn—Fred would check on him later—and headed to the surgical supplies store. The car warmed as the sun rose higher, but the kids just rolled down the windows and enjoyed the adventure. It was their first time out since the last summer.

There was a toy store down the street from Shaw's Surgical Supplies, so Ann gave Michelle a ten-dollar bill, telling her that the money was to last for the whole trip. With the kids happily ensconced in the toy store, Ann returned to the supply house and, with trepidation, entered. A man greeted her. She thought, *This is not good.*

"Are there any women salespeople?"

He pointed with his chin to a door in the corner.

An older woman sat at the only desk in the room. "Hello," she said. "May I help you?"

"I … may be in the wrong place. I'm sorry to have disturbed you." Ann's courage had fled.

"I'm Mrs. Anderson, the breast prosthesis counselor, if that is who you are looking for," the older woman said, smiling.

"This is really embarrassing. I …"

"You need not be embarrassed. I had cancer, and I wear one. You're having backaches, right? Come on in, and let's see what we can do."

Two hours and a hundred and fifty dollars later, Ann had accomplished her mission. She left the store with the latest model and Mrs. Anderson's business card. All that money translated to guilt, but she stepped out onto the sidewalk as if it were a new day. The information alone had been worth it, and now she knew there were a lot of women like her, with the same issues.

Rather than drive, Ann walked down to the toy store, swinging her arms and even swaying her hips. A car with teenage boys drove by, and one of them whistled. They couldn't tell either! As her feet sprang along the sidewalk, the world moved in a different way. Michelle and Holly were sitting under a maple tree to get out of the sun. Both girls looked puzzled. Something was different.

Now I can live a normal life.

◆   ◆   ◆

Along with the kids, Ann went back to school in the fall. Occasionally another teacher would ask about her operation, but by now, she could handle it. If a female asked, she was honest; if a male asked, she answered using nonsensical wording, leaving him to scratch his head.

Life was good, but still the loneliness was there. She missed Bob. Looking back over the past few months, she began to question her own role in their rift. She wanted to talk to him, at least. *He must be in San Francisco,* she thought. He hadn't left an address in the note, as she recalled, but the company's name was Aseptic something. She had to try to find him somehow. One day, on an impulse, she picked up the phone and dialed directory assistance.

"I'm sorry, ma'am, there is no listing starting with Aseptic."

A couple of days later, Dad called. He was now in the habit of going to town and getting Elsie to dial for him.

"Dad, do you remember the name of that company Bob was going to work for in San Francisco?"

"No, I don't remember. Why? You going to patch things up?"

"You think I should?" Discussing personal issues with her dad was not normal, but now it was comforting. "You know, Dad, Bob just needed to find himself, and it came at a bad time in my life. The timing was off." Excusing his behavior didn't sound right. "What would you do?"

"I don't think I can answer that. Your mom and I had our ups and downs, but when things got tough, we pulled together. How long has it been since he left? Six months? Seems to me that's a long time without letting you know where he was, don't you think?"

"I don't know. Maybe. I have to try."

"Then call his sister or dad and find out if they know where he is. What about that job he had before the last one? I recall something about the new job having to do with that company."

"You think I'm foolish, chasing after him, don't you?"

"Follow your own path. Don't matter what others think."

"Thanks, Dad. I'll try to contact his family."

The old man added, in a monotone, "Course, I could ask your Aunt June to give you a call, and you could talk it over with a real expert."

◆   ◆   ◆

No one knew where Bob was. Ginny, his sister, did know the name of the company in San Francisco and its phone number, but the service was disconnected when Ann called. She called Bob's old place of employment, a janitorial service. The owner was not happy with his supplier in San Francisco, which had gone bankrupt, owing him hundreds in credit. He said he would ask around to see if any of the employees were in touch with Bob.

A couple of nights later, she received a phone call. "You Mrs. Garrity?"

"Yes. Who's this?"

"An old friend of Bob's. He don't know I'm calling, but I always thought you got a raw deal. Call this number, and see for yourself." The caller gave her a number, then disconnected without a further word.

It took a couple of days to muster her courage, but on Friday night, after the girls went to sleep, she dialed. The phone rang five times, and she decided to hang up, but on the sixth ring, a female voice answered with a hello.

"Who's this?" Ann demanded.

"Who are you calling, please?" The voice on the other end was formal, courteous, and maybe sultry.

Ann, suspecting a wrong number, said, "Is Bob there?"

"Yes, but he is indisposed at the moment. May I take a message?"

"Ask him to call home when he is more disposed," she responded, then hung up. Embarrassed by her response, she picked up the phone again, then gently replaced it. Legs weak, she sat on a dining chair. For some reason, she had always thought he would fail and come back. Now there was another loneliness she had never known existed. She sat, waiting, but the phone never rang. The calendar above the phone declared the date: Friday, the thirteenth of October. *I've lost something else this year,* she thought.

Chapter 8

Spring 1973

During the fall and winter, Yoty stayed around the corral with the horses and slept in the barn. While his wild counterparts foraged for food, he became healthy on alfalfa hay. The fall hunting season was no problem, as he was too small and young. Besides, he never left the farm, even though he was healthy enough to jump the fence from a standing position. One time that fall, an old buck came though the farm, heading up the mountain slope. Yoty tried to follow, but the buck lowered his head and charged, forcing the young deer back to the safety of the barn. By spring, Yoty went into velvet with his insignificant spike antlers. He also developed curiosity about the rest of the world and wandered, now that he could outrun dogs. Late one spring evening, Ann got a call from an irate neighbor. Yoty was not discriminating. Newly started tomato plants were just as good as roses.

She called Fred. "Yoty got in trouble with the Hobsons this week. Seems he took a fancy to their tomato plants. It's time. Yoty needs to be with his kind. You got any ideas how I can get him into the mountains?"

"You won't be able to shoo him away. He's a pet now."

"Help me out here, Fred. I know that."

"We have a transport trailer to haul captured elk and bighorns. If we tranquilized him, we could get him in the trailer and haul him away."

"Sounds cruel."

"Can you think of a better way?"

"I guess not. When can you do it?"

"This weekend, I suppose."

"I'd rather not have the kids see it. Could you do it on a weekday?"

"I guess so. How about Wednesday?"

"Will he make it?"

"He's made it this far. He's pretty tough."

That morning, the kids took the bus. No sooner was it out of sight when Fred drove up with the trailer. She had hoped to have some time alone with Yoty.

There were two other Fish and Game people. One of them pulled a rifle out of its scabbard, while the other loaded a syringe. Now was the time. Before she knew what was happening, the rifleman aimed and shot the dart into Yoty's rump. The deer jumped, ran around the corral once, jumped the fence, and staggered into the snowberry bushes. Then it went up the slope of the runoff dam and onto the berm, where it collapsed. Ann rushed up the hill, and the men followed.

Yoty lay in the same place where she had originally found him. His eyes were glazed and his breathing labored. Fred pushed her aside. She turned away, sobbing. The men monitored the deer's breathing; satisfied, they dragged the animal down the slope, just as Ann had a year ago. She followed with her head down, not wanting to look in its eyes, even if it was sedated. Once in the trailer, she sat on the floor, stroking Yoty's neck as tears streamed down her face. Even Fred was teary-eyed.

Fred tugged at her arm. "You can't go, Ann."

She nodded, hugged Yoty one more time, then rose and closed the door behind her. She turned back to the house and quickly walked away. As the truck started to move, she turned and waved. "Wait! Wait!" she called, but the truck did not stop. She watched until it was out of sight, then sat in the grass staring at the place where it went out of sight. *Thank you, Yoty, thank you!*

◆   ◆   ◆

All three Garritys pined for weeks after the deer left, but life returned to normal, as it always does after a change. Two weeks later, Fred phoned in the evening.

"Hi, Ann. How's it going now?"

"Pretty good, Fred. I meant to call and thank you for what you did. I couldn't have done it without your help. You won't get in trouble, will you?"

"Shouldn't. We transport wild animals all the time. Listen, Ann, I may be out of line here, but I was wondering if I could come over now and then to see you."

"I'm married, Fred. Perhaps someday. I have children … I'm not healthy."

"Yeah, I'm sorry. It was thoughtless of me—"

"Good night, Fred."

Ann hung up so fast that the handset missed the cradle and crashed to the floor. Kneeling, she picked it up to replace it, but she spotted a picture on the second shelf down from the top. Sitting back on her legs, she hesitated, then reached for it. The frame was silver and the matting black. Bob and Ann had dressed formally that night. In the picture, they stood in front of Bob's 1957 Ford station wagon before leaving to the prom. The corsage of orchids was pinned on her gown. Both breasts stood out. She yearned for more than that.

"You okay, Mom?" Michelle stuck her head into the room just then.

"Yes, dear. I just dropped the phone and was picking it up."

She busied herself in rearranging the shelf. Dwelling on it would not help. She now had only one objective in life: to live long enough to raise the kids. Yet, there was still longing. She wanted to be nurtured too. Her goal, to raise the kids, was noble and necessary but perhaps too altruistic. Deep inside, she didn't want to be a martyr. Aunt June's comment echoed in her mind: *Who cares what men think?* Easy for an eighty-year-old woman, but did it apply to a thirty-three-year-old woman? There was a hint that Aunt June knew the answer. What had she said? Something like: to be attractive, fix the bra. Why fix the bra just to raise kids? No, there was more to it than that. After all, the new bra had brought back good feelings. Maybe playing a martyr was just an excuse to simplify things and to avoid issues. But it was easier this way.

◆　　◆　　◆

On a Friday just before school let out for the summer, Ann was grading papers at her desk when the school secretary, Karen, knocked on the door. Karen and Ann had common equine interests. Michelle and Karen's daughter had competed together at horse shows over the past year.

"Come on, Ann," said Karen. "Let's have fun tonight! A few of us girls are going to the Branding Iron for dinner and drinks. You know that saying—all work and no play ..." She cocked her head and smiled.

"Thanks, Karen, but I have to get home after grading these papers."

Karen was persistent. "Oh, come on, Ann. You need a break from kids. Come with us. Michelle and Holly are old enough to look out for themselves for a few hours."

The four women walked in at about 7:00 PM. Not only was the Branding Iron the best restaurant in town, it was the local watering hole. Adults congregated after work to unwind, socialize, and conduct business, if needed. Outside the country club, this was the only social scene in town; the crowd was a little rougher than the country club set. Ann felt apprehensive as she glanced around. Would people look at her? Was she a freak? Would she make a fool of herself?

"Come on, Ann. Loosen up. You remember how to socialize, don't you?" Karen teased.

The place hadn't changed since Bob had last taken her there. The deer heads were still on the walls, draped with ornaments from the last holiday season; in fact, one deer had a red flashing lightbulb on its nose. The tavern was noisy, and the jukebox cranked out a song of lament about a frog named Jeremiah, or something like that. The music permeated the restaurant side. Ann couldn't hear much else, so she smiled and glanced around, uneasy. The other girls laughed as they ate or commented about that man or that couple or some woman. Bored, Ann wished she could leave, so after dinner, she excused herself. *Enough is enough,* she thought.

As she walked through the tavern side, Fred bumped into her. His eyes were glassy, and his speech was slurred. "Hello, Ann. What you doing here?"

"I gotta go."

"What's your hurry?" he asked as he grabbed her arm.

She twisted free and turned to the door.

"You too good for me? I was all right when you needed help. You always use people like that? Don't give me that 'poor me' stuff. I know about your illness, you hotsy-totsy poor-little-me with only one breast. You think people don't know? Get off your pity-potty, and join the human race again!"

The whole place turned silent; even the jukebox was between tunes at that moment. Ann bolted out the door and ran through the parking lot, her eyes blurred.

◆   ◆   ◆

On a lonely stretch of farm road halfway home, she pulled over to the side. There was a quarter moon, and the sky was clear. She sat gazing upward, sighed, then climbed out. The field next to the road was filled with mint; the fragrance was strong and sweet. A warm breeze from the east and the silence of the night gave her a sense of security. Thankful to be alone, she walked out to the middle of the field, sat down, and cried until she couldn't cry anymore. Try as she might, there were no more tears. The sky was cloudless, and the stars were bright. A shooting star held her attention now. Nothing else in the world mattered.

The Milky Way was faint, but an evening planet, probably Mars, shone bright. The nearest star was four light-years away from her. "Let's see, that's about twenty-four trillion miles. If I started now at a hundred miles an hour, I would get there in ten billion days, or about twenty-seven million years. With my bladder size, I would need about a hundred million rest stops."

"Lady, what the hell you doing out here?"

Startled, she jumped. So engrossed by the stars, she had not been not aware of anything else.

It was a big man with a flashlight and a shotgun. Shining the light into her face, he noticed her bloodshot eyes, dried tears, and sad face. His mood softened. "Oh, family problems, huh?" He put down the gun, turned off the flashlight, and plopped down beside her, as if they were close friends. "Sometimes I got to get away too. Usually I go to the top of the haystack, but I've sat out in a field before. You ain't going to commit suicide or something like that, are you?"

Now over the shock of seeing another human being in her universe, Ann laughed. "No. I have two children who need me."

"What's going on out there, John?"

Ann couldn't help laughing again. "Farmer John?"

They both laughed as another woman appeared. "This is my wife, Edith. Sit, Edie. This woman is studying the universe. Maybe we can learn something."

Instead of running away, she had found entertainment with new friends. As it turned out, John and Edie knew a lot about astronomy and acted as guides to the constellations for Ann. She in turn dazzled them with astrophysical facts and theories, including Hubble's Big Bang. By midnight, the ground was getting wet and cold.

"I have to get back to my kids." Rising, Ann hugged John and Edith.

Edith escorted her back to the car, and upon closing the door, she told Ann, "Next time, stop by the house first. You're always welcome."

In the darkness of the trip home, the incident with Fred went through her head again. Although drunk and vitriolic, he did have some valid points. She had used him. *Maybe self-pity plays a part in who I am now.*

◆   ◆   ◆

Monday, after school, she returned home to find the girls sitting in the front room. *Unusual,* she thought. "What's the matter with you guys?"

Michelle spoke solemnly and slowly, to be sure her diction matched her role as the spokesperson. "Mom, some kids were talking at school today about you. Is it true you have only one breast?"

Ann froze. She didn't know how to handle this one.

"Come on, Mom. We aren't that dumb. We've talked, and now we know the secret. It explains a lot, like how come you come out of the bathroom in the morning with two lumps but only one showing in the evening."

"Yes, I had an operation two years ago, and they had to remove my right one." She blurted it out.

"Why?"

Ann crossed her arms and looked at the faces staring up at her. *They're so young. Why now?* "I had cancer. They had to remove it to cure me."

"Yeah, but why did they take off your breast?" Holly's face contorted in disbelief.

"They had to remove the breast to be sure they got all the cancer."

Holly looked to her sister for guidance, but none came. She was on her own. "Do you still have cancer, Mom?" she blurted out.

"I don't know. It is too early to tell, but the doctors say they can find no evidence of it now. And after two years, it may not … won't come back."

"I don't want it to come back. Did I cause it?"

"Why do you think that?"

"I don't know. It just seemed like you didn't want us no more, so I thought maybe I did something wrong. Even Dad left. Did he cause it?"

"You're being silly, Holly." Michelle tried to cover but couldn't. "Mom?"

Ann said, "I want you two more than anything in the world. I just was so afraid of everything then, and I didn't know how to handle it."

"Did you want Dad too?"

"Yes, Holly, I did. But your dad needed to go … and find himself. We didn't do anything to make him leave." She sat down between them, and they huddled together.

◆   ◆   ◆

After dinner, Ann took the garbage out to the shed to keep wild animals from getting it. Coming up the drive was Fred's pickup. Ann dropped the two sacks, ran back to the house as fast as she could, and grabbed the old L. C. Smith single-barrel twelve-gauge shotgun. Fred stopped in the driveway and got out.

Ann stood at the edge of the porch with her legs apart and the gun raised. "You're trespassing, Mr. Block. One more step, and I'll shoot."

"Please, Ann, hear me out. Then, if you want, shoot me or call the sheriff, or do whatever you have to do. But just listen for a moment." He turned his head toward the mountain and sighed, then turned back to her. "I … I did a terrible thing Friday night." He paused again.

"You were crude, and if you ever talk about me again in public, I will neuter you on the spot. You got that, big mouth?" Spittle shot from her mouth. Embarrassed by her own energy, she stopped and looked at him. "What happened to you, anyway?" She pointed the gun down but kept it cradled, just in case, as she inspected his face. There was a laceration over his left eyebrow, and he had a swollen right jaw, a split lower lip, and bruises on both cheekbones.

"Let's just say I have friends that taught me some manners."

"Do you remember what they taught you?"

"Yes, ma'am, I do."

Ann lowered the shotgun and looked beyond him for a moment, then dropped her head. "To be truthful, you were right. I did use you, and I have hidden from the truth. Maybe if I had friends as open and honest as you, I would be a better person." She raised her gaze and smiled.

"I only wanted to be your friend," he said, then turned and walked back to the truck. At its door, he turned to face her again. "I'm very sorry."

"You know Fred, maybe you could come over every now and then. But no booze."

Chapter 9

1997

Holly was hot and wanted to go down to Baskin-Robbins for an ice cream sundae. Instead, she got ice cubes out of the freezer, placed them in a plastic bag, then draped it behind her neck. The ice cream sounded better, but she had to watch her weight. Her life centered on that. Anything she ate required conscious deliberation of the consequences. She was sure she would weigh two hundred pounds if she ate what she wanted. To be a professional dancer required self-discipline.

She looked in the mirror as she passed the bathroom. A ballet dancer had to be lithe. She pressed the ice to her forehead as she inspected herself: willowy arms and well-proportioned legs with developed calves that offset the larger thigh muscles required of ballerinas. In her field, breasts were not an asset, and, like her professional peers, hers were small, almost inconspicuous. The breastless look augmented the Balanchine body of ballerinas: thin, figureless, sticklike. She was proud of the look, as she had to work hard to maintain it. But the appearance achieved and so admired in American female dancers had become an obsession. Was that a little pooch below her waistline? She turned sideways to check it out. She knew that the competition to look like walking sticks drove many healthy females out of the profession, leaving the remaining majority neurotic and ill equipped to a life outside ballet. Not her, of course.

She replaced the ice pack around her neck, sighed, shrugged her shoulders, then went to the window and opened it so she could crawl out on the fire escape landing. Hopefully, there would be a slight breeze. Below, cars moved, but there was no foot traffic. On occasion, a taxi horn blared, but otherwise, the night was unusually quiet for 10:30.

She leaned back against the brick wall, but it too was hot, so she leaned forward, grasping her legs. At thirty-three, Holly's life was limited. She was married but childless. Her years of training, first in Los Angeles and then in New York, had required living alone in dorms or apartments since the age of seventeen. Even then, she had started a dancing career late. Many of her peers started at twelve, and she rationalized that her mediocrity was because of the late start. She presented well and always impressed at auditions for support roles. It was almost as if she was selected for her mediocre skills and fine body, so as to augment the lead dancer. At five feet four inches tall, she didn't tower over the others, but she was tall enough not to stand out in the background. Still, she would not quit, always dreaming of the big break. She was always fighting health problems: tendonitis, stress fractures, muscle strains, dehydration, and bulimia. At most, her body would allow this profession for another six years.

She gazed upward, but there were no stars. She missed that about the farm. A sound from the street distracted her as a garbage truck backed up to a dumpster. A man got out and pulled some levers, causing a whining sound; a warm breeze came up from below, as if he had caused it. The dumpster was lifted into the truck with a loud crashing sound that carried between the building walls as if they were canyons. So much for the quiet of the night.

The phone rang. It must have been eleven o'clock, but there was no need to hurry to answer it. Her roommates were still out, so the noise wouldn't bother anyone. She didn't want to move right now; it was too hot. Besides, it was just George. He called every night. Sometimes she felt guilty. Her marriage was for convenience. He was not handsome or athletic, but he was intelligent and wealthy. She had met him at a party for the opening of *Swan Lake*. She'd had a solo performance for that production, so she had been invited to the gala afterward. Such attendance was mandated to impress potential investors and others that could influence the general public. The spotlight only started on stage, then narrowed down to parties. It was all a part of the ritual. The austere lifestyle of a dancer was based on these brief moments of recognition. She opened the ice pack and removed an ice cube to suck on. The phone stopped ringing, and as if by signal, the garbage truck left. Quiet returned, and she slipped back to her thoughts.

He had been shy at first, and he was out of his element as an organic chemistry professor at a local college. That night, though, he had represented his family: wealth and social power. The ballet director had fawned on George, introducing him to the entire cast in order of importance. When George took a special interest in Holly, the director had given him a disapproving look and tried to refocus his attention onto other cast members. Even Holly's attempts to thwart George could not dissuade him, try as she might, to appease the director. George just looked at her. He had not spoken, just stood there, and the silence had gotten embarrassing.

"Are you involved with ballet, Mr....?" She had forgotten his name early on.

"Ah, no. I'm not. Newman."

She had reached for another glass of champagne as the server passed. "Pardon?"

"Name's Newman."

He was tall, about six feet four inches, and she had been forced to look up to make eye contact. Fortunately, the director had taken him by the arm and glided away to another group. She had exhaled as if she had been holding her breath during the encounter. Even then, George had kept looking back at her. It was awkward, yet he was intriguing in a strange way, in his rumpled light-gray suit with sleeves that were too short, giving an arboreal quality to his overall appearance. His white shirt had carried a coffee stain, and a blue bow tie completed the picture of a social incompetent. If appearance reflected anything, it did not fit with her concept of self. Something though, was an attractant; maybe his lithe appearance was animus to her anima. But she had dismissed George from further thought.

About three weeks later, there he was again, at another postproduction party. This time, he followed her around the room, to the dismay of the director. She had even gone to the powder room to escape, but when she returned, there he was.

"Remember me? George Newman?"

It was difficult to interact due to the twelve-inch difference in height, which at party-close range seemed insurmountable. "Yes, of course, Mr.... Newman. I remember. So nice of you to remember me."

"Would you ... consider ... going to dinner with me some night? I know you are busy."

To escape, she had consented. He was not challenging, and he was downright boring; his talk about substitutions on the benzene ring had no meaning to her. His attention brought new status for her, though. The director took notice, as did the whole retinue. She commanded more solo parts. Six months later, George had proposed, and she had accepted, to cement her newfound status. The apartment shared with two other dancers had been replaced by a house of her own. No longer were there overdraft charges on the bank account. There was a price to pay, though. She had to look up all the time and act interested in jargon she didn't understand or care about. His small circle of friends was equally boring. His mother was delighted with the marriage: a commitment to social responsibility for the performing arts. At first, this elevation in status was exciting, but soon she had realized that her role was just the opposite. Instead of independence and status, his mother and her social circle dominated her. After three years, she longed for what she had once had: the struggle.

So here she was, in a distant city on a hot summer night, sharing a room with other struggling dancers, trying to beat the heat with ice cubes. Discipline and challenge to be better drove life and the reward: recognition, no matter how brief or significant. She rolled to the side and crawled back through the window. George would continue to call until she answered. This arrangement seemed acceptable to him. When they were together, the relationship was dynamic, even interesting, with mutual respect. Mother was out, directors were out, and he entertained her with his recent research, something to do with forecasting a molecule's function on biological systems, and she would revel in her latest solo performance. He still was laconic and still gazed at her with adoration. But she liked that. After a few days, old feelings returned, and they separated to go their own ways, until the next encounter necessitated by loneliness and proximity. She knew it was an arrangement of professional gratification while avoiding personal growth.

What would happen when she couldn't dance anymore? She didn't want to think about that now as she paced. She wished he would hurry and call back. It would be difficult enough to sleep, because of the heat, but she needed rest. The day's rehearsal had been long and strenuous, as it was the last one; tomorrow was opening night. The sole of her left foot hurt already—probably another case of plantar fascitis. If it got any worse, she would not be able to perform. That afternoon, it had been hard to hide the limp, but she had succeeded, by stuffing a paper tissue in the shoe and faking motion, particularly petit allegros, when no one was observing. Maybe some rest and ice would eliminate the problem. If not, a substitute dancer would take her place. At her age, substitutions signaled unreliability, and directors looked at such issues when auditioning dancers. Finally, the phone rang. Grimacing, she hobbled to the phone. Her foot needed rest.

George was excited. "Hello, dear. Guess what? I'm one of the candidates for department head, with full professor rank! If this latest paper is accepted, I will have the magical twenty-five articles, which will give me the professorial rank, but the department head position is unexpected. At forty-two, I'll be the youngest department head at the school."

"Great, George. I'm proud of you. When is this going to happen?" Before he could respond, she continued, "Listen, I won't be coming home next week after the production. Shannon and the girls want me to go with them to a dinky little town in western Oregon. Apparently this place has an annual dance festival and this year is putting on three performances of classical ballet during the early fall. They need Russian technique performers, and there is a good chance I could get a big solo part. The *New Yorker* wrote about this little festival for its uniqueness last year. If I get a part, I could get a lot of notice. Everyone will be there. Besides, I would be able to go home for a while to see Mom. I haven't seen her since Christmas at your mother's place two years ago."

"Oh. I was hoping, you know ... that we might...." he stammered. "When will I see you?"

"I don't know for sure. I'll call you in a couple of days, once the plans are firmed up. That's great about the job." Holly had no idea of the magnitude of his promotion. Right now, she had to nurse a painful foot.

The foot was worse the next day, and another dancer replaced her.

◆   ◆   ◆

Released from the troupe because of the injury, Holly flew to Portland and rented a car. She had calculated that if she got there before Shannon and the others, it might mean a better solo part for her. Auditions were not starting until the next week, but there were always ways to secure parts if the right people noticed you. Gripping the wheel and gritting her teeth, she took the curves on the coastal highway with resolve.

Leonard Gregowich was the ballet company director, and she knew him from previous productions. She wondered how a famous director had come to be at this out-of-the-way place. Renting the car had maxed out her credit card. While driving, she calculated her finances in her head. Without support, she only had enough in the checking account for a week, at most. Darkness prevented her appreciation of the coastal beauty, but she didn't care; her journey had a different focus.

A motel at the end of town still had a vacancy for an exorbitant price. It was a generic roadside room, where cars parked right outside the door, in front of the wall-mounted air conditioner/heater. Several of the units were humming away, and with thin walls, the noise was as bad as the city at night. Holly wondered why they bothered, as it was cool on the coast. Later that night, the sounds of carnal pleasure next door woke her. Sleep would not come easy in this environment, and she was up early, to start the search for Leonard.

A server at a small but crowded café called the Egg and I informed the newcomer that the performing arts center was on the cliff overlooking the town and shoreline, about two miles away. She even drew a map on a napkin. People here were sure cooperative.

An elderly woman in the next booth turned around to face Holly. After a quick inspection, she started up a conversation, with a slight Slavic accent. "I'm sorry, but I overheard you talking to Julie about the performing arts center. Are you involved with them?"

"Well, yes and no. I would like to be. I'm a ballerina, you see."

"Good for you, dearie. We need good ballerinas. Are you seeing Lenny? I think he is there this morning."

Small town, thought Holly. Calling Leonard Gregowich "Lenny" was inconceivable to her. Holly tried to pry herself away from the talkative old lady, but she was forced to hear about the festival, its productions, and the town pride—chit-chat in which Holly never could maintain any real interest. Even after she yawned several times, the older woman did not get the hint. She kept right on expounding as Holly paid her bill and headed toward the door.

◆   ◆   ◆

"Holly! It's so good to see you again! What are you doing here, in this small place?" Leonard, as always, presented an upbeat appearance, at least until rehearsals started—then he did his famous Dr. Jeckyll and Mr. Hyde routine. After a lengthy wait, Holly had able to get in to see him that morning.

"I know it's early, but I had some time to spare, so I thought I would sightsee along the coast and drop in to see if you needed a solo dancer for this production." Actually, she didn't even know what the production was, but Leonard was of the Vaganova school of ballet, like her.

Leonard paused and changed his inflection. "Well, the production is *Giselle,* and the parts are by invitation only for leads and solos. We don't really need dancers now, but we will audition for subs, starting next week, if you would like to be considered."

Time to drop a name or two, she thought. "Oh, I must be misinformed. Shannon told me you wanted a couple of solos, and we were coming out next week. She will be disappointed, as will Darlene."

She knew that Leonard knew these names. He was a noted womanizer, and past indiscretions gave both Shannon and Darlene leverage. Leonard stared at her, then rose and came around the desk to stand in front of Holly. He perched on its edge with one leg, hands clasped. "Frankly, Holly, I noticed a limp when you walked in. Plantar fascitis? You can't sustain. I took the liberty of calling around before the secretary showed you in. You were replaced twice in the last year. Maybe it's time you hung up your shoes." He rose and walked back to the chair, then continued. "I know why you invoked Shannon and Darlene. I will make a deal with you, if you want. I won't tell them you came early, if you don't audition. I need an assistant choreographer. You can have that job, but that's the best I can do. I'm acting in good faith, given your ... handicap."

An assistant choreographer title was not a challenging or prestigious position. It would be lower in status than a dancer and lower in pay. How could she face the other girls? "Let me think about it. Can I let you know tomorrow?"

"Okay, but no later than tomorrow."

She rose to leave, but curiosity caused her to ask, "Why are you here, at this small spot on the map?"

He smiled. The question had hit a nerve, and he changed his demeanor. "Western Oregon is a beautiful place, particularly in the summer, when the rains quit. The temperature is usually sixty to seventy degrees and never gets above eighty during the day. This little town comes alive in the summer with visitors from around the world."

He stood, stretched and went to the window before continuing. He was like an actor now. "There is a lot of money in tourism, and Bandon leaders recognized that and built a performing arts center. They didn't have any idea how to market the thing, though, until a performing arts director, retired from San Francisco's Ballet Company, and one of the retirees took it on."

He turned to Holly with a smile. "She knows most everybody in the business and had done a lot to advance many careers. Many people, including myself, owed favors to her, and failure is never an option, so she proposed to the city council a concept to bring ballet."

He stopped talking then, as if he knew she was bored. She urged him on with a nod..After all, she had asked.

He went on, "After ten years, the program was a model for other small communities. Guest professionals from around the world come for summer performances by invitation. Throughout the time they are here, local families eagerly house them and entertain them in small gatherings such as beach parties, golfing, fishing, and horse riding on the beach. In return, we organize, rehearse, and perform—a kind of busman's holiday with pay. Because of this model, Bandon is able to attract the best directors, who attract the best performers, who attract the best audiences." He waved his arm to try to buffer his lack of modesty and continued. "These annual endeavors give status to the performing arts scene that has caught national attention from publications such as *Sunset* magazine and the *New Yorker*, and this hamlet is now the cultural center of coastal Oregon."

Now she knew why he was here. It was for the same reason as hers: attention. "Thanks for the background," she said.

Leonard was already turning back to his desk, as if tired from his performance. As she went through the door, he mumbled, almost to the wall, "No later than tomorrow."

◆   ◆   ◆

The view from the performing arts center was spectacular. Driving up, Holly had not noticed it, but now, as she left the building, the view captured her attention like a big explosion. Leonard's lecture had succeeded. Looking down on the little town below, she felt insignificant yet comforted, in a strange way, by this insignificance. Not religiously or even spiritually inclined, Holly never dealt with issues she could not control in her life. Now, like it or not, her career was out of control and could not be fixed. If Leonard had been able to find out about her injuries that quickly, it meant she was blackballed. It was over.

She limped painfully across the lawn to the promontory. Looking straight down frightened her at first. Then a thought of hurling herself to a certain death flitted through that part of the brain that makes impulsive decisions, but it was overridden by her rational self in an instant. She looked over the view again and discovered she was not alone. Down below, small ant-sized humans walked the streets, unconcerned about her problems and going about their day-to-day lives. She envied them. Along the coastline, there were distant mountains extending to the sea where the beach ended. Across the harbor was a small lighthouse; it was surrounded by beach grass that undulated in the breeze. It was all so peaceful.

The small harbor bustled with fishing boats, kayaks, and sailboats nonchalantly plying the protected, quiet inlet. Beyond the jetties, the water was turbulent from the sea breeze; the sun warmed the water. Whitecaps churned as she watched a small fishing trawler exit the safety of the harbor and climb a wave, then descend as it passed. At first, it appeared that the boat would capsize, and it looked like it was not making any perceptible progress. *Why doesn't he turn around?* she thought. The effort seemed futile to her as she watched, mesmerized for the moment. Yet slowly, ever so slowly, the little boat progressed to open waters, followed by others with equal determination. Even in these peaceful surrounding, there were struggles.

What did it all mean? She was contemplative as the gentle wind blew her hair and dress. She had her arms crossed, as if to protect herself. Protect from what? Herself, perhaps? There was serenity here, though. George would love it here. She missed him for the first time.

"Hello, dearie! Beautiful, isn't it?"

The voice broke her reverie. Holly turned to see the woman from the restaurant climbing up the hill. She had been startled out of her solitude and was resentful of the intrusion.

"I hope I'm not disturbing you, dearie."

"No, I'm just looking," she lied.

"I come up here every morning to look. My late husband and I used to come up here and just sit and gaze for hours. I guess it was our church. We always left feeling we belonged to the world, instead of being its center. Our problems melted. Ralph and I never fought. We just looked for a while, then everything was all right."

Both women just looked. Holly understood what the older woman was saying: everything was all right for the moment. Later, they turned to walk back to the cars.

"My name is Mila," said the woman. "What's yours?"

Uncharacteristically, Holly felt inclined to talk. Now the tables turned as Mila listened, unlike earlier this morning. The communication was cathartic for Holly, and it continued as they leaned against the car. She even candidly talked about her marriage to George. For some reason, Holly couldn't help herself. Leonard came out of the building, walking briskly, as if late for something.

"Hello, Lenny! Come here and meet Holly. She's a dancer and wants to talk to you."

Leonard paused at the sidewalk entrance to the parking lot, smiled as if his face had been programmed to do so, then walked over to the two women. Each step seemed painful. "I talked to Holly earlier this morning," he announced in a quasi-whisper. He regained his composure and displayed his famous, disarming smile. Holly could sense that, for some reason, the last person he wanted to alienate was Mila. "We already discussed arrangements. Holly needs to make a decision." As an afterthought, he added: "Hello, Mila. Holly."

"Oh?" said Mila. "What decision is that?" She turned to face Holly.

"Mr. Gregowich has offered me an assistant choreography position."

Mila nodded. "Ah! The limp. You are injured. Right?"

"Yes. Mr. Gregowich feels I am getting too many injuries and should change my focus in life. He may be right, as much as I don't want to admit it. I guess my dancing career is over. He was kind and let me down by offering this position." Holly couldn't believe the admission had come from her mouth and that she had any semblance of gratitude to Leonard. Mila had some kind of effect on her. Even Leonard relaxed and showed some sympathy in his expression.

Mila said, "Well, are you going to stay and take the job? It doesn't pay much—not as much as a dancer makes—but it will give you a couple of months to decide what to do with your life. This is a good place to make life decisions, you know." She nodded toward the promontory.

"I'm not sure I can afford to live here. I could ask George for money …"

"Yes, maybe you should. But in the meantime, why don't you stay with me and sort it out?"

"Oh, I couldn't!" The thought of a stranger offering anything, let alone sharing her shelter, was alien to Holly. She was embarrassed and frightened. Sure, it was easy to share an apartment with other dancers—that was expected. But she felt uneasy about sharing lodgings with anyone else. Yet she was running out of money. Did she want to stay here? Part of her wanted to, but part of her wanted to run away. Maybe she should see Mom and George first. Maybe she should just go back to George anyway.

Mila said, "Nonsense! Sure, you can stay with me. All the performers here live with locals. You can't afford to live in a motel if you take the job."

"That's true. I would like to go home first, then come back."

"Then it's settled. You will move in with me and take the job with Lenny. Lenny, when do you want Holly to start?"

"We start next week," he said. He turned to Holly. "Can you get back here by then?"

Holly was overwhelmed. Did she want to do this? *Why not?* "Yes."

Mila said, "Now, you run along, Lenny. We are going to lunch and discuss arrangements."

Dismissed, Leonard walked back to his car as Holly puzzled over the effect this little old woman had on people and how she could command without offending.

"Follow me down to the restaurant," said Mila. "I'll have to hurry. I have a one thirty appointment at the doctor."

Following in her car, Holly pondered. She had woke up this morning with a life of her own, but now she was following an old woman down a hill for lunch—probably things like hamburgers and French fries served with catsup, a week's worth of calories—and she had given up her life's dream just to become a gopher for a skirt-chaser in a small production far from the real world, and she was dependent on a granny who dictated her every move. *What am I doing?*

They arrived at the restaurant, and Mila said, "You'll like this restaurant, dear. They serve small portions, all healthy. I know the owner. She moved here from southern California. She owned a chain of health food stores down there—until one day, she woke up and wondered why she worked so hard. So she started this small café. Works just as hard, but no smog or traffic." Mila hardly stopped talking to breathe as they entered the building and saw a woman come out of the kitchen with both arms carrying plates of food. "Oh, here she is now! Holly meet Andrea. Andrea, this is Holly. She will stay with me the next couple of months. I know you're busy now, but I have to be at the doctor's office in forty-five minutes. Can we have that little table in the back?"

Andrea pointed to the table with her chin. "Go for it, Mila. Nice to meet you, Holly. I'll send Jeff for your order right away."

Mila commanded everyone, and everyone accepted it, as if honored. *What charisma!* thought Holly. She groped for something to say. "I hope your doctor visit isn't anything serious."

"I have advanced breast cancer and have to go every month and see Dr. Young. He keeps me alive. He's young enough to be my grandson, but he is a great doctor. I just love him!"

Holly was taken back by her candor. She didn't know what to say.

Not missing a beat, Mila continued, "I'm amazed at these young doctors. They know so much! When the cancer came back nine years ago, the doctor told me there wasn't much to do. Of course, he was just a family doctor. He took care of Ralph before he died. My daughter is a pharmacist back at the university in South Carolina and wanted me to go there, but I asked around. Our oncologists are just as good, so I stayed here. They have given me nine years so far."

"You have cancer still in your body?"

"Well, it comes and goes. Mostly it's in my bones. At first, they put me on pills, but now it's in my lungs, so I've been taking chemotherapy. Just finished three months ago, and now Dr. Young wants to see if they got it all."

"Wow, you've had cancer for nine years? That seems unbelievable. You still have all your hair. I thought you lost your hair with chemotherapy."

"Well, I've had chemo and lost my hair. That was about three years back, I think. Depends on which chemo drugs they use. Dr. Young just gives me a different regimen when it comes back. He always has something new to offer me when it rises up. I can't complain. It works whether I lose my hair or not."

"Do you get sick? I heard that chemotherapy is bad."

"Some of it is bad, but the other option is worse. You do what you have to do. I can't complain. I'm able to do what I want in life. Nine years is pretty good, I think. Someday it probably won't work anymore, but for now, it's working."

"Do you ever think about when it won't?"

"I used to, all the time." Mila paused. "Why do you ask?"

Now it was Holly's turn to pause. Why was she asking? She searched for the answer but decided to work it through out loud. "I don't know for sure. My mother had breast cancer when she was only thirty-two. I'm thirty-three now. I remember when Mom came home from the hospital. My sister and I knew something was wrong, but we didn't know what it was. We thought Mom would die. I would lie awake at night and wonder what would happen to me if Mom died. After a while, I started to wonder if I would get cancer and if I would die."

She turned her head to look out over the bay to the abandoned lighthouse on the other side. It looked lonely perched on the point, overgrown with grass. The view made her want to keep talking. "The thought that I would not be here anymore, and that my death would signal the end of everything, overwhelmed me. I would not have any existence, just ashes that didn't think or feel. It was so scary that I had to think of something else. I dreamed a lot then. You know, fantasizing. At first, I would fantasize just when I went to bed until I fell asleep. If I woke up during the night, I would continue the fantasy. Soon, I was living in two worlds—reality and fantasy. I liked the second world best, because I could control what and who I was, just by thinking what and who I was. Sometimes I wished I could just stay there—in my fantasy, I mean. As I grew older, the fantasies waned, but the fear is still there. Does it ever go away?"

"You mean the fear of dying?"

"I guess. I'm not sure I can express the feelings. I get so frustrated thinking about it. I want answers, but I don't know the questions."

"Well, I don't know either the questions or the answers. Yes, I fear death, but it's different for me. I know I'm dying with a pretty good timetable. You don't. When I was your age, I was afraid to think about the hereafter. When I was first diagnosed with breast cancer about twelve years ago, I thought the doctors were wrong. This couldn't happen. The fear was overwhelming, and I couldn't deal with it. I had to believe that the surgery and radiation would cure it—there was no other option. Then, when it came back two years later, I had to accept that I was dying. I didn't want to, but there was no other way. It was harder on Ralph than me, I think, but day by day, I learned to live with it. Each day became a blessing, and I became so grateful for that day that nothing else mattered. You see, that was my fantasy. Like you, I would lull myself to sleep with that gratitude, and I would do the same if I woke during the night. Then, eventually, my reality changed to fantasy only. That way, the fear isn't so bad."

"I can't believe those feelings of long ago still control my life. I have never discussed them with anyone before. I hope you don't think me selfish, when you are the one dealing with … the issue."

"That's all right, Holly. I appreciate your candor. I'm really not dealing with any issues. You are. I changed when Ralph died. Life lost its meaning, not because of the cancer, but because of loneliness. I miss Ralph, not my life as it was."

Jeff presented the salads and iced tea, and Mila stopped talking for the first time and ate. Holly couldn't eat. This was heavy stuff they were discussing. An old fear was rising.

Mila broke the silence. "Is your mother still alive? What about your dad?"

"Mom's alive and kicking. She lives on the same ten acres where I was raised. She is cancer-free after twenty-five years. She just retired from teaching and now raises wildflowers from seeds and sells them to research botanists. I haven't seen my dad since I was eight."

"I didn't mean to pry."

"That's okay, I think. I haven't talked about my life like this before. It is a bit scary, but talking, somehow, is ... I don't know. Maybe ...?"

"I know, dearie. I didn't talk about things until after Ralph died and Dr. Young insisted I go to a support group. At first, I resented it, but after a while, I just blurted out whatever was on my mind at the time. Never solved a damn thing, but just expressing things seemed to keep issues from getting too big to handle. Besides, I found out I wasn't alone."

"I could never do that. I'm amazed I've told you as much as I have. My husband doesn't even know these things about me."

"From what you have told me, I doubt you've given him much of a chance to know you."

Holly looked like she had been hit between the eyes with a hammer.

Mila stopped chewing. "I'm sorry, Holly. Sometimes I have a big mouth. That was not appropriate."

"No, you are right. Yes, it hurt, but I needed to hear it."

Mila tried to shift the conversation. "What was your fantasy?"

"You mean when I daydreamed as a child? I was a ballerina, and everybody noticed me. I saw some ballets on television, and it seemed they were going through life with grace and ease. Everybody was happy."

Mila rose, looking at her watch. "Oh, my gosh! Look at the time! I have to go now. I'll be late. Here's my card with my telephone number and address. Call me when you get ready to come back, and I'll have the spare bedroom ready. If you need to store anything before you go, Andrea can give you directions. Here is a spare key. Oh, by the way, don't worry about the lunch bill. Andrea will put it on my tab. Bye." Like a whirlwind, she was out the door and gone.

For a moment, Holly wondered if the encounter had happened or not. Already, she missed the old gal.

Andrea gave her directions. Holly decided to leave one of her suitcases at Mila's house. She could have taken it; after all, she only had two. But leaving it behind confirmed that she would come back. "I have never been this impulsive before, but there is something magical about all this. Will it last?" she mumbled to herself.

The house was back on the cliff overlooking the ocean; it was a modern home with all the latest conveniences. The back lawn actually ended at the cliff edge. As she glanced around at the scenery, she thought perhaps she should just stay. This place was gorgeous. After depositing the extra bag in the hall closet, Holly enjoyed the view for a while, then turned to leave. A fireplace caught her eye, and she wondered why anyone would need a fireplace on the coast. Holly examined it.

The mantel was massive and covered with pictures. It was as if the fireplace was not for fires but instead existed to provide a place for the mantel. There were images of groups and portraits, lots of them. One in particular caught her eye: a black and white glossy with a dark background, a sage scene of a male dancer holding a ballerina high by one hand, as if she were flying. Her arms were outstretched with a patagium of gossamer silk as her head arched back; one leg extended high, while the other was bent so that its foot touched the outstretched thigh. A written note at the bottom right-hand corner read: TO RALPH. HOPE TO SEE YOU AGAIN. MILA GORSKY. At the top of the photo was a printed title: MOSCOW'S BOLSHOI BALLET, NORTH AMERICAN TOUR, APRIL, 1959. PRODUCTION: THE DOVES. The print was a promotional photo. Mila was more than just a little old nosy lady.

Chapter 10

Late July 1997

Holly drove straight through to the farm: fourteen hours, with three stops for fuel and coffee. The trip was a time for reflection. Her life was changing fast—too fast, in many regards. For the first time, she wanted to be with George, but he lived there, and now she was here. This job would be for two months, but afterward, moving back with George and dealing with his mother didn't sound appealing. At the first stop, she called him.

"Hello, George. I'm sorry to bother you at work—"

"Holly! Where have you been? I've tried to call you on the cell phone for days. Are you all right?"

"Yes, George. I'm fine, and it hasn't been days—I just left yesterday. I came out west to get a solo part in a small coastal town. It's just beautiful out here, George. I love it. I met this wonderful old ballerina, and she's helping me. George? My dancing career is over. I think I may be blackballed because of too many injuries. I'm going to try choreography, if I stay in dancing."

There was a long pause before he responded. "I don't know what to say. This is so sudden. You could come back to me. Would you?"

"George, I've been thinking about a lot of things today. I don't have it all straightened out in my mind. Please don't complicate things just now. I don't know what I want to do with my life. I may just stay here in this little town. It's so peaceful. If things work out with Leonard, I may go with him."

"You mean you'll leave me for him?"

"No, George, that's not what I'm saying. Leonard is a company director, and he is the one giving me a chance at choreography. It may or may not work out. If it did, I would work with him in the future. Do you see now? Give me some time, please."

"I'm sorry. I love you, is all."

"I needed to hear that. I'll be at Mom's place for a week, then I'll go back to this place, Bandon. I'm going to do a lot of soul-searching this week. I have to go now."

"Turn your cell phone on so I can get hold of you."

"George, this is the Wild West. Cell phones don't work everywhere out here."

"I'll call you at your mom's. Okay?"

As she continued down the road, the thought occurred that she hadn't told him she loved him. She had wanted to, but things got too involved. Too much was happening too fast.

It was about four in the morning when she opened the gate leading up to the house. The moon was full, and it lit the whole valley. The gate was the same old one that Michelle and she had swung on as they waited for the bus in the mornings. The snowball fight had happened in that field by the fence twenty-five years ago. The images flooded her mind; it didn't seem that long ago. They had been so desperate then. Now those feelings seemed childish, that fear of the secret. It sure had been real then, though, and as she reminisced, the feelings rushed back upon her like a wave. They had been two children trying to be adults but not knowing how or why.

She closed the gate and latched the chain, so the horse couldn't get out. Turning back to the car, now inside the gate, she stumbled, exhausted. The pause enhanced the memories of that spot where Michelle had wrestled her to the ground. There was no snow now, but she could almost hear the laughter from long ago. Dropping to her knees, Holly started sobbing.

"Am I going to die?" she cried out, not understanding why. She tried to figure it out, but it didn't make sense. She curled up in the soft grass by the path and went to sleep, exhausted.

◆   ◆   ◆

The sun peeped over the eastern mountains, sending its rays across the valley to chase out the shadows of darkness left over from the night before. Across the old lakebed, the sun's rays danced with glee as the darkness retreated, announcing another day. The rays hit the western slope, where Ann's property was exposed, then danced on Holly's eyelids. Holly opened her eyes to see her mother standing over her, pointing a shotgun at her. Then Ann pointed the shotgun barrel upward and dropped to her knees in front of Holly.

"My God, Holly! What are you doing here? I thought you might be one of those people doped up on methamphetamine and maybe dangerous. You all right?"

Holly didn't speak. She wrapped her arms around her mother. It felt good. They hugged and rocked until Ann lifted Holly upright, brushed her hair, positioned her in the car, then drove back to the house. Arm in arm, they walked into the house, where Ann put on coffee and made huckleberry pancakes. "You remember how you loved huckleberry pancakes?"

Holly started to cry again, but through the tears, seeing her mother brought joy. She was a little girl again, and someone cared. Mom was older and heavier now but still Mom. The robe silhouetted the remaining breast while showing the conspicuous absence on the right side of her chest. It wasn't all a dream, then.

Ann looked puzzled as she stood with a spatula in her right hand. "Do you want to talk now? Or eat?"

All Holly could do was shake her head. Ann handed her a tissue and a stack of pancakes.

Two full stacks later, Holly pushed away the plate. "Please, Mom, no more. I haven't had pancakes for years, and I have to watch my diet." Funny that these had been the first words to her mother. "You got any peanut butter?"

They both laughed until their sides hurt and they had to pee.

◆   ◆   ◆

That night, as was Ann's custom in the summer, they dragged an inflatable mattress out onto the porch to sleep under the stars. They lay there together, looking up at the vastness. It was the season for shooting stars, and tonight there was a meteor shower—better than the Fourth of July. They counted thirty-six of them before Holly sighed then said, "Do you think we are alone, Mom?"

"You mean in the universe? I think it would be egotistical to assume we are. Look at how many stars there are in the galaxy—and how many galaxies. Most certainly, other Earthlike environments are out there. The question should be 'how many?' Why do you ask?" Ann turned from looking at the sky to her daughter.

"I don't know. Looking up at the stars makes me feel … insignificant. I guess that makes me lonelier."

"Lonelier? Dear, you have friends—lots of them—and a wonderful husband too. Your family loves you. Your loneliness is inside yourself."

"I know, Mom, but it's really funny. Sometimes I don't think much of myself, but all I think about is myself. Do you think that's crazy?"

"Ever since you were a little girl, you were something of a loner. Were you lonely then?"

"I wanted to escape. So does that mean I was lonely?"

"Really? Escape from what?"

"I don't know. Maybe your disease, or to be with Dad. But I don't know for sure. Sometimes I would feel guilty and not know why, then want to run away from it all."

Anna cradled Holly in her arm as the meteor shower continued. Silence lulled them to sleep.

At sunrise, Ann woke Holly to coffee and muffins. It was nice to have Mom to herself; it was just what she needed now. The leisure was short-lived.

Ann handed her a pair of leather gloves, a hat, and duck boots. "Let's go. We have a lot to do today. The weather this spring was wet, and we are already into the second cutting, which is dry and baled." Holly pulled on boots as Ann continued. "Sharon and Ted can't load it. Ted had emergency heart surgery two days ago, and we have to put bales in their barn for him. Sad, really. They don't have much money, and this surgery will probably ruin them. They might have to sell the farm."

How could Holly say no? But she wished she could just sit on the deck all morning. "Mom, I can't lift bales," she whined, hoping for a reprieve.

"Sure you can, dear. They're only sixty-pound bales."

Holly spent most of the morning dragging bales. At her weight of a hundred and two pounds, a sixty-pound bale was formidable.

After stacking the hay and after lunch, Ann announced the next project to her fatigued daughter. "Charlie just brought a truckload of tamarack that we need to split and stack."

"A little early to be gathering wood, isn't it?"

"Not really. The Forest Service is really restrictive anymore, and finding a dead tamarack means you have to get it now, or else someone else will. Charlie was lucky."

The sun beat down hard as it started into the western sky. Holly was thirsty, despite drinking water every few minutes. The drinking spells gave the only respite from chopping. She hoped the sun would go down soon, but it took its time, as it always does. The fatigue caused a strange euphoria that opened doors in her mind.

"Mom," she asked, "do you ever think about the cancer?"

"Strange question, Holly. What brought that on?" Ann slammed the back of her axe onto a wood-splitting wedge.

"My friend, the woman I told you about. Mila has breast cancer that came back."

"I used to lie awake at night, wondering if the cancer was still there. Sometimes I thought I could feel it eating me away. I was so sure it was still there that it felt like I had a crystal ball to see into my future. Every day I checked myself over, looking for a new lump. Sometimes I found something new, but it just turned out to be a part of me that I didn't realize was really me. I couldn't run to the doctor with every little thing. Finally, I decided I could go crazy … or go on. It was hard, but I just went on. What else could I do, really?"

Holly just lay there after the sun went down, too tired to eat. The phone rang, but the effort to answer wasn't worth it. Ann came to the bedroom door: Michelle wanted to talk. It had been at least two years since she had last talked with Michelle. It wasn't that they didn't care; they just had lives of their own.

Michelle said, "Hello, Brat. How's it going? I haven't talked to you in a while. Are you still with George? How's the dancing business treating you?"

It felt good to talk to her older sister—just like old times. She retorted, "Yeah, I am still married—much to your surprise, I'm sure. How's that nerd of yours? What's his name again? Petey?"

They carried on as if they were kids waiting for the school bus. Later came a pause, as if they were talked out. Then Holly asked, "Michelle, do you ever wonder if you are going to get cancer?"

"Yes, at times, I suppose. Maybe it's inevitable. According to what I read, it can be hereditary." Michelle responded philosophically.

"That's scary. But I guess I have always thought, in the back of my mind, that I would eventually get it. I haven't given it much thought until now. I met this neat old lady who has advanced cancer. She went three years after her breast surgery, then it came back in her bones. She has lived with it in her body for nine years now. Twelve years is a long time to live with cancer, isn't it?"

"Wow! I guess so. I always thought that if you got cancer and it wasn't treated, you would die soon, like within a year."

"I got to thinking, after I met her, that if cancer can be in your body for twelve years, then it must be there long before there is a lump or a test that shows it. Maybe we have cancer now and don't know it."

"Holly! Why are you thinking like this? There is nothing we can do now. Just live each day until and if it becomes a problem."

"Michelle, you ever have a mammogram?"

"No, have you?"

"No, but maybe we should. You're thirty-five now, and I'm thirty-three. If we caught it early, then we might be cured."

"I don't think we are old enough yet. I read that they didn't recommend those things until forty or fifty years of age, because of the risk of radiation."

"That doesn't make sense for us, Michelle. Mom was thirty-two when she got cancer. We're both older than that now. Do you have insurance?"

"Yes."

"Why don't you see a doctor and ask?"

"What about you? Do you have insurance?"

"No. I wonder what a mammogram costs."

"I'll find out and let you know. Assuming, of course, that I can get hold of you."

"Do you examine your own breasts?"

"No, but that is how Mom found hers, so I think it would be a good idea. I'll ask the doctor how to do it."

As Holly readied for bed, she examined her breasts, first the right and then the left. *Is that a lump? No, it can't be cancer—there are others. Maybe I have a lot of cancer. No, that is just the way they are. Why is the outside of the breast lumpier than the inside? I'm not sure. They are so small. They can't get cancer. What does cancer feel like? Like this? No, this is ridiculous.*

Later that night, as Ann and Holly lay under the stars, Holly felt like talking. "Mom? I never told you, but I am so sorry that I didn't come when Grandpa died."

Ann stared upward for a while. "He loved us. You don't need to feel bad about not being there. He wanted it this way. He died out on the ranch, not like Mom. He used to call me every Sunday morning to see how I was doing. He'd get Elsie to go to the phone exchange and call. I always wondered if he and Elsie had something going besides phone calls on Sunday morning. If they did, I'm sure he was doing it to get access to phone me." She sighed. "There was no funeral. I got the old gray mare and hauled his body out to the old grove and buried him there. That's the way he wanted it."

"You remember Yoty?"

"Of course I do! I think of him often and wonder if he lived to a ripe, old deer-age. You know, if it wasn't for him and you kids, I probably would still be in a robe, just wandering around the house, afraid of life. He helped me a lot at the time."

"Funny you look at it like that. We kids thought he was our pet, not yours."

"Having him around helped all of us, I think. After Fred took Yoty into the mountains, I tried to get him to tell me where, but he would just point to the eastern mountains and shrug."

"What would you have done if he'd told you where Yoty was?"

"I would have found him, then stood guard during hunting season."

After another fit of laughter, they looked for shooting stars until clouds obscured the sky. Holly pondered the vastness of the universe and wondered if it centered on this deck tonight. She gazed east across the valley formed by a collapsed mountain, then dosed off. Storm clouds arrived, sneaking over the western mountain and dropping their load onto the valley. The first few drops were light, but soon, large drops pelted Ann's deck. Both women sat up as the heavy rain came down. It seemed to take a long time to struggle out of the sleeping bags, then they scrambled for shelter. The wind blew one sleeping bag off the deck. Laboriously gathering up the other bag, Ann rushed to the cabin door, only to find it locked.

"I'm sorry, Mom. In the city, I always lock the door. It's just automatic."

"I don't even know where the key is. I haven't locked the door in years. Cover yourself with the sleeping bag while I go around to the back." Soon she returned to the front door, soaking wet. Rain beaded on her face and dripped off her hair, nose, and chin. "You locked the back door too! Come on, let's run for the barn."

As they raced for shelter, lightning flashed, followed in seconds by thunder. By the time they were safely inside the barn, both were soaking wet. Ann groped in the dark to find the light chain. The resulting sight was eerie: their shadows were projected on the walls, while rain pelted the doorway, as if beyond it was another dimension. The dim lightbulb hung by a short cord, but the wind racing through the door caused it to sway. Each pendulum swing enhanced the shadows, causing them to move back and forth about the room.

Ann rummaged around and found two old shirts. "Here, get out of those wet things, and change into this. Fred left them here."

Ann disrobed; the sight mesmerized Holly. She had never seen her mother without a robe or other garment. Was it real? The dim light, shadows, and lightning combined to make the vision eerie. The right half of her chest was nothing but lines crisscrossing ribs, as the light was too dim to see skin. As she moved and breathed, the scars seemed to migrate on her chest. The weirdest feature, though, was her ribs, which made Ann look like a skeleton-costumed dancer at Halloween. Yet the rest of her body was normal, giving an illusion of erosion. The waxing and waning of shadows in the background added to the illusion. For an irrational moment, Holly feared her mother would erode. The sight frightened and at the same time embarrassed her. She felt intrusive. Her mother didn't look like Holly's childhood image of her. Mother had a dark side that even today, twenty-five years later, was shocking. Holly wanted to hug her but couldn't.

She diverted her thoughts by bring up another subject. "Mom, what happened to Fred, anyway?"

Ann was hanging up the wet garments. She dropped them to her side and was quiet for a moment. Holly was afraid she had gone too far into her mother's life, but finally Ann responded. "Let's just say that Fred loved his booze too much. Every time he came around toward the end, he had alcohol on his breath."

"Did you love him?"

"Who? Fred? I loved Bob, and I liked Fred for what he did for us. Look, Holly. It was hard when your dad left. Fred helped us. He moved on, is all."

"It's just that Fred was there for us when Dad left."

"Really? You thought that much of Fred?"

"Of course, Mom. I know you tried to hide his ... your relationship from us. Michelle and I knew what was going on."

"Yeah, I tried to ... pretend. I would sneak over to his house after you guys went to sleep, so you wouldn't know. I guess I was the only person fooled."

Holly felt embarrassed but wanted to know. "So what happened to Fred?"

"He just moved on," Ann said again. Then she looked sheepish and added, with a sigh, "I went over there one night, and he was drunk ... with another woman."

"Sorry, Mom. It's none of my business."

Lightning flashed through the window, lighting the inside of the barn and outlining Ann's face. Holly began to realize just how difficult her mother's life had been.

◆   ◆   ◆

The rest of the week flew by fast—too fast—and Holly was reluctant to leave. The time alone with her mother had been a first. She had seen things in herself that were not apparent before, and the fear she had experienced that rainy night had given her a different perspective on suffering. The skeletal image would never leave her mind.

As she drove back to the coast, thoughts of her own life seemed inconsequential and petty; the week's experiences had been spiritual and had forced her to confront her emotions. She wanted to see George and share the experience. Halfway to the coast, she called him.

"George? Sorry to bother you at work again, I'm heading back to the coast. How are you?"

"I'm fine," he said coolly.

"Sorry I haven't called." There was a long pause, and she wasn't sure what that meant. "George? You still there?"

"Yeah, I'm still here. I tried to call you but got no response. Look, Holly, I know I'm not a great catch for you, but I do need some encouragement, you know. Maybe we should just bag it."

"Listen, could you break away for a couple of weeks and come to the coast?"

"Yeah ... okay."

Chapter 11

Late July 1997

On the night of the storm, Michelle lay in bed, in her suburban neo-Victorian home about three hundred miles away. The night was hot despite the air conditioner, which was humming away at full blast. The largest city in the Northwest had experienced a brownout; electricity had been rationed for air conditioning only for the sick and elderly. The curfew had lifted at 6:00 PM, and now the house was too hot for the unit to be effective. Finally, she tossed off the covers, rose, and went out to the deck. It was more than heat that bothered her; the discussion with Holly kept reverberating in her head.

"What's wrong, hon?" her husband, Pete, called. He yawned and shuffled through the French doors to the patio.

"I called Mom last night, and Holly was there."

"So? It's been a long time since you talked to Holly. I'm glad. You two seem so close, yet it's been a couple of years, hasn't it?"

"Over two years. We talked for two hours last night. She seemed … needy, I guess. A lot of reminiscing about when Mom came home from the hospital and we didn't know what was going on. Holly's going through some crisis with her dancing. Apparently injuries are plaguing and jeopardizing her career. It sounds like a midlife crisis, I guess. Anyway, she met this older woman with cancer, and now she is afraid she will get it too, given that Mom had it."

"She still with George?"

"Off and on. They have a distant relationship."

"I liked him. A little nerdy, though."

"Pete, it's all relative. Some think you are a little nerdy too."

"True. We are getting off the point here. Why is Holly's neediness keeping you awake?"

"I guess I'm afraid too. We talked about seeing a doctor, and getting mammograms, and learning how to do breast exams. After we hung up, I tried to do a breast exam, but all it did was make me nervous—I feel lumps everywhere. It got me thinking about the girls. If I have a bad gene or something, did they get it? Is there anything we can do to find out? What difference would it make? Some-where, probably on the evening news, I remember a report of a new breast cancer test. If there is one, then maybe it would be worth pursuing. But even then, do I really want to know?" She waited, as did Pete, since the question was rhetorical. "There's something about cancer every day in the news. It seems like every female celebrity that gets cancer is touting her story as a victim, overcoming hardship with the courage to fight it, as if only they can overcome such adversity. Now the government is saying that one out of every nine women will get breast cancer in her lifetime—hardly rare enough for only celebrities. The latest thing I heard is that DDT causes breast cancer."

Pete just nodded as he sat in a lounge chair, gazing up at the moon.

Both were silent for a short time then Michelle said "I'm overwhelmed by all this information. Holly said something about knowing, in the back of her mind, that she would get it someday, like she has some kind of crystal ball. Darn Holly anyway. She is such a worrier. The conversation last night opened up many con-cerns that I have not thought about before." She looked directly at him before continuing. "Pete? Would you leave me if I only had one breast?"

Pete paused, as if his response was important and he wanted to say the right thing. "Would you leave me if I had only one eye, or one ear, or one testi—?"

"Oh, shut up, smart-ass."

"Treatments today are a lot better than in your mom's time. Breasts don't need to be removed. My secretary, Ginger, got breast cancer and only had the lump removed, followed by radiation." He plowed on, taking a different tact. "Would it be helpful for the girls if we had them tested? I agree, it is worrisome if breast cancer can be inherited. But at the same time, would the knowledge alter their … well, normalcy?"

Michelle nodded and was about to speak but Pete continued. "Giving them a head start might be worth it, if there is something that could be done but right now, we don't know enough. Maybe you should see a doctor, just to talk about these issues."

"It's just that … well, you know. This merger business has really been stress-ful, and I don't have the time right now."

"I'd go with you. I have a right to know too."

"Yes, but when? You're busy, and I'm busy. I can't just walk out of these nego-tiations and say sorry, I have a doctor's appointment, just to ask some questions."

"How's the negotiation going?"

Michelle sighed. "I wish the accounting firm was like it was when it was just Margie and me. Life was so simple. Now we are so large that I don't even know the first names of many of my employees."

"So what's the problem? Sell out to Texas. You have the money."

"I could say the same of you, you know," she countered.

"It's not the same. I'm just the vice president in charge of research and development."

"No, I meant you have enough stock, so you don't have financial worries. You could quit, and we both would look after the kids."

"Really? You know as well as I do that there is more to life than that."

"That's my point. I can't just walk away from my responsibilities. I have to think of the welfare of the employees too."

"Texas doesn't want them?"

"Not all of them."

They sat looking upward. To the west, the glow of the city dimmed the stars, but the rest of the sky was clearly visible.

"Is that the Pleiades over there by Orion?" Pete asked. "Remember when we used to spend hours looking at constellations?"

"Yes. It seemed like all we had, when we first dated, was looking at the stars and being poor. I remember you were so shy, while I had to do all the entertaining for us." Michelle chuckled at the memory.

"Well, you were so adept. Remember? You passed the certified public accountant examination while taking college final exams. You had three accounting firms competing for you, then you chose the largest firm in the Northwest, bought a new car, got an apartment, and worked twelve to sixteen hours a day. I had to follow you to the big city and take a career in the computer industry." There was no rancor to his voice as he continued, "We were both in the right place at the right time."

"Looks like it. Pete, when's the last time we just looked at the night sky? Seems like it was back when I first got promoted." It wasn't long until her firm had promoted her to division manager, then executive manager, and finally vice president. There had been no senior female executives before her.

"Yeah, it was about then. Seems like everything got out of control for us. You were just too damn good. Even when you quit and started your own little business, things just got busier." Pete yawned and stretched his arms to indicate that it was only a statement and not a challenge.

"You forget—you were all for it, as I remember. We both wanted a family, and I started my own business so I could take control." Michelle was on the defensive now. "My mistake was taking a sample of good clients with me. Looking back, it appeared to some in the corporate world, that the move signaled success." She pondered then continued." ... and many companies transferred their accounting services to my fledgling business."

Laughing now, she shrugged her shoulders. "Instead of controlling a business, the business controlled me. The company grew so fast that I had to hire many of the employees from the old firm. The environment was the same, but I was on top."

"You act like you were a victim of circumstances. As I remember it, you liked it at the top until we moved out here and Nicole was born. You liked being the CEO of your own accounting company, with employees that used to be your bosses. Remember when that magazine ran feature biographical articles about your success? It took you five years at the top before you wanted to sell and have more time with the children." Pete's voice tapered off, and he sneezed. "Must be pollen out here."

A large company in Texas had gotten wind that Michelle was thinking about selling the firm. Acquiring Michelle's company would give them a firm base in the northwest. Secret negotiations and clandestine meetings took up most of her time now. "I wish we never had to go back to the city," Michelle said to the sky as she continued to gaze.

"For someone who is so goal-oriented, you sure dream a lot lately. We're only thirty miles from downtown, and in a few more years, this place will be surrounded by tall buildings too. I don't think you will last as a stay-at-home mom if you do sell the business. You've got to have the challenge, Michelle."

"You're wrong. I would like to try it and see. We have the stable just down the road, and I could teach the girls to ride. I would like to dig my fingers in the soil in this five-acre lawn we have and raise a flower garden. I think there is enough to challenge me." Michelle crossed her arms and pushed out her lower lip. "Pete? You remember Granddad Dan's ranch? Well, since he died two years ago, Mom has not done anything with it. We could buy it and run the ranch."

He squirmed in the lounge chair and continued to look up. "What about the girls?"

"It would be perfect for them. They are still young enough to learn to appreciate the great outdoors." She tightened her folded arms around her waist as she leaned forward.

"What about me?"

"What do you mean?"

He sighed and dropped both arms to his sides. "Look, Michelle, be reasonable. I have a great job. I'm not like you. You were magna cum laude, while I was just a B student. I was a nerd, while you were in *Who's Who of American Universities*. You were the popular one with all your plays and student body things, and you were homecoming queen. They even mispronounced my name at the graduation ceremony. Why me? I always wondered. Why me?"

"I loved you … because you were so helpless. What's your point?"

"My point is that you can jump from one job to another and always be successful, while I can't. I lucked into this job, and to this day, I don't know why I am good at it. Oh, yes, I accept that I'm good, but I don't have talent like you. And if I pulled up stakes and left, then found out I didn't like the next job, like being a rancher, then I couldn't get another job like this. I didn't get to where I am by talent. I got here by luck."

"You and your damned 'It's all fate' attitude."

They were silent again. Crickets started strumming by the pond. Cars could be heard passing by on the distant freeway.

He asked, "Why did you go into accounting anyway, if your heart is outdoors?"

"I was good at math and got a scholarship for college."

"Look, why don't you back-burner the ranch stuff and see how you feel in a year or two? You may change your mind. If not, then we'll talk about it."

"I won't change my mind, so get used to it. Oh, look, Pete! There's a satellite. There's another one! Aren't we lucky?"

They watched for a while, then Pete got up, stretched, and leaned over to peck her cheek. He said good night, then went back in the house. Michelle knew she needed to go in too. Tomorrow meant more negotiations.

I'll go see my gynecologist anyway. Damn the negotiations.

Chapter 12

Early August 1997

Michelle fidgeted in the small examination room. The appointment was already thirty minutes late. She had decided to see this hotshot doctor about genetic tests, at the recommendation of her gynecologist after a mammogram. Things were getting out of hand. To top off this silly quest, the mammogram needed repeating in six months. The whole experience was ballooning out of control.

Now she sat, waiting, while there were other important things to do. Already nervous, she thumbed through two *People* magazines (with contemptuous disgust at the celebrities), one *Time*, one *Newsweek*, and an unfamiliar magazine called *Cope*. The latter was about cancer issues for patients; it was not a rag she wanted to read while waiting there. It was funny, though: a lot of the advertisements were about herbs and supplements. That didn't seem to bode well for the oncology profession. She grabbed another outdated *People* as the doctor came in. He walked to the small desk, sat down, and perused her chart, without a salutation or any recognition of her presence.

Finally, she announced, "Hello, I'm Michelle Garrity-Keebler. Are you the doctor?" She thought she might as well slip some Socratic irony into the situation.

Still, he did not respond, but continued to study the chart. To her knowledge, there wasn't anything in the chart to study, since she was a new patient. At last, he closed the folder and turned to her. "I am a doctor, but not *the* doctor. Why is your last name hyphenated?"

Taken back by the abstruse nature of this introduction and annoyed, she retorted, "Why is your last name Nielsen? Irish?"

"Irish Jew, actually. I'm sorry. I can be abrupt. Can we start over? I'm not good at social interaction."

"I'm not here to socialize, doctor. Let's get to it." She began to dominate the interaction, a role in which she was comfortable. "Look, my mother got breast cancer when she was thirty-two years old, and now my sister and I are concerned that we might get it. I went to my gynecologist because I read somewhere that there is a test that can tell if you are going to get it. My gynecologist recommended you as the expert. She did a mammogram that was—how do you people put it?—inconclusive."

He listened attentively until she was through, as if intimidated. Then he started into teacher mode. "There are two basic types of breast cancer, Michelle—hereditary and nonhereditary. To be classified as hereditary, there have to be two or more breast cancers in first-degree relatives, and usually the cancer occurs under the age of fifty. These are not hard and fast rules, but they give a hint of a hereditary cause. With your mother getting cancer at thirty-two and your grandmother dying of cancer, there is concern. We are just now beginning to understand something about hereditary cancers. I may not be able give you definitive answers, and certainly not today. We might be able to identify some factors involved, but only in about forty percent of hereditary cancer families. The tests are expensive and really only investigational. However, I would be willing to do the studies if you wish, but you need to decide first if you really want to know—and what you are going to do with the information. Why don't you think about it and let me know?"

He left, then a nurse in a white cap and a young assistant came into the room before Michelle could leave. "He doesn't have the best bedside manner does he?" Michelle fumed.

The nurse said, "He's brilliant in his field, but tact isn't his strong suit. Can I answer some questions or help?"

Michelle was overwhelmed and needed to talk, so she nodded. All three women sat, the nurse scooting her chair right up to Michelle and putting her hand on her chin, as if ready to listen.

Michelle was uncomfortable with the silence, then blurted something off the top of her head. "I don't understand any of this. I'm an executive, and I make decisions all the time, but I don't like being treated like this! I'm doing this for my kids. What's the matter with you people? You treat me like I was a piece of meat or something."

The student drew back in her chair, but not the old nurse. She continued to look at Michelle.

Michelle asked, "Am I going to get cancer?"

"Let's go over the situation and see if we can ease the confusion. Genetic testing is a new field, and we don't know how to handle it, to be honest. Let me try to give you some data—but you interrupt at any time to ask questions. About four years ago, investigators found that some women that developed cancer at an early age, with a history of cancer in family members, had an abnormal gene.

This gene, called the BRCA1 gene, was a mutation that caused breast cancer. If a woman has this mutated gene, she runs a high risk of developing cancer, and these scientists can now determine how probable this is, based on age and family history. An affected woman with several cancers in her family can have a probability of over fifty percent—again, depending on her age. If you know you have this mutation, then you might be able to prevent getting cancer."

"How?"

"Well, lifestyle changes such as exercise and watching your weight can help. Getting regular mammograms and even removing the breasts are options being explored now. Other things that are being looked at are removing the ovaries or taking anti-estrogen drugs, since these cancers seemed to be fed by estrogen."

"Some of the options don't sound too good."

"Everyone has to consider their comfort level. To compound the issue, now there are two recognized mutations—BRCA1 and 2—and there will be more. If you do not have these two, you may still be at risk."

"What about my girls? If I have a mutation and they have it, will it harm them psychologically to know?"

"That's a hard one to answer. There is a study out of Georgetown University suggesting that the impact will be minimal. To be honest, I think it will be an issue for all of you, and you will have to work through it. How did you feel when your mother came home with cancer? Was it better to know what was going on?"

"It's not the same."

"No, of course not. But it is a close analogy, isn't it?"

The nurse and Michelle talked for another hour as the student sat in silence. The nurse kept repeating many of the same ideas until Michelle grasped the concepts. "Can we start the test today?" she asked, feeling like something needed to be done besides talking.

"I'll ask Dr. Nielsen to come back. But there are other issues."

Inwardly, Michelle sighed. "Such as?"

"Well, the impact on you is the most important. And, as we discussed, the girls. But there are others—your sister, mother, and husband too. Social factors come into play as well. If the defect is present, you then have a label. You could consider it to be like having a crystal ball. It is conceivable that insurance companies, employers, and others will hold it against you. Who knows all the ramifications?"

"I can relate to ramifications. My dad left Mom with two kids after the cancer. We lived on a farm, isolated."

For a moment, the nurse just sat and stared at Michelle. Then she glanced at the name on the medical record sitting on the desk. "Garrity-Keebler? Are you Ann Garrity's daughter?"

"Yes. How did you know?"

"I use to work at the hospital there. I took care of your mom and…. How could I forget?"

"Small world, isn't it?"

"How is she? No, we'll talk later. Let me go get the doctor before he scoots out of here."

Dr. Nielsen came back into the examination room to explain the procedure and its cost: three thousand dollars, which the insurance company would not cover. He would send the blood to a special commercial lab in Maryland. He explained that he was doing research on the BRCA2 gene and that if she had this mutation, he could study it further without cost.

Two weeks later, Michelle was back at the clinic. Today, she would get the results. The magazines were the same, and the doctor was late again, but this time the wait was tolerable; Sharon, the nurse with the white cap, was there. Dr. Nielsen waltzed into the room with a smile and a bright salutation. Sharon rose from the stool to stand behind Michelle, anticipating a need to be supportive. But Michelle guessed what the faux bonhomie meant. In a calm, rational voice, she said, "Did the test show the mutation?" She now knew the lingo.

"Yes, you are a BRCA2 mutant."

Michelle flinched. "Where do we go from here?"

"Well … there was a paper published just this year, by Berry at Duke University, about the probability of developing cancer in the BRCA1 mutation, depending on age and family involvement. Assuming the penetrance is the same for BRCA2—"

"Give her a break, doctor. Spell it out in plain English!" Sharon fumed.

"Well, at thirty-five, the probability of cancer is about ten percent and rises to eighty percent by the age of eighty, given her history. Whereas a woman without a mutation has a probability of less than one percent at thirty-five, rising to about ten percent by the age of eighty."

"So what you're telling her is that she has about a tenfold increase in the risk to develop breast cancer during her lifetime, and that her chance of not getting cancer is about twenty percent," Sharon said.

"Ah … something like that. Of course, there are other cancer risks too."

"What other cancers?" Michelle sounded anxious.

"Well, we call these mutations BRCA as an acronym for breast cancer, as they were first discovered in women with breast cancer, but the defect can be in other tissues and cause cancer there. The ovaries are susceptible, and a woman with the BRCA mutation—either one or two—can get ovarian cancer with a cumulative risk of about fifty percent by the age of eighty. The defect has been found in prostate cancer in affected males, melanoma of the eye, and even pancreatic cancer. The breast is the most susceptible, probably because of an estrogen influence."

"Good grief! You are signing my death certificate! What about my daughters and sister?"

"I'm sorry, Michelle. I don't know what to say."

"Well, say something! I need some advice here. What about my children?"

"We would have to test them to see if they have the gene. There's a fifty-percent chance. But are we opening up Pandora's box? I mean, do we want to look that far into the crystal ball? Science doesn't have all the answers, and right now, all we have are questions. I honestly don't know where to go, but I know your daughters are not at risk today and probably not in any danger until they are over thirty. By then, science will have better tools and knowledge."

"Okay. That makes sense. What about my sister?"

"It would be wise to check her, if she is comfortable with the knowledge. We can also just screen for breast cancer, but that's up to her."

"Can you do the tests if she agrees?"

"Yes, my grant is to study the BRCA2 gene in families. But to justify the work, we would have to have the whole family."

"You mean Mom. I never thought of Mom."

"Yes, Mom, Dad, and any other relatives. What are you going to do?"

"I don't know where my dad is, but I'll contact Mom and Holly, then let you know." She turned her wrist to look at her watch.

"No, I mean, what about you? Do you have any idea—or feelings about your options?"

"I don't know. I need to think about it some more. Can you give me something to study?"

"Yes, but it's technical, for the most part. Sharon would be a good resource, and she can interpret things for you. I will answer any questions you have. Why don't we set up another appointment in, say, a couple of weeks to revisit these issues?"

"That's a plan. Okay."

Dr. Nielsen rose, reached for Michelle's hand to help her rise, then hugged her. He was human after all.

Michelle drove back to the office, numb. What had started out as a simple quest for answers was now a complex maze that involved several people. The two people that had most motivated her to begin this adventure were out of the picture; at least the girls were safe ... for now. Her risk still seemed difficult to comprehend, but there was no need to panic today, as decisions required more input. At least that was what she thought while driving down the freeway.

Panic set in when she remembered that the mammogram had been abnormal. She almost rammed her Chevy Suburban into the wall two feet beyond the reserved parking space, but her dazed state gave way to reality in time. She sat in the big SUV, with the air conditioner running at maximum, and thought about it. *The girls might not be a priority right now, but they will perceive something's wrong, just like we did as kids. Can't keep it a secret. How will Pete react to this information, and how much should I tell him now? All of it, of course. He has a right to know. First things first, though, and the first thing to do is get back to business. I'll tell Pete tonight, and we'll discuss it. After we have a plan, we will tell the girls. I'll call Holly and—*

"You okay in there?" There was a metallic tapping on the side window. The lawn maintenance man, key in hand, stood at the door, looking concerned.

She rolled down the window. "I'm fine. I was just thinking about something."

"Could you back up a little, so I can mow in front of the building?"

"Yeah. Sorry."

In the elevator, life returned to normal. In an hour, there was a meeting with the corporate bigwigs and their lawyers from Texas, and she still hadn't decided how to deal with the transaction. She was holding out for a better plan to transfer her employees into their company while maintaining some control for herself in the new scheme of things. Texas, however, was not too interested in her having a big role. They thought it might harm their relationship with the power company. Today was the showdown.

"How did the doctor visit go?" Kathy, the secretary, asked as her boss emerged from the elevator and headed to her office.

"Great. Don't disturb me until the meeting. Okay?"

Later, she walked into the conference room to greetings from the chairman, the CEO, the CFO, the two negotiators, and four lawyers from Texas.

She said, "Okay, boys. Here's the deal, and let's get it done today. I walk away with no further association with the firm, but you hire all my employees who want to stay. I walk out of here today with a deal, or we drop the whole thing."

The lawyers seemed disappointed when she agreed to all their nitpicking concessions. The executives left, owning a new northwestern branch with employees already in place, ready to work. Michelle went to her office, threw everything into the trash, and left to fight the evening traffic, knowing she would never go back.

◆　　　◆　　　◆

Peter went ballistic on hearing the news. He would not believe there was a test that could predict cancer with that accuracy, although he did concede that cancer was a risk, given the family history. Maybe it wasn't so much the ability to predict as it was his inability to accept. At any rate, he was irate. Michelle had never seen this behavior before, and at first, she cowered. But as he pursued his emotion, she became resentful; after all, it was her problem, and potentially one for the girls. She had expected him to be supportive—his usual response. His continued anger undermined the focus she wanted now. The girls cowered too. Nicole looked like she was on the verge of tears when Michelle shuffled them off to bed. She returned to the living room, hoping he would help decide how they should proceed. She listened as he picked up his cell phone to call the head of his company.

"Bill? Hey, this is Pete. Sorry to bother you, but I was wondering if you could do me a favor. You still a regent at the university? Great. There's a quack doctor there that saw my wife today, and he frightened her with some poppycock about getting cancer. His intimidation was inappropriate, and now she is a basket case. Do you think we could get a hold of the president and get this straightened out? This guy should be fired!" He continued his vitriolic diatribe for another five minutes as Michelle watched him. Finally he hung up, drummed his fingers on the desk, then stood and began pacing the room.

She stood, walked to the window, and leaned against the frame with her arms crossed. Outside, the night was silent; distant lights flickered across the lake. A breeze was probably causing the trees to sway. She wished she was out in the forest now. Pete continued to pace. Both remained silent, waiting. Not ten minutes later, the phone rang again. *Things move fast at the top of the food chain,* she thought, as Pete picked up the phone.

"Oh? What the hell is a BRCA gene?" He listened. "Really? Okay, thanks, Bill." He punched the cell phone dead, looked away from her, then hung his head as he left the room.

Michelle slept with the girls; Pete slept alone. Nothing much was said in the morning. He left early, after a cup of coffee, while Michelle nursed her cup at the dining table. A civil good-bye would have been nice, but she didn't feel prone to civility. After a few moments alone, she dropped her head into her arms and cried. There was nothing else to do.

That night, after the girls were in bed, he finally spoke. "I went to the university hospital today and talked to Dr. Nielsen. He's a geek, you know."

"No, he's strange. You're a geek."

Pete continued, ignoring her backlash. "I didn't like him at first. He was condescending, but he does know his stuff. He gave me some published materials, and I have been reading all day. I've researched on the Internet too. I called my old roommate, Tom, at UCLA Medical Center, and he called Dr. Nielsen too. Tom's boss is the head honcho at the cancer center down there and does research on breast cancer—something to do with a her-2/neu receptor. Anyway, I have an appointment for us this week to fly down and see him."

Michelle just sat there.

"I'm sorry, Michelle."

After a deep breath, she spoke. "If I ever needed you in my life, it was last night, and you weren't there. I needed you to help sort out all this stuff that will change our lives. What did you do but go off on your own emotions? You scared the girls and me. We are the ones that have the problem, Pete, not you! How dare you take this issue into your own hands! It's my body and perhaps the girls' too. You have no right to treat us this way just because you are afraid. You have no right to direct things without sharing with me first. We can make mutual decisions, or I can make decisions on my own."

"Do you want me to cancel the appointment?"

"Is this expert in the field of cancer genes? What is a her-2?"

"Her-2/neu. I don't know what it is. He knows about breast cancer, is all I know."

"I don't have breast cancer ... yet. I have a genetic defect. We should see someone who knows about my defect if we are going to consult anyone. We don't need to see a friend of a friend just to placate you!"

That night, Michelle slept with the girls again but woke early to a revelation. *Was this how things went with Mom and Dad? Did Mom drive Dad away by excluding him?* She threw back the sheet and slipped out of bed, trying not to disturb the kids. Pete appeared asleep on his side when she entered the bedroom and sat on the edge of the bed. He was pretending, because there was no snoring, and soon he opened one eye to look at her.

"I'm sorry too, Pete. I was hurt, and wanted to hurt you back. Let's work through this together."

"Yeah ... okay."

Chapter 13

August 1997

The view from the top of the mountain took her breath away again. She was glad to have reached the summit. Now she could just sit and take in the scene below. Today was exceptional: no clouds or rain. This trek, done once a week in the summer and early fall, rejuvenated her spirit, and she equated it with going to church. Although not religious in the sense of organized religion, Ann was spiritual: she worshiped nature and her small place in it. She performed her ritual every bit as faithfully as most churchgoers. Every week, she would reflect on the big scheme of things, her insignificance, and the wonder of the universe. *Funny, feeling insignificant makes me spiritual.* Even humanity's achievements added to her religion. This reflection gave her time to be grateful for her life. After her diagnosis of cancer, she had questioned—or at least was angry with—her creator. Standing on this pinnacle, in awe of all that was around her, her attitude changed. Instead of *why*, it became *how*; instead of *poor me*, it became *why not me*. Whenever her life was not going as she expected, this hike realigned things. Today was one of those days.

Michelle had called the night before to say she would arrive in the afternoon; she said she wanted to talk to Ann about the family and cancer but would not be specific. "We'll talk tomorrow, Mom." All night, Ann had worried. Perhaps Michelle had cancer too. She was dreading this meeting.

Ann gazed out as far as she could see. Her eyes took in the vast expanse while her ears heard things that were not normal in the city or even at her farm, things like coyotes playing in a meadow below the promontory where she sat, or elk stepping through the woods on the slope to her right. She could smell things, too, like pine sap from the trees when the breeze came up the slope. Every now and then, she would stand up to restore her circulation, then sit back down. At about noon, she ate a banana and an apple for lunch, then gazed to the far eastern mountains and squinted, as though she could see finer details—like Yoty. It was ridiculous, of course, but she would look. It had been twenty-five years, and he had to be dead, but she kept the memory alive. *Crazy,* she would remind herself.

We are just products of our experiences, good or bad. As the sun tipped west, she looked at her watch. It was time to go, if she was going to be home by the time Michelle got there.

The house was in sight as she climbed over the back fence and tore her pants leg on the barbed wire. "Someday I ought to put a gate back here," she said to herself. No sooner had she started walking again than she saw the big Suburban come though the front gate. The meeting time had arrived, but at least she could see her granddaughters.

Michelle said, "Hello, Mom. You been on the mountain?"

"Yes, I was. Let me see those babies." She opened the side door. Kira, now four years old, just looked at her grandmother, but Nichole, tired from the trip, started to cry. Ann was in her element as she removed the crying baby from the car seat and held her.

Michelle said, "The girls are tired. We got up at six to beat the traffic out of the city. I didn't stop, except to buy gas, so the girls need some food and a change of pace from those car seats."

"You look tired too, dear. Let's go in, and I'll make you guys some lunch."

◆　　◆　　◆

Michelle stood at the kitchen window as Ann fed the kids. Gazing up the mountain, she asked, "You still go up there every week, Mom? I remember I always used to want to go with you, but you always went alone. Holly and I used to go up there, but after that time we saw the rattler, we quit. You ever run into rattlesnakes?"

"Sometimes. I just stay out of their way, and they don't bother me. It's their home too. As long as you don't get on sunny rocks, or stick something into a crevasse, they won't be irritated. You want to go up there?"

"Not with the girls. They need a nap right now." Nichole was already asleep at the table.

Later, Ann and Michelle moved to the deck. There was a warm, gentle breeze, so there were no insects to bother them. Michelle stretched out in the recliner with a sigh. Ann sat at the patio table, sipping an iced tea. She too wanted a nap. "How come you're not at work?" she asked.

"It's Saturday, Mom."

"I know that. You know what I meant."

"I sold the business to an outfit out of Texas. I think I got out at the right time, Mom. The heyday of the big accounting firms is going to crash. Some of their accounting practices are questionable, and I don't want to be in it when the hammer falls."

"You always had the vision for business, Michelle. That's why you were so successful. What are you going to do now?"

"Be a mother and a wife. I don't need any more money, so why not?"

"What's Pete's take on all this?"

"Oh, he's okay with it. He could quit too, if he wanted. But he enjoys it—I didn't. He wanted to come today but had to go to India to check on his team there."

"What's this about our family and cancer, Michelle?" She might as well get it over with.

"You remember when Holly and I talked last month?"

"So?"

"I got to thinking and went to my doctor. She sent me to a specialist."

Ann leaned forward, heart pounding now.

"This specialist is at the university, doing research in cancer genes."

"So it is inherited." Ann almost whispered.

"Well, it can be. Most cases, as I understand it, are not, but a small number can be. He wants to test us to see if we have a cancer gene."

"Us? You mean me too?"

"Yes. You, Holly, Dad—anyone who is still alive in our family."

"Why? What difference would it make?" Ann was defiant now.

"Well, it may. This research is new, and no one knows what to make of it yet. There is some indication that there are some things that can be done to prevent cancer."

"Like?'

"Remove the breasts, or take antihormones, or remove the ovaries or—"

"Good grief! That sounds drastic! Remove the breasts?"

"That's just one option, Mom. If you think about it, that would still be better than getting cancer, wouldn't it?"

After the initial shock, Ann pondered for a moment. "Perhaps you're right. I don't know. This researcher sounds cold, Michelle." Deep inside, she wondered whether he was cold or she didn't want to know.

"What makes you say that? I have to agree, though—he isn't the friendliest person I've met, Mom." Michelle chuckled, then went on. "He does know his stuff, and he is trying to help."

"You didn't say 'me'."

"What do you mean?"

"You didn't include yourself when you said he wanted to test us. You already know, don't you?" Fear almost choked out the last word.

A flicker cried up the mountain, as if to confirm the question. The warm breeze quit; there was no other sound.

Michelle was motionless. Then she took a deep breath. "Yes. I have the defect. It's called BRCA2. I have an eighty-percent chance of breast cancer in my lifetime and a fifty-percent chance of ovarian cancer."

Ann gasped. For twenty-five years, she had dreaded this moment, and now it was here. Neither woman spoke; they just looked across the valley. The only activity was some giant irrigation sprinklers shooting large volumes of water over fields of green potato plants, mesmerizing the two mothers.

Kira interrupted the trance as she slipped out the kitchen door and waddled across the deck to her mother. Naptime was over. For the rest of the afternoon, Ann directed her attention to the grandchildren, while Michelle went around the farm, reminiscing. That night, after the kids were asleep, she asked, "Mom, is there someone who could watch the kids in the morning, so we could go up the mountain?"

"You're not afraid of the snakes?" Ann teased.

A neighbor's daughter agreed to babysit, as the task got her out of Sunday school.

The following morning, after giving the sitter a ride, mother and daughter climbed the mountain. Ann carried a pack containing breakfast. Michelle, out of shape, lagged behind, but youth provided her with the necessary stamina. By the time she reached the mountain peak, her mom was already sitting on the point, drinking a cup of coffee from a thermos.

"Beautiful, isn't it? What do you think of my church?"

"Yes, it is beautiful. It's my church too, and you can share it," Michelle retorted with a smile.

They gazed on the sight before them as they munched fruit and drank coffee. Never had Ann felt so close to her daughter as now. "What does Pete think?"

"At first, he was angry and incredulous. I wanted to run away. But we worked it out, and he has been supportive since. He's not emotionally very strong, Mom."

"Neither was your dad.

"Is that why he left us?"

"I guess so. Your dad was a dreamer—always looking for a big break. He hated the farm and wanted to go the big city and find … something."

"Did he? I mean, did he find something?"

"I doubt it. That something was in himself."

"Where is he now, Mom?"

"I don't know. He went to San Francisco, following what he thought was his golden opportunity. But I couldn't go. I wasn't strong enough at the time, either physically or emotionally. Looking back, I wish I had gone, in some ways, but in others, I'm glad I stayed here."

"You're isolated, Mom. Still are, for that matter."

"Yes, I am isolated. Easier that way."

"What do you mean?"

Ann just shrugged.

After a while, Michelle said, "Did the surgery affect you that much, Mom?"

"I guess. My only goal was to raise you kids. But I yearned too. After you left, I didn't have a goal anymore, so I just stayed. I love it here."

Michelle decided to take another approach. "Did having only one breast influence things?"

"Why do you ask?" Ann didn't want to think about it.

"Please, Mom. My best chance may be to have my breasts removed. I need to know."

Ann sighed. "One day, many years ago, I ran across a term in the dictionary at school. *Lusus naturae*. It means freak of nature. I thought, that's me. Yeah, it influenced me and who I am. My relationship with men changed. Even if I wanted a man, I was afraid he would look at me like I was a freak. I think Bob was like that after the surgery. He left for other reasons, but I suspect that was part of it. Fred usually got drunk before.... Anyway, one night I was coming home from a meeting in Seattle. It was late, and I was hungry and tired, so I stopped at this bar and grill, the only place open in this little town in western Washington. There was a man there, handsome but drunk. He came over to the counter where I sat and put his arm around me, then rubbed my prosthesis in front of the rest of the crowd in that greasy spoon. I was humiliated."

"What did you do?"

"I kicked him in the groin."

"That's it? What's the point of the story, Mom?"

"He vomited after that, and the rest of the women in the place cheered. I ran out, because I heard a siren coming. That's all."

"Mom! I don't get it."

"Later, after I calmed down, I wished I was normal, so I could have *felt* like a woman when he touched me. That's the point of the story."

They were both silent again. A jet contrail streaked overhead as an eagle soared on a thermal current below them, looking for game. The sensation of looking down on the eagle was exhilarating, as though they were at the pulpit of life. They scanned their world for a long time, until Michelle screamed, then jumped, pulling her feet up from the shelf below them. Ann put her arm out in front of the startled woman, as if to restrain her. They looked down to see a rattlesnake between Ann's legs.

Slow and focused, Ann reached down to the motionless animal, out to sun itself, and then grabbed the creature behind the head before it could react. Lifting her prize as it wrapped its body around her arm, she looked at its head. Its mouth was open wide, fangs extended. It did not rattle. She studied it for a while as Michelle looked on from a distance.

"See? It's just as afraid of us as we are of it. Look."

"No! Get that thing away from me!"

Ann uncoiled the animal from her arm and placed it back onto the ledge, as if it were a baby. She watched in fascination as the snake oriented, then moved back into the recess of the ledge to escape. So much for sunbathing.

"Let's go back, Mom. You know, it's ironic that you have no fear of a poisonous snake, but you hide from the rest of the world."

"No, I don't. I have friends."

"Yeah? Who?"

"Karen, for one. You remember Karen's daughter. You use to ride with her. Then there's John and Edie, and—"

"Okay, I'm sorry. I was being smart. Do you ever take a stand for a cause?"

"What in the world does that mean?"

"Well, I was looking through your old college yearbook last night, and it looked like you were involved in many activities, including causes like political and moral issues. I was surprised, as I didn't know you did that kind of thing."

"Yes, I guess I did. I haven't thought about that stuff in years."

"Why did you stop?"

"I don't know. When I got … cancer … it didn't seem that important anymore. I didn't know … how long. I just focused on one cause—you two kids. There was no other mission. I just wanted to live long enough to raise you two, and nothing else mattered."

They started down the mountain. Michelle kept slipping on the talus rock, as her running shoes did not have traction like her mother's hiking boots. Concentrating on the route, she said nothing until they descended into a grove of trees.

"Mom, do you feel guilty about the cancer?"

"Boy, you sure have a lot of questions. I guess I do, in a way. I always feared you or Holly would get it. Sometimes, right after I was diagnosed, I would suddenly think about it and become real afraid. Sometimes I would blame my mom, just so I wouldn't feel guilty. Strange, huh? I didn't mean to give it to you, and I know Mom didn't mean to give it to me, but I had trouble for a long time before I could be rational about it." She stopped and turned toward Michelle. "You feel that way too, don't you?"

"I don't want to, but I am so afraid for the girls that I feel guilty. Yet I know it wasn't my fault. At the same time, I feel shame, like I am a—what's that word you used?—lucas something."

"*Lusus naturae.*"

"Yes, a freak. Maybe these feelings are irrational, but they are there—guilt and shame. Maybe we should call it guilt-shame."

"Yes, I like that word. Guilt-shame. It isn't guilt, and it isn't shame, but it's still there, rational or not. Quite an albatross to carry around one's neck, isn't it?"

Silent now, they descended the rest of the way. Each woman was deep in her own thoughts. Ann cursed as they climbed over the fence; she tore her pants leg again.

◆   ◆   ◆

While preparing dinner and feeding the girls, Michelle started again. "Will you have the test, Mom?"

"I don't know. I mean, why? If you have it, you got it from me, so why test me? I agree that Holly might want the test. If we are just doing it so some professor can write another paper, then I don't want to do it. Part of me just doesn't want the objective confirmation of something I have feared for twenty-five years."

"I talked to Dr. Nielsen about the tests. He is pretty adamant. He wants all possible members of the family to be tested. I'm not sure I understand why either, but he'll do the tests for free. And believe me, it's expensive. This may be the only way we can get the test for Holly, unless George pays for it."

"That's a point I had not considered."

"This Dr. Nielsen is trying to get his name in lights, I'm sure. But some good may come out of it."

"What do you mean?"

"Well, this BRCA2 defect is on the thirteenth chromosome, in a specific location. If we can identify that location, then maybe they can correct the gene."

"That sounds like science fiction."

"Dr. Nielsen says that they are starting trials in patients this year at the University of California Medical Center in San Francisco, using gene therapy in patients with brain cancers."

"I … if it might help you or the girls, I guess…. What would I have to do?"

"Just have some blood drawn. I talked to the laboratory technician, and she is going to arrange to have your blood drawn at this hospital, then shipped up there. Neat, huh? Oh, he also wants you to sign a release, so he can get your medical records. I have the form in my purse."

The next morning, Michelle strapped the girls into their car seats. Ann stood there, tearful, as she closed the doors. The trip to the coast was an eight-hour drive, and Michelle wanted to get there before dark. As she opened the driver's side door, she stopped. "Do you have any idea who I could contact to find out about Dad?"

"You still going to try and find him? Well, I don't know. I use to trade Christmas cards with his sister, but we haven't done that for fifteen years or so. I don't know if she is still alive. If you want, I will dig through my address book and see if I still have an address. There was a man at the janitorial business in town who knew where he was, in the beginning. You might contact him. I don't know his name, but I can get the number for that business, if it still going."

"Oh, I almost forgot. Did you know a Sharon Townsend, Mom?"

"No, I don't recall the name."

"There is a nurse at the university who claims she took care of you at this hospital when you had surgery. She went on to get a PhD in nursing and now is head of the oncology nursing program there."

"Medium-built woman that wears a white nursing cap?"

"That's the one."

"For Pete's sake! I always wondered what happened to her. She was the one that first helped me through that ordeal. She was a gem."

"She still is, Mom. Bye. I love you."

As Ann watched the Suburban drive away, she was alone again. Guilt-shame crawled back out to bask in the loneliness.

Chapter 14

Late August 1997

Michelle pulled the big Suburban off the road as she approached the freeway intersection. The girls were restless, not wanting to be restrained in their car seats for another long trip. Yet it wasn't the children that had caused her to pull off. She had a decision: to go on or turn back. Now, after the visit to Mom, the mission of this trip seemed less defined and purposeful. Starting out, Michelle had been sure that her quest to inform Ann and Holly, then get them tested, was noble. Now, she wasn't so sure. Mom had reacted differently than she had predicted; she had not really wanted to do the test. Sure, she could be convinced, but was it worth it? The visit had been traumatic, and the revelations about Mom, although giving her insight, were stressful.

"Am I opening up a can of worms? Maybe I should just let things alone. Yet if I can forewarn them by having them tested, it may save their lives. Yes, that's the decision. I will go on to Holly for that reason, no matter the consequences." She looked in the rearview mirror at Kira as she spoke. The child cocked her head, not understanding.

She pulled back onto the road, but doubt still lingered, and she almost convinced herself to turn back. She could just call Holly. After all, she could always talk her little sister into doing anything. Only a coward would deliver such an important message by phone. To reinforce her resolve, she remembered it had been a long time since she had seen Brat. Besides, the southern Oregon coast might be worth visiting. Now was the perfect time.

By the time she reached the summit of the first pass and viewed the panorama to the west, self-doubt about the mission had faded. At times like this, she regretted her decision to take up the indoor profession of accounting and wished she had become a forester or rancher. Sometimes, when Holly and she explored the woods behind the farm, they had talked of the future; Holly had always wanted to be a dancer, but even she had dreamed of owning her own farm someday. They had even fantasized about running away to Alaska together.

The kids were fidgety as Bandon came into view. After leaving the freeway, it had taken them about two hours to go down a winding canyon road with a river on one side and large road banks on the other. It may have been beautiful, but the road had required all of the driver's attention, and the children hadn't cared.

She drove to the performing arts center, only to find it closed. A poster announced that last night had been the final performance. After driving up and down side roads, trying to find Mila's house, Michelle gave up, pulled out her cell phone, and dialed.

"Hello?" a voice responded.

"Is Holly there?"

"Yes. Are you Michelle? We have been expecting you. Your mother called, wondering if you made it okay. Oh, my. I'm so rude. I'm Mila. Where are you, dear?"

"In Bandon, at the corner of 9th and Sutter."

"Can you see the ocean from there?"

"Yes."

"Just turn into the next driveway with the pink mailbox, dear. You're right here now."

Michelle felt a little foolish as she turned into the driveway, where a spry-looking little old lady and Holly stood smiling. After introductions, they unpacked as Michelle admired the location and the house. She wondered if Pete would like it here.

"You two girls need to talk. Why don't I take the babies down to the ice cream parlor?" Mila offered. She packed up the kids and scooted out the door before Michelle could object.

"She is delightful, isn't she?" said Holly.

"Is she always bubbly like that?"

"Always. Even when I take her to the doctor."

"I see, by the poster, that the production is finished. What are you going to do now?"

"Well, Leonard is impressed with my work and wants me to go back to New York with him, but I said no. George and I just love it here, so we are purchasing land about one mile down the coast, and as soon as the architect finishes, we plan to build. In the meantime, Mila needs help, so I will stay here. She is getting weaker, and the pain is worse."

"She doesn't seem … ill."

"She is a strong person, but she needs help. Her daughter in South Carolina refuses to deal with her mother unless she moves back there. Of course, Mila doesn't help. She's very stubborn and wants to be independent."

"She's accepting your help."

"Yeah, but on her terms. There's a difference."

"You mentioned George. I'm surprised he wants to leave the university and move here. Even more, I'm surprised you are going along with it. I thought your relationship ... was best at a distance." Michelle was uneasy, but Holly laughed.

"Yeah, so am I. George came out here a couple of months ago, and we hammered out our future. He didn't get the department chair, so he doesn't see a future there, and he doesn't like the squirrel-cage environment. We discussed what we want out of life and decided to move here. I decided that the most important thing in my life is ... well, life itself. And George."

"Wow! Have you changed!"

"Yeah, I guess so. When I couldn't dance anymore, I didn't know what to think. My image of myself was just as a dancer. Shallow? You bet, but I had to find out who I really was, and Mila pointed me in the right direction. You can't be around such an energetic and positive person without having some of it wear off. She even taught me that sharing was the most important thing." Holly turned her head sideways at an angle to her sister. "You're not here to talk about my lifestyle. What's up?"

Holly just listened as Michelle started telling her about breast cancer. Then she said, "You're up to something, aren't you?"

"No," Michelle lied, wondering why, since telling the truth would be easier.

"Yes, you are. Don't lie to me, Bossy."

"Now listen, Brat—"

"No, you listen to me. It doesn't make sense that you are going around drumming up business for some doctor. You would only do it if you were scared. Until I talked to you a couple of months ago, you hadn't even thought about cancer."

"That's not true."

"Come on, Bossy. Let's go walk the beach and talk. This stuff is too heavy for me to listen to while just sitting. You're telling me there is a test they can do now that tells you you're going to get breast cancer? That's ... not natural. That's a crystal ball."

The two descended a long flight of stairs leading from the cliff, where the house perched, down to the beach: ninety-seven steps, with a landing in the middle. At first, Michelle felt dizzy and feared looking down. She grabbed the side rails with both hands.

"Afraid, big sister?" Holly challenged, taking two steps at a time.

A fog bank lay at the water's edge, so the view tunneled as they descended from the cliff. Michelle felt cold, but the weather didn't seem to bother her sister. "You get used to the chill," she proclaimed, as if she were a long-time resident.

At the bottom, the beach was eerie; the cliffs were to the east and the fog bank to the west, as if they were in a canyon. The fog moved, and as they walked, large rocks would suddenly appear as shadows out of nowhere. The sound of waves, amplified in the fog, would interrupt the silence, and the smell of salty ocean spray was heavy. Daylight from above kept the scene from being sinister.

Michelle found herself breathing hard, and her calves started to ache. "How far are we going to walk?"

"Down the beach about a mile. I want to show you our building site. You'll love it. Right on the beach. Remember when we used to take hikes and pretend we were in Alaska? Well, I hike down here and feel just like that. Kinda all alone with nature."

"Funny, I was just thinking about Alaska this morning. You miss those times too?"

"Yeah, in a strange way. We were two scared kids then and wanted to escape. But now I just enjoy the outdoors. Sometimes I will run on the beach, and sometimes I just walk to take in the view. It's all so ... spiritual, I guess. Sure beats the cities I've been in."

"You still want to dance?"

"No, I never was a good dancer, but a dreamer. I miss the glory, but being here with Leonard and learning by teaching made me realize I'm not good. It's funny how when you see someone else do something, it looks so easy, but then you try it, and it is so difficult, even after years of practice. Dancing was hard for me, but I didn't know it until I instructed this summer. Kinda like life."

"What do you mean?"

"You go through life making it hard on yourself, until finally you realize it ain't easy the way you are doing it, so you have to change."

Michelle stopped. She was amazed by her sister's newfound insight but didn't really understand; to her, if things were difficult, you worked harder. Holly kept walking, forcing her to take up the pace again. "How will you know where your lot is in this fog?"

"I'll know." Holly chuckled, then added, "If there is a test for breast cancer, why isn't it being used?"

"The test isn't good on every woman, only those who have a type called hereditary breast cancer."

"Is ours hereditary?"

"Ye—what do you mean, ours?"

Holly took a deep breath, stopped, turned to her sister, and hugged her. They separated and looked into each other's eyes. Now they were just two little girls, sharing their fears with an unspoken communication, as only children can. Michelle tried not to sob.

◆   ◆   ◆

After Michelle put the children to bed that night, the three women gathered on the deck and gazed out to sea. The fog bank was still visible offshore in the full moonlight. To the north, an isolated thunderstorm pushed toward the cliffs.

Mila broke the silence with a blunt approach. "Cancer isn't so bad, you know. I've had it for twelve years now. With all the doctors can do now, it's amazing. Holly will be cured, I know."

Michelle said, "You are always so optimistic, Mila. Doesn't anything bother you?"

"Of course, but sometimes you have to have faith in others. Dr. Young and Dr. Peterson know what they are doing. You just need to have faith in them now, and the fear will go away."

"I find that hard to accept. Holly, when do you have surgery? I would like to be here."

Holly said, "Next week. Dr. Peterson will do it on Monday. He is going to inject some kinda dye into the tumor to see if it's spreading, then remove a lymph node. If it hasn't spread, then he will take out the lump."

"If it has? Spread, I mean."

"I don't understand all of this. but he will remove more lymph nodes. I guess."

"Shouldn't you get a second opinion?"

"Dr. Young is Mila's doctor, and he has reviewed the reports too. Dr. Peterson and he presented my case at a conference—called 'tumor board,' I think—and everybody agrees this is the best way to go."

"Wow! Sounds like they are … conscientious, anyway."

"Dr. Young is the best!" Mila bristled.

"You'll have to excuse us, Michelle, Mila and I like our doctors."

"Was the biopsy difficult?"

"No, I went in one morning, they x-rayed the area on my breast, then stuck a needle in it, and that was all there was to it."

"Sounds a lot different from Mom's surgery, doesn't it?"

"I don't even remember Mom's operation, just the silence afterwards. Do you remember all that stuff?"

"No, just that she came home different, and it took a long time for her to recover, and she changed afterward. I wonder if they had tumor boards then."

"Tells us more about this test you are talking about. We are a club," Mila chimed.

"Yes, I guess we are. You have lived with cancer for a long time, Holly has cancer, and I will get cancer. Some club. Anyway, about four years ago, some researcher discovered an abnormal gene in women with breast cancer that ran in their family—"

"How can that be? I mean, how can a gene become abnormal?" Holly seemed interested now.

"Defective genes can occur due to insults like radiation and chemicals or even damage due to oxidation, but they can also be passed down as defective. A cell cannot function if it doesn't have proper genes." Both sisters looked at each other in amazement as Mila talked. "If the code is defective, then the cell loses that function. If the function is to regulate cell reproduction, then the cell might reproduce too much, and that is cancer. If a code regulates death and becomes defective, then that cell may not die, becoming immortal, and that too is cancer. Defective genes in these regions of the genetic molecule are called oncogenes, or cancer genes. Oh … I'm sorry. I just got carried away. Please excuse me. I'll go get us some tea, while you two talk."

"They can identify these defective genes now with this test?" Holly continued as the older woman left.

"Not all of the defects, but certain ones. Not even all breast cancers, so there is no single test. In my case, the defect is called the BRCA-2 gene. Only about five percent of breast cancer patients have it, but if there were cancers in the family, particularly in young women, then the chances are higher." Michelle felt her explanations were not as good as Mila's. "If you have the cancer gene, then your chance of not getting cancer during your lifetime is slim, about twenty percent."

"I bet I have it too, don't I?"

"Yes, probably. Mom too."

"You came here to tell me that for a reason, Bossy. What is it?"

"I wanted you to be tested too, but now it seems moot. You and Mom have cancer, and I'm positive."

"Is there anything they can do to help you?"

"There might be. It's too soon to know, and studies are under way now. I am wrestling with the options."

"What are they?"

"Well, I could have my breast removed or my ovaries, or take a pill called tamoxifen, or just watch and wait."

"Why the ovaries? And what's tamoxson?"

"Tamoxifen. It is a drug that inhibits estrogen. Estrogen makes the cancer grow. That's one reason to remove the ovaries. Another reason is that the cancer can be in the ovaries too."

"Really? A double whammy."

"Yes, I understand the cancer gene can cause cancer in other organs too. Even men with the oncogene can get cancer."

"What about your girls?" Mila asked, coming through the door, carrying a tray with tea and cups.

"They have a fifty percent chance each of having the BRCA-2 gene."

"I feel ... defective," said Holly.

"Mom and I call it guilt-shame."

Mila said, "Are you going to test your girls, then? Seems to me that's a real burden to put on their little shoulders, don't you?"

"What do you mean, Mila?"

"Well ... if I knew, when I was a little girl, that someday I would be like this.... Well, I don't think I would have tried to do the things I did. I would probably just have given up, thinking, what's the use? Humans shouldn't have a crystal ball. Even for you, knowing it now must have some effect."

"Yes, it does, I think. Thank you for that insight. You are right. I could have them tested and not tell them the results...."

"No, dear, that won't do at all. Children are very perceptive, and you are not an actress, to go around pretending all is well. No, that won't do at all."

"She's right, Bossy. You remember how we picked up on Mom's cancer, even though she tried to hide it? The secret? Remember the secret? What about you?"

"Until Mila mentioned it, I thought I was handling it well. But she is right. I did give up. I sold my business the same day I was told about the oncogene. I gave up."

"You give up, you die," said Mila. "Well, dears, I am off to bed."

The sisters sat in silence, listening to the night sounds. Off in the distance, to the south, they could hear laughter and see a fire: young people having a beach party at the park. Life was all around them.

Michelle said, "She is quite insightful, isn't she?"

"Yeah, and she doesn't mince her words, either. I don't know if I could have handled it if it wasn't for her. Just being around her has done me wonders. I'm not afraid anymore."

Michelle wished she weren't afraid either.

◆   ◆   ◆

The following morning, Holly shook Michelle from sleep. Looking up at her little sister startled her at first. She rolled over and looked at her Rolex: 6:00 AM, still dark. She groaned when Holly shook her again.

"Come on, let's go," said Holly. "We never did get down to the building site yesterday, and I want to show you."

"It's still dark outside!"

"Won't be for long. Come on. I have an extra pair of running shoes and shorts you can wear. If we go now, we can be back before the girls get up. Besides, this is the best time of day, and you're missing it."

Holly was in the driveway, doing stretches, as Michelle exited the house, dawdling, trying to avoid the agony. She hadn't run since college and wasn't sure she could make it a mile and back. She hoped no one would see her, as the shirt Holly had provided was George's, and imprinted on the back was a statement: IF YOU THINK I'M UGLY, YOU SHOULD SEE MY DOG.

They started slow, but even then, Michelle was breathing hard before they went a block. Soon, daylight lit the way, and the sun rising over the hills showed a scene that made her forget the breathing and the pain. Holly left the road then, and they went through the dunes and down to the beach.

Running in sand caused her calf discomfort, but the feeling was exhilarating as waves lapped at their feet. Michelle's breathing evened out, and for a time, she could almost keep up with her sister. For the first time since hearing the letters BRCA, she was living in the moment, not in the future or the past. Eight minutes after starting, Holly accelerated and seemed to jet ahead. She turned into a speck down the beach, then stopped.

"How far now?" Michelle asked breathlessly as they met again.

"This is it."

"Where? I don't see anything but dunes and beach. What's that big shrub with the little yellow flowers?"

"That's Scotch broom. A Scot named Lord Nelson brought it over, and now it is a weed all along this stretch of coastline. The locals hate it and its cousin, gorse, because if a fire gets started in it, you can't put it out."

"You are building in a fire hazard area?"

"We have to take it out first. That's what George and I are going to do this weekend—pull it out with a tractor. If you stay, you can help."

"When is George getting back?"

"Should be back anytime. He had to go back east and take care of some business with his mother. Anyway, what do you think about the location? Let's walk up to the site, and you can look around."

"I can't tell what it will look like, but the area is so … pristine. You sure you want to destroy it?"

"If we don't, someone else will. This whole stretch is for sale."

"It's beautiful. You can walk or run the beach every day from here. Come on, let's go back before the girls wake up. First, though, let's walk a bit. Would it be okay if I called Dr. Nielsen this morning to see if he wants to test us now?"

"I have been thinking about it all night. I want to know if I have it too. I'm not sure why, because it isn't going to alter anything for me. But I have a … well, a curiosity, I guess. I think, though, that if I didn't have cancer already, I wouldn't want to know. Crazy, isn't it?"

"No, not really. I wanted to know for the girls' sake, but if I didn't have children, I don't know if I would want to know, unless it was a factor in my decision to have children. Mom doesn't want to know."

"You're not going to go ahead and test them, are you?"

"No, especially not after talking to Mila last night. But someday, it will be an issue for them."

"How much will this test cost me? I don't have any money, but George will pay if I ask."

"Nothing. It's a research project for Dr. Nielsen. Do you or George have insurance?"

"No, he lost his when he quit."

"How are you going to pay for your treatment? Medical bills are expensive."

"We'll manage."

"I didn't mean to pry. I'm sorry. It's just … well, if you need help, I can—"

"That's okay. Don't worry about it. We'll manage."

"I'll always be here for you. You know that?"

"Thanks, I appreciate that. But George has a trust or something. That's why he went back to talk to his mother."

"How did he take the news?"

"You mean when I told him I had cancer? He yelled and called Dr. Young a quack. I was afraid he would go see him. Finally, he calmed down, and we worked through it, step by step."

"That's how Pete took my news too. What is it about men? They act like cavemen sometimes."

"George acted as I would have acted. His chest-thumping was different from my sulking, but the emotion would be the same—fear. That's all it is, fear. He just reacted and lashed out at the doctor because of that fear. Now he worships the ground Dr. Young walks on."

"Thanks, Brat. You just cleared up a problem between Pete and me that I didn't understand. How did you get so smart so fast?"

"Running makes you think better. Now, let's run home."

◆   ◆   ◆

She could tell that George was nervous that morning. He never said much, at least when she was around, and it was hard to picture him yelling when Holly had told him about the possibility of cancer. Today he just fidgeted, picking imaginary lint off his coat or pants, rearranging the magazines in the waiting room, and things like that. Mila just sat there and read her novel, something about a soldier in the Great War.

Actually, Michelle felt more nervous than they appeared. Looking after the girls helped to while away the time, but she kept glancing up at the big wall clock that appeared way too large for the room. The hospital didn't want visitors to forget time. Waiting is hard enough without always being reminded how slow time goes by when you want answers now. She sighed again. Michelle's patience was limited, even under the best of conditions. Pete used to remark that if she were in the back of a rocket, traveling at the speed of sound, she would complain about not being in the front, to make time go faster. She chuckled to herself at the thought. Einstein would have been proud of Pete. The girls were well behaved, which didn't give her enough to do, and for once, she wished they would act up a bit. No, she just had to sit and watch the clock.

It wasn't until early afternoon that Dr. Peterson finally walked in, six hours after walking out that morning, telling them the surgery would probably be a couple of hours. She was sure things had not gone right after the third hour; by the fourth hour, she was sure the operation was a disaster and she should have insisted that the operation be done at Mayo Clinic. By the fifth hour, she knew Holly had not survived, since the public address system announced, "Dr. Heart to ICU, Dr. Heart to ICU," and people came rushing down the hall, toward the sign directing them to ICU. By the sixth hour, she just knew the doctors didn't want to come and tell them the bad news. Dr. Peterson looked tired, which was augmented by the string indentations on the sides of his face from wearing a surgical mask, but he was smiling. *He has a morbid sense of humor, if he is telling us bad news,* she thought. But it wasn't bad news.

"Holly is doing very well. She is in recovery and about to be transferred back to her room. You can go see her in about half an hour. The cancer was larger than suspected, about three centimeters, but the first draining lymph node at the armpit was negative, so I just removed the tumor. She has a seventy-percent chance of cure but will have to have chemotherapy and radiation after she heals from surgery. I'm sorry for the delay, but there were some technical problems with the lymph node biopsy that slowed things down."

After the doctor left, Michelle sat down and sighed. George looked like he had been up all night, but after a few minutes of silence, he asked, "She's all right, is all I got out of that. What did he say?"

Mila said, "The operation went well. The delay was due to technical problems, probably with the radioisotope preparation. She had the lump removed, but it was bigger than the X-ray suggested, and because of that, she will have to have radiation and chemotherapy, starting in a couple of weeks. The cancer did not spread to the lymph nodes, so there is a seventy-percent chance of cure." The old woman hadn't even looked up from her book.

"You are amazing, Mila," said George. "I don't know what I would do without you."

Michelle agreed. The older woman's interjection had saved her from embarrassment, as she couldn't remember all that had been said either. She gathered the girls, who were playing in the corner with wooden toys, to go to the cafeteria to get something to eat. She needed to move on. The children did not seem cranky about missing their lunchtime, but it was best to feed them now. George and Mila would visit Holly in the meantime.

Michelle waited until late afternoon to go to Holly's room, as the nurses asked her not to visit until then. She felt slighted. Mila and George had gotten to go in, so why not her sister? Just the same, Holly was all right, and that was all that mattered now.

The room smelled like disinfectant, and the only familiar thing was a television hanging on the wall. Holly's hair was disheveled and ratty-looking. Normally she was always coiffed, as far back as Michelle could remember, and unlike most redheads, she had a thick head of hair that allowed her to wear it in a short and easily managed cut. Her eyelids were puffy, as if she had been crying. Her skin was pale. A tube came out her nose, while another snaked from a bag at the side of the bed, going up and under the sheets. The bag had urine in it, so much so that it looked like it might burst. Two more bags hung from a pole, and their lines emptied into a single one going to her left arm. Michelle wanted to take control. *It isn't right, these strangers doing these things to my sister. I should be taking care of her.*

"Hello, Bossy."

"Hello, Brat." She started to tear up. "You okay?"

"Yeah, it hurts a little, though. But I'm okay. They got it all, and it wasn't in my lymph nodes. They tell me that's good, and I've still got my breast."

"I'm so glad it went well. I ... love you."

"Don't get mushy. You have always been there for me, haven't you, Bossy?"

"Now who's getting mushy? We are ... close, though."

"You know, it's funny. I woke up expecting my breast to be gone, even though the doctors assured me they wouldn't remove it. I was so happy to find I still had it." Holly licked her dry lips, reached for a glass of water but continued. "Can you imagine what Mom felt like when she woke up? That seems so barbaric now, doesn't it?" Michelle helped her with the straw when water dripped down her chin. Holly didn't seem to notice. "Poor Mom. She went through a lot. I can appreciate that now. Looking back on it, all she had was us kids. Nowadays, there are all kinds of support and information. I knew exactly what to expect and what would happen. Mom didn't have anything. No wonder she didn't tell us, since she didn't know herself. And no wonder she felt isolated." Both women were silent for a while.

Holly broke the silence. "She had to do it all herself, while I sit back and every expectation is met for me. Medicine has come a long way in twenty-five years."

"Yes, it has. You are already facing issues Mom never has faced. You won't wind up alone, like she did. Of course, you have a husband that will stick by you."

"Do you ever miss him?"

"You mean Dad? I used to, but he did a terrible thing to us. That's hard to forgive, even now. Yet, for some weird reason, I would like to know what happened to him and hear his explanation."

"So would I. Will you find him for us?"

"Do you know what you are asking? I have had enough angst about this whole issue of digging into our genetics. If we find Dad, we may be opening doors in our psyche that should remain closed. We may not have healed from the past, but at least we function with the past."

"I want to know him. I think he owes us that much."

"Ah ... I'll try. Okay."

Later, she had doubts; three lives had been changed forever because of him, and now she was going to find out why. It might change them again. She thought, *We don't need him, even for the genetic stuff.* Deep down, though, she wasn't sure. At one time, he had been a part of her "higher power," and she needed to know why such a power had forsaken her. Good or bad, there was something there, like an empty vessel that begged to be filled. Holly felt it too. Maybe even Mom did too and didn't know it.

Chapter 15

Early 1998

Holly woke early as the winter storm passed through, dumping its moisture on the coast in the form of rain—lots of it. A giant winter tide lapped the beach. Holly made coffee as she gazed toward the ocean. George would sleep for another half-hour or so. With coffee, she would sit on the deck, just to watch another day begin. These early morning reflections were her motivation to start the day.

Funny, she thought, *Mila isn't up yet.* Usually the older woman waited until she heard Holly in the kitchen, then she would get up, dress, and—after allowing Holly some solitude—show up to share the view. When Mila still didn't show, Holly went looking. She searched the whole house before waking George to help. Frantic, they looked everywhere.

Holly peered over the cliff and saw that the tide was up to the cliff top—and a body was at the bottom of the stairs. Yelling at George to follow, she rushed down the stairs. It was Mila, with her arms embracing the lowest anchor post, her fingers interlocked. Her body washed in the tide, as if she were tethered like a boat to a dock. Holly focused as she reined in her descent. Mila clung to the post, eyes wide but without any other indication of life. Was the look imploring help or asking to be left alone? The rescuer wasn't sure as she straddled the body and begged the older woman to release her grip on the post. Holly pried fingers apart, one by one, until Mila's hands could not hold, then dragged her body up the first step above water level.

"Hurry, George! The tide's still coming in!"

Water from the giant winter waves lapped their legs by the time he reached them. He could not separate their entangled bodies, so he grabbed a couple of arms and pulled until they were safely above the waves. As they rested and watched the churning water below, Mila started talking.

"I'm sorry. I wanted to walk with Ralph this morning for the last time. It's been a week, and I know I won't have strength to get down here again."

"Who's Ralph?" asked George.

Holly said, "Her husband. You knew that George."

Mila went on, "Ralph built these stairs, you know. He was a perfectionist. Took him a year to build it. See? The supports are anchored in cement bases, and each is supported by a deadman to stabilize the stairs. The steps are attached by bolts, not nails. That cliff might slip away, but these stairs would stay. Every time I come down here now, I remember. Before this project was done I loathed the effort, but now ... well, now every step is a shrine. Ralph saved our lives today, didn't he? Funny, I was caught as the tide came in and didn't have the strength to outrun it. A big wave came in and washed over my feet, burying them in the sand as the wave went back out. As I stood there waiting for the next one, I thought it wouldn't be a bad way to die. I could just quit fighting, and the next wave would knock me over, and I could be washed out to sea. I wanted that, but I looked at the stairs, and Ralph told me it wasn't time yet. Oh, I didn't see him or hear him—I'm not daffy. I could see his workmanship, and I knew he wanted me to use it today."

"Mila, you're rambling. Let's get you up to the house and out of those wet clothes. You're breathing hard. Maybe I should call Dr. Young."

"I could *feel* him today, my Ralph. I doubt he is waiting beyond for me. He's just in my mind, and soon there will be nothing. Life will go on, but I won't be a part of it. Sad but natural, isn't it? I don't want to die, but my body is worn out, old, consumed with cancer and the effects of fighting it. It's almost time to go."

"She's delirious," said Holly. "Come on, let's get her out of here. I'm scared. George, can you carry her?"

Mila said, "Ralph spent hours down here on the beach, looking for Japanese fishing balls. I didn't have the heart to tell him that they were made of plastic now. Some of the neighbor men would brag about finding one, but I doubted it. George wanted to brag too, so his quest was that much more ... intense. Once, on a trip to San Francisco, I bought four of them at an import store on the wharf. The price was outrageous but worth it. I shipped them home by FedEx at another exorbitant price, then put them on the beach just before he went out to search. I felt like a parent watching a kid at Christmas. He only found one. The others washed out to sea, I guess, but he had his glass ball and bragging rights. That damn ball was the size of a basketball. It was green with air bubbles in it. Ralph put it in the front yard so everybody could see it, but some kids stole it one Halloween. Nowadays all you find on the beach is plastic buoys, bleach bottles, whiskey bottles, and used diapers."

Holly said, "Mila, save your strength. We're almost to the top."

Mila said, "I saw one of those big freighters dump their garbage out at sea, just on the horizon. Why can't they dump it at the garbage dump?"

George said, "Go on up, Holly, and call 911 to have an ambulance meet us."

◆   ◆   ◆

George and Holly were waiting in the Intermediate Care family room when Dr. Young came in. "Mila is stable," he said. "I removed two liters of fluid from her left lung, and she can breathe better now. The cancer in her lungs caused a buildup of fluid and made her breathing difficult. Except for exhaustion, she suffered no ill effects from her ordeal this morning. I want to give her a couple of units of blood, to see if correcting her anemia will give her more strength. I'll check back tonight to see her progress."

When the doctor left, George turned to Holly and said, "I really like that doctor. Let's go see the old gal now."

Mila was sitting upright in bed. Oxygen was flowing through a tube into both nostrils, and she was eating a sandwich. She seemed embarrassed when they entered, and she stopped chewing and looked at them. "I'm sorry for the trouble I've caused you."

"Why did you do it, Mila?" George challenged..

Instead of answering, Mila changed topics. "What do you want to do with me? Put me in a nursing home?"

"Heavens, no! What do you want, Mila? That's more important now

"Will you tell my daughter?" Mila asked.

"She has a right to know, don't you think?"

"She'll want me to move back there, you know."

The three of them talked into the afternoon. Holly was committed to staying with her as long as she wanted, but she insisted that Mila's daughter, Marilyn, be told about her mother's deteriorating condition. Mila objected but gave in. Holly did not intend to give her another choice. It would soon to be over, and Mila no longer controlled her life. Marilyn would want to take control. There would not be another dance season for the old ballerina.

Holly returned to the house, and George went to the construction site. She spent the afternoon looking for Marilyn's telephone number. Mila did not keep a directory or an address book downstairs, and Holly did not wish to intrude by going into her bedroom. After a thorough search, she was about to give up, but then she found a torn corner of a newspaper in the telephone stand's drawer. Scribbled in pencil on the edge of the paper was a phone number with a South Carolina area code. Perhaps it belonged to Marilyn or at least someone who might know how to contact her.

After the third ring, a voice announced, "Pharmacy."

"Is Marilyn there?"

"You mean Marilyn Carter? She just got off shift. Should be able to catch her at home in about an hour. I would guess."

After extracting Marilyn's home number, Holly hung up. She hadn't known Marilyn's last name. Gorsky was Mila's maiden name. It was funny how she had come to feel so close to Mila and yet she didn't know that much about her, not even her married name. Carter? It was possible. She dialed the number, and after three attempts, someone answered.

Holly asked, "Ah … is this Marilyn who has a mother in Oregon?" Holly explained the recent events. The conversation was one-sided. At times, Holly wasn't sure the connection was still open, and twice she asked, "Are you still there?" Then, with nothing further to say, Holly quit talking. Silence prevailed.

Marilyn asked, "Why are you doing this?"

"What?"

"Looking after my mother. Are you some kind of weirdo that preys on old women, hoping to get their estate when they die? Are you trying to kill her?"

"Look, I'm a friend, that's all. She is very sick and in the hospital."

"I just talked to her last week, and she was fine."

"She isn't fine. She has cancer and is receiving blood as we speak. Why don't you call her? Here's the number." She recited the hospital's phone number. "She's in room 5A."

"Why are you in her house, then?"

"Just call her, okay?" Holly hung up before she could hear another outrageous response. It had been a strange conversation, to say the least. She went to the bedroom to change into running gear. George had promised that he would run with her from the construction site. Pulling on her running shoes, she noticed a flashing light outside. A city police car was at the front of the property. She ran outside as two police officers were getting out of the cruiser. She closed the gate and approached them.

"You live here?" one asked.

She tired to explain the living arrangement to them. One officer explained that they had received an anonymous phone call saying that a burglary was in progress at this address. Dressed in shorts, running halter, and shoes, without stolen property in hand, she didn't look much like a burglar, and they seemed convinced that there was no harm here. She refrained from telling them about Marilyn, thinking it would not serve anyone well, least of all Mila. They took down her name, then left.

She started to run. Why would a burglar call a daughter in another state, while in the act? Why would Marilyn assume Holly was trying to kill her mother? For that matter, why assume she was after her mother's estate? None of it made sense. Maybe George would understand it. Maybe it wasn't Marilyn that had called the police.

George didn't say much, but he was out of breath most of the time; he wasn't in such good shape. Holly set the pace, staying two steps ahead. It was working, though. He had dropped fifteen pounds in the last month, and she was trim at 108 pounds. Five days a week, they ran at least two miles a day. Today, though, she was obsessed with the phone call and could not be distracted. He suggested that they talk to Mila and tell her. No matter how bizarre the behavior, this did not seem like something to share with a sick woman. Just the same, they could not explain it, and the repercussions could be detrimental. Mila needed to be in contact with her daughter, no matter what transpired. In the meantime, George and Holly decided to minimize their exposure to Mila, for fear of retaliation by Marilyn. They wouldn't abandon her, but they would be careful not to incite a situation.

After supper, they drove back to the hospital. Mila was watching a show about people surviving on some uninhabited island. It didn't make much sense. Holly nudged George to speak, but he only mouthed: *Why me? You made the call.*

"Mila, I did call your daughter today."

"Oh. Did she seem strange to you?"

"A little bit. Can you tell us what's going on?"

"I'll try." Mila sighed then paused as if she really didn't want to go on then suddenly continued. "You see, it was hard for Marilyn to accept Ralph's death. He died after a stroke." She chuckled as she thought out the next sentence. "They expected me to die first, and Marilyn just couldn't handle both scenarios, I guess. She was so upset that I quit telling her about my health. I just said that the cancer was under control and I was fine. We had quite a fight when the cancer returned." Mila looked up at George and Holly for the first time. "She insisted I go down there and see her doctors. Something about having a bone marrow transplant, I think. I refused, and then when Ralph died, she wanted me to move there again. Insisted, in fact, until I said the cancer was gone—then she left me alone. I continued the lie, just so I wouldn't have to move. I haven't seen Marilyn since the funeral five years ago. Sometimes when she calls, I get my story mixed up, so I told her you moved in because you were destitute and needed a place to stay. That way, I had someone. She was suspicious, but I couldn't tell her I needed help, because if I did, she would move me to South Carolina." Her story was coming out fast now. "I hate South Carolina! It's so hot and sweltering there that everyone lives in air-conditioned houses, offices, and cars."

Mila stopped chattering, embarrassed. "I'm sorry I made you the bad guys. It was just convenient and got her off my case. Besides, Marilyn is like me—she has to be independent and in charge all the time. Must be in the genes or something. Why she called the cops, I don't understand. Perhaps to intimidate?"

George said, "Well, it worked. Holly and I feel it would be best if we moved. In that regard, Marilyn is right. We have taken advantage of you ... but we did it unintentionally."

"You didn't do anything I didn't engineer. Having you guys with me gave meaning to my life."

Holly said, "I told Marilyn to call you. I said the cancer was spreading and you almost died today."

"I have to face the music, don't I?"

"Tell her the truth when she calls. She may not take it the way you hope, but she has a right to know. Things are not okay, Mila."

On the television, a group of half-naked people were sitting around a fire and voting about doing it again next week. Holly couldn't understand why anyone would watch next week anyway and wished she could shut it off. It was close to 8:00 PM, and a voice on the public address system announced that visiting hours were over in five minutes. The noise was loud enough to shake the windows. *If anyone here is near death, that announcement would push them over the edge.*

Dr. Young entered. After the usual bedside salutation, he announced, "Mila, your daughter called me this afternoon. I was a bit taken back. I have never talked to her before, and she was angry. I must admit, I thought Holly here was your daughter. I need your permission to give out information about you. Can you give me some guidance?"

Mila retold the story about keeping her daughter out of the loop.

The doctor said, "I don't have to tell her anything, Mila, if that is your wish. But she is your daughter."

"I don't have power of attorney or even a will. I always thought it could be done some time in the future. I guess the future is now."

"You have fought many battles, but it's not realistic to expect to win the war. We are running out of options, Mila. Maybe you should see a lawyer. But in the meantime, tell me who I can talk to about your medical situation."

The old woman gazed at Holly and George, as if checking if it was all right. Then she answered, "I would like to have Holly and George be in on it."

The doctor said, "Okay, I can tell them everything about your health. What about your daughter?"

"Please let me think. I don't know if I want her to know, at least not yet."

"Will you see an attorney?"

"Okay."

Dr. Young turned to Holly and asked if she had any questions.

She said, "This puts George and me in an awkward position. Marilyn has already tried to make things rough for us. If she can't get information and we can, that is just going to make things worse for us. Mila, why not let her have information?"

"Okay, I will. But you won't ... leave, will you?"

"We will always stand by you, but we do not want to interfere with Marilyn's right to be your daughter. Do you understand where we're coming from?"

Driving home, Holly and George discussed the situation. It was obvious that Mila didn't want Marilyn to control her life. But was she being reasonable?

"Her deteriorating health means she is not independent," said George. "In a sense, she used us to extend her independence. Marilyn has a right to feel hurt, but at the same time, she doesn't do anything to help, except insisting that Mila move. She hasn't been to Bandon since her father died five years ago. Maybe if she visited now and again, she could assess the situation. Mila might be more receptive to moving in Marilyn's presence. No, there's culpability on both sides of this situation." George was passionate.

The hospital was thirty miles from Bandon. They continued to discuss the Mila problem until Holly noticed they were not on the right road.

"I know," George said. "We need a diversion, and this road will wind up in Bandon."

They fell silent as the winding road climbed through a cathedral of trees and darkness progressed. Houses and farms were sparse here, and lights could be seen every now and then between the trees. On occasion, lights flashed up ahead as a car approached from the opposite direction. Both of them were deep in thought.

The road peaked, then started to descend into the darkness, and a fork presented two options. George turned west, toward the coast, on a gravel road that continued downward until reaching a creek bed. There were no other cars. He pulled off the road and got out a map.

In the headlights, Holly could see a blackberry bush, so she grabbed George's straw gardening hat and picked the fruit, using the hat as a container. She wasn't sure what to do with all the berries she was collecting, but it was fun, in a primordial way. Here she was, gathering food, while the male stood guard. *No, that doesn't fit. The male is lost, and I'm filling in time.* Still, *feelings* were aroused. Generations ago, she would have been gathering food and tending the children, while he hunted and provided shelter. *There are no children,* she thought remorsefully. She continued to pick berries until she could see no more, then she turned back to the car and concentrated on George.

She asked, "Did you figure out where we are yet?"

"Somewhere in Oregon, I guess. Let's just continue down the road. It might be a little late to find a farm with occupants still awake, but if we do see someplace, I'll stop and ask. Ooh, blackberries! My favorite."

They started down the road, popping berries in their mouths, like eating popcorn at a theater. The road climbed a hill, exiting the trees, and at the top, they could see southward, down the coast. The moon was full, and to the right was the ocean. It was light enough to see waves breaking; farther down the coast, they could see the lights of Bandon. All they had to do was continue south, and soon they would be home. Holly placed her hand on George's forearm to indicate she wanted to stop here. The view was spectacular in the semidarkness and provided a scene they had not appreciated before. They sat in the dark, taking it all in, until her thoughts overflowed.

"George, did you want children?"

"What do you want, Holly? It has to be rough knowing you have cancer and that if you do have children, it is likely they will get it too. I can't even imagine what it's like."

"No, George. You turned the question around and didn't answer."

He bent his head forward and turned it back and forth, eyes squinting. "Hard to see this road. I ... that's a hard one to answer, you know. It's complex, to say the least. Yes, a year ago or so, I would have said it might be fun to have a kid or two. But it's never been about kids for me."

"Just drive straight, and don't get in the ditch. What do you mean, it's never been about kids?"

"Damn, this road has a lot of potholes! I hit another one like that, and it will knock the car out of alignment. I just wanted you, is all. My career made me very happy until you came along. Then the only thing I ever wanted was you. I never did understand how I was so lucky. I always thought my career was enough, and I never wanted a wife, let alone kids. Never. You changed everything. Life used to be so simple. I just worked in the lab, gave a couple of lectures to keep the chairman happy, and every now and then, Mom would force me to go to some charity function. I was happy, then I saw you. I even thought about a family after that. Now I'm driving down some old dirt road in the middle of the night, afraid of some old woman's daughter, building a house on sand, and trying to keep up with the woman of my life. Does it get any better than this? Now I have to think about kids too?"

"Don't hit that hole! Whew, that was close. This road is getting worse the closer we get to Bandon. You mean you never had a woman before me? Doesn't say much for me, does it?"

"What in the world does that mean?"

"Oh, I don't know. Maybe it means I was the only one you could catch."

"Probably true," he teased.

"I'm not saying we should have kids, George. I just wanted to know how you feel. For me, it seems like a bad idea. Now, with the genetic information and cancer, it wouldn't be fair. Besides, I'm getting too old. Michelle is lucky. She had her family before we found out about the secret. How would I feel passing on a gene that could affect my children? I don't know. How does Mom feel? She must have thought of that issue. Poor Mom. If I had a daughter, would she treat me like Marilyn treats Mila, and would I resist like her?"

George swerved again but hit the soft, sandy shoulder, and the car plowed into the ditch, burying the right front tire. Holly screamed and grasped the door handle. The car slid to a stop.

George said, "Great. Now we are stuck. Looks like we will have to walk back to Bandon now. There's no bus service in the country. I haven't seen a single house." He got out and surveyed the damage.

The right side was leaning into the sand and Holly couldn't open her door, so she crawled out after him. "Boy, you sure know how to treat a girl on a date. We'd better get walking." She turned to leave, then looked back at the car. "We could have been killed."

"It wasn't that bad. Look at it this way—this evening's experience is different from what we normally do. Besides, now I have an excuse to get one of those SUVs."

The moon provided enough light to see the road ahead without groping in the dark. The slight breeze landward made the walk pleasant.

"Life is so precious. One minute we are alive, and the next minute we just missed death," she said in a flat tone, as if thinking out loud. "George? What about kids?"

"Are we still on that? Why are you asking me? A minute ago, you said it was a bad idea."

"It's not what I think, dear. I want to know what you think. You have sacrificed a lot in this relationship, and you have a say in it too." She stopped in the middle of the road.

He continued walking a few steps, then stopped too. "What's wrong?" he shouted back.

Holly thought, *This is the first time I have ever thought of how he feels instead of how I feel.* George came running back. She said, "Nothing is wrong. I just want to know."

"I don't want kids, for the same reasons as you. But if you didn't have the gene, and if we were younger, and if you didn't have cancer already, and if I could take care of more than one—then yes, I would."

"What do you mean by 'more than one'?" In the moonlight shining through the trees, she could just make out his facial features, shadowed on one side.

His smile appeared sardonic. "I have one now that I can't handle, don't I?"

She hit him in the chest, then they continued down the road, holding hands.

◆   ◆   ◆

A week later, Holly was packing for the move to a trailer. George had bought a small camping trailer and placed it on their site. For now, it would suffice.

Mila watched her pack. "Will you guys come see me?"

"Of course, Mila. We are only moving a mile down the road. I'll run by every morning, then George and I will run by at noon, and we'll come back at suppertime to fix your meal. It will be just about like it is now. We love you and are not about to abandon you."

"I know. It's just that I don't want you to leave at all."

Holly stopped packing and hugged the frail woman. Her ribs beneath the blouse were prominent to the touch, and Holly was afraid that squeezing too hard would break them. She saw Mila every day, but she hadn't realized how emaciated Mila was until hugging her. *It can't be too much longer. Maybe we should stay.* Holly wanted to call Marilyn with the news, but she knew it would just incite more conflict. "Did you make an appointment to see a lawyer about a living will and all that?"

The older woman avoided eye contact and didn't respond.

Holly persisted, knowing that the chance of getting through was slim. "Did you tell Dr. Young he could talk to Marilyn? Mila, you have to do something!"

Exasperated, she turned and picked up a suitcase. She turned back to Mila. Mila stared, then turned to the phone but did not move. Holly shook her head and left.

◆   ◆   ◆

The doctor's office was busy, as usual. So many people had cancer, it seemed. Holly and Mila were ushered into the examination room by a petite young nurse dressed in green scrub pants and a brightly colored top printed with wild animals. Her nametag gave her title: nursing assistant. She was pretty, and Holly wondered what had motivated her to take up this profession.

Holly sat in the corner, looking at the picture on the wall: a watercolor of the beach, with dunes in the background. The scene was familiar, and she was trying to place it when Dr. Young came in. He smiled. Looking concerned, he asked what Mila wanted, as she was not due back in the clinic until the next week.

Mila answered, "I've been thinking about what you talked about in the hospital. I don't want you to talk to Marilyn, my daughter. I want you to help me. I've been reading about this new law."

"What new law?" He was squirming.

"I called the Compassion in Dying people and got all the particulars," she said. "They say to talk to you, and you could help me or point me to who will. I want to die, and I can't do it myself."

"Mila, I don't know." The doctor seemed reluctant to continue. He sighed, then as if he was reading a response prepared a head of time, started again. "Society is pushing this new role onto physicians. Normally, the role of physicians is to help—but toward health, not death. Even then, medical advancements should drive change, whereas this role is being driven by politics. I don't know where I stand on the issue. I've always been taught never to do harm, you know—the Hippocratic oath. I took it during graduation ceremonies when I got my medical degree, and now I have to set it aside. My religious training as a Christian forbids it." He smiled now, pleased with the explanation. "Yet I have to admit, there are times when it may be appropriate to help someone die, if there is suffering. Are you suffering, Mila?"

"It depends on how you define suffering, doesn't it? I am not in a lot of pain, and the pain medicine works, except for the constipation. I take a pain pill, then pills to open my bowels, then pills to close them. My life centers around pills, but that, I can tolerate. No, the suffering is different for me. My daughter will force me into a situation I don't want to be in, my best friends have been scared away, and I can't live alone and do the things I want to do now. Is that suffering to you?"

"Mila!" exclaimed Holly. "We weren't scared away …!"

Patient and doctor stared at each other, then at Holly. The look was not stony but inquisitive; each tried to understand the others through unspoken communication.

"Mila, what about hospice?" said the doctor.

"I thought about that a lot. Don't get me wrong—they are a good organization, and they do wonderful things. I listen to many patients in the group talking about how great the service is. But that won't help me much, except for physical comfort. I am in pain, doctor, but it isn't physical. I can talk about my demise and accept it. I don't believe in God, like you do, but I am at peace. What could they do to make things better? What I want is to go out as who I am now, before it's too late and I am nothing but a body that needs to be cared for all the time. Do you understand?"

"This is all new to me, Mila. I don't know what to do. Let me call the state health department and get legal advice on how to proceed, and talk to other doctors that have more experience. I need to search my beliefs and soul too, before I can make this decision. Can you understand that?"

"Of course I can. I just wrestled with it too. In the meantime, would you note in the chart that I made this request? If you can't do it, would you see if there is a physician you could recommend?" She reached into her purse and pulled out a folded letter, handwritten, requesting assisted suicide. She was following the law to the letter with a letter.

The older woman was smiling, and there was a sparkle in her eye. She walked out the room as if she were twenty. Holly was amazed as she fell in step behind. On the way home, Mila gazed out the window while maintaining a constant chatter about what had happened here or there, local history of such depth that Holly was always amazed; Mila also spoke about ballet. At home, George, not always attuned to a woman's mood, commented on her ebullience.

The next morning, Holly got out of bed in agony. Camping-trailer design did not afford the type of comfort she was used to, and the thought of spending a couple of months like this was discouraging. The bed could pass for one of those beds of nails used by clerics in India. The bathroom would be small even for a contortionist. To make bad matters worse, the physical activity was taking its toll on poor George, causing him to sleep deeply, and his sonorous snoring made her sleep difficult. She would just have to get used to it.

She stretched, which helped the aches and pains, then put on running gear while George slept. The floor creaked despite her tiptoeing, and the door squeaked even though she opened it slowly. She would run up, check Mila, then return and make breakfast. The rafters were going up today. It was amazing how much work George was doing. She had always thought of him as a head case, but he had turned out to be quite good with his hands. He had even helped pour the cement last week for the tarmac and driveway. He presented quite a picture at the end of a workday, reminding her of a small boy who had been out playing in mud. She even surprised herself as she went about domestic duties with relish. It was funny how simple things could be so meaningful.

She started running down the hill. The sun was up, but it was not hot; it never was on the coast. Her breathing became regular, and she ran with an efficient stride. Neighbors were used to her running by in the morning, and they waved. She even knew some of them by name and called out as she passed. This new role of belonging was gratifying.

The house was empty when she examined it. She rushed down the beach access stairs as quickly as possible. Relieved not to find Mila collapsed at the bottom, she scanned the beach both ways. At first, there was no one to see, but soon a figure emerged from behind one of the haystack-shaped rocks down the coast. Holly ran along the beach toward the figure, and as she approached, she could see that it was Mila. *Thank goodness she's all right.* Her assessment proved wrong when she slowed to a stop in front of the older woman. Mila was breathing hard and her lips were dusky.

"Hello, dear. I'm a little out of breath this morning. I think that darn fluid has come back in my lungs. I don't think I can climb back up."

Holly assessed the tide; it was still going out, so they had time. She turned Mila around and headed further south. They would walk to where George would be working, then get a vehicle down on the beach. There was a beach access for dune buggies about two miles below the new house. The trip proved to be slow, and Holly worried. She sat Mila in the dune grass above the tide level, just in case they couldn't get back in time, then ran up the dunes to the house.

George was already at work as she approached. One of the construction gang was a young man, almost a boy, who owned one of the balloon-tired jeeps that were ubiquitous along the coast for joy-riding on the beach. The contractor was not too happy when George commandeered the boy and his jeep; work was being done at an hourly wage. All three hung on as the vehicle took the corner into the state park down the road. A gate closed off the beach access road, but the boy wasn't deterred; he maneuvered the jeep over a dune and around the gate.

They raced up the coast to where the patient waited. At first, Holly could not find the spot. but then the new house came into view for reference. There was Mila, still sitting on a dune in the grass. Except for the labored breathing, she seemed content and appeared to want to stay there all day. Back at the house, they transferred her to Holly's car for the trip to the hospital.

Dr. Young came to the waiting room for the second time in two weeks. The fluid had reaccumulated, but removing it was proving more difficult. He suggested a procedure to try to prevent it from coming back by scarring the lining of the lung. To do that, she would have to remain in the hospital for a few days. A surgeon was putting a tube into her chest to drain as much fluid as possible before they would add a chemical to cause the scarring. After explaining, he lingered in the waiting room, as if something was bothering him. He glanced across the room at other visitors, then decided to take his leave. Holly puzzled over the behavior, then dismissed it. *It has to be hard being an oncologist,* she thought. Probably he was just upset because he was always the bearer of bad news.

Later that afternoon, Dr. Young called Holly's cell phone. There was a complication. Mila had gone into shock as the fluid drained out the larger tube in her chest cavity. They had moved her to the intensive care unit, where she was stable. Again, Holly sensed hesitation in his voice.

He asked her, "Did Mila get a living will and power of attorney?"

"Not that I know of. I asked her to make an appointment, but she didn't. I would have been the one to take her. Why?"

"Well, if she goes into shock again and it persists, we could be faced with life support issues here. I need to know who is going to make that decision."

"It will have to be her daughter, Marilyn."

"Do you think you could stop by my office? Say at five? I have a dilemma I need to talk to you about."

George drove her back to the hospital. A nurse allowed them access to the intensive care unit. Mila was sitting up in bed, reading a menu for supper. She didn't seem sick enough to warrant intensive care. Holly looked around at the other patients as they entered the unit. Each patient was in a separate room with sliding glass doors. Some were conscious, but most were not; they appeared to be bodies kept alive by machines.

There was one old man, shriveled and emaciated, hooked to a tube from his right nostril to a machine larger than him. The machine had gauges, lights, and knobs that reminded her of an airplane cockpit. Another tube exited his left nostril to connect to a plastic bottle on the wall labeled SUCTION. There were two poles with machines clamped on each, like monkeys on a tree at a zoo. Bags of fluid hung above them. One bag was yellow, like urine, and the other was white, like coconut milk, while two others were clear liquid. The solutions, including the milk-and urine-colored ones, were going through a tube into his chest. A bag hung on the bed frame with a tube snaking under the sheets to his crotch. Both of his eyes were held closed by tape over cotton balls. It took a full-time nurse to monitor and adjust his equipment. Holly looked on in horror.

Even Mila, upon inspection, had tubes. A large, almost garden-hose-sized tube ran from a plastic rectangular box on the floor to her chest, where it snaked under a white dressing that covered most of the left side of her chest. Another tube ran from the box to the wall, where it plugged into the suction apparatus. There was bloody, urine-colored fluid in the plastic box. Mila had a tube around her neck, with prongs sticking in her nose to provide oxygen. The oxygen whistled, and her voice resonated from its flow. There was an IV tube in the right arm. Overall, it looked like it should be painful, but Mila didn't appear to be in any discomfort. In fact, she was cheerful. "My breathing is much better!" she exclaimed when she saw them.

According to the rules, they could only spend five minutes visiting. Assured things were okay, both were glad to leave. The unit made them anxious, with all those sick people and machines. Holly could not get the image of the old man to go away.

After a cup of coffee in the cafeteria to kill time, they proceeded to Dr. Young's office for the meeting. For the first time since she had been coming to the clinic, the lobby was empty. It reminded her of a tomb. Even George appeared nervous as they sat down after looking around for something to read or fiddle with. The wait ended with the little nursing assistant ushering them into a small room with a desk surrounded by chairs. There was an X-ray box on the wall. Dr. Young was standing by the table. He encouraged them to sit.

"I don't know how to begin. Well, given what has happened today and the fact that she doesn't have a living will, I must tell you. She did give me permission to talk to you, so I don't think it unethical. Mila forbade me to talk to her daughter. Now, today, the only person who can make decisions, if Mila can't, is Marilyn—but the only people I am supposed to talk to are you two. She has no power of attorney or living will to guide us. Do you think Marilyn will come out here and help us out if you call?"

"Mila is alert now. Why can't she call?" George knew the answer even as he asked.

"If she will. It seems to me that Mila drags her feet when it comes to dealing with Marilyn. I'll ask her again tonight to call her daughter." Dr. Young looked at Holly. Holly hoped she wouldn't have to call Marilyn.

The following morning, Holly asked Mila about the call, knowing the answer beforehand. The woman just couldn't do it. It was amazing. Here was a person who could cajole and manipulate some of the world's greatest performing artists, producers, directors, and choreographers—not to speak of all the business people and dance lovers—but she couldn't even stand up to the one person who should help. They talked about the situation, and Mila promised again to call her daughter.

After three days, it was obvious that she wouldn't. Holly sat in her car in the hospital parking lot, looking at the cell phone on the seat. *Why do I have to do this?* She picked up the phone and dialed. Marilyn picked up at the second ring. Holly stammered at first, then went on without stopping, but the interaction was similar to the last call. She implored Marilyn to come and see for herself, while wondering if the line was dead, as there was no response. Out of frustration, she asked if Marilyn had any questions, but all she got for her effort was a click.

"At least I tried," she said, trying to console herself. She went in to see Mila. There was a sign on the door: NO VISITORS. The nurse informed her that Marilyn had just called and insisted on posting the sign. Dr. Young rounded the corner, saw the sign, and looked at Holly with a puzzled expression. Then he entered, and she followed.

He said, "Mila, are you not feeling well today?"

"I'm fine today, doctor. See? I'm down to 50 cc of drainage in the past twenty-four hours, so today you are going to put the tetracycline in my chest, right? I can go home tomorrow, right?"

"If all goes well, yes. Why is that 'no visitors' sign on the door?"

Holly said, "I just asked the nurse, and she said that Marilyn insisted on it."

"Did you call her, Holly?" Dr. Young seemed confused.

"Just before she called the nurse. I'm afraid she is not buying any of this from me."

Mila said, "It's all my fault. I'm sorry, Holly. I wanted to call, really. Now I've messed up everything."

◆   ◆   ◆

Mila was in good spirits riding home. Every now and then, a bump made her grimace, but for the most part, she was her old self. Holly dropped her off and made sure she was comfortable; groceries were available, and snack foods were in the refrigerator. George and Holly resumed their routine of three visits a day. Twelve days later, Mila and Holly drove to the doctor's office again.

Mila said, "It's been two weeks, Dr. Young. Will you write the prescription?"

It took trips to four different pharmacies to find a pharmacist who would fill the prescriptions for Nembutal and Reglan.

The night was clear and well lit by the moon, and a slight ocean breeze cooled the beach. Holly was restless as she stood at the trailer door and looked toward the house on the hill. Tonight was different. She wondered what was going on, as there were no lights. She swung her arms as she walked through the sand to the berm edge. She looked toward the house again, sighed, then gazed seaward. She sat until her shoulders shook from the chill; her only other motion was an occasional glance at the house. The moon went behind a cloud as she trudged back to the trailer. She tried one last look, but all she could see in the moonless night was an outline.

The following morning, she prepared for her jog; she knew she had to go. The house loomed large as she approached, and she called out but knew there would be no response. The body lay in bed with a peaceful face. A book rested at its side, and the sheets were smooth, without a wrinkle.

◆　　◆　　◆

Holly had moped around for two weeks after the event. She sat on a dune, looking out to sea as the morning wind shifted inland, undulating the needle grass around her.

"You okay?" George walked over the dune to sit next to her. He plucked a grass stem and put it in his mouth.

"Yeah, I guess. I don't know whether to be angry at her or glad it's over."

"Why would you be angry?"

"She was like a mother to me. Mom never talked about things, but Mila did, and that helped me a lot. All my life, I have depended on people, even when I tried to be independent. First, there was Mom. Then, when she couldn't do it any more, I relied on Michelle until we grew up. Then Mila. They were my examples, my mentors. My best mentor did the one thing I can't forgive—she committed suicide. Now I have no one to … show me. I'm not strong enough, George. You will have to be my Mila now. Will you? I want to live, and I don't want to die like that. It's strange, I can accept death now. But when my time comes, I want to be surrounded by friends when it happens, not alone in some big house, afraid of the one person that I want to love me. I want you to be with me. I need you to take up where Mila failed. Promise?"

"What if I die first?"

She put her arm around his waist and her head on his shoulder. She smiled. "Does it matter? You will still be with me, won't you?"

Chapter 16

1998

Michelle's stomach churned as she sat in the gynecologist's waiting room. She didn't want to be there, and she didn't want to make the decision now. It had been over ten months since Dr. Nielsen had diagnosed the BRCA2 abnormality, and she still had not decided to have anything done that might help prevent her getting cancer. Every morning she would wake up with a resolve to decide that day, but by the time evening came, she was as wishy-washy as ever. Pete tried to help, bless his heart, by digging out research articles and talking, but the more information she consumed, the more confused she became. Pete was losing patience, as was Dr. Nielsen. Both of them were adamant that she should be in a research protocol using one approach or the other. At least that was one decision she had made: she would go on a protocol. But which one?

She rose and walked around the room. It was small, and the attempt was futile. Another patient looked up from her magazine, as if disturbed by the pacing, so Michelle sat down, crossed her legs, and swung the upper one. The other patient still seemed annoyed.

As Dr. Nielsen had explained, she had four options: watch and wait, have her breasts removed, take anti-estrogens like tamoxifen, or have her ovaries removed. All of them were unpleasant. It frustrated her that she couldn't decide; all her life, she had made quick decisions, which had done her well. But now, with her own life at risk, she didn't know what to do. She was leaning toward having her ovaries removed. Her mammograms had come back normal this time, but if there was any question about it, she would have the mastectomies. Since her breasts were normal, she cringed at the thought of removing them.

From the door, the assistant called for Michelle to come inside. Anxious and weak, she stood and walked to the room, her heart pounding.

The doctor came in almost behind her. She said, "I haven't seen you since our conversation last summer. Dr. Nielsen called me about the cancer gene. It was a good thing I sent you to him."

"Yes, I suppose...."

"You don't sound convinced. Have you decided on an oophorectomy?"

"A what?"

"Oophorectomy. It means to have your ovaries removed."

"Oh. I wish I had never started this … adventure last year. I'm a basket case, and I can't decide what to do. My sister has gotten cancer, and my mother is reluctant, to say the least. Now, every time I look at my girls, I want to cry. If that means it was a good thing you sent me to him, then I'm damn lucky, ain't I? Do you have any idea what it's like to have a crystal ball to look into your future? What it's like to have to decide whether to mutilate your body, and no one knows whether it will do any good or not? What happens to your body image afterward? My mother had a breast removed twenty-six years ago, and she has been isolated since then. Yeah, I'm lucky, all right."

The other woman flinched and drew back. "I see your point. I have not looked at it that way. I'm sorry. Sometimes we doctors just see things from a scientific point of view and not from a patient's one. Yes, that would be tough, having a crystal ball. I have enough trouble just looking ahead to the bills at the end of the month, let alone issues that could affect my children. What are you going to do?"

"I don't know. When I talked to Dr. Nielsen and Sharon Townsend last week, it seemed like a good idea to have an oo—my ovaries removed. Now that I'm here to schedule the operation, I'm having second thoughts."

"Okay. Why don't you think about it and give me a call?" The doctor seemed anxious to leave.

By the time Michelle got to the SUV, she was embarrassed. "What a waste of time," she said to herself. "I wish I could make up my mind." *Maybe someone else can make the decision. Pete? No, he already has—ovaries out. Dr. Nielsen? No, all he'll do is just quote another latest article on the topic. Sharon? She seemed to be the most sympathetic, but would she be if Dr. Nielsen weren't there?*

She picked up her cell phone. "Sharon? Sorry to bother you again. Would it be possible to meet me for lunch today? I still can't make up my mind. What? Yes, I did go to the gynecologist today, but I make a fool of myself, and she suggested I think some more about it. Great! Say one thirty at the Sandpiper? See you then. Thanks, Sharon."

◆   ◆   ◆

Sharon was at a table when Michelle came in. "Hello, Michelle. You look like you didn't sleep last night and you need a drink."

"Yes, I would like a martini. I haven't been sleeping much, what with the pressure to make a decision and all. I felt like a fool this morning."

"What are you going to do now?"

"I don't know. I was hoping you could help me."

"I can give you advice, Michelle, but the decision is yours to make, not mine."

"There are so many options, and it is so technical. How can you people expect a patient to be able to evaluate all of this information and make a wise decision? I have no experience, and I can't even understand half of the words. I'm educated and not stupid, but it's like a different language."

"You're right, of course. It does take a lot of time on a subject that you really don't want to face. It seems like it would be better to have someone just tell you what to do. But Michelle, the consequences are with you the rest of your life—and may even mean your life—so you can't just leave it to someone else."

After a second drink, the conversation started in earnest. Sharon said, "Well, Michelle, you have a life-changing event. That's rough, but you have to do something, and soon. It's been, what? Nine months since Dr. Nielsen did the test? You still have not done anything to prevent cancer, and the longer you wait, the more risk. Sometimes we don't know what the future has in store, but we must act, right or wrong, then accept the outcome, right or wrong, and not look back. Heaven only knows I've made decisions that were right and some that were wrong." With that said, she raised her glass high and signaled the maître d' for another round.

Sharon went over the options again, giving the pros and cons of each one. However, three martinis each, on empty stomachs, were having an effect on both of them. Sharon started slurring her speech, and Michelle started talking louder. It was late in the lunch hour, the staff had to prepare for the evening meal. Concerned about their sobriety (and its repercussions for him), without asking, the maître d' brought out an appetizer of rye bread and smoked salmon with onions and capers. Overhearing parts of their conversation had made him tolerant—until Michelle blurted out loud:

"Fuck it all! I'll just have that quack whack out my ovaries and be done with it!"

The entire lingering lunch crowd and restaurant staff, including the dishwasher in the back room, heard her decision. After a moment of silence, Sharon giggled. The maître d' stiffened. Laughing, the two gobbled up the appetizer using both hands, then paid the bill with Michelle's credit card and staggered out the door.

"I can't go back to work like this," Sharon said. "Hell, I can't even drive."

"Let's call a cab. Okay?"

"Sure. Where's your cell phone?"

"Shit, I lost it somewhere. I don't want to go back in there now. Let's just sit in the truck until we are sober. Why did you leave?" Michelle asked.

"What do you mean? I didn't leave—we did."

"No, why did you leave the hospital twenty-six years ago?"

"Oh, you mean Valley Hospital? I was asked to leave."

"Fired? Why?"

"Your mother's case. I helped her, as best I could, to understand what was going on. And the surgeon didn't like that, so he got me fired."

"Really? What did you do that he didn't like?"

"I changed her dressings and told her what the surgery was all about."

"That doesn't sound like something to get fired over."

"Today it's not, but in 1972, it was. Nurses didn't talk about things like that then. The doctors were om … nip … omnipotent then and didn't like nurses showing them up. Wow, I'm still loaded! Can't even speak."

"You must really be angry at him," Michelle said.

"Dr. Long? No, not at all. Oh, I guess at first I was. It's like what we were talking about at lunch. You make a decision, right or wrong, then live with it. I got fired and made a decision, because of that, to go on and get my PhD to teach. At the time, I had just divorced an alcoholic bum, so I picked up the kids at school, packed the car, and drove here. I made the right decision at the time, Michelle, and didn't know what the future would be."

"You're trying to tell me something, aren't you?"

"Make the best of a bad situation, and get on with your life."

◆   ◆   ◆

The night before the scheduled surgery, Michelle woke with a start. She was still afraid, even though she had made a decision. Perhaps there were better options. It wasn't that she needed her ovaries; they didn't want more kids. It was the invasion of her body and the question of whether this was the best way to go.

She crawled out of bed and dressed, without waking Pete. She would go to a bookstore and browse. One of the talk shows that afternoon had presented a topic on alternative medicine. Perhaps she should consider that option, she thought.

At the bookstore, which was open all night, she asked the clerk where to look for books on breast cancer and cancer prevention. There were only a few people there that late at night, and the young woman led her to the area where she might find what she wanted, then departed. Michelle glanced over the selection and was impressed. There were books on nutrition to prevent cancer, spiritual guidance on dealing with cancer by self-proclaimed gurus, and alternative treatments written by physicians who had graduated from places like the International University in Calcutta, India. She wanted to buy all of them, but she realized most of them probably wouldn't help. She did buy one each on alternative medicine, nutrition, and spiritual guidance. How did a person unfamiliar with cancer know what to read and how to interpret what was valid? *The guru book might be helpful,* she thought. *It just makes sense that a positive attitude will help.* The other books were full of ideas based on theories proposed as scientific fact, and she had doubts.

"Did you find anything useful?" the clerk said as she rang up the sale.

"I'm not sure. I just got a few to see."

At home, she went to the computer to see what she could find on the Internet to support the books' hypotheses. There wasn't much. The International University of Calcutta site confirmed her suspicions. The university offered medical degrees and PhDs in alternative medicine. The curriculum format was two years of correspondence courses, waived if the applicant had a degree—any degree—and $750.

The nutrition book started out strong, with a lot of information supported by the U.S. Department of Agriculture and its recommendations for good nutrition, including the food pyramid. However, by the last few chapters, the theme was not good nutrition, but high doses of vitamins. "If high doses are good for you, why aren't there high doses in nature?" she said aloud. The last two chapters advocated such things as grape seed extract, special diets to reduce toxins, and coffee-ground enemas. "That's the last place I would put coffee!" She threw down the book in disgust. She turned off the computer and rubbed her tired eyes. "At least I considered everything. Now I can get on with my life."

◆　　　◆　　　◆

Three weeks after her surgery, Michelle received a call from Sharon. Dr. Nielsen wanted to see Holly and Michelle about the results of the BRCA2 tests.

"I thought I already got the results of my test last year. Why do I have to be there, and why can't you just send Holly the results?"

"It could be done that way, I guess, but he wants to tell you in person. The tests he did are far more complete than the mutation screening test you had last year."

"You mean I might not have it? Could the screening test be wrong?"

"No, if that test was positive, you have it. These tests are experimental, to see where the defect is. Please, Michelle, there is nothing new you need to concern yourself about. You are all right with what you've done. Surgery was the right decision, no matter what type of molecular defect you have. Should I call Holly and set up the appointment?"

"No, I'll do it. When do you want us there?"

Holly arrived two weeks later for the meeting with Dr. Nielsen. She had lost some weight from the chemotherapy and radiation. The chemotherapy had made her lose her hair. She wore a wig but kept scratching under it. "This thing is driving me crazy, now that my hair is coming back. I tried one of those scarves, but I look funny in them, so I use a wig when I go out. How long do you think this meeting will last?"

"I don't know Brat. We'll just have to see. I wouldn't worry about the hair loss. Dr. Nielsen and Sharon have seen it all. If you want, just take it off."

The sisters were looking for the conference room where they were to meet. Heart pounding, Michelle pushed Holly along, so as not to be late. For some reason, she had a bad feeling. *Why is he so secretive about the information?* she wondered. Her sister's fidgeting suggested that she too felt nervous.

Dr. Nielsen and Sharon were waiting when the two sisters arrived. His expression was serious, which added to their anxiety.

Michelle said, "Sorry we're late, but I couldn't find a parking space."

"Let's get down to business," said the doctor. "I appreciate you coming all the way here, Holly. I know it is an inconvenience, but I felt we should talk about it, rather than have you read a report. This way, we can ask questions too. How are the treatments coming along?"

Holly said, "I'm through with the chemo, and I just finished the radiation. My skin is still red and burning, but my hair is coming back."

"Do you have the path report I asked for?"

"Yes, it's here. Why is that important?"

"Just to be sure. Yes, I see it was an infiltrating ductal adenocarcinoma, three centimeters, with no lymph node spread. That's good. Umm … aneuploidy with a high S fraction." He was engrossed.

Sharon coughed, and that seemed to bring him back to the moment. He said, "Now, let's go over things. You both have the same defect, a BRCA2 mutation.

About five years ago, a very good researcher named Easton discovered a genetic defect in families that had a high incidence of breast cancer. He called it BRCA1. In the following year, he found another defect and named it BRCA2. Studies have now located the defects on the seventeenth chromosome for BRCA1 and the thirteenth for BRCA2. We still don't know why these two regions are important, but we know that a mutation here causes estrogen-sensitive tissue like the breasts and ovaries to be very susceptible to cancer. We are trying to figure out how and why. My research is looking at families with the BRCA2 defect to see if we can determine where defects cause the damage. I have examined thirty-four families so far. You guys have a unique defect."

Michelle glanced at her sister, whose eyelids were drooping. Even Sharon had started to yawn. "What do you mean by unique?" Michelle said, mainly to keep from nodding off herself.

"Well, the BRCA2 region is large, about five million base pairs, with twenty-seven different exons—"

"Whoa! You're way over our head. What's a base pair, and what's an exon?"

"DNA is the genetic material that determines what we are. This information is transmitted by a sequence of molecules that are paired. We call these molecules 'base pairs'. DNA is composed of many sequences, some of which don't appear to have any function. Those that do function are called exons."

"What does this have to do with us? I mean, our cases."

"Well, so far, there have been seventy unique mutations, and now you are seventy-one."

"So?"

"Most of the mutations have altered the size of the protein that the exon has coded for. But in your case, the code is too big, so the protein doesn't work. That's called a duplication defect."

"If all of these seventy-one defects cause the cancer, what difference does it make?"

"It may make a difference. We don't know. That's why we are studying it. In your case, the defect is unique. All of the other seventy are frameshift, splice-site, or nonsense mutations on exons above nine. Yours is a duplication on exon eight."

"Oh, good grief! I don't understand any of that. Just tell us what we need to do and what you want from us."

Holly said, "Bossy, just calm down. He's trying his best, I think."

Nervous now, the doctor shifted in his chair as the two sisters sparred. Sharon smiled. "Bossy? That's unusual."

"She has called me that since we were little," Michelle said. "I call her Brat. Fits, doesn't it?"

The doctor cleared his throat. "Let's get back to the issue. I want to study your family further and see what kind of pattern there may be."

"You mean my children?" asked Michelle.

"No, I don't want them … yet. But your mother and father, as well as their brothers and sisters."

"You mean Mom didn't have her blood drawn?"

"No. We never received it. I got a letter from that hospital, and they said they were in the process of converting all their medical records before 1990 to micro-fiche documents, and they would send them to me when they were through. But I never got any blood."

"Mom was reluctant, but I thought she would do it. How important is this?"

"I would like to have her blood, yes."

"What do you think, Brat? I really don't want to ask her again. I think she doesn't want to do it. She feels guilty enough now. No, I won't ask again. I opened up Pandora's box with this stuff, and I don't want to make it worse. There comes a time, doctor, when science needs to respect people's feelings. This is one of those times."

"Okay. What about your father?" he persisted.

"Brat and I don't know anything about him. We wanted to find him, and I looked last fall, but it's like he fell off the face of the Earth—or else he's dead. The last person that knew where he might be was a fellow worker, but I can't find that guy either."

The room fell silent, as if there was nothing further to say. Holly glanced at her sister, as though to ask permission, then turned back to the doctor. "Should I be doing anything else?"

"You need to get annual mammograms, as a minimum. But you might want to consider other options, like your sister did. You still have breasts and ovaries that can get cancer. There is a review from Mayo showing that removing the breasts works, but those studies are not conclusive. There is a protocol now look-ing at that issue. Removing the ovaries, like Michelle did, may protect you from both types of cancer. And, as you know, there is a study that your sister is now part of. Is your oncologist going to put you on tamoxifen? That may work."

"He said I should, yes."

"You might ask him about using another drug called an aromatase inhibitor. That may prove to be a better drug, but we are still studying it."

"Okay. Anything else?"

"No. Just eat your vegetables and fruit. Do lots of exercise. Women with breast cancer have a lower recurrence of cancer if they exercise."

They were silent during the walk back to the car. Once she was inside the vehicle, Holly pulled off the wig and rubbed her head vigorously. "You know, Bossy, I just can't think like I used to. That chemotherapy did something to my brain. I don't get it."

"What don't you get?"

"Well, it seemed to me like he was trying to help us and at the same time, study us. Is that so bad?"

"No, of course not."

"Why did you get mad, then?"

"I don't know. I didn't want to. It's ... just that I feel overwhelmed by all this stuff. They tell us all kinds of facts. And then, when you want to know what to do, all they can do is tell you they are studying it now. There's no end to it. Get on this protocol, or get on that one, we don't know yet, we want more.... It just goes on like we are cattle to be pushed and prodded."

"I don't feel that way. I think it's kind of neat to be unique like this. It sets us apart."

"Oh, great! We are unique in that we have a duplication mutation in the eighth exon on the thirteenth chromosome. Cancer. Yeah, that's really something neat."

"Come on, Bossy. What's really eating you?"

A horn blared behind them as Michelle navigated the freeway. Both fell silent after the driver pulled alongside and extended a middle finger in their direction while mouthing one word.

The next morning, Holly made ready to return home. Michelle walked to the car with her, and she loaded the suitcase into the trunk. Since the freeway incident, they had kept the conversation light, but now Michelle felt she must say something. "I don't really understand my emotions with this stuff. When I started, it seemed distant. But the more I live with it, the more fear I have."

"That guilt-shame stuff you and Mom concocted?"

"I don't want to die."

"Neither do I. But all we can do is live for now, right? Why worry? What did Grandpa Dan use to say? We worry when something bad happens. We worry when something good happens. We worry, but something always happens."

"Yes, I remember that. He was down to earth, wasn't he?" She studied her sister for a moment. "You're such a philosopher now. I can't get over the change in you. What caused that?"

"Easy. I learned from Mila. I wished you could have learned from her too. Grandpa too, for that matter. Life isn't that hard, you know. Maybe you're trying to make it something harder than it needs to be."

"If it was just me, perhaps I could. But I have two children."

"So? Someday they may have to deal with it too. But that's their future, not yours, and you can't do anything now, so why make it a big deal? Unless, of course, you enjoy playing the victim."

For the rest of the day, Michelle worked. Since she had quit working, she found it gratifying to work with her hands, in the yard, for instance. Three acres was a lot to tend, even with a lawn service. Just the same, it gave her a chance to think. Today she had a lot to think about, and her own behavior the day before with Dr. Nielsen puzzled her. Anger never solved anything, and Holly was right to question her. What Holly had said made a lot of sense. Pete would be home tonight from one of his overseas trips, and maybe he could help sort it all out.

With the girls in a wading pool, she worked in the rose garden until Pete returned late in the afternoon. After the children were asleep, she sat on the deck, nursing a gin and tonic, wearing her nightgown. The landscaping lights were still on, and she could see strips of grass she had missed when mowing this afternoon. She took another sip of gin. *Bitter. Must have scrimped on the tonic water.* It tasted like it had come right off a juniper bush.

A frog croaked by the pond. She missed the night sounds of the farm, where owls, coyotes, and bats kept the night alive. Here it was cars, jet airplanes, sirens, and horns, even as far out as they lived. The frog's sound was music to her ears. Soon a cricket joined in, and Michelle gazed at the sky. There were a few stars, but not many, because of the city lights. On the farm, there were always lots of stars. She remembered many a summer night when Mom would rouse them out of bed and pack them in the pickup. They would journey down into the valley to John and Edie's place, just to sit in the field and watch the heavens, late into the night, undisturbed.

"Kinda warm out here tonight." Pete was sitting right next to her now, and she hadn't even heard him come out of the house. She reached over and stroked his thigh with the back of her hand. After a bit, she quit stroking, and dropped her hand to the side of the lounge chair. "How did it go yesterday?" he asked.

"I made a fool of myself. Dr. Nielsen has confirmed that Holly and I have the same defect and that it is unique to us. Now he wants to study Mom and Dad, but I put my foot down and told him Mom has had enough."

"Sounds reasonable to me."

"Holly thinks I'm playing the victim too much and that I need to accept things as they are and not get upset about things I have no control over. What do you think?"

"You handled this well, after you made your decision about the oophorectomy. What happened?"

"I don't understand what happened. I think all that scientific stuff made me frustrated, and when he said Mom didn't get the test, I got defensive. I feel like we are dealing with issues no human should have to deal with, or something like that."

He rose and gently put her arms to her sides, got both arms under her body, and lifted. He staggered through the door and into the bedroom with his load. A couple of times, she thought he would drop her. On reaching the bed, he heaved her onto it, then gasped for air and sat on the edge to compose himself.

"Thanks, Pete. Now, that was gallant—even if it wasn't romantic."

"You could have helped, you know." He tickled her ribs, and they laughed together. He crawled into bed.

"Pete? In the big scheme of things, this is just a small ripple, isn't it?"

"Yeah. I'm glad you can see it that way."

Chapter 17

2005

It would be another hour before George came home. Dinner was in the oven, the house was warm, despite the ocean breeze, and all the windows were open. It was one of those unusual hot days on the coast, where a temperature of eighty degrees was intolerable. She would walk on the beach, as the air was cooler there.

More people lived here now, not like when she first fell in love with the area eight years before. She reminisced as she walked, but solitude was impossible, as others would stroll by and greet her. She knew most of them, as the locals always walked the beach, while the tourists would just drive by on the cliffs above, stopping to take a picture, then hurrying along. Down here, everyone knew everyone else. Gone were the days when it was just Mila and her.

Holly glanced up the cliff as she approached the old stairs Ralph had made. An oil company executive had bought the old place after Mila died, but he never seemed to be there. A maintenance crew kept the lawn and garden looking nice, but the house itself was deteriorating as the weather took its toll. Houses required upkeep; the salt air was corrosive. The stairs, however, were as solid as the day Mila and she had hung on for life until George had dragged them to safety. Holly chuckled at the thought as she stopped and rubbed the railing.

She remembered Mila rambling that day about feeling Ralph's presence. At the time, Holly had thought the old gal was delirious, but now she knew better—she could *feel* Mila here now. She rubbed the rail with affection. She thought, *Funny, I can hardly feel the wood.* She looked at the palms of her hands. The creases were almost invisible, replaced by thick skin, giving the appearance of calluses. Upon closer inspection, the calluses were more like ridges, and her palms looked like the tripe she saw in grocery stores. Both hands had this unusual appearance. She made a grip a couple of times, then looked again, but there was no change. "Doesn't hurt. Maybe it's just something to do with an allergy or the heat," she mused aloud. Then she dismissed the concern and headed back home, so she could have dinner ready for George when he got home.

George was already there when she got back. He was dishing out the food on the dining room table, where candles and flowers were arranged as a centerpiece.

"My, why the formality?" she said. "This is romantic!"

"Thought we needed to take some time for ourselves," he said, placing a hot dish on the table. "Do you realize this will be the first sit-down meal in a long time? Usually I'm off on county commissioner or hospital board meetings, and you are off to visit a hospice patient, so we never have an evening alone. Let's take advantage of it."

"Sounds nice to me. I do miss our time together." She hugged him while rubbing his back. She couldn't feel his back.

Later, as they prepared for bed, she looked at her hands again. The appearance was the same. She was puzzled.

George asked, "Why do you keep looking at your hands, dear?"

"Look at this, George. My hands look like tripe."

"What's tripe?"

"You know—cow's stomach. You see it in the stores. Some people eat it."

"Oh, yeah. Cook it with hominy. You're right. Your hands do look funny. How long has that been going on?"

"I don't know. I just noticed it today. It doesn't itch or hurt. Must be an allergy."

"Yeah, it'll probably be gone tomorrow."

◆   ◆   ◆

Two weeks later, the lack of feeling in her palms was worse, prompting Holly to see Dr. Young. She was due for an annual checkup anyway. The clinic had expanded in the last few years, but the waiting room was unchanged, except that now more people filled it. The old feeling of warmth just wasn't there. The staff was all business as they rushed people through. Gone was the beautiful young assistant in the colorful uniform, replaced by a stern one in street dress, who ushered her into a room with few words. Dr. Young had not changed, though, and Holly felt at ease again.

"How are you during? You look great. How's George managing at the college? I have a young patient who takes his chemistry class and thinks he is the greatest. I got a note from the Bensen family after their mom died, and they appreciated what hospice did. They commented on your effort as if you were a godsend. Great job, Holly. Is this just your annual visit?"

"Yes, I'm still taking tamoxifen. It's been seven years now. Is there any new data?"

"Just came out. It looks like long-term use, beyond five years, is more beneficial than stopping the drug at five years. Of course, in cases of hereditary cancer like yours, no one knows."

"Good. I'm glad we decided to stay the course beyond five. Otherwise, I'm fine—except this strange thing with my hands. I can't feel with them like I used to, and they have this funny appearance."

The doctor examined her hands, his brow furrowed. Then he pushed back in his examining stool, as if she were contagious. Apprehensive now, Holly waited.

He asked, "Anything else? Weight loss? Shortness of breath? Bone pain?" Staccato questions—not like him.

"No, I feel fine. What is it?"

"I'm not sure, but we need to do some tests, Holly. Let's get them scheduled today, and I'll see you back afterwards. In the meantime, stop the tamoxifen. It could be a drug reaction. Why don't you bring George when you come back?"

"You don't think it's the drug, do you?"

"Could be. Let's just check things out, okay?"

She left the clinic, numb all over.

◆   ◆   ◆

Over the next week, she was in and out of the clinic and radiology department as she underwent CAT scans, bone scans, and blood tests. The last test was a biopsy: a needle inserted into her right lung. Although not painful, it did add to her anxiety, so that by the time she returned with George to see Dr. Young, she was convinced the results would be bad. With shaking knees, they entered the office. *This can't be good,* she thought, *if he needs the office instead of the exam room.* On the X-ray viewing box, there was a CAT scan of a chest.

The doctor came in. Without making eye contact, he went to the viewing box. "Good morning. I have here the scan we took last week. The right lung has a large mass in the upper portion. This is the area, Holly, where the radiologist did the biopsy. The path report shows cancer."

"What ...? What ... kind of cancer?" George squeaked.

"It's adenocarcinoma, and it looks just like the breast cancer specimen from eight years ago. It even has the same characteristic markers."

"You mean it came back?" George asked.

"Yes. The scan also shows a lesion in the liver, and the bone scan shows it in the bones as well."

"Good grief!" said Holly. "It's all through my body. I don't feel that bad. The tamoxifen didn't work. I should have done something else."

"We don't know that. It is most likely that the cancer had already spread eight years ago. And the medicine suppressed it for this period of time but now is losing its effect."

"What do we do now, Dr. Young?" She turned her palms upward and stretched her hands toward him. "Is this cancer too?"

"No, your palms are an effect of having cancer. It's called paraneoplastic syndrome. When the cancer is controlled, that will go away. We can't expect a cure now, but we might be able to control it for awhile. Like we did with Mila."

"When does she start chemo?" George asked, his voice cracking.

"We'll put a venous catheter in tomorrow, then start Monday. Is that okay with you, Holly? You can get a second opinion if you want."

"Monday is fine. What good would getting a second opinion do? It would just waste time. George? What do you think?"

"No, getting a second opinion isn't going to change things." He was trying not to sob, but his voice was high-pitched.

They spoke little on the way home. Holly felt numb, as though her emotional self were somewhere else. The news had not surprised her, as she had expected it, but the confirmation had affected her just the same. She looked at her husband as he drove. His face was ashen, and he stared ahead, his features fixed. His driving was all right, but his hands appeared frozen on the steering wheel. She looked forward again and watched the trees go by. For eight years, she had traveled this road as a hospice volunteer, to support a family or patient through the final stages, but now she didn't know how to support her husband.

At home, she dressed in her jogging outfit and headed toward the beach. George just watched her without a word as he sat at the dining table. After a mile of running fast, she slowed to a walk, hoping her emotions were as fatigued as her body. Up ahead were the stairs. She sat on the lowest step and gazed out to the sea. She wanted her mind to quit, but it kept going. Going where? It seemed to jump all over the place: first to the bus stop where she and her sister had wrestled with the secret, then to the doctor's office; then it bounced all over and back again—no rational thoughts, just thoughts. A fog bank was moving in, which reminded her of the meeting with Michelle and how she had told her about the cancer. She would have to tell them again. Mom would take it hard, and Michelle could not handle this cancer gene stuff at all. Her thoughts moved on. A boy came down the beach with his dog, smiled, and threw a stick into the surf for the dog to retrieve.

"Hi, Holly," he said. He seemed to sense that things were not right, and he moved on before she could respond. She watched them until they were out of sight, and Yoty came to mind. The sun dropped over the edge of the fog bank to set in the horizon. It was starting to get dark. She looked down the beach and saw George walking toward her.

"I thought you might be here," he said. "I got worried when you didn't come back, and I was afraid you—"

"No, George, that's one thing I won't do. I needed to *feel* Mila, not act like her. How you doing?"

He sat beside her, arms on knees, and sighed. "Okay. What happens now?"

"I go back tomorrow to get the catheter."

"No, what are we going to do?"

"George, you're not making sense. Spit it out."

"Well, do you want to stay here, or move back closer to your Mom, or plan something else?"

"I don't have plans, George. *We* have to plan. I don't want to move. This is my … our home. Why leave?"

"Maybe you should get a second opinion."

"Is that what this is about? I know you want to do everything possible, and I know you are so shocked that you don't want to believe it. And I suspect you are grasping at straws now. Am I right?"

"I guess so. When you get the news that the most important person in your life has incurable cancer, you want to do everything possible. Is that so wrong?"

"No, it's not, and a part of me wants to get every doctor in the world in on my case. But that's just an emotional thought, George. It's not a rational thought. Stop and think about it. We have been around enough cancer to know there is no cure at this stage, and running around to get the same answer isn't going to help the situation. We need to focus. Besides, it would just delay any treatment that might help. Do you agree?"

"My rational mind says you're right, but—"

"There's no 'but.' Mila lived, what, eight to ten years after it came back? That's pretty good. Yes, we have a crystal ball into the future. I don't know how long I have, but I do know we need to enjoy what's left—and not listen to this or that doctor telling us ifs or whens or maybes, or whatever they say when they don't know the answer. That's not a life. That's living on false hope. I'm sure you can find somebody out there that will guarantee a cure, or agree with you that Dr. Young is wrong, but it isn't going to change anything."

"Your sister was right."

"What does that mean?"

"You have changed, and I can't believe how wise you are."

She smiled, looking into his sorrowful eyes. She wanted to make it all go away for him, somehow. "Not wise, George. Just objective. If we let fear control, then what do we have?"

◆   ◆   ◆

After dinner, Holly started cleaning the kitchen as George cleared the table. "Don't you have a meeting tonight?" she asked.

"Yes but I want to stay here with you. The hospital board can function one night without me."

"Okay, stay home. I'm going out on a hospice call, so you can just sit here by yourself."

"How can you do that? Today you found out you have it, but now you are going to help others."

"Get off your pity-potty, George. This isn't about us. It's about life. What better way to have a life than to function *as* a life. You need to move on too. I sat with Mila this afternoon, too shocked to think, until you walked up and forced me back to thinking. We need to get on with life—that's what it's all about. I do the things I do. You do the things you do. I'm not going to sit in this house all day, waiting for the reaper. He can damn well search for me."

"What about us? I want to spend time together."

"No, George. You don't get it. We spend time together, and when we do, it's wonderful. But if all we do is spend time together, it loses something. It's like a drug. A little bit is good for you, but a lot is toxic."

"I'm an addict, then. I want more."

"Then go to your meeting, and afterward, I'll give you more."

◆   ◆   ◆

At first, the chemotherapy wasn't that bad. She wasn't fooled, though, remembering how the treatments had gone eight years ago; it wasn't bad at the beginning then either. But this time, after the third course of Adraimycin and Taxotere, things got worse. She lost her hair, and her fingers and toes started to tingle, but the worst effect was the vomiting. It started about six hours after the infusion and lasted for three days, despite the new wonder-drug injection that was supposed to stop it. Yesterday she had gotten the fifth course, but before another one, Dr. Young wanted to scan her heart again because of possible heart toxicity. She had received Adriamycin the first time in 1998, and the cancer had come back, so she doubted it would work this time.

In the middle of the night, the nausea started, so she got out of bed (so as not to disturb George) and went down to the basement guest bathroom. She lay on the cold tile floor, waiting for the next wave of nausea to herald the need to vomit. "Man, this tile floor is cold," she said aloud. George had wanted to put a floor heater under the tile when the bathroom was under construction, but at the time, that had seemed foolish; winters in Bandon were never cold. Now, though, she wished they had put in the heater. George was a pushover if she insisted. This time, she had been wrong, and she wished he had disagreed. Sometimes, right after vomiting, the cold floor did feel good when the sweating and dizziness started, but two hours on the tile was just plain cold.

Why doesn't that new antivomiting drug work? she thought. *It's just like water. Wonder if that pharmacist diluted it.* There had been a story a while ago about some pharmacist in the Midwest who gave diluted doses of chemotherapy to make more money. No, Rick wouldn't do that; it was just crazy thoughts to pass the night away.

Oh, good grief, there's a mouse! As she lay there, the rodent scurried along the wall, then abruptly stopped to look right into her face. Her initial impulse was to get the broom and whack the little bugger to death, but it appeared concerned about her. It rose on its hind feet and stared, twitching its nose. It dropped down to all fours and advanced with caution a few steps, then rose up again up to stare. Holly did not move, fascinated by the behavior. The animal showed little fear, although it was cautious, and as long as she remained quiet, it was content to continue its evaluation. The mouse provided distraction from the cold and nausea. She raised a hand to reach out to it, but that was too much, and its bravado evaporated; it turned tail and ran.

"Here I am on a cold floor, sick, while my best comfort comes from a tiny rodent. There's so much in life I have not appreciated. I am grateful for you, my little friend," she called out. "I hope to see you next time … if there is a next time."

She stood up and flushed the toilet again, even though it was empty. It was ritual, but lingering smells connoted bad experiences. She went to the kitchen to start a pot of coffee. Smells were still nauseating, but it was about time for George to get up; it was best not to interrupt the routine. She slipped through the patio door and went onto the deck to avoid the smell.

As dawn approached, a brisk breeze pushed out to sea. A storm last night had left the deck wet, and the moisture in the air made the breeze cooler. It was not a good idea to be outside with nothing on but a nightgown. She slipped back inside and pulled George's cardigan off its hook in the mudroom, then went out again. Dark clouds gathered over the coast in both directions, moving from southwest to northeast: a winter storm pattern.

Daylight broke through the clouds, shining rays like spotlights onto the ocean. Ever since her first storm, she marveled at this scene and found it spiritual: rays from above signifying power from beyond. Many artists, both contemporary and Renaissance, used this image in their paintings to signify spirituality. *Will there be spiritual feelings when I die? Maybe this will be the last storm.* She turned her focus on the beach. The waves were high, breaking offshore, and flotsam washed in—even logs. It was fun to walk the beach after a storm, just to see what the sea had brought in.

"Maybe I will if I feel better this morning. I wish George didn't have to work today and he could go with me."

Behind her, George opened the door and walked out in his underwear; it was a nice thing about being the last house on the beach. Unshaven, with disheveled hair, he yawned and stretched, then smacked his lips, as if to be sure his mouth worked. "What are you mumbling about? You okay? You didn't sleep in bed last night. Vomiting?"

A nod was enough. She didn't want to talk just now. Besides, he would just lecture her about taking the antivomiting pills and the need to avoid dehydration. He had become quite the expert in the last year. He went to every doctor visit with her and asked so many questions that the doctor and the nurses would anticipate answers, to preempt his questioning. He would go with her to the cancer support group and sit in the back until someone asked a question; then he would stand, as if at a lectern, to answer. Everybody enjoyed his performance as well as the useful information. If a question stumped him, he would research the topic on the Internet or ask the doctor at the next visit. She lived cancer; he managed cancer.

He leaned over the rail and glanced sideways at her. The wind was blowing her gown between her legs from behind, and her arms were folded, holding the cardigan tightly to fight the cold. Her legs were just spindles from all the weight loss.

"You hungry?" he asked. "I can make a Scandishake or a can of Ensure."

"Please, George. The thought of that crap is nauseating." He tried to get three or four cans of the expensive supplement down her, but the more he forced, the less she could drink. It tasted too sweet, and even mixing it with ice cream and making a milkshake didn't help. She just couldn't eat. She had lost a pound and a half last week alone. Soon she won't have any muscles left. "I saw a little mouse last night."

"What? Where? I'll put out poison."

"No, George, don't you dare. He was just trying to help. He came out onto the bathroom floor and just watched me. He was curious, and it seemed like he was concerned about my health. It was … sweet."

"Are you hallucinating?"

"No, I'm not. The mouse was real, and when I tried to touch it, it ran away. Have you ever looked closely at a mouse? They are so cute. Back on the farm, we used to kill them, because they got into everything. But maybe they have a right too. After all, they have a life with needs and wants."

"Good grief, dear. You are not making a lot of sense."

"George? What would you say if I stopped chemo?"

"I'd say no. Why?"

"Well, it's been almost six months now, and my palms aren't any better, and I'm weaker and losing weight. The chemo is making me real sick, and it isn't working."

"Your palms do not have cancer. That's just a cancer effect. The rest of your symptoms can be explained by the drugs."

"No, Dr. Young said my palms would get better when the cancer did. It isn't working, I know. I could put up with this if I thought it would help, but it isn't, so I think it's best to stop and enjoy life."

They watched a large log turn in the surf. George turned to go back in the house.

"George? When it's time, will you take me home?"

"Home? You mean to your mom's place?"

"I want to see it one more time. Maybe Michelle would come too."

"Now?"

"No, but soon. I want to be able to walk in the woods, climb the mountain, and lie under the stars while Mom points out the universe."

"Don't you think its time to tell them you have the cancer again?"

"No, not yet. They have their lives to live in the meantime."

"It's Thursday. Are you going to the support group?"

"Yes, I'd better get ready. You coming?"

"No, not today. I have a meeting."

She knew he was lying. He didn't want to face the group with the decision. It would be hard on all of them.

The cancer support group met every Monday morning and Thursday afternoon. Usually they lasted about an hour, sometimes more. People that didn't feel well weren't able to take much and wanted to go home. That's why the group tended to be composed of cancer patients who had already gone through therapy. Those patients had a sense of accomplishment. After all, it was an elite group: survivors. They welcomed newcomers, and their collective experience provided a foundation of courage for the uncomprehending and struggling neophyte. The new patients got support, while the experienced patients got validation. Everyone benefited.

It was, in many ways, a religion without the guilt. Many patients prioritized the meetings over other events in their life. When one of the experienced patients relapsed, the whole group took on the issue, and the behavior was a phenomenon in itself. The group would be concerned but remain aloof. It signified mortality to each member, like looking in a mirror while the image is fading away. They could be next, and the fear of cancer returned. Every day, the subliminal thought came back to the surface, and it took energy to suppress it: *It's not me today, but it could be me tomorrow.* Seeing the latest victim just meant the need for more energy. The group stayed together because of the bond.

As Holly entered the meeting room, she thought about the new patient coming today. At least it would provide a diversion for her and the whole group. The new patient was a single man; this was unusual, since wives, determined to do everything possible to save their mates, brought most males to the group. This guy was different: a bachelor with a sheepdog. He announced, "I ain't coming in unless the dog comes too." The group allowed it.

The diversion was invigorating. He demonstrated naiveté and humor. Dealing with topics such as dog wills and canine cancer proved challenging as the group tried to get him to deal with his issues. The atmosphere was lighthearted, and Holly appreciated the change in mood.

Driving home, she reflected on how the meeting had made her situation tolerable. Everything was relative, and each person's prospective was different. She thought about what Mel Brooks had once said: "If I fall into a septic tank, that's tragic. But if you fall in, that's comedy." The new man's issues were just as real to him as Holly's were to herself. It wasn't so bad when you shared and saw others struggle too. She felt better. *Strange, I made a decision today to face my own mortal-*

ity, but it took a mouse and an old man with a sheepdog to make me appreciate what I have left.

Chapter 18

January 2006

Michelle didn't know why it took so long for Kira and Nicole to get ready every morning. Their uniforms were set out the night before, and all they had to do was wash, comb their hair, dress, and eat breakfast. Kira was getting to that age, though, where a girl thought she was a young woman; it took time, no matter how efficient a mother might be. Nicole, only two years younger at ten, was also straining with gender issues, but at an accelerated pace, because of her older sister's behavior. Michelle remembered how Holly had done the same. *Holly and I were more efficient,* she thought. She yelled up the stairs to hurry the girls along.

Today, Michelle had an appointment and didn't want to be late. She would have just enough time to drop the girls at school, then she would have to hurry across town to the university, during the rush hour. The previous afternoon, Sharon had called to ask her if she could come over and see Dr. Nielsen. Apparently, he had some new knowledge about the cancer gene that he wanted to share.

"Kira, please," said Michelle. "I'll be late if we don't go now."

"In a minute, Mom."

Michelle was ambivalent; after all, this whole issue of oncogenes just caused a lot of trouble for the family, and every time Dr. Nielsen wanted to see her, it seemed to make things more complicated. Back in the late nineties, she'd done what she had to do, and now she just wanted to forget it, at least until she was forced to face it with the girls. If she didn't think about it, she didn't get the guilt-shame, that feeling she and Mom had described on the mountain, years ago. Sharon was insistent, though, and Michelle had agreed to the meeting.

The story of the monkey came to mind. The monkey couldn't resist the empty coconut shell containing a rock. Every time it shook the shell, it could hear a noise, and curiosity demanded that it try to get it out. The animal would stick its hand into the hole and grab the rock, then wouldn't let go. *I'm just a monkey,* thought Michelle.

It would be nice to see Sharon, who seemed more like a benevolent aunt these days. They talked every now and then on the phone, but they had not met since the lunch meeting where they'd both gotten tipsy eight years ago. It was strange; they were less than ten miles apart but never saw each other. Back on the farm, friends that lived fifty miles or more apart would see each other every couple of months.

"Come on! We are going to be late!" she yelled again.

The two girls ran down the stairs. Kira's lips had a hint of color. On any other day, Michelle would have objected and made her wipe off the lipstick, but that would just delay them more. Kira would argue. Michelle mumbled to herself, "No, just let it go. It takes too much time and energy," and pushed the girls toward the door. The girls looked at each other, not understanding the comment.

Traffic was light, and she let her mind wander. She was thinking about Holly. Her younger sister had called a couple of days ago to arrange a family reunion. Her voice had sounded strange, maybe weak, but she had said she was all right. Just the same, Michelle was concerned. George had talked for a while too, and he had sounded evasive. Something was wrong. She would deal with that issue next.

Michelle parked and walked into the building. There was a lot of construction going on. It seemed like the medical center never had enough room, as there had been a lot of construction eight years ago too.

Michelle knocked at Sharon's office door, and Sharon greeted her. "Good morning, Michelle. My, you look nice. The years have been kind to you." The older woman was the same, except for a few additional pounds. She still wore a white nurse's cap. "Let's have a cup of coffee before we go up to the meeting. Dr. Nielsen is now the head of the department, so he has his own office now. Nice, too. He has rounds this morning, so he will be a bit late anyway. How's your mother?"

The two women talked for another fifteen minutes, then took the elevator to the eighth floor. Dr. Nielsen had a corner office with large windows to the south and west. The walls were English walnut paneling with built-in bookshelves. His desk was walnut and large enough to qualify as a conference table; it was positioned diagonally across the room. The chair was one of those swiveling executive types, and it faced the table away from the windows. There were no visitors' chairs, just a large, curved sofa with a low profile, so a visitor had to look up at the desk.

Michelle thought, *He must turn around all the time to take in this view. I'd never get anything done in this office.* A glance around the opulent space was enough. "I don't like this room. It's intimidating," she announced to Sharon as they sat down.

"Neither do I. I feel like a school kid in a principal's office. You can't even see the view from this sofa."

"Researchers must make a lot of money to have offices like this one."

"Dr. Nielsen inherited it from the foundation director."

Both women were now uncomfortable, and they grasped at small talk. Another ten minutes transpired before the doctor showed.

"Sorry," he said. "Rounds took longer than I anticipated this morning. The residents just rotated today, so there was a lot of confusion. Thanks for coming in, Michelle. I appreciate it. I have come across some puzzling information. After thinking about it, I thought you might want to hear it too. It's kind of complex, so we will have to walk you through it. It's about your oncogene."

"My oncogene?"

"Well, yes. Your family's oncogene. What we have discovered is that the BRCA2 region on the thirteenth chromosome is so large that virtually all defects occurring in that region are unique to each family with the oncogene. So to find two families with the same defect is really unusual. Scientists working in this field decided to keep a database of the types of defects, to see if any differences or patterns occur. So far, we have not noticed any patterns that will help patients. It seems that any defect in this region will cause cancer, indicating that there is only one protein expressed from the region—"

"You're losing us, doctor. Try to make it so Michelle can understand." Sharon, as always, assumed the role of interpreter.

"Sorry. Anyway, we keep a data bank, and it is unique to see two different families with the same exact defect. I was perusing the data bank a couple of weeks ago and found another family with an identical defect."

Michelle was not impressed. "Seems to me that if you look at enough DNA, you are going to find others with the same thing. Only stands to reason, doesn't it?"

"Yes and no. Not that many cases have been studied yet. The clinical test, like you first had, just reports a defect in the BRCA2 region, not the specifics within the region, like researchers do with specific exon probes. Clinicians just want to know if there is a defect, not what kind of defect. So there could be more. At the same time, in the past ten years since we have been probing this region, yours is unique on the eighth exon. All the others have been on nine or above, and most are on the eleventh. So I was curious when another family showed up in the data bank with the exact same defect on the eighth exon."

"I still don't get it. What's this have to do with me or my family?" She tried to look out the window.

"Well, the defect becomes a genetic marker that could be used as a genealogy tool."

"You think we are related?" Her voice showed energy now.

"Yes, that's a distinct possibility."

"Wow, that's interesting. Where is this family?" Leaning forward, she unfolded her arms and looked him in the eyes.

He shifted his eyes to the window, then back. "I ... don't know. The database doesn't give personal information, and the new laws about patient confidentiality make it difficult to find out. I think we could, but it would be difficult. This new HIPAA law is very hard to interpret."

"Then why did you bring this up? I don't see any reason to pursue it if we have to run up against the bureaucrats. I had my fill of them when I ran an accounting business." She leaned back again.

"There's ... more. I told you this was complicated. After I found the other family's data, I pulled your family research file to confirm the defect's identity. You may not remember, but when Holly and you were here in ... let's see, it was 1998 ... we didn't have your mother's results, and you didn't want me to pursue it, so we just dropped the issue. Remember?"

"Yes. So what?" Michelle crossed her arms again.

"Well, we had sent for your mother's medical records from the hospital where she had her surgery. They couldn't send them in time for our meeting then—something about getting past records filed in the microfiche system. Anyway, about a year later—1999, I think—they sent them. The whole record and more. I didn't think them important at the time, because we were not studying her, so I just put them in the research file and didn't even look. There were about a hundred pages. I guess whoever copied them from the microfiche files didn't read that all I wanted was the pathology report, or else they felt it was important for me to have everything. Anyway, two weeks ago, I pulled out your mother's path report when the other family showed up. Since she signed a release, I can let you read it too." He searched for the file and handed Michelle a photocopied page. It had a sticky note on one corner, with a handwritten word: PATH.

Valley Hospital
Department of Pathology

Joseph Black, MD, FCAP 18 April 1972
Director

Patient: Ann Garrity
Hospital number: 1689273
Accession number: 72-0349
Specimen date: 12 April 1972

The submitted specimen has four pieces.
Specimen A: A 3-centimeter diameter yellow tissue labeled biopsy. This specimen was initially submitted for frozen section, then blocked for H and E staining. The cut surface showed a small nodular density, about 1.5 cm in diameter, slightly pale in color and harder than the surrounding adipose tissue. Frozen sections revealed too much artifact to interpret with disruption of cell membranes and freezing artifact. The H and E stains confirmed the nodule was composed of fibrous tissue. Diagnosis: fibroma.
Specimen B: An amputated breast, reported as right breast weighing 232 gm. Sections revealed adipose tissue and normal ductal elements. Random H and E blocks showed normal tissue only.
Specimen C: Muscle, pectoralis with fragments of skeletal muscle, fascia and adipose tissue, normal. No suspicious lesions.
Specimen D: Axillary tissue containing 33 lymph nodes. None of the nodes were grossly suspicious. Random lymph node sections on H and E showed normal architecture.
Diagnosis: Fibroma in an otherwise normal breast, skeletal muscle, adipose tissue and lymph nodes. No evidence of cancer.
Addendum: 27 April 1972. Block of specimen A and blocks from specimen B referred to Dr. C.D. Anderson, University of Chicago. Results: concurrence with the above diagnosis. Report on file.
Addendum: 23 May 1972. Block of specimen A and blocks from specimen B referred to AFIP, Washington DC. Results: concurrence with the above diagnosis. Report on file.

Michelle looked up and handed the report to Sharon.

Dr. Nielsen hesitated, then said, "The reports from Dr. Anderson and the AFIP are here too." He seemed anxious now.

"This means my mother ... didn't have cancer? I don't believe this." Michelle's eyes were closed, and her lips were drawn tight.

"No, it's true. Your mother had a lump that was just scar tissue," the doctor mumbled, almost to himself.

"Why did they remove the whole breast, then?" Michelle asked, opening her eyes wide, like a lion about to pounce on its prey.

"I'm not exactly sure, but the records have some clues. You know, Sharon, you have notes in here too. Just two days of nursing notes at the beginning."

Michelle turned to Sharon. "Did you know that my mother didn't have cancer? Is that why you were so nice to her? Why didn't you tell her then?" Michelle could feel the anger becoming uncontrollable.

"Calm down, Michelle," the doctor said. "You're not acting rational."

"What do you mean, 'not acting rational'? My mother's body was mutilated, and she crawled into a shell afterward. My sister and I have been told we got it from her, and now you sit here and tell me it is all a mistake—and you expect me to act rational? What the hell is wrong with you people? What can we believe? Is this crazy BRCA crap real? Does it mean anything now? What in the hell am I supposed to do with this? I can't go home and tell my mom that her whole life was turned upside down by a mistake. Come on, doctor! Quit with the perhaps, the maybes, the we-don't-knows, the ifs, and all that hedging you academics do, and help me here. I want answers, and I want them now!" *Shit! I'm out of control,* she thought.

The room was silent; Michelle glared over the desk at the doctor, then at Sharon and back. Her nostrils flared, and she breathed loudly. Then she looked down and started sobbing. Sharon tried to put an arm on her shoulder, but she pushed it away. She was still angry.

"I want all that BRCA2 stuff confirmed," Michelle said. "I want the pathologist to suffer for what he did to Mom. If there is a conspiracy here, you will all feel my wrath." She was sobbing as she talked, then she reached a point where there was no more energy. It was as though the tank of her emotions had run dry. She took a deep breath as rational thought returned; she raised her head to stare straight into the doctor's eyes. This time, she even smiled at her own embarrassment.

"Let's take each point, one at a time. Sharon? Did you know?" Dr. Nielsen asked.

"No. I was fired by the surgeon on the second post-op day. How could I know?" said Sharon. "The path report came out about five days later. I didn't even have an inkling. The surgeon, Dr. Long, would be the one to make the decision to remove the breast, not the pathologist, I would think. Unless the pathologist made a mistake on the frozen section."

Dr. Nielsen said, now satisfied that Sharon was not involved. "I have some information about that." He turned back to Michelle. "But before we go into that, I think we need to clear up more of Michelle's concerns. It is possible your mother still has the BRCA2 defect. After all, we just assumed she did, and your grandmother did have breast cancer, so there is a history. However, it always bothered me that your grandmother got hers when she was in her late fifties. It could be that she was just part of the one out of eight or so of women who will get cancer. Usually, but not always, hereditary cancers occur at younger ages."

He got up and turned to the window and gazed out for a moment with his hands clasped behind his back, then turned back to the women. "As I remember, there were no other cancers in your mother's family, so the history is suspect. The other possibility is that the BRCA2 gene came from your father. We have no information about that, but again, we jumped to conclusions. Now, to the question if the BRCA2 defect in your sister and you is valid. I went back to the work notebooks from when we did the tests. We did three replicates, with the same results each time in both samples. There was one probe, the exon 27, that the manufacturer recalled as defective that year. We replaced the lot, and the tests were the same. But even if we used that lot, your defect is on the eighth exon, so it would have made no difference."

With confidence and finality, he concluded. "The data have been confirmed, Michelle. You and your sister definitely have the BRCA2 oncogene. Don't forget, your sister has cancer, so it fits."

Michelle said, "I'm … sorry. Please forgive me. I don't know.…" It was time to let the anger go. This time, she let Sharon put her arm around her shoulders.

The doctor asked, "Anything else you want to know?"

"How am I going to explain this to the others? They're going to react too."

"Yes, it's difficult, and I don't have the answer, but there is more information here that might help."

"Do I want to know?" She squeezed out a smile.

"Maybe. Remember, we have a surgeon and a pathologist who could have made the mistake. These records may offer a clue. For some reason I don't understand, whoever copied them just copied everything related to your mom's case, including special confidential files." His eyes went to Sharon.

"Mom had confidential records?"

"No, but her case was pivotal to an investigation conducted by the Board of Medical Examiners. All those confidential records wound up with your mother's file. Whoever did this seemed really incompetent or else wanted someone to know." Again he looked at Sharon. "You can study all of these if you wish, but there are three reports I think you should see. Here, read this one first." He handed her the paper.

This one was an original, not a photocopy like the pathology report. It was yellowed and had fold marks, like it had been in an envelope. One of the folds was torn on the side.

Verbatim Affidavit taken from Dr. Charles Long, June 1, 1972
Examiner for the Board: Mr. Hugh Carpenter
Location: Valley Hospital Administrator's Office

I was supposed to operate on Mrs. Ann Garrity on the morning of April 12, 1972. She was the first patient on my schedule. The pathology department was advised a few days before—I don't remember the exact day—that we would need frozen sections on this case. I was informed by the surgery nurse that there would be a delay because Dr. Black had not yet arrived. I was naturally upset, as it would put me behind, and I had another patient after this one. Besides, I was tired. The other surgeon in town, Dr. Anderson, was on vacation at the time, or so he says, and I covered the hospital and his patients for three days straight. During that time, I had several emergencies and only had about three hours sleep during the whole period. I was going to do my two cases, then go home to nap. When things go the way I expect, there are no problems, so I felt comfortable doing these two cases, even though I was tired.

Dr. Black is an alcoholic and can't be trusted. I told Mr. Jones, the administrator here, on several occasions to get rid of him, but nothing happened. In my capacity as lead surgeon, I threatened to stop using this hospital if he didn't do something. I insisted, for the sake of these poor patients, that he contact you guys at the Board for disciplinary action, but all you did was drag your feet, and now look at this mess. How can you possibly think I did anything wrong? I'm the best surgeon in this state, and I have made this hospital what it is, and this is the way you treat me. That Dr. Black just made the complaint to get back at me for insisting he be removed from the staff, and then got that madman to attack me. Who you going to believe: a pillar in this medical community, or a drunk?

The standard of surgery for a breast cancer is a radical mastectomy. I practiced the proper procedure and did a radical mastectomy. Oh, sure, some of these young hotshots want to do it other ways, but I trained at John Hopkins Medical Center in Baltimore, where the great Halsted did his pioneer work at the turn of the twentieth century. Halsted was the first to show that breast cancer could be cured by removing the breast and all tissue down to the ribs, then removing as many lymph nodes from the armpit as possible. Cure rates as high as 50% documented. Yes, I did a Halsted; I trained that way.

Some physicians, like this new young Dr. Anderson, leave the chest wall muscles and don't remove all the lymph nodes from the armpit, calling their procedure a "modified radical mastectomy," but until studies show it is better, I'll stay with the time-tested procedure. After all, Halsted was the first to recognize how breast cancer spread: first to the armpit nodes, then throughout the body. It makes sense to remove the source, then follow potential spread areas. Since local recurrence is about five percent, removing the muscles seems like a good idea. After all, it is better to be cured than cancerous, no matter what the procedure.

At the last American College of Surgeons meeting, there was a talk by a young whippersnapper named Bernard Fisher, imploring surgeons to involve their patients in a study comparing mastectomy to just removing a quarter of the breast that contained the tumor. He even had the audacity to call the procedure a quadrantectomy. Halsted would roll over in his grave! Fisher claimed the Scots and Finns have been doing quadrantectomies since the late forties, with results equal to our Halsted procedure, but where's the data? He also referenced that wild Englishman, Baldwin, who is just removing the part of the breast segment that contains tumor. Are we plastic surgeons or real surgeons? All these approaches are just fads. Even when I was in training, there were fads: the super-Halsted procedure that removed the neck nodes and breast-plate was no better than the Halsted. That crazy radiation oncologist down at M.D. Anderson Tumor Institute just irradiated the tumor. After the initial report, there was no further mention of primary treatment with radiation. Those surgeons down there must have tarred and feathered her.

Besides, we now have Medicare. The government isn't going to pay for experimentation. Also, we have to be aware of the ambulance-chasing lawyers. Any procedure that is not the standard of care leaves a surgeon vulnerable. Did I do it without pathology? I tried to get that drunk to give me an answer, but he wouldn't do it. He was just doing that to get me in trouble. He wanted me to wait until the permanent sections came out. Why, that would take a couple of days. I would have had to wake the patient and tell her, "I'm sorry, we don't know if it's cancer or not. We'll know in a couple of days, then we'll operate." Oh, by the way, the anesthetic we use is halothane, and the more you are exposed to it, the more likely you will die of chemical hepatitis. No, I did the right thing.

"Through? Here's the second document." Dr. Nielsen brought her back to the present as he reached over the desk with another piece of paper and took the first one back. This document was yellowed and folded, like the first one.

Verbatim Affidavit taken from Dr. Joseph Black, June 2, 1972
Examiner for the Board: Mr. Hugh Carpenter
Location: Valley Hospital Pathology Office
I knew I had a surgical specimen case that morning of ... April 12, I believe. I even got up extra early to be there on time, but I live forty miles away and had to come over the pass. There was construction that morning; they were blasting part of a cliff, and so I was delayed. I have four hospitals I serve—kind of an itinerant, since no one hospital needs a full-time pathologist. It takes a lot of time to do what I do. Anyway, I tried to be on time, as I'm very conscien-

tious. I was maybe a half-hour late at the most, but then I couldn't find a parking space, so that took another ten minutes.

I notified the OR when I was ready, and about forty minutes later, we got the specimen. I cut it open and carefully processed it with my technician, Sue. She's very good. We did it right the first time, but the knife on the tome must have been dull, because I couldn't make out any discrete cells. Everything was distorted. In retrospect, all we were looking at was fibrous tissue, but we didn't know that at the time. Sue made some more cuts, but the results were the same.

I called down to the operating room, as there is an intercom directly to it from the lab, and told Dr. Long the problem. He got all mad and yelled at me to come down there. I did and met him in the OR office. He broke scrub to come out to talk to me. The other nurses all left. Everyone is intimidated by that guy. Someday, someone is going to flatten him. Anyway, I told him there was not a pathologist in the world that could interpret the frozen sections, and the only thing to do was to wait for the permanent H and E slides that would be ready in a day or two. I even told him that the university was starting to do that anyway, rather than rely on the frozens. He just got madder when I said that. Really, I was afraid he would hit me.

The H and E sections showed there was no cancer. When the final report was done, Dr. Long called me a liar—said I made it up just to get him in trouble. Why would I say she didn't have cancer if she did? He insisted I get a second opinion from a reputable pathologist, even said he wanted Dr. Anderson at Chicago to do it. I sent the specimens to him, and he called me a couple of days later. Boy, was I embarrassed. He said I was right—like I really needed a second opinion to say everything was normal and a small fibroma could be cancer. Any second-year medical student could have done that. Anyway, Dr. Long didn't like that answer either and insisted that the Armed Forces Institute of Pathology review it. Jesus, can you believe it? AFIP confirming normal tissue? I refused at first, until Mr. Jones, the administrator, insisted. Why can't anybody in this hospital stand up to that bully? I wish it had been me that turned him in to the board. Do I drink? Yes, I do, a little bit. If you had the stress I do, you'd drink too. But I don't overdo it. Ask Sue. She'll tell you I function well at work.

Michelle just shook her head as she handed back the paper and took the third page from his outstretched hand. It was yellow too.

Recommendation to the Board of Medical Examiners, June 21, 1972
Examiner: Mr. Hugh Carpenter
Enclosed are the affidavits from the two physicians in question, Drs. Joseph Black and Charles Long. In addition, I interview the OR nurse, Mrs. Sally Hart, the administrator, Mr. Matthew Jones, and the laboratory technician, Miss Susan Foote. They confirm the essentials of the story. Dr. Black has a

drinking problem, and Miss Foote, only after skilled coercion, states he had alcohol on his breath that morning. Mrs. Hart confirms that there was an altercation in the OR office and that Dr. Long was out of control. Mr. Jones confirms that the two physicians had a grudge. Given the results of the final path report, it appears the removal of this woman's breast was based on equivocal data and the pathologist was acting appropriately to recommend delay. The Board should further review the reports and consider sanctions on the surgeon. However, given the alcohol problems, the Board should consider Dr. Black's ability to perform his duties as a pathologist.
CONFIDENTIAL
NOT TO LEAVE THE OFFICE

"Poor Mom. She got caught in quite a mess, didn't she? Why didn't the hospital or the doctor or the Board of Medicine tell her of the mistake?"

Dr. Nielsen said, "I don't know that answer, but I would assume it was the responsibility of the surgeon to tell her. The stuff from the Board of Medical Examiners shouldn't have even been in the hospital's own files. That stuff is strictly confidential and should have stayed at the Board's office in the capital." He glanced once again at Sharon, who just stared, as if listening to a lecture. "What do you want to do with all this ... data?"

"Well, there's still the issue of the BRCA2 gene. Do you really think my dad could have it? If so, should we try again to find him, warn him? Maybe this other family could be a link to him. Mom said he had a sister but she lost contact years ago. Maybe this family is his sister's. I still don't want to tell Mom, but I'm uncertain. Will it do any good? I can't think of anything good to come out of it, except...."

"Except what?"

"Oh, nothing. No ... yes, it is something. Mom and I have talked about the emotional effect of having this thing. We call it guilt-shame. Maybe if she knew the truth, she wouldn't feel that way."

"Are you going to try to get her tested?"

"I don't know. Part of me wants to protect her from all this. I started it, and now I feel ... well, guilt about creating a monster. I don't want to hurt her any more, but if we could put a positive spin on this data, it might help her. I just don't know. I think it would be better if we could approach the father angle with this other family. If we can find him and test him, then I would feel better if we needed to test her. Am I wrong? If we connect that family to my dad, then Mom wouldn't have to be tested?"

"Yes, you're right. It's a long shot, though," Sharon interjected. Michelle thought Dr. Nielsen shot a glaring glance at the nurse.

Michelle asked, "What do you mean?"

The doctor said, "Well, that family may not be connected to either of yours. We may not be able to find them, and if we do, they may not want to share. We will have to get the reporting investigator to tell us what he knows. He may not know much personal information, because of confidentiality issues. This new HIPAA law is strict yet ambiguous, and the feds are already showing teeth in its enforcement. The FBI can get involved. It could get ugly. Are you willing to take the risk?"

"How can they think this is a breach of confidentiality when there may be lives on the line, Dr. Nielsen?" Disgusted, she added: "On second thought, don't answer that."

"Before we start, I think you ought to see a lawyer to be sure we do things … well, legally. Even then, I worry. This is a new law, and already there have been ambiguities, particularly with this issue of cancer tests. A couple of months ago, a woman sued a doctor because he didn't tell her a sister had an oncogene—yet the HIPAA law forbade him to do so. Go figure. I also recommend that you get a private investigator to do the legwork. That is, if you want to spend that kind of money."

"Money is no problem."

Chapter 19

Late January 2006

The meeting with the lawyer was short. The only way to do this within the framework of the law would be to contact the investigator and ask him or her to contact the family to see if they wanted to have their information disclosed. If they didn't agree, then the inquiry was through, and any further attempt to find them would be illegal. Simple. They could go to court to challenge the HIPAA law, but that would be expensive and time-consuming, and they might not win.

"Everybody is afraid of this law," Michelle said. "What does HIPAA stand for, anyway?" She was obviously frustrated.

The lawyer said, "Another bureaucratic acronym—Health Insurance Portability and Accountability Act. It was enacted in 2003, primarily to ensure that electronic medical information was handled properly. But provisions about patient confidentiality protection were added, and that is the part you are dealing with." She said it as though it were obvious. No one wanted to take on the government.

Michelle left the office, discouraged. The SUV hybrid didn't have the power to squeeze into the freeway as fast as she hoped. The two cars behind her honked, but she was deep in thought. She tried to organize all of the information, but it was confusing. She sighed and recited a mantra: "One issue at a time." The first thing to do was to go back to Dr. Nielsen and have him contact the reporting investigator for the family and see if that person would intervene with this request. She thought there were too many intermediaries, too many things that could go wrong, but there was no other choice. She tried to imagine how she would feel if someone wanted to contact her about the oncogene.

"Would I cooperate? This thing has been such a complex issue, and part of me feels like it is something to hide.—that damned guilt-shame stuff. I don't even tell friends about it. No, I probably wouldn't want to tell a stranger about it ... yet if it could help someone else? Yes, maybe I would. It all depends on how it's presented to me. That's the important thing—presentation. If Dr. Nielsen presents it right to the other investigator, then that person presents it right to the family representative, then the family representative presents it right to the family…. Too many ifs." She looked at the car on her left. The passenger, an older lady, was staring wide-eyed at her as the car passed by. At first Michelle didn't understand, but then she realized she had been talking to herself. She shrugged and laughed. Everybody seems to be doing it anyway since the advent of cell phones.

Pete came home late, which was not unusual. His job demanded more of his time now. Although he didn't travel as much, he spent evenings at meetings and dinners, so the family saw even less of him.

"Evening, dear," he said to Michelle, "I'm home. What are you doing?" He reached into the refrigerator for a carrot and some buttermilk, then came into the study, where Michelle was on the computer. "Oh, no! You're drinking a gin and tonic and on the Internet. Bad sign. Something's up," he joked.

"Maybe you could help me, Pete. I know it's been a long day, but I have been on this thing all afternoon, and I'm getting nowhere."

He sighed. "Where do you want to go?"

"I'm trying to find a data bank."

"I'll need a little bit more information than that. Does this have something to do with your mother and that family?"

"Yes. I saw a lawyer today, and she says the only way to do this legally is to have the doctor get hold of the family representative and see if they would be willing to share information. Otherwise, there is no other way, unless we go to court. But she thought we would lose in the end."

"Okay, that makes sense. So why are you trying to find a database?"

"Bank, data bank. Dr. Nielsen said he found the family on a data bank. I want to see how much information there is in it and who the investigator is that did the tests."

"Why don't you just go to Dr. Nielsen and have him pull it up for you?"

She pulled back from the screen and took a sip of her drink, then let out a breath and looked at Pete for the first time. "I could, I suppose, but something about all this is bothering me. He tried to play down his role in looking for this family, but he was very liberal with the hospital information about Mom. He's the one who wanted me to see a lawyer, but he didn't think it would do any good. He also suggested a detective. Strange, don't you think? I think he wanted me to tell Mom, but at the same time, he acted like the answer was with this family. Strange…."

"Yes, it sounds strange. But what good is all this? I mean, does it matter if the oncogene came from him or her? I can't see how it changes anything. Yes, it's a tragedy about the mastectomy, but running down this family and telling your mom isn't going to change anything. Let sleeping dogs lie."

"I suppose you're right. But Pete, you don't have the gene, and you don't have the ... feelings like Mom and I do. Suppose for a minute, just suppose the gene came from Dad. If Mom knew that, then maybe she wouldn't feel the way she does about passing it on to Holly and me. Hell, if I knew that, maybe I wouldn't have so much trouble understanding how I feel toward her and my children."

"Michelle, that's illogical. She's your mother, and you're Kira's and Nicole's mother. Nothing changes."

"I said you were right about the logic. But you're wrong about the feelings."

"Okay, okay. So what does all this have to do with the data ... bank."

"Well, I could go to Dr. Nielsen, and he could go to the other doctor, and on to the family—but it loses a lot in translation. Whereas if I can cut out a middle-man or two, then my chance of success increases. I want to see what's in that data bank."

"Michelle. Dear. I think you are obsessed. Why don't you just go to Ann, lay it out in a logical way, then ask her to be tested? Simple. Leave this family stuff alone. It's too complicated, and you could get in trouble."

"I can't." Michelle put an elbow on each side of the keyboard, to support her head. The posture distorted her lower face into a grimace. "First off, I have to protect Mom. She's suffered enough, and I already feel guilty for starting this whole business of the oncogene. I don't want to tell her anything unless I can put a positive spin on it. If the gene came from Dad, that's a positive, but if it came from Mom, that's not. Simple? No. Besides, years ago, Holly and I promised to find Dad. And now, if it is possible that he has the gene, then maybe we can get him some help. The only clue we have is this family." Her eyes pointed at the screen.

"Why help him, after what he did to you?"

"He did what he did, I don't know why. But I'm sure it was hard on him too at the time. I used to hate him, but now both Holly and I want to hear his side of the story before we judge him. He did us wrong, but remember how you reacted when I told you about the gene? Well, George did the same to Holly. You guys reacted. So did Dad."

"Yeah, but we stayed with you."

"True. What if I had not come to you that night and asked to work together? If I hadn't done that, would we still be together? Mom didn't ask."

"Okay, I surrender. You want to get into this data bank, and you are willing to risk criminal charges. I'm going against my instinct, but I'll help. Do you have a name for this bank?"

"No, he just called it a data bank. But it's where scientist working in the field of oncogenes posts their findings."

"You looked under oncogenes, BRCA, BRCA2, cancer genes, breast cancer, inherited breast cancer …?"

"All of those."

Pete shrugged. He paced the floor, hand on chin, then pulled out his Black-berry and pressed one button. Michelle looked on, pleased.

"Dracula? Pete here. Got a problem. Need to get into a data bank but don't know its name and don't have a password…. Yeah, I know we expect a lot from you…. Yeah, I know you can…. Well, drop that project for one night…. Okay, be there in forty-five minutes." He punched another button and dropped the unit back in his pocket. "Okay, let's go." He lifted her up by the arm, and they scooted out the door.

"It's late. Where are we going? I can't leave the girls like this."

"You wanted to get into a bank, so now we are going to play robbers. The kids will be fine. They're asleep anyway."

"Pete, tell me where we are going! And who's this Dracula creature?" Michelle rubbed her arms to warm them; Pete's 1931 Ford Victoria didn't have a heater, and he had rushed her out of the house so quickly that she hadn't had time to get a sweater.

"We're going into the recesses of hell to see the greatest computer hacker in the world. He goes by the moniker of Dracula because he only works at night, avoids most people, and sucks the electronic blood out of viruses, worms, and other little creatures that invade our computer systems. Our platform is vulnerable to these nasty infections, so most hackers use it to infect, then we get blamed. So we have a corps of hackers to help us debug and tell us where we are vulnerable. Besides, if we hire them, they won't attack us. Be aware that Dracula lives in a different part of town."

The old Ford could only do a maximum of fifty miles an hour, so a different route than the freeway provided views of residential areas with many stop signs. Pete had insisted on taking this vehicle, despite having four others in the garage—cars that had modern conveniences like heaters, shock absorbers, and brakes. Sometimes he could be melodramatic.

After half an hour, the shipping docks came into view. The Ford traversed the perimeter gate and wound through the cargo containers to a little shack in the back of the lighted loading yard. There were no lights coming from the shack, but there were two windows, both with old carpets tacked over them. Pete knocked at the door, which opened a crack to reveal an eyeball attached to a huge head that nodded when the eye recognized Pete.

"Jesus, this is like something out of an old B-grade gangster movie," she whispered to Pete as she got out of the car. Pete pushed open the door. Inside the room was a sink, a toilet, a refrigerator, and a stove on one side, with a bed in the middle. On the other side, an array of electronic and computer devices extended to take up half of the room.

Pete said, "Michelle, meet Dracula. Dracula, this is my wife. We need help."

The pale, chunky man with a full beard could have been thirty or fifty-five years old. He grunted in acknowledgement, then spoke. "So you want to get into a data bank, but you don't know its name. Well, tell me all about it. Don't leave out anything. Let me be the judge of what's important or not. Every detail, please. I'll interrupt from time to time to ask questions, but for the most part, the stage is yours. Want a cup of tea first?"

Michelle was taken back by his articulateness, which did not fit his image. It was obvious that Dracula was intelligent. She told the whole story of the oncogene and her family in about forty minutes as Dracula sipped his tea while Pete stood and fidgeted.

Dracula said, "Well, it's more a problem of finding the bank than robbing it. Let's start with Dr. Nielsen. Where's he at?"

"He's at the University Medical Center, Department of Molecular Oncology."

"Ooh. Getting into the university system is no problem, I do it all the time. Their security is a joke. Let's see.... Okay, here it is. How do you spell oncology? What *is* that, anyway?"

Michelle spelled it, wondering whether her earlier assessment of his intellect had been right.

"Here it is," said Dracula. "Busy little beaver, isn't he? There's all kinds of things on here. Yes, there are several data files." He kept mumbling as he scrolled. "Here's a data file ... from the lab, apparently some kind of results ... exons with people's names. Interesting. No reference to a national data bank. What did you say your exon defect was? Eight? Here's your name, and this must be your sister. Holly? There's two other names here."

Michelle bolted out of her seat to look over Dracula's left shoulder at the screen. "Hello, Dad," she whispered with a smile.

The trip home didn't seem too bad; in fact, Michelle felt euphoric. She gazed out the window at the passing houses, admiring them for the first time: old Queen Annes, gothics, and ranch houses from the early fifties. These old, restored beauties reflected bygone eras, and riding along in the 1931 Ford just added to the ambience.

"How come Dracula lives on a dock? Why doesn't the shipping company throw him out?" she asked Pete.

"Can't. He owns the dock. Been in his family for years, and he inherited it. The company would love to get him out of there, but he won't go."

"I wish he would have helped find Dad for us. Why did he look at you that way when I asked him to find an address for Dad?"

"Dear, you have to accept some things in the computer industry. Dracula is not interested in punch-and-search details. He is a hacker and gets his kicks from doing what others can't do. He knows I can do all that stuff, and he even knows that I could have gotten into Dr. Nielsen's data bank. He was doing me a favor, is all."

"Then why didn't you help me in the first place? What's going on here, Pete?"

"Look, I am a senior vice president of one of the largest software companies in the world. What do you suppose would happen if I got caught? Dracula knew that, but he doesn't care about legality. He's in it for the thrill. Once we got in, it wasn't a challenge for him anymore. Anybody can do the work now."

"Will you do it for me?"

"No, Michelle, I won't, and it's not because I don't care. This is your quest, and I have other time-consuming projects that rob from the family as it is. Do as Dr. Nielsen suggested—see a detective. Speaking of Dr. Nielsen, it looks like he threw you a curve. He knew that one of those new BRCA2 patients was your father. I wonder why he lied."

Almost yelling over the sound of the Model A motor, Michelle said. "Actually, Pete, he didn't throw me a curve, and he didn't lie. He just didn't tell all. I thought it strange, remember? He tried to get me to decide the next step. He recommended an attorney, because he knew that avenue was a dead end, and he wanted me to find out on my own. He couldn't just come out and tell me, either, because of the HIPAA law. Clever, I think. He knew there was a lot of information and that I would probably react—which I did, to my own embarrassment. So he gave me the options and hoped I would work it out. The clue was the recommendation to get a detective. Stop and think about it. Have you ever been to a doctor that recommended a detective?

The question didn't require a response. Suddenly, a cat darted out between cars as Pete swerved to miss it.

"Whew, that was close. Was that cat all black?"

Michelle ignored him. "Dr. Nielsen knew that if I would go after the family, I would have to do it on my own, and somehow he figured I would try to find Dad. Yes, I'm impressed. I have come to admire that doctor. If I would have talked Mom into the test, he probably figured everything would still come together. He did the tests on Dad and that woman, Edie Blankenship, then went back to our data files and found, as he said, the medical records. It was all too complex, with too many options, so he just threw all of them on the table for me to sort through."

She smiled. "Clever, very clever. What he didn't count on was the resources of a very loving husband. Thank you, dear, for what you did tonight." She scooted over next to him, careful not to hit the gear shift in the middle of the floor.

"You're welcome, but I think your quest has just begun, not ended. Now you have to go to a detective and find your dad, if you are still committed to the rationale you stated before we saw Dracula. I suspect you have some more twists and turns in your adventure. I just hope you don't get too … disappointed."

Chapter 20

Late January 2006

The appointment for the Acme Detective Agency took place the next afternoon. Michelle felt foolish going there. First off, the name was a turn-off—and right out of the 1930s. She felt like the "dame" in a Dashiell Hammett or a Raymond Chandler gumshoe novel. She expected an office in the seedy neighborhood of town on the second floor, no elevator, with a partially frosted glass door with the name stenciled on the glass. There would be a secretary in a dimly lit but small outer office, and the detective would be sitting in the inner office in a rumpled suit and loosened tie, with a lit cigarette hanging out the corner of his mouth. His feet would be propped on the desk, revealing a hole in the sole of one shoe. He would feign lugubriousness as he listened noncommittally to her problem and would only take the assignment after being enticed by a large retainer. She thought about how the image fit with her escapades last night.

So much for images. The office was on the top floor of a large building in the commercial section of town. The city view was spectacular from all rooms. The reception room was spacious, lavish, and decorated with taste. Two receptionists, not one, were dressed in suits, and both were men. She didn't have to wait long before she was ushered into one of many soundproof offices. One of the receptionists held a leather library chair for her, then offered coffee or tea, with or without cream and sugar.

The woman on the other side of the desk was dressed in a pinstriped suit with a hem above the knee. She came around the desk to shake hands. A short, utilitarian haircut offset the high heels and Chantilly lace blouse. She explained that modern detective work was in demand by the corporate world and that most of their efforts entailed computer work. Right up front, she announced that her company did not spy on wayward husbands or wives. They would look for missing persons if the assignment did not involve legal issues. Finding Michelle's dad would be challenging because of the cold trail, but if it could be done, it should not take too long.

Michelle hadn't even finished her coffee before the detective rose to indicate that the meeting was over and she was anxious to get started. Billing would take place after services were rendered, and no retainer was required after filling out the application; services would start after the credit check. All business.

Michelle walked back to the parking lot, somewhat disappointed. It would have been nice to at least see some feet on the desk and maybe even a cigarette. She still didn't know what to do with the information if they found him. Maybe sleeping dogs should stay asleep, but would they? Perhaps not, if it meant clearing up family secrets that had been dormant too long.

◆   ◆   ◆

"Why does that damn phone always ring when I am in the bathroom?" The answering machine was already regurgitating its contrition at missing this important call. Would the caller please leave a message? The recipient would drop everything as soon as possible to fulfill the recorded request.

She interrupted at the beep with a hello. The detective agency had results. Would she like to pick up the dossier, or should they send it by Federal Express? The billing cycle was the end of the month. *Good grief,* she thought. She had been there only two days ago, and now they had a dossier on him. She felt like a sneak.

The following morning, the FedEx truck arrived with an impressive bundle. How could they have found so much on him in such a short time, when the family didn't have a clue to his whereabouts? There were several documents: birth certificate, marriage license, Selective Service data, addresses where he lived since birth, college records, employment records, credit reports, and even medical records before 2003. She felt like he was in her hands, all three by nine by eleven inches of him. All day, she studied the documents as the rain came down outdoors. In the Pacific Northwest, rain defined the area as sunshine defined the Caribbean; it was the perfect time to read about her dad. She curled up by the fire and read.

After leaving Ann, Michelle's father had moved around, taking various jobs. Sometimes he quit, and sometimes he left upon being requested to do so. There was a hint of alcohol trouble in some of the documents. He changed career three weeks after leaving Ann, as that company had gone bankrupt; he then had gone into the construction field as a bookkeeper. In that position, he had found employment with a worldwide construction company based in Omaha,

Nebraska, and advanced to project office manager in exotic places like Saudi Arabia, Venezuela, Australia, and Portugal.

In 2002, he had developed a brain tumor, which was treated with surgery and radiation. Although the treatment was successful, he did not return to work, because of progressive dementia compounded by excessive alcohol consumption, according to a doctor's report. His last known address was in a small town in Montana. How he wound up there in 2004 was unknown. He did have a Social Security disability determination on file, but it was not accessible. A new power of attorney for an Edie Blankenship had replaced one revoked in 2004 for a Mrs. Ginny Bayes.

Interesting, she thought. *This explains the other person on the oncogene study—either an illegitimate daughter or a niece.* Yawning, she rose and walked around the house, then put the dossier in the bottom of the suitcase as she packed.

◆   ◆   ◆

There was a freeway all the way to within 150 miles of the small town on the Missouri breaks. The hybrid SUV made good time and got decent mileage. They had downsized the vehicles as gas prices rose. It wasn't that they couldn't afford the gasoline; it was a conscientious effort to conserve. Pete drove the Ford Victoria to work, and she drove the hybrid. Of course, there were still the Hummer, the Corvette, and the Mini Cooper in the garage, just in case.

She made good time on the freeway, but it was boring, and she tried to sort out the events of the past couple of weeks. Her life had seemed so mundane before that, and now she was seeing an eccentric man in the back of a shipping yard at midnight; dealing with lawyers, then detectives; and now she was on the road to meet a stranger who might be responsible for who she and her family had become. Her father. How did she feel?

Yawning, she reached over the seat and grabbed the thermos, then held the steering wheel with her knees as she poured hot liquid into the cup. The SUV drifted into the outside lane, where a trucker was trying to pass. His horn blast brought her attention back to the road, and she smiled up to his cab when the truck was alongside the car. Perhaps fortunately, she could not see his face.

She settled back down to drive, and did not plan to stop until leaving the freeway. As she sipped the hot coffee, thoughts arose again. How did she feel about this man, her father? It wasn't love for him, just curiosity—that was the only conclusion she had for now. It was a waste of time to put any more thought into it, she concluded, and she drained the cup.

After five major mountain passes and eight hours, the scenery changed from steep mountains and evergreen trees to rolling hills and junipers. She turned north off the freeway, fueled at a truck stop at the junction, then continued another 150 miles on a two-lane road that rose and fell like a roller coaster. Daylight turned to dusk, then dark—darkness unlike any she had seen in the city or its surroundings. She could see the town's lights ahead when she crested a hill, only to have it go dark in the vale, then return as she crested the next one. Except for the headlights and distant town lights, there was nothing to see, which caused her uneasiness.

She was glad to see the city limits sign proclaiming a population of 324 people, 128 dogs, 456 cats, 29 horses, and 65 children: PLEASE DRIVE CAREFULLY. It wasn't really a town. It had one small motel in the old 1950s style, where you parked your car in front of a bungalow that had two metal chairs on a little porch in front, so that visitors could look out at their cars while relaxing in the shade.

Michelle filled in the registration form as the old man scrutinized the credit card. "Ain't seen one like this before," he said. "Guess it looks like you."

"Where would I find this address?" She pulled out the slip and handed it to him.

"That's Davis's trailer park up the street, end of town. Can't miss it," he said, writing the registration information on a piece of paper. He printed with purpose, sticking his tongue out of the corner of his mouth as he wrote. "There's only one café in the center of town, but it closes at nine, so you will have to wait till seven for breakfast. The gas station has snack foods, if you want something tonight."

The little bungalow had a bed (somewhat lumpy), a big refrigerator, and a sink. The place was clean, but the refrigerator fired up every now and then with a lawnmower sound. She had just gotten to sleep the first time it took off; after the second time, she pulled its plug, and the rest of the night was quiet. It was eight thirty in the morning before she woke.

The café was full, with locals drinking coffee and discussing issues ranging from the war to how the park service had screwed up again. There was even some gossip at the women's table in the corner. The room went silent when she entered, making her feel self-conscious. She sat at the counter, since there were no tables. The coffee tasted bitter, but the orange juice was cold and refreshing. The crowd went silent again when she asked for a poached egg, and she ate fast, so she could leave.

She walked to the trailer park, which she could see up the road. The address she had was a vacant spot. The trailer park manager watched her from his office window, then came out as she stood in front of the vacant lot.

"You looking for someone, lady?"

"Yes, I was told a Mrs. Edie Blankenship or—"

"She's dead. The state killed her. Died last month, and the repo company didn't even wait for the body to cool before they yanked her trailer out of here. Couple of weeks ago."

"Oh, I'm sorry. The state executed her?"

"No, but they might as well have. Wouldn't treat her cancer. Bastards."

"Was there a man living with her?"

"Yeah, old Bob. Moved in a couple of years ago. Kinda daffy old coot at times, but harmless enough. She said he was her uncle, but most folks hereabouts figured she took him in to get the welfare money. Foster home, my foot."

"What happened to him?" Her heart was pounding now.

"Don't know. Big state car—you know, one of them brand-new SUVs—showed up after Edie died and packed him away. Why does the state need those big, fancy SUVs? Waste of taxpayers' money, if you ask me."

"Do you know where they took him?"

"No. They probably took him to another foster home. Maybe down in Billings. That's where they have their Gestapo offices."

"Would anybody else around here know?"

"Doubt it. You might ask Mrs. Gore down in slot six. She used to take Edie to that hotshot doctor down in Billings before she died."

Before she could knock on the trailer door at slot six, it opened to reveal a lithe, little woman who reeked of tobacco and looked like she had spent her whole life washing clothes with an old Maytag washer. *She may have even gone through the wringer a couple of times herself,* Michelle thought.

"Hep ya?"

"Yes, I'm looking for Bob Garrity, who lived with Edie. The manager told me you might know something about him."

"Why? Ya from the state or feds? You guys did dirt to Edie, and now old Bob is alone again in some stinkin' foster home."

"No, I might be related, and I'm trying to find him."

"Really? I didn't know Edie had a sister. Well, come in. Let's talk."

"Cozy place you have here."

"Yeah, after my husband died, I moved here. You know, I kinda liked Bob. Hope he's all right. I don't know where they took him. Just showed up one day and hauled him away. People here ain't happy about all this Gestapo stuff. Poor Edie tried to get help to prevent gettin' cancer, but the state wouldn't pay for it without proof that she would get it. Old Bob and her got tested and showed she would, but by then, it was too late. Bob got brain cancer, you know. Edie's family was riddled with it. Her mother, Bob's sister, died at forty-one. Poor Edie was only thirty-seven. How come I never met you before?"

"I'm not her sister. I'm Bob's daughter, and we didn't know where he was. If I had known, I would have been here sooner. Do you know where they took him?"

"Naw. Them Nazis just snuck in here and whisked him away. The manager even asked where to forward his mail, but they just said they would take care of it. You ever see that movie where the government controlled everyone, and in the end, the guy just escapes into his mind to get freedom? That's Bob."

"Any ideas about where I could look?"

"Might try Gestapo headquarters down in Billings—all I'd know. But don't get your hopes up. Them people's mean."

"Thanks. Well, I'd best be going." At the door, a thought struck her. "Do you remember that doctor down in Billings that Edie used to see?"

"Sure, that's Dr. Hawn. Nice man. He tried everything to help Edie and Bob. He has an old medical school buddy in research out on the coast somewheres that could do the tests for nothing if Bob and Edie together got tested. The state wouldn't do it, that's for sure."

Michelle hurried back to the motel to collect her luggage and drove out of town, glad to be leaving, but even then, she felt like eyes were watching her departure. Trust, in a small town, had to be earned. She contemplated the warmth the two local people had for Bob. Would she be warm, or would she be cold like the bureaucrats? She understood their problem too. After all, he was disabled and needed care. Just the same, it did sound like Gestapo tactics, the way the locals presented it. *It's all about communication.*

The State Division of Human Services building was a modern edifice with a fenced parking lot reserved for employees. Several white Suburban SUVs lined the perimeter. *Must be twelve or so,* she thought as she climbed the steps to the lobby. She actually gawked at the opulence as she tried reading all the signs telling visitors where to go. A receptionist in one of the large side rooms was busy on the phone as Michelle walked in. The room was massive, with cubicles to hide the employees. The receptionist cupped the phone and asked, "May I help you?"

It turned out that Michelle was in the wrong room, and the receptionist directed her two flights up, to an identical room, where another receptionist was on the phone. After repeating her story, she was ushered into a caseworker's cubicle to repeat it again to a skeptical-appearing, plump woman, whose glasses, with a string around her neck in case they fell off, sat on the end of her nose. Michelle fought the urge to push them back up.

"I'm sorry, Mrs. Keebler," the caseworker said. "There's nothing I can do at this time. You will have to document your relationship to Mr. Garrity before I can disclose any information about him. We have to protect those we serve, you understand."

"What kind of documentation? My driver's license shows my maiden name, same as his. Wouldn't that work?" The brick wall of bureaucracy was impenetrable as she argued her case. She needed proof that she was the daughter, with permission from the next of kin to visit him. Discouraged, she left the building.

The Hilton hotel's restaurant offered a refreshing respite from the day's adventure. Frustrated, she contemplated having a glass of wine with her late lunch, then decided to forgo the pleasure as another plan fermented that would require her full attention. While the server brought a fruit salad, she called Dr. Hawn's office on her cell phone and was lucky to get a late afternoon appointment, after pleading with the scheduler, claiming to be from out of town and in need of an oncologist. The salad didn't last long.

Dr. Hawn entered the room as if this was his last patient of the day and he was anxious to go home. Middle-aged and bald, he seemed sympathetic as she laid out the whole truthful story, except the part about hacking into Dr. Nielsen's files.

"How is Doug?" the doctor asked. "I haven't talked to him since he did those tests for us. What a tragedy. But she already had cancer, and we didn't know it at the time. Let me tell you, dealing with all this bureaucracy was quite an experience. Opened my eyes. Now we are dealing with this HIPAA law, and I can't tell you much. Bob is still my patient, but he really doesn't need an oncologist. Now, if I were to put his chart in the chart box outside this door and go to rounds at the hospital, who knows who could look at it until Debbie locked up? Sounds legal on our part, wouldn't you say? We can't put the address on the front of the chart anymore, but I think it is posted on the back, inside of the folder. Have to be careful who sees it. We comply with everything. Why, just the other day, the FBI was up in the chart room, looking for infractions. Have to be careful about these things now. Can you find your way out, say in five minutes?"

She waited, reading a *Sports Afield* magazine, until she heard the sound of a chart sliding into the chart box outside the door. The hall was empty as she reached around and pulled it into the room with her. An address and a telephone number were on the back cover, attached with a paper clip. Written in pencil on the corner were the words: GOOD LUCK.

The address was right outside Billings and easy to find, in one of those new developments where every third house was the same. It was a ranch-style house with an addition where the garage used to be. Two cars parked in the driveway almost blocked a wooden post with a swinging sign proclaiming this to be the foster home. A woman in her twenties answered the door. She had an infant cradled on her left hip.

"You must be Mrs. Keebler. The doctor's office said you were coming. Please come in. We just finished dinner, and the patients are watching *The Price is Right*. Let me talk to you briefly before you see Bob. Please sit."

The room was small and had a desk and two chairs; it was probably a converted bedroom. The young woman yelled in the doorway for a man to take the infant. *Must be her husband,* thought Michelle.

The woman said, "In case you're wondering, my husband and I run this home. We started about a year ago, as it was the only way we could afford a home. We added three bedrooms and a rec room, then qualified as a foster home. Neighbors weren't too keen on the idea, but it has worked out so far. Bob only joined us two weeks ago. He has had trouble adjusting. He'll wander around at night, and one night, he tried to get in bed with one of the females. He gets confused. You're lucky today, as he is having a good day. Some days, he is real lucid, and others, he is so confused that he gets agitated. When he has a good day, it's hard to believe he has dementia. I'll go get him now and leave you two alone. If he gets agitated, don't react. It just makes it worse."

"What if he doesn't recognize me?"

"I think he will. I told him his daughter was coming, and right away, he said, 'Michelle?' He's excited, and he couldn't eat. Oh, by the way, don't be surprised if he asks if you have any alcohol. Does it to everyone, even the postman."

An old man stood at the doorway. He had gray hair, and he was wrinkled and gaunt. She recognized him anyway. "Hello, Dad. Remember me?"

He came into the room without a word, his eyes glued to her. Then he sat down and stared. His face appeared bright, with a slight smile and twinkling eyes, as he surveyed her face, then her body. At first, she was apprehensive, having never been around a person with dementia and not knowing what to expect.

Soon, he spoke, alleviating her anxiety. "What's it been? Thirty years? You look just like your mother. Is she still alive? I really would like to see her. Tell me all about yourself. How's Holly? Oh, my, I'm rambling. Your turn."

She told all, and he sat looking into her eyes the whole time, never interrupting or moving. He seemed to be soaking in the history she gave; she left out the oncogene information. Then she couldn't hold it back any longer. "Why did you leave us, Dad?"

For the first time, he flinched. Michelle became afraid again. His pupils constricted as his eyelids widened. He took a deep breath. "Knowing what I know now, I wouldn't have left at all. Funny how you go through life, making mistakes that you look back on as so dumb you don't know how you could have done it in the first place."

He shrugged. "Your mother and I tried to make it go. We were both teachers in the beginning, but I wasn't any good at it, and she was. I think I was jealous. She got a raise, and I didn't. Everybody wanted her, not me. I know the only reason I got that provisional contract renewed after the first year was because your mother told them she would leave if they didn't. That's how good she was and how bad I was. The following year—you were about five, I think—the principal called me in and suggested a new job. She even had one for me if I would leave, working as a janitorial supply salesman."

For the first time since starting, he took a breath again, then looked out the window for the next memory. "I wasn't good at that either. Then I got this offer to go to San Francisco. It was my chance. I hated that farm stuff—your mother was even a better farmer than me. I wanted the big city, and she wanted the country life. Anything I wanted to do, she didn't. Looking back on it, she was dominating, and I was too dumb to know that I was outwitted."

He stopped again, with his head down and his hands clasped between his knees. "Anyway, that damn San Francisco job came up right when she was in the hospital. I remember that day as if it was yesterday. I was so excited to tell her: look at me! I'm going to be successful! But when you just had a breast removed, it isn't a good time to look at transitions or even somebody else's success. I didn't realize that at the time and left the hospital with a 'poor me' attitude."

He paused again, frowned, and fixed his eyes on hers again, like a child about to confess. "I went to San Francisco. I wrote her a note saying to follow if she still wanted me, but she didn't come. I rushed home and checked the mail every day, hoping for a letter saying you guys would be coming. I was alone and afraid. Then the company went belly up, and I was left with no money and no future. I couldn't come home with my tail between my legs. Part of me wanted to, but I couldn't. I got a job as a dishwasher just to pay the rent, always dreaming that I would be a success someday, then come back and be your hero."

The clock in the hall chimed as he went silent with his head down again. She could hear the pendulum ticking. He said, "Ha! Some hero. Anyway, I thought a lot about swallowing my pride and coming home, but I didn't. Did get a job in a construction camp, impressed the project manager with my skills, and worked up to office manager. Surprised me. I can't add or subtract unless I use my fingers and toes, but I could manage by not managing. People who worked for me liked me, because I left them alone to do their thing. I got jobs all over the world. I had other women—lots of them—but I never stopped thinking about Ann and you guys. I was just too scared to do anything about it, like call or write."

He squeezed his eyes closed to conjure up the next thought. "Oh, I did call a couple of times, but I got a man's voice. I expected to get divorce papers any day, but nothing happened. I did get the local newspaper, never saw anything about Ann, always thought she would be the queen of the town, like she was the queen of that college."

He slapped his thighs as another thought occurred to him. "I did read about how you graduated at the top of your class, and how Holly got accepted to that fancy ballet school down in Los Angeles. I was proud, real proud." He straightened up and looked around, as if puzzled. He stared at Michelle until she became uneasy. A trembling smile formed as tears filled his eyes. She reached over and massaged his hand, never taking her eyes off his.

The owner came to the door and interrupted. "Bob, time for your medicine. We were supposed to give it to him in the morning, but it upset his stomach and made his mouth dry, so the doctor changed it to after dinner, and it seems to work now. The medicine is Aracept. Supposed to help the memory. You think it helps, Bob?"

"I don't know. Makes me have trouble peeing, is all I know." He was acting normal now.

Daughter and dad sat in the office and talked until the owner came back to announce bedtime. He got up to leave, then turned back at the office door. "You know we got a curse, don't you? Came from my family. Poor Edie died from it, as did her mother and my mother. A lot of breast cancer, but all kinds. My grandmother died with a swollen belly. Everyone thought she looked like she was pregnant, but she had her womb removed years before. You better watch out too. Edie and I had some fancy test, but I tried to tell them they didn't need tests—we got it."

"Thanks, Dad. We'll talk about it tomorrow. You had better get some sleep. Okay?"

He nodded. "You wouldn't have some whiskey in that purse, would you?" He pointed his chin at the purse while licking his lips.

Michelle spent a week in Billings, sitting and listening to Bob's stories. He'd had a full life, and he told wonderful stories about snakes in Venezuela, large lobsters and shrimp in Australia, paella in Spain, and running with the bulls in Pamplona. She left every night entertained but sad that she was just now getting to know him again. His personality hadn't changed from what she remembered as a young girl. In some regards, it was best that she and Holly had hated him after he left, as the affection she felt now would have been detrimental then.

On the sixth day, Bob was having trouble. He kept stopping and asking, "Who are you?" But after she identified herself, he would go on with the conversation until he became confused again. She could tell he was tired, so she decided to leave. At the door, he turned again and asked if she had any whiskey, but then he rushed back into the room and hugged her, as if sensing that this would be their last meeting.

The trip home was uneventful. She glided along the freeway, wondering what to do now that she had found the past, and wondering how to deal with her mom, as this thing was getting bigger and bigger instead of smaller and smaller. *Everything just gets more complicated,* she thought.

Chapter 21

February 10, 2006

The sun was shining, and there was no wind. It was a beautiful late winter day in the northwest. All the rain in the past few weeks had produced a significant amount of flowers and with them, pollen. Both Michelle and Sharon were sneezing before they went a hundred yards into their walk in the park by the bay. After returning home from Montana, Michelle had pondered her next move. Pete had felt she should just be done with it, and he tried to discourage further action. In some regards, she thought he was right, but something inside was bothering her.

Sharon was a good listener, but neither of them wanted to repeat the restaurant incident, so they had elected to walk in the park. It was the perfect escape from the dank indoors, where confinement limits interaction. Out here in the fresh air, even with the pollen, things didn't seem so bad. The two laughed as they walked, reminiscing about Michelle's first meeting with Dr. Nielsen, then about the restaurant escapade. It was a good time to be alive.

"I found my dad," said Michelle.

"I'm not surprised," Sharon said. "Dr. Nielsen figured you would."

"He knew Dad was the carrier, didn't he?"

"I don't really know, but you're probably right. Tell me, how did it go?"

Michelle told her of the battle of anonymity she had overcome and about the wonderful doctor that had just looked the other way. She even recreated the scenes of paranoia and government mistrust in the small town. "It was a real eye opener for me, yet I found those people very helpful in their own way. Once they decided I wasn't a threat, they told the whole story, at least how they saw it. I don't even blame the bureaucrats. They were defensive too, just like the little town's people, but they looked at it from the opposite side. I could have been a person out to do some harm, so it's nice to know they do their job to protect people like Dad. That's what these laws are supposed to do. At the same time, though, laws are blankets of policy that do not allow for exceptions to the rules. I'm sure the protection clauses of the HIPAA law were constructed by well-meaning folks, but they had tunnel vision, and people like us suffer for it. I feel sorry for you guys in the medical field. Maybe laws like this should be designed by people that know the field, rather than bean counters on the third floor of some building back in Washington. Sorry—got on my high horse, didn't I?" She turned to the older woman, like a little girl who had been walking at her side.

"You go, girl! Yes, it's frustrating. Go on … with your story, I mean."

"Dad is sixty-five now, but he has dementia. I'm not really sure I understand all that. He was a heavy drinker, it sounds like, and when he got brain cancer, they radiated his brain after the surgery. Does radiation cause dementia? I never heard of that. You hear a lot about Alzheimer's, but I didn't know other things caused dementia."

"Yes, whole-brain radiation causes memory problems, but usually it takes some time to develop, and older patients may not live long enough to show it. But in your father's case, it sounds like the cause might be complex, and a pickled brain didn't help. Sometimes things like radiation or certain drugs or even head injury can usher in underlying Alzheimer's. Many things can cause dementia, even depression."

"Is it something that comes and goes?"

"What do you mean?"

"Well, he was sharp as a tack during the time I was there, until the last day. Then he seemed confused at times and often asked me who I was. I thought maybe he was tired."

"Were you tired at the time? I imagine the experience was draining for you. Well, he was drained too, and when there is early dementia, patients can function well until they become fatigued or frightened or physically ill, where things like that insult their body. As long as they don't have to learn new skills, they can function well. We had a doctor in his seventies, still practicing until he needed to know new drugs to treat his patients. He couldn't learn them. Had a heck of a time getting rid of him, as most people thought he practiced good medicine. So what are you going to do now? Here you have evidence that the oncogene came from him, your mother didn't have cancer, and your father is in a foster home. Wow, this is like a soap opera." She continued to walk, and she turned toward Michelle and slapped her thighs.

"What should I do?" Michelle interpreted the gesture as a prompt.

"Why do you have to do anything? Maybe that's your problem."

"What do you mean?"

"Well, you always have to fix things. Sometimes the best thing to do is accept things as they are, not try to change them." They walked by two woman with their hands out. Sharon shook her head as they passed. "Like these panhandlers, for instance. They want you to fix them up with a handout, but it wouldn't change anything, as they would just spend it for smokes or drugs or alcohol, then hit up someone else to feed the behavior. Is that fixing, or enabling?"

"Are you telling me I should leave well enough alone in my family?"

"No, I don't know the answer for your dilemma. You need to decide—I can't. What I'm saying is that you have to look at the problem from your viewpoint, not theirs. You can't fix your dad, but you can see that he is all right. You can't fix your mom, but you can be there if she needs you. We have to help others as long as we don't enable them to continue being helpless. That's all I'm saying."

"Maybe I shouldn't have started all this stuff with the oncogene to begin with."

"Looking back isn't going to help. You did, and that's that. You said you wanted to find your dad, and you did, through the oncogene study. You were the first born, typically the overachiever of the family who tries to fix everyone else. That's your destiny, and you are not unique. Accept it, and live your life." Sharon shrugged.

"You aren't helping."

"That's the point! There is no help. You are the panhandler now, and I will not give you what you want, because you will continue doing what you do. You want help. It has to come from within."

They walked up to the old electric plant that hadn't functioned for years; it would have been demolished, but someone had seen its potential as art, then saved it for all to enjoy. The two gazed at the engineering and pipes painted in many colors.

"You know, Sharon," said Michelle, "my dad is like this plant. An engineering marvel with a flaw in his design. But now he's just a relic with some redeeming color. I think he is worth saving, and he won't affect me."

"How about your mom?"

"You're right about me. I can't fix her but if she needs help, I will be there. Say, there's an al fresco café at the entrance when we came into the park. They serve wine. Think we can handle it this time?"

"It's a beautiful day to sit outdoors and drink a glass. Let's do it. Reminds me of Hemingway in Paris. It won't be long before I will be able to do it as often as I like."

"What do you mean?"

"At the end of the month, I am retiring. I've been at this for thirty years, and I'm tired. Besides, the new nurses know more than me, and I don't want to be like that old doctor I told you about. Better to just go out while I'm still respected."

"What are you going to do?"

"I'm going back to the valley where your mom lives. That's my home. Dad had a ranch near there, and I still own it, so I want to go back. Funny how old people migrate back to the places of their youth. Must be an instinct thing, I suppose. I plan to revise a manual I wrote for student nurses and try to get it published."

"What's it about?"

"It's about how to deal with patients with terminal illness. How to avoid burnout and guilt, understanding issues so they don't assume they are the problem, and things like that."

"Sounds like it might be a good guide to life for all of us. That's what you have been telling me, isn't it?"

"In a way, I guess it is. We all have the same emotions, just different experiences."

The café was empty, as it was the middle of the week. They ordered glasses of white wine and sandwiches. The umbrella over the table shaded them from the sun. When the drinks came, each woman fell into her own thoughts for a while. The air was heavy with the fragrances of lilacs and hibiscus, even though it was still winter, albeit a mild one.

Michelle broke the silence. She glanced out to the lake, then glanced at Sharon, hesitated, then began speaking. "Sharon, do you remember that meeting last month, when Dr. Nielsen told me about Mom's medical records?"

"Of course. How could I forget? What about it?" Her tone was suspicious. She set down her glass.

"Well, I don't know for sure, but it seemed odd that there was all that information when all Dr. Nielsen asked for was the path report. But instead, he got copies of everything, including confidential investigation reports from the Board of Medicine that shouldn't even have been there." Michelle twisted the wineglass stem as she talked.

"You think I had something to do with that?"

"Did you?" She looked up at Sharon.

The older woman leaned back in her chair and said nothing at first, just looked at Michelle. "I may have, but I didn't do it on purpose, as I didn't know those things about your mother's case."

"Care to explain that?" Michelle asked, head down.

"Back in 1997, when we first started, Dr. Nielsen asked me to call the hospital and be sure they would cooperate after your mother signed the release form. I called the administrator. It was the same man as when I was there. I knew him well, as he was the one that fired me, Matt Jones. Anyway, Matt was glad to hear from me and said he had always regretted what he did, and he asked if there was any way he could make it up to me. I told him just to send your mom's records. I forgot all about that incident until last month."

"You think this Mr. Jones did it?"

"That's all I can figure. He took a lot of heat from the physicians over this case, I'm sure. I think he had an in at the Board of Medicine and collected as much as he could to send to us. I think he wanted me to find out what happened after I left."

"Why didn't he tell my mom?"

"Afraid, I guess. Matt wasn't the strongest administrator, and he wouldn't do anything if Dr. Long didn't approve. Besides, it was Dr. Long who should have told her." Sharon signaled the end of the story by finishing her wine in one gulp.

Later that night, Michelle waited up for Pete to come home. He showed up at about eleven o'clock and went straight to the refrigerator for his evening fix of buttermilk. Just watching him nauseated her. She had never understood the ritual. Michelle would normally be in bed rather than watching him tip the glass back, the chalky liquid going into his mouth. He would empty the glass in one gulp, leaving the glass caked, then lower the glass to reveal a white mustache, which he would remove with his tongue. That's when she would gag and look away. He seemed to enjoy the effect on her, and sometimes he would reach into the refrigerator for a second performance.

"Enough, Pete! How you can drink that stuff is beyond me."

"You're the country girl, and you can't stand it? I thought all you farmers drank buttermilk. My grandmother use to churn cream by putting it in a gallon glass jar, then shaking it until the butter separated. We kids were always delighted when the butter churned and we could drink the warm buttermilk." He smiled mischievously.

"Oh, Pete, that's disgusting! That crap is bad enough cold."

"One man's medicine, another man's poison. To what do I owe the presence of the lady of the house in the kitchen at this late hour? You're not going to ask me for my sage advice that you really don't want to hear, are you?"

"I listen and appreciate your advice. That's a mean thing to say."

"Okay, maybe that is a bit harsh. But usually when you wait up for me, it's because you want something. What is it? Not another bank, I hope, or another plea to move to your grandpa's old ranch."

"I want to go to Bandon and see Holly. Can you get away and go with me?"

"Can't. Right in the middle of an acquisition. Why now?"

"I want to tell her about Dad. I could just call, but it would be better if we could spend some time talking about it. I suspect she will want to go see him too. Also, I just want to see her."

"Why? Something wrong?"

"I haven't seen her since they first moved there. Last I talked to her, she sounded … weak, I guess. She says things are okay but … I don't know."

"Funny how we don't live that far apart but we never see each other. How's George doing with that teaching job at the community college there?"

"Holly says he loves it. They are pretty involved with the community. She's a hospice volunteer and raises a lot of funds for the organization. She puts on a ballet every year, like Mila did, but the proceeds go to hospice."

"It's amazing. Your sister never thought of anyone but herself before."

"That's not nice, Pete."

"Well, it's true. When are you going?"

"Tomorrow, if you can handle the girls for me again."

◆   ◆   ◆

Although there was urgency to the trip, Michelle took her time and drove down Highway 101 along the coast, even stopping at several tourist shops along the way. By the time she crossed the bridge entering the Bandon area, she had purchased two myrtle-wood bowls, a myrtle-wood clock, a dream catcher (which she later discovered was made in Korea), and smoked salmon. Up the coast, she stopped for lunch and left with taffy that she was still munching as she neared her destination.

Somewhat sick to her stomach, she drove down the beach road beyond Mila's old place, toward the new house. She had never seen it before, but it was hard to miss, even if she had not been to the building site: a large, three-story contemporary house with gray cedar siding. It looked more like a modern castle than a residence. The sun was far to the west as she parked in the driveway. She knocked and yelled, "Hello, anybody home?" then opened the unlocked door. The house had an odor: aseptic, like in a hospital.

George came around the corner from the study. "Hello, Michelle." He seemed startled.

This was understandable, but she became nervous just the same. She went inside, still somewhat confused by his behavior. "Everything okay, George? Where's Holly?"

"I don't know. I just got home and was searching the house when you showed up. She isn't inside. I think we should search outside. It's getting late."

His anxiety puzzled her. "Probably down on the beach, wouldn't you think? She's okay. She *is* okay, isn't she, George?"

"Ah … yeah, it's just that I expected her here. Come on, let's hurry." They exited the back door, went down the steps to the bottom deck, and walked out into the needle grass.

"Something's wrong. This is all bizarre," she mumbled, hurrying to keep up. The path led through the grass, then over the sand berm down onto the beach. The wind blew a thin layer of sand across the beach surface that bit at her shins as she ran. George was running up the beach toward the old house. She could just see him. The stairs came into view.

He was no longer in sight. Michelle slowed to catch her breath. Out the corner of her eye, she noticed a head bobbing above the berm. Curiosity forced her to detour to see who it was. The berm here was not too high, and as she topped it, she found Holly sitting in the grass.

Michelle gasped. What she saw was a pale, emaciated woman. Holly's eyeballs seemed to protrude. Michelle pictured a concentration camp. Only her red hair and her nose indicated the old Holly. Holly's blue lips pursed with each exhalation as she labored to breathe, and she held her arms straight in the sand to help inhale, her hands made into fists. She looked up and seemed to recognize her rescuer but didn't have the strength to respond; all of her effort went just to breathe.

Michelle froze, not knowing what to do. George was yelling on the beach. She turned to the berm, yelled back, and continued until he came into sight, then waved. She motioned him on with both arms, almost flailing. She wasn't sure whether she was doing it out of need or hysteria. "Hurry up, George!" Yelling at the top of her voice didn't seem effective in the wind.

He slowed at the berm, breathing hard.

"Quick, George! She's up here!"

"Oh, my god!" he exclaimed. "Holly, darling…." He dropped to one knee and stroked her hair off her brow. "She needs her oxygen. We can't move her like this. I'll run back to the house and get the Helios bottle. You stay here on the berm, so I can find my way back."

Michelle watched him run down the beach, then turned back to her sister. Part of her didn't want to look, but she had to, for Holly's sake. *Try not to look afraid, Try not to look afraid.*

The eyes under the red hair just stared at her, as if they wanted to be amiable but couldn't. Holly was fighting for her life and had no spare energy to be social. It seemed like a long time before George returned, but it couldn't have been more than three or four minutes. Michelle stood on the berm, as instructed, and yelled into the wind, "Here, George! Here!" until she saw him running up the beach.

He carried a bundle in his arms that made his running look awkward—more like he was bouncing. His progress seemed slow and even surreal. She rushed down to help him with the load. They climbed the berm again, and he unraveled the oxygen line and placed the oxygen tube prongs in Holly's nostrils. The machine seemed to come alive with intermittent pressure-releasing sounds. For a few moments, it seemed as if the machine wasn't doing any good. In fact, the patient shook her head to fling the tube from her face, as if it obstructed her breathing, but George held it in place. Soon Holly quit fighting as the oxygen reached her lungs, and not long after, her breathing slowed down. She still pursed her lips, and Michelle noticed for the first time that her neck muscles strained with each inhaled breath.

George said, "We'll sit here for a little while, to let the oxygen take effect. Then you and I need to carry her back to the house. We'll take her to the hospital from there."

Holly started shaking her head vigorously when he mentioned the hospital. All three sat in the sand. At first, George tried to shield her from the breeze, but she raised an arm to motion him to the side; the wind helped her breathing. Soon the wild look in her eyes subsided, and she could breathe easier. They pulled her up to a standing position. George slung the oxygen bottle over his shoulder, careful not to dislodge the nasal prongs, then put one of her arms over his shoulder and motioned for Michelle to do the same with the other arm. Together they lifted Holly over the berm for the trip back down the beach.

◆   ◆   ◆

Michelle sat in the waiting room as George admitted Holly to the emergency department. She saw a bank of vending machines, two dining tables, and rows of chairs. *How ironic,* she thought. *A vending machine for cigarettes and others for snack foods. The hospital supports the things that cause people to need to come here, and it makes a profit, to boot. They know more about business than health.* With nothing else to do, she sat and watched the people.

George came back, looking beat and dejected. "Dr. Young is coming in to see her. They will admit her for tonight."

"How long has the cancer been back, George?"

"Oh, about two years now."

"Why didn't you tell me?"

George went ballistic as his frustrations and fears boiled up into an answer. "You Garrity women are just too damn stubborn and independent. She wouldn't let me, that's how come. She didn't want you to know until the end. I am not at fault here, so don't accuse me."

"I'm sorry, George. I didn't mean it. Yes, I can see she would try to hide it from us. Kind of like Mila in that regard. Please, don't take what I said personally."

"It isn't Mila's fault. Your sister just wanted to protect you and her mom, that's all," he said tersely.

"Can I see her?"

"No, not till morning. Let's go home." He turned, without waiting. Michelle followed meekly.

◆   ◆   ◆

The trip back to the hospital the next morning was entertaining; the sun peeked through the trees like a strobe light as she drove north. George had left earlier to see his wife, then he wanted to go to the college for a morning faculty meeting. Michelle was impressed by how he was able to continue functioning despite the crisis.

"You learn after a while," he had told her. "We both decided to try and keep our lives as functional and normal as possible. Holly would want me to go to work and not sit at the foot of her bed like a vulture."

The parking lot was empty this morning, not like the previous night. "I guess people get sick at night around here," she said to no one. She tried to get directions to Holly's room from a volunteer at the front desk, but the poor old woman just mumbled, and a younger woman with her kept chewing gum as she spoke. At least they managed to convey a room number, so she just needed to be logical. Holly was in room 324, so it must be on the third floor, since the first number was three. She was proud of her logic as she stepped into the room.

A handsome middle-aged man in slacks and a short-sleeved shirt with the word ONCOLOGY embroidered over the left pocket stood next to Holly. He gave Michelle a quizzical look until Holly identified her. "Dr. Young, this is my sister. She saved me last night."

"Oh, yes. Nice to meet you. Your sister is doing well this morning, so I think we will let her go home today. We gave her three units of blood, and it did wonders. She was really low last night, and that is why she was in so much trouble."

"Why can't you keep her blood up?" Michelle asked, somewhat defiantly.

"The cancer is in her bone marrow now, so she can't make her own. We have to transfuse to maintain her." He turned back and leaned over so his face was in line with Holly's as he continued to talk. "Someone in this room doesn't keep her appointments so we can transfuse in a timely manner to avoid these little mishaps. Isn't that right, Someone?"

"I'm sorry, doctor," said Holly. "Can I go home now with Michelle?"

"Yes, but I want to see you in a week." He stood up and shook his head.

Driving home, Michelle said to Holly, "You shook your head no last night when George mentioned the hospital. You aren't keeping appointments, either. What gives?"

"I don't know. I want to live, but I feel so … dependent. I get tired of going to the hospital all the time. We stopped chemotherapy a couple of years ago, and I got real bad until Dr. Young insisted I go back on it. He changed the drugs, and it was easier to take. I got gemcitabine with Taxol instead of that damn Adriamycin crap, and I did well until the cancer got in my bone marrow and I had to quit. It's been up and down, and now I'm just coasting. Yesterday, I wanted to walk on the beach, as I know there won't be many more times I can do it, but I got too far away from home and crashed. If you hadn't found me when you did, I would have been a goner for sure. I'm reaching the end, and sometimes I think getting more blood and medicine just … prolongs. I need you to do something for me." She reached over, grabbed her sister's arm, and squeezed. "Okay? Promise me, okay?"

"Okay, okay. What?"

"I want you to tell Mom for me and set up a reunion for us, all of us. Pete, the girls, George, you, me, and Mom. I want to go home, then come back here to die. Can you do that for me?"

Michelle took her eyes off the road, saw the desperation chiseled in her sister's face, then turned back. She didn't answer straight away. *Here I have enough money to buy anything, anything but my sister's life.* "Yes, I will. But can you make it? There's another issue, Brat, that you need to think about too."

"What's that?"

"I found Dad."

Holly didn't speak for the rest of the way home. She sat looking out the window. Michelle thought she could hear an occasional sob.

◆   ◆   ◆

Michelle left the coast the same day for the farm. Prior to her departure, Holly promised she would keep her doctor appointments, as she would have to get her strength up for the trip. Michelle was to be the vanguard, warning Ann and arranging the reunion as quickly as possible. After leaving the coastal mountains, she reached for the cell phone.

"Pete? Sorry to bother you at work, but I'm going over to Mom's place now. I may have to ask you to drop everything in the next day or two to help me. Can you arrange that for me? This is important, Pete.... Thanks. I'll call as things develop. Holly's cancer is back, and she doesn't have long to live.... Thanks, I'm sorry too. She wants all of us to get together at Mom's for a reunion, so you will bring the girls ... I don't care, we'll just take them out of school. This is a priority over school. I probably won't give you too much advance notice to come, so be prepared. I may have another task too, but I need to talk to Mom first. Do you think you could get the corporate jet for a couple of days? Great! Oh, do you like myrtle wood? It's a wood from the coast. I bought some.... Well, if you feel that way, I'll just give it to Mom. Tell the girls I love them and miss them. Thanks so much, Pete. Remember, be ready with the jet. Yes, I love you too."

It was early evening when she turned off the paved road to the county road. A grader went by, smoothing out fresh-laid gravel, so she slowed, then turned into the drive. There was a new horse in the pasture, and it came up to the gate as she entered, looking for a handout. She had to shoo it away before she could get the SUV through the gate. Ann was working in the garden when she parked the car. She looked up, squinting, and recognized Michelle. "My, what a pleasant surprise! Hello, Michelle! What are you doing here?"

"I'm here on a mission, Mom. Get dressed. I'm taking you out to dinner."

They engaged in small talk about the kids and Pete as the older woman changed. Even in a dress, she looked rough, with dark-brown, wrinkled skin, pale in the crow's-feet around her eyes, dirt under her nails. She pulled her hair back under a baseball cap as they got in the SUV. "My, this is exciting. I haven't been to town for ... three weeks or more. Where do you want to go? We only have two good restaurants—the truck stop and the Hillside. I guess there is a new Mexican restaurant, but I have not been there."

"Let's go to the Hillside, then. For some reason, a truck stop just doesn't set the proper atmosphere for me."

They were early enough not to need a reservation. After the wine arrived, Michelle decided to reveal all—well, almost all. "Mom. There's a reason I'm here. Holly's cancer is back, and she won't live much longer." There, it was out.

Ann set down her glass of wine and lowered her head in silence. For a moment, Michelle thought she had gone to sleep, but then she saw the discharge dripping from Ann's nose. She squirmed and glanced around as her mother wiped her nose on her sleeve, then left.

Michelle found her in the restroom, stooped over the basin, washing her face. She moved into the small room and stood over her mother, not knowing what to do. At one point, she raised her arm to place it on her mother's shoulder but suspended the motion in midair, shook her head, and let her arm drop back to her side.

She had known that this would be difficult. She had planned the scenario before arriving: dinner out, to get Ann away from the house, to focus on the issues. But this was not how she had thought it would go. In fact, now it seemed to be a lousy idea, and she wished they were at home. Women kept coming in, seeing Ann, and leaving, embarrassed.

"Come on, Mom. This was a bad idea. Let's go home."

"No, go back to the table. Give me a minute, and I'll be there." Ann enunciated each word with conviction.

Ann returned with red eyes but tried to smile as she ordered a broiled salmon steak. She gulped down the wine and ordered another before the server finished writing. Michelle was impatient for the young man to leave, but it took so long that it seemed like he was writing in Greek.

After he left, Ann started talking. "I knew it. Her voice is getting weaker every time we talk on the phone. I suspected but didn't want to believe it. How long has it been back?"

"Two years. The chemotherapy has kept her going till now, but it is in her bone marrow, so they had to stop treating her. She has to have transfusions to live. It won't be long."

"Why didn't she …?"

"She didn't want us to worry until about the end. She and George have tried to maintain a normal life as much as possible. She went into the hospital last night for a transfusion, and George even went to work this morning. I have to admire how they are dealing with it."

"How did you find out?"

"I went down there to discuss … another issue with Holly and found her like that. I came right over here today."

"I want to see her."

"That's why I'm here. She wants to come home, have a reunion, before she…. Anyway, we have to arrange it soon. Are you up to it?"

"Of course. Let's have it tomorrow. Get her over here now."

"It's not that easy, Mom. She may have to take a transfusion before she can come, then she can't stay too long. There's another problem that complicates the issue, too."

"And that is?"

Michelle took a gulp of wine, then a deep breath. She looked into her mother's eyes. "I found Bob."

Time stood still. Only the chatter from the other tables indicated that time was still moving.

Ann did not breathe at first. "My Bob?"

Michelle thought she could detect something warm in the question. "Yes, Mom. Robert Hugh Garrity. The man you married in 1962."

"I thought he was probably dead by now. How is he?"

"He's had a pretty hard life, and his health is not good. He lives in Billings, Montana."

"Oh, he is with his sister, then."

"No, his sister died of breast cancer, and her daughter just died with it too. He is in a foster home. He had brain cancer about three years ago and now has mild dementia."

"Poor Bob. Does he … does he … remember me?"

"Yes, he remembers all of us. He even remembers the day he left and why he couldn't come back to you. He says he wrote you a note, saying to follow him."

"Yes … he did." Ann hung her head.

"Holly wants to see him before … she dies. But she doesn't have the strength to go there and here too."

"Why don't we all go to Montana?"

"That's a possibility and something we need to consider. but there may be another option." Ann looked puzzled, so Michelle continued, "We could bring him here. That way, she could see you both, and she could see the farm. She wants to lie on the deck and look at the stars with you. This is her childhood home, and coming here has meaning. Besides, it's closer."

"Here? Bring Bob here? You mean, to visit? Would he come? Can he come?"

"The mechanics of getting him here will be difficult, but the question is whether or not you are receptive to the idea."

"Bob, at our house, with us. I...."

"You don't have to, Mom. It's just an option."

"Do you really think he would come? I mean, will he want to come? All these years, and now, he might come back. I ... can't believe it."

"Like I said, Mom, it's just an idea. There's all kinds of problems we face. You live in an isolated world. Believe me, dealing with bureaucrats is not easy. We would have to get permission to let him leave the foster home. Then we would have to be sure his medications are given right, and it won't be easy for him, either. As I understand it, taking them to a new place is very stressful. They can get agitated and even violent."

"What do we have to do?"

"First decide if you want to dig up the past, and realize he is sick. It could be hard on you too. This whole thing may backfire in the end."

"I've always wished he would come back," Ann whispered.

"Are you still married to him?"

"Yes. We never divorced."

"That may make it easier. I'm no lawyer, but you are probably his legal guardian. I'll call Pete, when we are through eating, and see what his lawyers say about all this."

"Who's going to get him? Can he travel alone?"

"Why don't you go? It's time to bust out of your shell."

Ann fidgeted at the thought. After dinner, they drank coffee (a French-roasted Guatemalan Huehuetenango: pretty fancy, for a small town) while waiting for the bill. Michelle wanted to bring up another issue but didn't know how to approach it or if the timing was right.

"Mom ... is Dr. Long still practicing?"

"Dr. Long? No, he died years ago. Committed suicide after a doctor got him in trouble with the Board of Medicine. I had to go to another doctor after I got out of the hospital. Dr. Anderson, I believe."

Michelle sipped her coffee. *That explains why she didn't find out. He died before telling her. One less battle to fight.*

Chapter 22

February 13, 2006

George wouldn't be back until late afternoon, so there wasn't much to do to make the time meaningful. She thought of hospice, but they had quit asking her to take on clients. In fact, no one asked her anything anymore. Just a year ago, the city of Bandon Council had wanted her to be the director of the Arts Festival again, but not this year. People just backed away, now that her cancer was bad. It was as though she were contagious, or perhaps they thought that associating with her would weaken them somehow. People used to come up to her in the street and talk about this project or that social need, but now she found that they lowered their eyes and scurried off at the first opportunity, somehow embarrassed. People were nice but distant. Usually the salutation was a hello, but if they asked, "How are you?" then the embarrassment started and they fidgeted and couldn't wait to leave. Some would rub her shoulder as they greeted her, then pat her on the back as they left, in patronizing benevolence. The intimate interaction of one human to another had vanished for her. Because of this, she too withdrew more and more. George and the support group provided her only social nourishment now.

Even the support group offered little refuge; when she entered the room, the eyes and faces of the other group members turned to stone. Every week, it was as if they expected her to die and not come back. How many times could they say good-bye? Only the old man and his dog seemed glad to see her. The dog would rush to her, wagging his tail, and stick his nose in her crotch, then run back to the table where the old man sat with the others. He would smile, which made his face wrinkle even more and revealed the yellowest teeth she had ever seen. His approach to life was simple, and it energized her spirit. He just told it the way it was: no-nonsense philosophy from a sheep herder, which motivated her to fight on, at least for another day.

It wasn't Thursday, so there was no meeting. She walked around the house aimlessly, running a finger over a dresser or a table every now and then. She looked out the window at the dunes; they were like an old friend calling. Mila used to walk the beach and get in trouble, then everyone would get angry with her. Now she saw what had motivated the old ballerina to take the chance. Between the air and water, there was no loneliness. She sighed and scanned the beach, as though she might see the old woman. Then she pushed away from the windowsill, shuffled into the kitchen, and sat. Wind gusted, making the patio door shudder. Holly got up and went to the deck to look again. There was a woman on the beach. For a moment, Holly's heart skipped a beat, and she straightened and leaned forward with a smile. She would chance it again today.

To avoid problems, Holly wore her oxygen tank. The nasal prongs were uncomfortable and dried out her nasal membranes, sometimes causing nosebleeds. The tube dug into her cheeks and rubbed against her ears. The tank was cumbersome; it was slung over her shoulder and hung to one side, reminding her that she carried a load. Sometimes she just wanted to throw it away, but like it or not, she needed it. Dr. Young had told her that the cancer had spread into the lymph of her lungs, causing them to be unable to get enough oxygen. Every day, her body became more cancer than Holly. Today, though, it didn't matter.

Jaw set, she walked at a turtle's pace over the berm and onto the beach. The tide was out, so the beach extended about a quarter of a mile from the berm. Up the coast, she could see the stairs, but the woman was gone now; there was only a couple walking a dog. She stopped, shook her head, then turned to go back, but she stopped again to scan the beach. She stood for a while, then started toward the stairs, staying close to the berm to avoid any trouble with waves in case the tide came in before she could react. Seagulls joined her, flying just overhead and hovering there, turning their heads left and right, seeking out something to eat. Sometimes she would stop just to get them to come lower, then raise an arm, and they would ascend effortlessly to just beyond her reach.

She passed the point where she had taken refuge before and continued on to the old stairs to sit. Mila was there today, in spirit. Holly sat at the spot where they had fought for life together and rubbed the wooden post as she looked out to sea. The intermittent sound of the oxygen tank regulator forcing oxygen into her nose interrupted her reverie. She tried holding her breath, but that just meant that the next few would be more rapid, making the sound that much more irritating. She reached down to turn off the regulator, but then she stopped and thought again of Mila. That would be suicide. She drew back her hand as if the handle were hot. There were reasons to live: going home to Mom and Dad. Indeed, when Michelle had said, "I found Dad," Holly's heart had thumped, as it did now. The thought of seeing them together again after all these years was the thrill she needed in order to go on. *What will it be like?*

Holly looked out to sea and placed her elbows on her knees with her hands holding her head. Breathing was easier in this position.

She remembered his face and smile. She remembered how he would always throw her in the air when he came home, up so high that her stomach flopped, and then she would descend into his secure arms, and he would laugh. Michelle had said he had changed. *Do we really change? I feel excited, like I did then, waiting for him to throw me in the air.* She smiled as she gazed at the ocean, but the machine reminded her of reality.

No, Mila, I won't follow you anymore.

She rose and shuffled home.

◆   ◆   ◆

She heard George in the kitchen as the garage door closed with a whirling sound; she had slept for four hours.

"Hello, dear," he said. "How did it go today? Any word from Michelle?"

"No, not yet, but I'm sure she will call soon. It takes time to arrange to get Dad, and Pete has to get the jet."

"You still want to go?"

"I have to ... go back. I need to go back."

"Holly, dear, I'm not sure this is such a good idea. A couple of days ago, you almost died less than a half-mile from here, and now you want to go over six hundred miles away. Is this realistic?"

"George, you promised. Remember?"

"Yes, I did. But we waited too long. We agreed to do it when the time came, but we waited too long. We have been fooling ourselves about when to do it."

"You're right. We always look to tomorrow. Maybe that's a human defect—always waiting for tomorrow instead of today. Let's go now."

"Leave right now? You said you wanted to wait until Michelle arranged things. You want to go anyway?"

"There may not be a tomorrow."

Chapter 23

February 14, 2006

Ann looked on helplessly as Michelle made calls to coordinate all of the activities. As her daughter talked on the phone, Ann began to realize the impact of the decision. She left the house and paced the deck, then stopped, looking back inside at Michelle. It was over thirty years since Bob had left, and now, out of the blue, he might be coming home. She would no longer wonder what had happened to him, and the yearning would not be there any longer. She wondered if those feelings were really what she was all about; she had made him a martyr from the past. *To live a life of yearning for something, then confronting it—it could mean my life was not real after all.*

Michelle came to the door and interrupted her thoughts. "Mom, is that old airport down the road still functioning?"

"Why, I think so. Yes, it is, now that I think about it. Dale, the farmer down the road, has a plane there."

Michelle went back to the phone, and Ann went to the door to listen. "Pete, there is an airport about eight miles down the road.... What? How would I know how long the runway is? You've got those fancy corporate pilots. Let them earn their money and figure it out.... Okay, we'll meet you guys there after you make arrangements. Call before you take off, so we will know when to be there.... No, Holly and George are coming by car. She isn't up to flying. George called last night to say they were leaving then."

After the call, the two women sat in silence. The horses started neighing at the gate, as was their custom when breakfast had not yet arrived. Ann rose to go and feed them.

Michelle asked, "You having second thoughts about this, Mom?"

"Come feed the horses with me."

"You didn't answer the question," Michelle said. She opened the barn door and grabbed a bale with the hay hook. "I get the impression you are not as excited about this plan as before." She dragged the bale out to the hay wagon.

Ann stood aside, not helping. She grabbed a halter from the fence post. "I'm not, I guess. I don't know. I mean, it has been over thirty years, and maybe I don't want to face reality. What if he is a ... cad? What if ... my life isn't what I thought it was?" She looked toward the mountains.

"Oh, Mom! You can't think like that. He went his way, and you went yours. Why didn't you follow him to San Francisco? Maybe you are just as guilty as he is."

"Yes, I suppose I am, in some ways. I'd just had surgery and was frightened, is all. I didn't know if I would live long enough to move, and I couldn't ... leave this place. Looking back, I could have done things differently, but the bottom line is still that he should have come back to us. I had cancer and needed help." She held the halter by its reins, twisting them as she looked down.

"You're right about that, but I get the impression Dad wasn't ... well, wasn't the stronger of you two and that you called the shots. Maybe he just wanted to be strong for once."

Michelle worked on in silence as Ann thought about those times years ago. She suddenly remembered him in the tuxedo. "I guess I want to see him. I don't know."

The cell phone in Michelle's jacket sang the opening bars of Tchaikovsky's *Piano Concerto No. 1.* Ann wondered what else she had missed throughout the years; even the familiar sound of a telephone ringing was gone.

Michelle said into the phone, "Yeah? Okay, Pete. Great job! ... Yes, she has the original marriage license. Let me ask her." She turned to Ann. "Mom, do you still want to go through with it? One of Pete's lawyers is a friend of the Montana lieutenant governor, and they can pull strings to get Dad over here if you agree to take responsibility as his legal guardian. He can go back after the reunion. Now is the last time to say no, if you want."

Ann stood stone-still; a cold wind blew off the mountain, and she felt a chill. The sensation was not the cold, but more like the feeling of a first date. She nodded.

"Okay, Pete. She'll sign the papers when you bring the girls over this afternoon. We'll meet you at the airport at one. Thanks, Pete. Love you." She closed the phone and glanced at her mother. "Mom, Pete's got everything arranged now."

"Yes, I heard."

"I feel in the middle here, Mom. Holly wants to see Dad, but you seem ... still ambivalent. Can you handle it? I mean, for Holly?"

"Yes ... for Holly ... of course." Ann put the halter back on the fence, then slapped her thighs and grabbed a bale.

"Pete has gotten the corporate jet and will bring Kira and Nichole here this afternoon. You will sign the papers, then he will fly them over to Montana and get Dad. Mom? This is going to happen fast. Do you know what I mean?"

Ann worked on in silence.

Later, the sound of a car at the gate interrupted the two women cleaning stalls, and both looked up. George and Holly drove up, and they all met in the drive-way. Ann gasped as Holly exited the SUV with George's help. Her skeletal daughter smiled and spoke, her voice deepened by the intermittent oxygen flow.

"Hello, Mom. We drove all the way. George is tired, but I slept most of the time. It wasn't as bad a trip as we thought it would be. Dr. Young said I might need a transfusion in a couple of days. He said to check at the emergency room then."

Later, the three women sat on the deck as George napped. At first, the scene was awkward. Then Holly stood with her hands on her hips and looked down at the others. "Look, you guys. Let's get real, here. I'm dying, and nothing is going to change that fact. I'm here to see you, but if all you do is sit around with long faces, I might as well go home. I want to enjoy this time together, like the old days. So get your crying over with now, so we can have some fun."

Michelle started crying. Ann lifted her by the arm, and the three hugged like a huddled three-man football team. They cried until Holly started to giggle. The other two just looked at her at first, then started to giggle themselves. Giggles turned to laughter. They were a family who knew how to struggle together, and they were reunited.

◆   ◆   ◆

The jet slowed as it flew over the airfield. Ann wondered if the pilot knew what he was doing, as his approach was perpendicular to the runway, but Michelle seemed calm as she watched. Ann brought her hand up to her mouth and turned wide-eyed to her daughter, who just smiled. She relaxed a little, fiddling with the scarf around her neck, as the plane banked north, then west, and turned south to line up with the runway. It seemed to her like the plane was coming in too high and fast, but it slowed, then touched down. The engines roared as though in defi-ance of this place as clamshells deflected their energy forward. There was almost no runway left when the plane stopped, then turned back to the tarmac.

Ann watched the whole event in awe, then dropped her shoulders, her tension easing. There was that chill again. The plane pulled up right in front of them, and the engines quit whining. The fuselage door opened to reveal the girls. Ann waved, excited. The passengers appeared to take in the occasion as seasoned travelers, waiting until the stairs extended for their exit. The girls bounded off the plane and into Michelle's arms, then moved on to their grandmother.

Ann remembered two other girls this age who had tried to hug her when she had first came home from the hospital and changed all their lives. Now, though, the young girls wore hip-hugging short skirts with T-shirts; instead of dolls or toys, they had electronic gadgets. Kira's gadget was a phone with some kind of homing device so she could tell Ann where they were and how fast it took to get there.

Pete joined the reunion on the tarmac. Ann hadn't seen him for years. She didn't recognize him at first, thinking maybe he was the pilot. He said, "Ann, are you still going through with this … adventure? If so, you need sign these forms for me. I'll fly them over to Montana and get Bob. We should be back tonight, but there are possible complications you need to consider before signing."

"Doesn't matter," she said. "Holly wants to see her dad." It was bravado that she didn't understand, coming right out of her own mouth. She held her hat as a gust came off the warm airfield.

"Yes, I understand that. But the social services people over there are not too happy with us pulling strings like this. They want documentation that you are still married and all that. If we bring Bob over here, they may not consider him eligible to go back into their system, if you are the true legal guardian and not a resident of their state. We can argue that he is a legal resident there, but it could get ugly. I just want you to know that we may have trouble down the road. My lawyers think we can make things work, but they have their concerns. You know how lawyers have to look at everything. And I don't want any surprises that could hurt you." He leaned close to her ear as he talked.

"Thanks, Pete. That is very considerate of you. I appreciate what you are doing. What am I signing?"

"An affidavit that you are still married, and a State of Montana release form. They don't want to be liable if something untoward happens while he is gone from the foster home."

She signed, and she gave Pete the yellowed marriage certificate. He kissed Michelle, then went back to the plane and waved good-bye to them. He was off to Montana. They watched as the plane took off. Ann's stomach churned as it pointed to its destination. For now, though, she wanted to get back to the farm and Holly. She will worry about the meeting with Bob later.

◆   ◆   ◆

At first, the girls acted afraid of their aunt. She laughed and played with them until they became more comfortable with her, but she tired. Ann tried to help. Later, Pete phoned to say that they had Bob and would be starting back. The excitement mounted as the time to go to the airport neared. Ann changed into a dress, and she combed her hair twice; the others giggled at her preparations. But the anticipation was contagious, and all five women preened. George just sat gazing at the valley below, commenting now and then about their activities but trying not to be chauvinistic. Ann noticed that he seemed more relaxed now that she had taken over some of the duties of caring for Holly.

Three hours later, Michelle's cell phone rang. Ann could hear her talking, then Michelle snapped the phone closed and announced, "Okay, everybody, listen up. Pete just called, and the plane is about to land. Let's go to the airport."

Ann rushed to her bedroom to get a scarf. Her trembling hand bumped a brush onto the floor, and as she leaned to pick it up, she noticed the framed picture on the shelf. She knelt down. There he was again, in the tuxedo. She kissed her index finger and touched it to the picture.

"Come on, Mom! Let's go!" Michelle was at the door.

Ann's knees creaked as she rose; her muscles were so weak that she had to prop her arms on the bed and the bookshelf. She was trembling, and she and almost fell as she slipped out the door.

Two cars hauled all six people to the airport. Ann sat in the back of one and watched Holly, in the front, leaning forward. Ann was doing the same thing. The sun set just under the mountains as the jet touched down for the second time that day and went through its braking procedure. The whole family lined up along the tarmac, as if they were a military formation. Bob and Pete exited the plane.

Ann strained to see Bob in the waning light. He had a slight stoop and a paunch and had difficulty with the steps out of the plane, but once on the tarmac, he straightened as he waited for the next move. To Ann, he seemed confused and frightened. At one point, he even turned back toward the plane, but Pete guided him by the arm to the silent group. Words could not express the moment. Ann just stood there with a dry mouth and a lump in her throat. *You bastard!* she thought. No, there were no words for the moment.

Holly broke the silence. "Do you remember me, Dad?"

Bob kept his eyes on Ann as he turned his head. A slow smile started as he focused on Holly. "Of course I do. You're Holly."

Pandemonium broke out as the women started talking at once, all but Ann. She stood and watched. On occasion, Bob would glance her way. There were still no words, and she would lower her eyes at his gaze. When he wasn't looking, she would stare again. *I'm doing this for Holly,* she thought.

Pete brought back order by announcing that they had to move, as the jet needed to turn around and return to its home base. Ann and Bob were to get into the back seat. Bob held the door and leaned over to take her hand, smiling. She smiled for the first time and held up her hand for him, then stepped into the car. It was just like prom night in college again—until he asked, "You got any whiskey?"

At home, Ann hurried to prepare dinner. It would be tricky, as Holly could not stand the food smells, so she improvised by cooking the meal out in the old cabin on the corner of her property. An old woodstove there still performed, despite years of no use, and the smells were far from the house.

Holly said she felt like eating. Being home with family seemed to revitalize her. However, after the first few bites, she just sat and observed the others.

The conversation was light until Bob spoke directly to Holly. "You okay? You don't look so good."

The conversations stopped. Holly said, "Dad, I have cancer, and it's worse. I don't have long."

"Oh, yeah. Michelle told me that the other day, didn't she? Seems she said you and she got it from me. Bad genes in the family, what with all us Garritys getting it. I'm sorry." He then turned to Ann. "You're lucky you didn't get cancer like the rest of us."

Ann froze then looked around at the others.

Nervous, Michelle tried to deflect the conversation. "Dad, we wanted to have you here because Holly needs us now—all of us."

"You didn't tell Mom?" Holly was nervous too.

"Tell me what?" Ann glared at her daughters. "What's going on here?"

"We got the cancer gene from Dad's side of the family, Mom. I just found out the other day. That's how I found Dad. He and his niece had the studies done too, and since our defect is unique, the doctor suggested I might be able to find him. And I did."

"I … don't … have the cancer gene?"

Bob seemed oblivious to the emotion. He blurted out. "No, you don't. Why would you? You didn't have cancer."

Everyone, even Nicole and Kira, looked from Bob to Ann.

Michelle said, "Dad, let me handle this, please. Mom, you signed a release for me to get the medical records for Dr. Nielsen, remember? He showed them to me the other day when he told me about Dad. Your path report was in there, and you didn't have cancer."

"That's ridiculous," said Ann. "Of course I had cancer. Dr. Long removed it." She shook her head.

Bob interjected again. "No, he removed your breast, but you didn't have cancer. I know. That last day I saw you in the hospital, I left because you wouldn't listen to me. I started out to the car, but instead I just sat on a bench out back of the parking lot and started to cry. This pathologist saw me—I don't remember his name—and started talking. He was a bit tipsy, but when I told him I was your husband, he got real excited. He said you didn't have cancer and that Dr. Long wouldn't listen to him when he tried to stop the surgery. I waited around until Dr. Long came, then I asked him why he went ahead with the surgery. He got real defensive with me. Said I wasn't a doctor, so I couldn't understand it. He said the pathologist was a drunk and didn't know what he was doing." Bob stopped and took a bite of roast beef, then chewed as the others just looked at him. He continued chewing until he seemed to realize they were waiting. "Oh, yes ... sorry. Where was I?"

"You were telling us about Dr. Long." Ann's voice was stern.

"Oh, yes. Now I remember. I got mad and told him I would kill him if he was lying to me. He just laughed, so I hit him, hard, in the head. At first I thought I killed him, but he started breathing again, so I ran away. I was afraid he would bring charges. That's when I wrote you that note. When I got to San Francisco, I wrote a letter to the medical board, asking them to investigate. I may not be able to remember yesterday or what happened to me this morning, but I remember the old days. I couldn't forget that episode. I thought you knew you didn't have cancer."

Michelle broke the silence. "So you are the one. I read the investigation report. Dr. Long blamed the pathologist, but you turned him in."

Ann felt like her head was spinning. *All these years ... all the fear, shame, and guilt. It defined who I was—am. Now I'm not. Who am I?* She flushed, then she smiled as all eyes turned to her to see her response. She glanced around the table and fidgeted with her silverware. Her head pounded as the silence wore on. Then she said, "That's very interesting, Bob. I didn't understand why you wrote that letter and what happened. Thanks for clearing that up. Does anyone want coffee?" She raised the pot to signify that the topic needed to change, but weakness prevented the gesture from being completed, and she lowered her arm. All eyes were upon her, but she didn't know what to do, and the pot crashed onto the tabletop.

Embarrassed, she jumped up and ran out the door. She wanted to run forever, but it was like a dream in which she ran but couldn't get away. She stopped at the tree by the road, out of breath.

She leaned over, her hands on her knees. The sobs began and made her breathing worse. Back up the road, Michelle and Holly started from the house toward her. *Oh, god, I can't let them see me like this!* She clutched her chest with one hand and rose as the girls approached. Holly was leaning on Michelle as they slowly came down the road, and Ann remembered that day, long ago, when she had watched them get off the bus while she hid behind this very tree. *So much has happened since then, but now I don't have cancer and don't need to hide. I need to help them!* She stood tall, stepped out, and walked toward the girls.

"Let's go back to the house now. It's cold out here," she announced as nonchalantly as possible. She helped support Holly, and the three of them marched back. *Just like the old days,* she thought. *The three of us facing the future.*

◆   ◆   ◆

Later that night, it started to snow. It was one of those winter storms that dumped a lot of moisture that could melt fast, causing flooding. The snowflakes were large and sticky; white covered the trees and ground. The storm didn't last long, but it left a couple of inches of snow on the deck, which gleamed in the light of the emerging moon. Ann took a broom and cleared a section of the deck large enough to put out sleeping bags. "Who wants to sleep out under the stars tonight?" she asked.

Michelle insisted that the girls sleep indoors, but she welcomed the outdoor adventure. The men opted for the comfort of mattresses indoors. Ann and her two daughters giggled as they ran outside in their nightwear and jumped into sleeping bags. Sleep did not come easy, nor was it invited. They lay watching the night sky.

"We have done this all our lives, Mom. Why?" Holly said.

"You mean, why do we lie under the stars and gaze? I don't know," said Ann. "I have always been fascinated by the universe. It seems to me that the answers are up there, not down here. But to be honest, I think I like to look up to escape from my problems—by looking beyond them. Does that make any sense to you?"

Holly said, "Yeah, in a way. What about Dad and what he said tonight? It has to bother you."

"I don't know. The whole thing is so bizarre that I don't know what to think. It doesn't alter the fact that I had a mastectomy years ago, and it doesn't alter the fact that you have cancer now and that Michelle is at risk, does it? Our lives are the same now as they were yesterday."

"I don't think so, Mom," Michelle blurted out. "You have lived with the guilt-shame stuff for years, and now you don't need to anymore. That's a big difference."

Ann said, "I suppose you are right, from a rational point of view. But I still feel ... I don't know. The feelings don't disappear just like that. I have had these feelings for years. They have become a part of me. Maybe I don't want to give them up."

"That's sick, Mom. You have hidden from the world because of this, and now you don't have an excuse any more. You don't have a crystal ball anymore."

"Michelle! You're being kind of hard on Mom," Holly scolded. "Cool it."

"Maybe she is right, Holly," Ann said. "I have to work through this—but not tonight. We are here under the stars, and I have my girls—just like we used to. What more could a mother ask for?"

They gazed in silence at the night sky for a long time. Then Holly said, "Mom? I read somewhere that only about five percent of places in the United States can see the Milky Way now, because of the lights on the ground."

Ann said, "We're lucky, then. We are fortunate to see it this time of year. I look for it every time the weather clears. It helps me keep my own world in perspective. If I couldn't see it, I would probably start thinking I was unique."

Holly asked, "You still think we aren't alone?"

"We are not alone. You and I are just a small piece."

"Small piece of what?"

"I have no idea, and it isn't possible for me to understand. I just need to know I am a small piece of something, and that something wouldn't be whole if I weren't in it."

"Sounds Donnish to me," Michelle interjected.

"Donnish?" Ann asked.

"You know, John Donne. 'No man is an island.'"

"Oh, yeah. Any man's death diminishes me, because I am involved in mankind. And therefore never send to know for whom the bell tolls. It tolls for thee." As soon as the quote was out of her mouth, Ann wished she could retract it.

After a moment of silence, Holly chirped, "I'm not lonely anymore, Mom." She was oblivious to Ann's recitation.

"What in the world do you mean?"

"Remember the last time we lay out here? I looked at the stars, and it reminded me how lonely I was. Well, now I can look up there, and I'm no lonely."

"Good, Holly! I'm glad."

◆   ◆   ◆

Later during the night, Ann woke to singing. The song was "Almost like Being in Love," and it was coming from the kitchen. She slipped out of her sleeping bag and tiptoed into the house to find Bob standing in the dark kitchen, singing. As she turned on the light, she wondered how the others could still be asleep. He stood naked at the closed refrigerator door, startled by the sudden light. He stopped singing.

"Who are you?" he asked. "Got any whiskey?"

"Bob, I'm Ann. Do you remember me?"

He seemed confused and frightened, like he had been when he got off the plane. He studied her for a moment, as if to decide whether to respond. She feared he might become violent, but then he spoke again. "Of course I remember you. What are you doing here, Ann?"

"I live here, Bob. This is my house. You came here this afternoon to visit. Do you remember now?"

"Yes, but what are you doing here at the foster home?"

She was frightened now, but she approached him just the same. He didn't seem to mind as she took his hand and led him back to his bedroom. She tucked him between the sheets and said good night. "This is where you sleep tonight, Bob. I'll leave a light on, in case you need to get up. Can you remember that?"

"Okay. You got any whiskey?"

She stayed until he went to sleep, then returned to her sleeping bag. As she slipped into it, she remembered time long ago, when she had slipped into a seat in the front row of the college theater. It had been an exciting time in her life. She had watched the production of *Brigadoon,* and Bob had sung "Almost like Being in Love" to the audience. It had seemed like he was singing it just to her.

Chapter 24

February 15, 2006

The following morning, Ann was up before the others. She went down to the old cabin to make breakfast. The snow was still on the ground, and the weather had not yet turned warm. Her footsteps crunched in the snow, adding a pleasant sound to the otherwise silent trek. She wanted to make huckleberry pancakes, just for Holly.

As she stoked the old stove, waiting for it to heat up the grill, she thought of how well Holly was handling her situation. She tried to put herself in the same predicament. *I can't even handle the fact that I didn't have cancer. How did Holly become so … accepting? She used to be fearful of most anything while growing up. Michelle was the strong one—stronger than I was, but not Holly. I used to worry that she couldn't handle things, and here it turns out she is the strong one.*

The first cake came off the griddle: *Always throw the first one away.* She made a stack, then trekked back to the house.

Holly was in the bathroom when she got back, and Ann could hear retching. Soon, Holly came into the kitchen, pale and weak. This would not be a pancake morning.

"The others are not up yet, Mom. Thanks for the pancakes," Holly said with flat affect as she noticed the plate. "I'm afraid I can't eat this morning. It's been wonderful being here with you … and the family. I feel privileged to see you and Dad again. Do you think you might get back together?"

"I don't think so. A lot has happened through the years, and I don't think I can … handle him. He requires a lot of energy and skilled care that I don't have."

"Maybe Michelle is right."

"What does that mean?"

"Oh, nothing. You know, about excuses, crystal balls, and needing a cause. Sorry, Mom. None of my business. I think I want to go home now. I have seen and done what I wanted to do, and now it's time to go. I hope you don't mind."

"This is your home," Ann reminded her.

"This is my childhood home. My adult home is Bandon. I want to live out my life there. Can you understand?"

Ann could only nod as she tried to busy herself setting the table.

◆   ◆   ◆

George and Holly left after breakfast. The send-off was emotional but controlled. This would be the last time. Ann stood leaning at the car door, trying not to cry. Neither Holly nor Ann spoke; there was nothing more to say. George put the SUV in gear, and Ann reached in and caressed her daughter's face, then stood back. Michelle ran down the snow-covered drive to open the gate as Ann and the others watched; some waved.

As the vehicle started to move, slowly at first, Bob put his arm around Ann's waist. Distracted for a moment, she glanced up to his distant gaze, which refocused on her face, as if wondering what was happening. Their pose reminded her of the prom photo as she turned back to look at the retreating vehicle. Almost in slow motion, she moved her hand down to pull his arm away, then stepped aside, concentrating on the last view of her daughter. She wanted time to stop.

Michelle was opening the gate as the SUV approached. It stopped, and Holly got out, made a snowball, and threw it at the back of her unsuspecting sister, then hurried back into the sanctuary of the vehicle. For a moment, Ann could see two children waiting for a bus. Michelle threw a snowball at the fleeting SUV, then she started walking back to the house, looking back and crying. She climbed the road to rejoin the group, and they all stood silently, with blank faces until Pete, nervous at this behavior, announced that it was time for them to leave too. "I'll call the plane and take Bob back to Montana."

That afternoon, they loaded Bob in Michelle's SUV for the trip to the airport. Ann said her good-byes to Pete and the girls, then turned to Bob. He stood by the car door with both hands at his sides, wearing a puzzled look.

"Bob, it was good to see you again," said Ann. "It's been a long time." She offered him her hand.

He looked at it, then at her face. She lowered her eyes at first, then rushed to hug him. Then she pulled away and hugged Michelle good-bye. As they drove away, she could see Bob in the back seat, looking out the window. He had that strange, fearful look again, only this time there might have been tears as well. Ann turned and rushed back to the house, but she watched from the upstairs bedroom window as they went out the gate.

Ann wandered around the vacant house. Memories flooded her mind. The fireplace, near which she had placed Yoty so many years ago. The kitchen, where Holly had asked for peanut butter. The counter, where Bob had left the note saying to follow him. Her gaze went to the mountain, where Michelle had asked her why she didn't have causes to fight for anymore. Suddenly it dawned on her. *I make my own misery!*

◆   ◆   ◆

She hoped she wasn't too late. The old truck wobbled down the road as it hit seventy miles per hour. It took all her strength to steer, but Michelle's SUV was now in view. She honked, but it wasn't doing any good; she couldn't hear the horn herself at this speed. She was gaining on the vehicle, and then it slowed and stopped.

She jumped out of the truck as it barely came to a stop, rushed to the SUV, and threw open the back door.

"Bob, you're coming with me," she commanded, with a sense of determination that surprised even herself.

Now she had a cause again.

Chapter Notes

Chapter 1: This story is set in a small community in the northwestern states circa 1972. Medicine was practiced as depicted here, but the quality of medicine was probably no different here than in most places at the time. Although barbaric and unsophisticated by today's standards, there were few options at the time. The radical mastectomy (Halsted procedure), as performed by Dr. Long, was still used in the early 1970s. This procedure had not changed since originally described by Halsted in the 1890s. His work was a hallmark, as it provided medical science with the first reproducible success in the treatment of cancer. It set the philosophy of cancer treatment for over seventy years. Usurpation of this procedure did not come easily, and it is still an option today. The procedure of doing breast removal at the time of biopsy, if the pathology showed cancer, has fortunately gone by the wayside. Many detractors now debase the procedure as cruel and insensitive, which today it is. However, it was routine before breast cancer treatment options existed. Back then, the decision that a specimen was cancer relied on limited-precision frozen sections. Today, biopsies are processed completely before treatment options are decided. It was true in the early 1970s, however, that attempts to minimize surgery time because of anesthetic morbidity were valid. Halothane, the main anesthetic of the era, could cause severe and even fatal hepatitis.

Perhaps the single most important social medical advance in the twentieth century was the concept of addressing dying. Unfortunately for Betty and her family, dying was a taboo issue in our society at the time. There was little help provided, and most of the medical profession was obsessed with living and prolonging life. Death was ignored. Many medical professionals simply did not understand how to deal with it. For most, it was uncomfortable to broach the subject, let alone deal with it head-on. Many patients and families suffered because of this lack of understanding. Fortunately, a pioneer work by Elisabeth Kübler-Ross opened the door in 1969 to issues of death and dying. Another important event in the mid-1960s was the concept of hospice. Hospice started in Great Britain but was not imported to the United States until 1974; it took another twenty years after introduction before its full potential was realized, particularly in smaller communities. Fortunately, politicians helped get the ball rolling. As early as 1974, Senator Frank Church (D-Id.) introduced a bill providing federal funds for hospice care.

Betty died due to a common complication of advanced breast cancer: hypercalcemia. This disorder consists of too much free calcium in the bloodstream and results in irritability, personality changes, weakness, constipation, urinary changes, and coma. Today, such complications are treatable, avoiding suffering. Pain control was an issue for Betty. Opiates have been available for centuries but have been poorly managed by the medical profession. Fears of addiction (stemming from post–Civil War experiences) caused federal regulation at the beginning of the twentieth century. Although regulation was important, effective opiate use suffered, particularly with terminal patients. Opiate overprescribing caused disciplinary action for physicians. It wasn't until the 1980s that pain control advocates like Dr. Kathleen Foley convinced mainstream medicine to treat pain aggressively with opiates. Today, many routes of administration and drug combinations are available. Patients can even determine their own needs. Gone are the days that Betty endured, when Demerol was injected into muscle every four hours if a nurse perceived the need. Gone are the days when the Demerol oozed back out the injection site and was therefore not effective for the patient.

Chapter 2: Ann's operation included a skin graft to the chest wall to fill in the defect produced by overzealous removal of skin with the mastectomy. The donor skin was taken from the thigh in this case, by a procedure called split-thickness grafting. Nerves were severed by splitting the skin, and many patients found the subsequent pain worse than the mastectomy pain. The role of nurses like Sharon was not as proactive as it is today. Many surgeons did not want dressings changed except by them, and they demanded strict adherence to their rules. This behavior contributed to poor communication.

Chapter 3: The gregarious nurse in this story is a real person. In 1972, many patients were left alone in the first few days after surgery. This nurse, like today's nurses, forced the patient to engage in early activity, which reduces postoperative complications: no pain, no gain.

Chapter 4: Ann's plight after leaving the hospital is not unusual, although today there are support systems to help cancer patients adjust. During the era of this story, support systems only existed in large communities, and even there, they were relatively rare. It would be a few more years before organizations such as Reach to Recovery became accepted. To ask for help may be considered a weakness in many minds. Patient support has become a societal responsibility. Certainly the medical profession has been negligent in its supportive role. Even today, most doctors rarely refer patients to support groups. The medical profession, though, has come a long way in helping patients understand their disease. In Ann's time, follow-up visits after surgery were to evaluate and treat complications. Ann was never advised of the availability of resources such as mastectomy bras and prostheses. Even worse, she was not given statistics about prognosis, complications, and morbidity. Today, such neglect is unconscionable. Most surgeons and oncologists have reading materials addressing issues and references to other sources; many have staff counselors. Support for family members is critical too. Children especially are in need. They are perceptive, but doctors often keep them out of the loop when dealing with a parent's cancer, claiming the children's limited experience as their rationale. Like Holly, children may feel guilty or estranged because they don't understand. Even spouses need help, like Bob. Often a patient will isolate himself or herself after recovering from cancer, leaving the partner unable to cope.

Chapter 5: A seroma is just a tumor of fluid that can accumulate after surgery. They are benign and eventually go away but can cause anxiety and disfigurement. Actually, Dr. Anderson would have been happy to treat such a benign disease by aspiration: everyone feels better by doing something. Rarely, a seroma can last for months and may require minor surgery.

Chapter 6: Complications after breast surgery will occur. Numbness in the arm after axillary (armpit) dissection is the rule rather than the exception. Limited motion, like Ann's, needs to be addressed early in recovery to avoid permanent changes and even pain. Physical therapy helps. Fortunately, Ann did not develop the dreaded complication, lymphedema, like her Aunt June. Many postmastectomy patients lose the ability to drain lymph fluid out of the arm on the affected side, because the lymph ducts are severed or damaged. In addition to being unsightly, the swelling limits motion, increases susceptibility to infection, and can give rise to a serious but rare cancer. In Ann's day, the surgery removed excessive amounts of nodes, causing lymphedema in up to 50 percent of patients. Limited dissections now only cause lymphedema in 3 to 10 percent of cases. The sentinel lymph node biopsy coming into play now should virtually eliminate this complication.

Chapter 7: Today, as in Ann's time, the best emotional support comes from other patients with experience. A patient is more likely to accept advice from a veteran, as it is hard to refute experience; granted, the advice can be delivered more palatably than Aunt June's.

Chapter 8: Ann's secret seems hard to believe today, yet for many patients, breast removal was a pariah label. The secret, as in this story, can have consequences.

Chapter 9: The Mila Gorsky of this story is remarkable but not unprecedented, living with breast cancer for twelve years. Most oncologists have anecdotal data about long-lived breast cancer patients. These physicians would like to believe that the result is due to their skills. However, there is scant data about the natural history of breast cancer, and perhaps some of these patients would live long lives without ministrations. The only support for this hypothesis is data from John Hopkins Hospital, where Halsted developed surgical treatment for breast cancer at the turn of the twentieth century. Since there was no treatment prior to his endeavors, it was noted that a minority of patients, about 40 percent, lived beyond eighteen months, with an annual attrition of 15 percent. If this is true, about 10–12 percent (out of the original 40 percent) would still be alive beyond ten years without treatment, even though they had cancer. It would be unethical, however, to test this assumption today.

Bandon is a real fishing village turned nouvelle vague, with wealthy retirees on the southern Oregon coast, as have most small nonindustrial communities on the coastline. The performing arts scene does exist in all of them, but the description here exaggerates a bit. There is no ballet performance in real life, but excellent classical music, jazz, food, and wine festivals permeate the whole coast. The photograph of Mila Gorsky referred to in the last paragraph actually exists, but the performer is the famous Bolshoi ballerina Maya Plisetskaya. This extraordinary person was the premier ballerina of the twentieth century. She was barred from leaving Russia in the 1940s and 1950s, because her parents were branded enemies of the state. Her father was probably murdered and her mother imprisoned, yet her talents made her the ballerina prima of the Bolshoi. After taking "political instructions," she was allowed to go on tour in 1959. Since then, she toured the world, became a choreographer herself, directed Spain's National Theater, and continued to perform at the age of seventy-one, an unheard-of feat in a profession where forty is old.

Chapter 10: The use of routine mammography has become standard practice. It is an excellent screening tool, but, as Michelle points out, when to start using it is controversial. Certainly a woman with a strong family history of breast cancer in young first-degree relatives should start younger than the current recommendations. The use in woman over fifty, done annually, is the current standard. That recommendation is based more on how many cancers the test can detect and not on how effective the test is for younger cancerous women. Routine breast self-examination is still a powerful tool in the early detection of breast cancer and is often ignored as a first-line test. If done right, the examination will pick up tumors as small as a pea.

Chapter 11: At some point, everyone has to face the potential to get cancer. A checkup is the best first step.

Chapter 12: Oncogenes, or cancer genes, probably are involved in all cancers. Cancer is not a single defect due to chemicals, environment, or heredity; it is a complex interaction of factors that lead to alterations in the genetic makeup that controls cell behavior. Normal cells are derived from primordial cells ("stem cells") that are turned on to mature into functional cells; then, after a period of time, a genetic code (or codes) signals death. Another cell replaces the first, and the cycle goes on. Defects anywhere along this complex cycle can trigger abnormal behavior. If the trigger affects cell growth, then cells can become immortal and/or lack maturation. If cells don't die and/or proliferate, that's cancer. Gene defects that affect rapid growth or inhibit death are called oncogenes or cancer genes.

BRCA1 and BRCA2 are just two of many oncogenes. Since their discovery in the early 1990s, they have shown promise, as described in this chapter. BRCA1's defect is on the seventeenth chromosome, while BRCA2's is on the thirteenth. The area on the thirteenth chromosome contains about a million basic codes with twenty-seven distinct regions called exons. Seventy mutations have been described in at least nine of these exons, leading to the BRCA2 defect. The defect in this story (a duplication mutation on exon eight) is fictional but possible. The normal function of this region on the thirteenth chromosome has to do with repairing damaged genetic material; hence, a defect here would not allow repair of cells harmed, say, by things like radiation, oxidants, chemicals, or even other coding mistakes. If coding is not right, then these genetically injured cells become unregulated.

It has been a concern, since the advent of oncogene testing, that insurance companies and employers with health plans could misuse the information to discriminate against risky patients. Some states, as well as the federal government, have laws protecting patients from such discrimination. The Americans with Disabilities Act bars using this information indiscriminately. The Health Insurance Portability and Accountability Act (HIPAA) is supposed to ensure confidentiality of records, to prevent information like genetic testing from getting into the wrong hands; however, implementation of this law appears so encumbered as to raise questions of its effectiveness. Genetic discrimination is still possible, but it is still unknown how probable the risk is. A real paradox has developed whereby non-disclosure of genetic testing has resulted in lawsuits by other family members.

Chapter 13: Guilt-shame is a fictional emotional complex in this novel. Theoretically, cancer and oncogene patients with poor or no counseling could find it real.

Chapter 14: Michelle tells Holly that cancer gene testing isn't good for all breast cancers, only those with hereditary types. This statement is not true. At least 60 percent of families with a solid family history of early breast cancer will not have the BRCA1 or BRCA2 defect. Many more are likely to be found. Even patients with no family history can be found with the BRCA defects.

Chapter 15: As bizarre as the story seems, all physicians have experience dealing with family issues, and they have stories just as bizarre, if not more so. Family interactions are unpredictable and can be charged with extreme behavior. Family members who have not seen a patient recently often react, first with denial, then by control. Marilyn is not unusual in her response. A strange relationship develops in some elderly patients where they cannot confront their children, as depicted here; desiring independence more than anything, they will minimize their illness. The procrastination about making a will, power of attorney, or directive to physicians is rampant. Most cancer patients don't do so and can end up with someone making decisions based on their own issues and not the patient's wishes. Many times, patients are kept alive at great effort and expense because there is no direction. Do you have a living will?

Marilyn's concern about caregivers and their motivation is realistic. Sometimes what motivates a caregiver is odious rather than altruistic. Usually it's drug seeking, but attempting to gain material wealth does occur. Although most patients prefer to remain at home if they can, it is not realistic to hire full-time caregivers; it is too much to ask of one or two individuals. Most caregivers, like Linda and George in this story, are scrupulous and caring.

Never a state to avoid controversy, Oregon passed an assisted suicide law in 1994. The issue divided the nation, but attempts to control the law have not been successful. Even in Oregon, a repeal attempt in 1997 failed miserably. The federal government repeatedly tries to thwart Oregon's law, for fear that other states might follow suit. Today, the controversy continues, but only a few of the projected candidates have opted for this approach. Those that do are cared for with compassion, and the results are perceived as humane.

Treatment of advanced breast cancer is palliative only. No cure exists once the tumor spreads beyond regional tissues. Once standard options are depleted, as in Mila's case, treatment is symptom control. Marilyn insisted that her mother go to Chapel Hill to get a bone marrow transplant; her age would have argued against this approach. High doses of chemotherapy might improve survival but require replenishing the bone marrow destroyed from the potentially lethal doses. Patient advocacy groups, helped by the legal profession, pushed this type of treatment beyond science. The procedure was, and still is, investigational, where select patients enroll in clinical trials to see if it is indeed effective. However, in the mid 1990s, the advocacy groups pushed to have it as a standard treatment. Lawsuits against insurance companies for nonpayment occurred, forcing them to cover the unproven technique. Use of this procedure gained widespread use in the United States by 1997, circa this story. Even the Red Cross jumped on the bandwagon to harvest and store bone marrow. However, the only large-scale trial found itself in trouble by 2000, when the positive results noted came solely from a South African investigator who subsequently admitted to protocol violations. Things changed quickly as lawyers turned around to bring lawsuits against those doing the procedure; the procedure was abandoned on a large scale.

Chapter 16: Since the BRCA2 abnormality acts as autosomal dominant, then one allele abnormality would confer a 50 percent probability of passing it to offspring. However, once the gene is present, things are not that simple when studied in large populations. A measure called "penetrance" means how frequently a disease will occur when the gene is present. For the BRCA abnormality, the penetrance is high (up to 80 percent of patients have breast cancer by eighty years of age) but not 100 percent as predicted by Mendelian statistics. This discrepancy is probably because other factors have to interact to cause cancer; the current hypothesis of multifactorial interaction seems valid. Genetic issues are complex, and because of this, genetic counseling is becoming popular and needed.

When the cancer gene test came into use, it was difficult to advise patients what to do if they had it, as there was no data. Recommendations were mostly prescient. As it turns out, those prescient recommendations were valid. Suppressing estrogen with an oophorectomy or anti-estrogens like tamoxifen or aromatase inhibitors offers patients options besides bilateral mastectomy. They all work to a degree, but it is still unknown which one is better. It does appear that aromatase inhibitors, like Femara, are more effective than tamoxifen.

The threat of cancer can prevent action, as procrastination and disinformation occurs until it may be too late. The mind has trouble accepting it, and unfortunately, many patients get their information from less reliable sources than medical professionals. Well-meaning friends and family members offer advice based on their experience, which may not be applicable. Charlatans and mountebanks prey on this behavior. As Michelle's experience attests, there may be more information available to the public on alternatives rather than orthodox methods. Fortunately, in recent years, there is now a plethora of legitimate references about specific health issues available. Nowhere is this more prevalent than with breast cancer. In fact, there are so many publications that there are books about the books available. *Dr. Susan Love's Breast Book* is still the standard for patients or nonmedical readers and has been updated frequently to stay abreast of progress. *Breast Cancer for Dummies,* in the *Dummies* series by Wiley Publishers, is an excellent resource if it stays up to date with the advances in this field. If anything, too many books can overwhelm the neophyte and perhaps misdirect. Certainly, a book that proclaims cure, written by a graduate of a correspondence course from an unknown university, should be red-flagged. Such books do exist. Patients and family should question any claim where the promised results are too good to be true. Coffee-ground enemas have been in use since the turn of the twentieth century as a cleansing nostrum to cure cancer. This technique has been repeatedly revived through the years, and its only potential benefit is to keep the lower colon awake and provide a temporary disposal for coffee grounds.

Chapter 17: Holly developed a paraneoplastic syndrome that can often present before cancer. These unusual presentations can go undiagnosed, because no one associates them with cancer until it is too late. Many times, the syndrome is a hormone effect, such as too much calcium in the blood, but skin manifestations are common. Most paraneoplastic syndromes are associated with lung and GI cancer, but almost all types of cancer can cause them. Holly has a skin paraneoplastic syndrome called "tripe palms"; the lesions look like cow stomach. This very rare manifestation can occur in breast cancer, but Dr. Young was wrong to assume it would go away; only about 30 percent of these "tripe palms" will go away with treatment.

Chapter 18: The state boards of medical examiners issue licenses for physicians to practice in a particular state and have the responsibility to the public to insure that each physician practices acceptable medicine. Any complaint to the board, no matter how ridiculous it may seem, is taken seriously and investigated. Information is gathered, and the board then acts on it. The files, unlike presented here, are kept confidential and do not wind up in a patient's chart or in a hospital's files.

Chapter 19: Hacking into university files happens, just like hacking into government files. "Dracula" exists and may be working for antivirus companies; he might be under twenty-five years old though.

Chapter 20: Bob suffers from dementia due to a combination of factors. Brain surgery itself is not culpable. Radiation can cause memory loss and mild dementia that can progress. Because of this, procedures like gamma knife radiation may help reduce this delayed complication, but only long-term observation will tell. Bob has a history of heavy alcohol consumption that probably contributed as well. Repeated trauma to the head, such as a boxer sustains, can lead to what is called pugilistic dementia or "punch-drunk." Repeated strokes are another mechanical cause of dementia, called multi-infarct dementia. Other dementias occur due to other hereditary diseases, metabolic disorders, electrolyte disorders, and depression. Only a few of the causes are reversible. Bob's behavior typifies the early-demented patient. Unfortunately, other family members also suffer. Many times, the last person to see or want to see the disease is the closest relative. Early in the disease, a demented patient can function in society—look at President Reagan—as long as new tasks are not required; they can perform normally with previously learned tasks and may be aided by those closest to them to mask it. Aracept is a drug that may (or may not) improve memory by enhancing neurotransmitters. A newer drug, Memantine, acts differently and may help more advanced cases. Together, they may be even more effective.

Chapter 21: Holly developed a serious complication of advanced breast cancer called lymphangitic cancer, which spread into her lungs, causing an inability to diffuse oxygen into the bloodstream, causing her to be blue. If the cancer is refractory to treatment, oxygen will only help for a while. Another serious complication is the replacement of bone marrow with cancer, leading to the inability to make red and white cells as well as platelets; this is called myelophistic anemia. Blood transfusions may help for a while.

Chapter 22: Holly's loneliness is realistic. Even family can ostracize dying patients, as everyone expects death, and if it doesn't happen as expected, emotions can be unpredictable. In nonscientific terms, this is sometimes referred to as the vulture syndrome.

Chapter 23: Moving a dementia patient to a strange environment can lead to unusual behavior. Nurses and house staff in hospitals have encountered this many times. A patient will seem alert until darkness falls, and then the patient becomes confused and disoriented. They call this sundowner's syndrome.

Chapter 24: Smells, particularly strong ones, can have adverse effects on patients whose bodies have started to shut down. Forcing terminal patients to smell or eat may make the experience unpleasant for them. Normally, eating is associated with good health, and well-wishers (like Ann in this chapter) try to force food when it may not be best. Even supplements like Ensure and Scandishake may only benefit the caregiver and the pharmaceutical industry, not the patient.

Glossary of Medical Terms

Adriamycin: a chemotherapy drug used in combination with one or more other drugs to treat breast and other cancers

allele: the genetic material on a chromosome that expresses a gene or code to make an inherited characteristic. Since chromosomes are paired, there are two alleles.

Aracept: a drug to improve memory in patients with dementia

aromatase inhibitors: a class of drugs that prevent the body's production of estrogen

axillary: armpit

BRCA-1: an acronym (breast cancer-1) used to define the first discovered breast cancer gene. The defective gene is on the eighteenth chromosome. Usually found in hereditary breast cancer, but not always. Other cancers can be caused by this abnormal gene.

BRCA-2: an acronym, (breast cancer-2) used to define the second discovered breast cancer gene. The defective gene is on the thirteenth chromosome. Usually found in hereditary breast cancers, but other cancers can be caused by this abnormal gene too.

cancer gene: a gene that is abnormal in its expression that then alters cell growth, cell repair, or cell death. All cancers are due to one or more cancer genes. See also **oncogene**.

DNA: an acronym for deoxyribonucleic acid. The genetic molecule that determines what a cell is and does.

ductal adenocarcinoma: a common breast cancer involving ducts leading to the nipple

duplication defect: a mistake in the genetic code of DNA that repeats itself to make the code unreadable

Ensure: a shake, drink, or pudding commonly used in cancer patients who cannot sustain nutritional intake. High in calories (about 250 calories or more per eight-ounce serving) and sugars.

exon: that part of an allele that expresses an active part of a code. A gene may be composed of many exons.

Femara: a type of aromatase inhibitor

Gemcitabine: a chemotherapy drug used effectively in breast cancer and other cancers

hereditary breast cancer: cancer that has an inherited pattern, usually occurring at a younger age than noninherited cancers

heterozygosity: where only one of the paired genes is expressed

infiltrating carcinoma: a cancer that extends beyond its origin into surrounding tissue

lumpectomy: a surgical procedure that just removes a tumor and a small amount of surrounding tissue

mastectomy: the removal of the entire breast

Mendelian inheritance: classical explanation of how chromosomes pass characteristics to offspring; usually termed as dominant or recessive

modified radical mastectomy: surgical procedure in which the breast is removed, but the underling tissue remains

mutation: change in the genetic material that alters its expression

mutation site: that point or even area of DNA molecule where the code is changed to cause a mutation

Nembutal: a type of phenobarbital sedative

oncogene: See **cancer gene.**

oophorectomy: an operation to remove ovaries

paraneoplastic syndrome: manifestation of cancer not directly due to growth, but by something produced as a by-product of cancer cells

penetrance: the actual rate of physical expression of a gene, such as an oncogene

radical mastectomy: the removal of the breast plus underlying tissues down to the ribs

Reglan: an antinausea drug

Scandishake: a nutritional supplement commonly given to poorly nourished cancer patients. High in calories (440 in each packet) and fat

seroma: a benign, cystlike tumor that occurs after surgery due to injury to the tissue

tamoxifen: a drug that inhibits estrogen's effects

Taxol: a chemotherapy drug used in breast cancer, derived from the yew tree

Taxotere: a chemotherapy drug used in breast cancer, like Taxol, but synthetic

978-0-595-44375-8
0-595-44375-3

Printed in the United States
125571LV00014B/77/A